Tell Me Everything

A NOVEL

———

AMY HATVANY

Cover design by Christine Coffey
Book design by Inkstain Design Studio

ISBN: 978-0-578-56190-5

Praise for
IT HAPPENS ALL THE TIME

"Bravely sheds light on sexual assault and consent." —**US Weekly**

"Intoxicatingly honest…a compulsory read." —**Redbook**

"With nuance and compassion, Hatvany reveals the fallout
of the ultimate betrayal of trust." —**Kirkus Reviews**

"A page-turner that's impossible to put down." —**The Globe and Mail**

"It will consume you, drawing you into the very real plight of the main
characters and leaving you hoping for a better future for us all."
—**Buzzfeed**

"Compelling…a must read." —**PopSugar**

"A full-throttle story with heart."
—**Deb Caletti,** *National Book Award Finalist*

"Hatvany takes a risk with this disturbing study of the sexual
and power dynamics of friendship and love…[She] keeps the pace fast,
slickly layering her two complicated characters…Thanks to Hatvany's
powerful storytelling, there is a richness in these conflicted characters
that makes changes of head and heart seem both possible
and unpredictable." —**Publishers Weekly**

"A raw and emotional journey, [it] capitvates from start to finish."
—**RT Book Reviews**

Praise for
SAFE WITH ME

"Amy Hatvany is a strong new voice in contemporary women's fiction."
—Kristin Hannah, #1 New York Times bestselling author

"Equally heart-breaking and heart-pounding."
—Allison Winn Scotch, *New York Times* **bestselling author**

"A delicately crafted story... Hatvany compels readers to examine a diverse number of issues—death, organ donation, single parenthood, abuse, self-respect—and handles each topic with sensitivity and compassion." **—KIRKUS REVIEWS**

"Hatvany does a marvelous job of not letting the plot get too maudlin or 'ripped from the headlines,' and her characters have warmth and depth. Readers will find themselves cheering for these women. A good pick for women's-fiction fans, particularly those who enjoy the realistic stories of Emily Giffin and Kristina Riggle." **—BOOKLIST**

Praise for
BEST KEPT SECRET

"Realistic and ultimately hopeful story of Cadence, whose glass of wine at the end of the day becomes two...then... three...then a bottle. I love that Cadence feels so familiar, she could be my neighbor, my friend, or even my sister."
—**Jennifer Weiner, #1** *New York Times* **bestselling author**

"Amy Hatvany grabs you from page one and doesn't let you go. I was transfixed by Cadence and her heart-wrenching dilemma. The writing is visceral, the problems are real, and there are no clear solutions. You won't want to put it down." —**Emily Giffin,** *New York Times* **bestselling author of** *Something Borrowed* **and** *Heart of the Matter*

"Best Kept Secret is touching, hopeful, and so real. Amy Hatvany writes with depth and compassion about a secret many have kept as she offers the miracle chance of starting over . . . I loved these characters and this novel." —**Luanne Rice,** *New York Times* **bestselling author of** *The Silver Boat*

"Rarely do I find a book that stays with me long after I've finished it, but this is one. The honest portrayal of the fallible but oh-so-human Cadence hit me straight in the gut. The writing is warm, witty, thoughtful and heartbreaking, and that ending—I'm still thinking about it" —**Stefanie Wilder-Taylor, author of** *Sippy Cups Are Not For Chardonnay*

"Best Kept Secret is one of the most compelling books I've read in years. This could be any woman's secret – be it your sister, your best friend, or the mother you see on the playground. Amy Hatvany's heartfelt, heartbreaking, and ultimately uplifting novel will start an important dialogue about the secrets we keep... and it could even save lives." —**Sarah Pekkanen, author of** *Opposite of Me* **and** *Skipping a Beat*

"Haunting, hopeful, and beautifully written, BEST KEPT SECRET takes a brave and honest look at the slippery slope of addiction and the strength it takes to recover. I couldn't put this book down, and I can't stop thinking about it." —**Allie Larkin, author of** *Stay*

"A love letter to women everywhere. Inspirational and empowering." —**Rachael Brownell, author of** *Mommy Doesn't Drink Here Anymore*

"This gripping novel probes the darker sides of motherhood and family secrets, and proves that redemption is never out of our reach. A captivatingly honest book that you won't soon forget." —**Lisa Tucker, author of** *Once Upon a Day* **and** *The Promised World*

"A testament to the power of a mother's love. Hatvany goes places in this novel that other, less courageous, writers might fear to tread. And I suspect this story will resonate with more women, more mothers, than this author might ever know." —**T. Greenwood, author of** *The Hungry Season* **and** *This Glittering World*

"A gripping story of pain, love and renewal, one that leaves you cheering for the imperfect heroine who in some ways represents us all." —**Kaira Rouda, author of** *Here, Home, Hope*

Praise for
OUTSIDE THE LINES

"A palpable love story, emotional search for and acceptance of a lost parent, and a bittersweet ending make for an enveloping, heartfelt read."
—Publishers Weekly

"There are no storybook perfect endings here, but this compelling novel raises the possibility of a hopeful way forward."
—The Seattle Times

"Will delight readers…vivid and written with a depth of feeling."
—Library Journal

"Like a gorgeous dark jewel, Hatvany's exquisitely rendered novel explores the tragedy of a mind gone awry, a tangled bond of father and daughter, and the way hope and love sustain us. This novel does what the best fiction does: it makes us see and experience the world differently." **—Caroline Leavitt,** *New York Times* **bestselling author of** *Pictures of You*

"This extraordinary novel about a woman's search for her lost father--and herself—touched me deeply. With her trademark insight and compassion for her characters, Amy Hatvany has written a beautiful and moving book. Were there Oscars for novels, Outside The Lines would sweep the categories." **—Melissa Senate,** **author of** *The Love Goddess' Cooking School*

"Outside the Lines offers a fascinating look at the interior of a mental illness—the exuberance and self-loathing, creativity and destruction that then reverberate against the lives of family and loved-ones. Hatvany's storyline is compelling, weaving back and forth between father and daughter, patiently explaining as it asks all the important questions."
—Juliette Fay, author of *Shelter Me*

"Outside the Lines is a tender and lovely novel that explores the boundaries of love and how we break those boundaries in its name. It's sad and funny, heartbreaking and heartwarming. You'll want to read this book slowly. When you're finished, you'll want to read it again."
—Rebecca Rasmussen, author of *The Bird Sisters*

Praise for
HEART LIKE MINE

"An uplifting and heartwarming experience."—**Kirkus Reviews**

"Beautiful and deeply moving, Amy Hatvany writes about the tangled web of family in a way that makes you laugh, cry, cheer and ache. This book has so much heart." —**Sarah Jio,** *New York Times* **bestselling author of** *Blackberry Winter*

"By turns gripping and revelatory, Heart Like Mine is a sympathetic exploration of blended family dynamics. In her affecting new novel, Amy Hatvany pulls no punches; her characters grapple with life's big moments--marriage, parenthood, death--but she renders each of them with compassion and understanding. Heart Like Mine tells an honest, hopeful story that resonates in all the best ways."
—**Jillian Medoff, bestselling author of** *I Couldn't Love You More*

"Fearlessly explores men and women desperate to measure up to the rigors of parenthood, but still failing their children. Hatvany brings sympathy and compassion to the page, while never losing sight of the damage children suffer when their parents make bad decisions."
—**Randy Susan Meyers, bestselling author of**
The Murderer's Daughters **and** *The Comfort of Lies*

"A heartfelt, moving story about the lasting effects of grief amidst family bonds and breakups, and the healing powers of love, honesty, and acceptance. Hatvany writes with such wise compassion for every one of her characters." —**Sere Prince Halverson,**
author of *The Underside of Joy*

Also by Amy Hatvany

———

"If it's both terrifying and amazing
then you should definitely pursue it."

—Erada Svetlana

"You can't have solutions for the
conversations you're not having."

—Kate Northrup

Tell Me Everything

Prologue

The first thing you should know about me is that I love my husband. The second is that I occasionally have sex with other men.

Here I am, on a Saturday night, in the arms of a man we found together. He is smart, funny. He understands our need for discretion. He knows that he is only a visitor.

I kiss this man. I undress for him and let him touch my body. He teases me, as I do, him. We fall into bed, and I memorize the taste of his skin, how it feels when he pushes inside me. The number of times he makes me come. I etch every one of his movements into my memory, filing them away, like dreams. Knowing that what happens between us is everything. And yet, at the same time, nothing at all.

When we finish, I leave, almost immediately, and go home to the man who cherishes me.

I find him waiting for me, always, knowing exactly where I've been. I hurry toward him, my flesh still scented by another man's caress, my body aching from the pleasure of what we've just done.

My eyes lock on my husband's. Our desire for each other pulses like a heart that has just been brought back to life.

When I reach him—when I am finally, truly home—he pulls me to his chest, his lips pressed up against my ear.

"Tell me everything," he says. "Don't leave anything out."

One

I t started, as most things do, in the smallest of ways. An invitation to dinner.

"Hey sexy," my husband's text said. "Wanna go on a date with me tonight? I was thinking Italian. Or Thai. We could go downtown. The kids are with Peter this weekend, right?"

"Yep," I responded, fighting a small ache in my chest. It was a Friday in early May, I was finishing up at the office, and my ex-husband, Peter, and I had been divorced for ten years at that point. We shared custody of our two kids, Ella and Tucker, but it was always a little hard for me when they spent nights at his house instead of mine: I missed the noisy, musical notes of their laughter bouncing off the walls and dreaded the sight of their empty, rumpled beds when I walked past their rooms.

When Peter and I decided to split, Ella had been three and Tucker, almost two. Barely adults when we met—both of us, twenty—we had known each other only six weeks before we got married on impulse and had two babies in rapid succession, our naiveté leading us to believe that love was all we needed to sustain us. Love, it turned out, was not the only necessary ingredient in a successful marriage. Our relationship decidedly lacked the others, like maturity, communication, and mutual respect. I once told my best friend, Charlotte, that Peter and I were what should have been a one-night stand that ended up lasting three years.

I met Jake a couple of years after the divorce became final, and waited several months to introduce him to the kids, fearful of bringing someone into their lives who might not stay. But I soon learned that Jake was a solid, reliable kind of man—the kind my mother immediately described as "someone who would stick with you through cancer." As an oncologist's wife, this is her go-to gauge for the true measure of a person's worth.

"Let's do Thai. I'm craving something spicy," I texted Jake, now, including a hot pepper emoji and a couple of winking smiley faces, hoping he'd pick up on the innuendo. I couldn't remember the last time he and I had had a date night—especially one that he suggested—so the fact that he'd texted in the middle of the day to ask me out gave me hope that he might initiate something more after dinner, too.

"Oh, I'll give you something spicy, woman!" he wrote back.

That sounds promising, I thought, though I tried to manage my expectations. Jake would often talk a good game about sex—he'd flirt and make suggestive comments—but didn't always follow through with the act itself. A couple of weeks ago, I'd sent him a selfie of me standing in front of a "sold" sign with a big smile on my face, and he replied, "Wow, that woman is *smokin'*. Think I might be able to convince her to sleep with me?"

"Let me ask," I said, waiting a few seconds before sending him a second text. "She says maybe. But only if you promise to go down on her."

"That's my favorite direction! How did she know?"

And yet, as soon as we were both at home, Ella asked Jake to run soccer drills with her, and after that, Tucker needed his help with science homework, so by the time we went to bed, my husband kissed me, rolled over, and promptly fell asleep. I didn't say anything, because how could I complain that he prioritized spending quality time with the kids? I knew from talking with other friends who were on their second—or third—marriage that not all men took to the role of step-father the way Jake had, so I told myself that I should count my blessings. This was just a sexual dry spell—all marriages went through them. I simply had to be patient, and eventually we'd go back to the way we used to be.

Still, I was determined to try to keep a flicker of our romantic life alive. I'd met Jake in the kitchen last Friday night wearing nothing but high heels, a lacy thong, and one of his favorite blue ties dangling between my breasts. I'd thought about that moment all week, knowing both kids would be at a friend's house for an overnight. Hearing his car pull into the garage, I struck the sexiest pose I could manage while teetering upon four-inch stilettos. My right hand rested on my hip, elbow jutting out.

"Hi baby," I said, as he walked in the door.

"Nice tie," Jake said. He smiled, taking a second to run an appreciative gaze over my body, before glancing at his phone.

I took a couple of wobbly steps toward him, high heels clicking on the tile floor, and then made a playful grab for his cell. "Please tell me my naked body is more interesting than whatever it is you're looking at."

He pulled his hand out of reach. "Sorry," he said. "I really need to reply to this email. It won't take long. Meet you in the bedroom in ten?"

I frowned and crossed my arms over my chest, cupping my shoulders in my hands. All week I had imagined him dropping his briefcase on the floor and tearing off his own clothes the minute he saw me, the way he had in the beginning, before we got married, on the nights the kids were at Peter's, or when we'd enjoy what we fondly called a "naked lunch." (Since both of us were self-employed, we had the kind of flexibility in our schedules to pull off a daytime tryst.)

One afternoon he had invited me over to his place, leaving the door unlocked so I could let myself in. "Jake?" I called out, once I'd stepped inside his condo. We'd been dating about four months at that point, sleeping together for three.

"In here," he replied. His voice floated down the hallway from his bedroom.

I found him on the bed, already naked, vanilla-scented candles lit all around—they were my favorite, in almost every room of the small home I shared with the kids, so he had bought some for his place, too, a gesture I'd found endearing.

But the candles didn't hold my attention for long, because his hand was between his legs, stroking. His gaze locked on mine. "I've been thinking about you all morning," he said, in a rough voice. "Your body. Your skin. I need your mouth on me. Now."

A zing of excitement bolted through me. It was a new experience, having a man speak in such blatant terms in the bedroom. I liked how it made me feel. Back then, it was clear that having sex with me wasn't only a matter of want for Jake—it was a need.

But eight years later, as I stood naked in front of my husband in our kitchen, he not only remained fully clothed, he was responding to an email rather than ravishing his wife. I turned around and headed upstairs to our bedroom, where he met me, as he had promised. I'd changed into my pajamas, and when he sat down on the side of our bed, I pretended to have my attention riveted on my iPad.

"Hey," he said, putting his hand on my leg. "I'm sorry, but I really did have to get that email out before my HR contact went home. She needed to know when to schedule the next round of interviews with her department managers." Jake was a headhunter who worked for multiple technology firms around Seattle; he recruited candidates from all over the world, and then presented a selection of the best and brightest to the HR departments of the companies he served. With a global territory, he often ended up working all hours of the day and night: calls with someone in Japan at ten o'clock at night, a Skype interview with someone in France at two in the morning. The only way he could unplug was to literally shut off his phone, which was almost impossible to convince him to do. I understood this—my phone was the crux of my job as a real estate agent, too; I hesitated to turn it off for fear of missing out on a potential new client or an offer on one of my listings.

"It's fine," I said, though my words were clipped. I wasn't angry; I was hurt, and more than a little sad. I told myself that it wasn't entirely his fault. I could have told him earlier in the week what I hoped our evening alone together might consist of. It wasn't fair, really, to spring my naked body on him and expect him to react exactly how I wanted him to.

"No, it's not," he said, taking iPad out of my hands. He set it on my nightstand and then kissed me, sweet and slow. "Let me make it up to you."

"I'm not really in the mood anymore," I said, not wanting to seem retaliatory, but unable to summon any enthusiasm for sex. My injured feelings had shut down my desire, so we settled for spending the evening binge-watching House of Cards while eating an easy dinner of cheese, crackers, and grapes in bed, which, when I really thought about it, was a kind of intimacy all its own. I loved spending any time with Jake, no matter what we were doing. He was my best friend—my "person" as a character on Grey's Anatomy once put it. Anything that happened to me, good or bad, the first one I wanted to share it with was him. I wouldn't change anything significant about him—other than how, over the last year, he had ceased initiating sex.

But now, Jake had suggested a date night. He wanted a do-over, and I was more than happy to indulge him. Maybe it would help us get back on track.

I sent a text to my ex-husband, making sure that he would be picking up the kids from school. I didn't want a scheduling issue to ruin my evening with Jake.

"I'm on it," was Peter's terse reply, and I had to restrain myself from reminding him about the Friday that Jake and I went out of town for the weekend, and Ella's third grade teacher had to wait two hours after school for Peter to show up. "Great!" I answered, knowing from past experience it was better to ignore his curtness and save my energy for the more serious co-parenting issues that might arise.

Several hours later, Jake and I exited a popular Thai place near the Space Needle, and then strolled toward the garage where we'd parked. It was a warm evening. The night air was scented with a mix of flowering plum tree blossoms and exhaust from the busy downtown traffic. The Monorail clacked along above us, and a muffled beat pulsed inside a dance club across the street. The music became louder as the bouncer opened the door to let more people inside.

"Hey," I said, stopping on the sidewalk and looking up at Jake. "Want to get a drink over there?" I wasn't ready for our evening out to end.

"Really?" he said. "At a club, like grown-ups?" His mouth curled into a smile that lit up his blue eyes—the first part of him I fell in love with. There was a kindness in them, the reflection of a calm, grounded soul. Looking into them gave me a sense of peace. Of course, it didn't hurt that he was also six-two, with short, salt-and-pepper hair, broad shoulders, and a charming smile, but if I had to pick a favorite feature on my husband, it would forever and always be his eyes.

"Yeah," I said, feeling emboldened. "We never come downtown. We should take advantage of it." Jake and I lived east of Seattle-proper, across the 520 floating bridge in a heavily populated, but picturesque suburb named Queens Ridge, which we chose for the excellent schools and the fact that it was on the outskirts of Redmond, where Peter now lived with his second wife, Kari, and their three-year old toddler, Ruby. The bulk of Jake's tech company clients were headquartered on the Eastside, and most of the properties I sold were in the same area, so neither of us had much reason to venture west, into the city.

"We could stop at the Tipsy Sailor on the way home," Jake suggested. "Might not be as crowded as a club."

"We always go there," I said, determined to shake up our routine. I tugged on his hand. "Come on. Please?" I batted my lashes at him like a full-blown Southern belle, and he laughed.

"How can I say no to that face?" he asked.

"Yay!" I said, and he laughed again as we jaywalked across the street.

The night suddenly took on a more adventurous note as Jake paid the bouncer the twenty-dollar-per-person cover, and we entered the club. It was the kind of place we'd gone to a few times when we were dating, the loud dance music vibrating in our bodies as we sipped cocktails and shouted at each other, fruitlessly trying to be heard. This club, the Cove, was mostly dark, illuminated only by the hammered-metal sconces that covered the gray walls with a hazy, purple glow. I glanced down at the jeans and red, strappy tank top I'd chosen to wear, hoping that the place wasn't swarming with college kids and that, at thirty-five, I wouldn't feel a million years old.

But as Jake and I slithered our way through the crowd to get to the bar, I surveyed the dance floor, full of bodies swaying and grinding to the thudding bass that pumped out of the speakers too loudly for me to identify a melody, and noticed that most people appeared either our age, or not much younger than us. Jake was thirty-six, only a year older than me. There were men in slacks and button-downs with the sleeves rolled up, looking like they'd come straight from work to hit on women in outfits ranging from flowy spring dresses to jeans paired with more revealing, form-fitting tops. People crowded around us at the bar; we were lucky to have found a spot.

"Can I get a double vodka soda with lime, and a whiskey, neat?" Jake leaned over to yell at the bartender, a pixie-cut blond girl in a tight black dress who looked barely old enough to drink alcohol, let alone be serving it. She bobbed her head, and I tucked myself next to my husband.

Jake put his arm behind me, resting his large hand on the small of my back. He leaned over just as the bartender delivered our drinks. "You look beautiful tonight," he said, loudly, over the music.

Even with the twenty additional pounds I carried after having the kids, Jake had, from the moment we met, told me I was the prettiest woman in any room. Thankfully, most of that post-baby weight had settled in my tits and ass, and I generally took good care of myself with regular facials and weekly blow outs for my long, thick brown curls. I had insecurities of course—oh, the cottage cheese swell of my belly that would never, ever go away!—but for the most part, I was okay with how I looked.

"Thank you, baby," I said, taking a long pull of my cocktail, feeling the warmth of the vodka hit my stomach. "Whew! That's strong!" I poked his chest. "Are you trying to get me drunk?"

"Maybe," Jake said. He grinned. "We can get an Uber home, if we have to. Or stay in a hotel."

"Ella has a soccer game tomorrow morning," I reminded him, and then wished I hadn't had to, because I loved the way he had suggested something as fun and spontaneous as staying at a hotel. *That* was the Jake I fell in love with, not the Jake who responded to emails instead of bending his practically-naked wife over the kitchen counter. But he was one of the coaches for Ella's team, and Peter was busy as head coach for Tucker's baseball team. With both kids having activities on Saturday mornings, there was always at least one of us there to root them on—one of the few upsides to co-parenting with an ex-spouse.

"Shit, that's right," Jake said. "What would I do without you?"

"Good thing you don't have to find out."

"Good thing." He knocked back his drink in one gulp, and then grinned again. "Wanna dance?"

I sucked down my entire drink, too, cringing at the alcoholic burn, and nodded, puckering my lips. Something about the way the vodka immediately loosened the tension in my body felt extra pleasant. It had been a rough week, with four closings crowding in on each other, and two new listings. What better than the combination of drinking and dancing to lead to some ripping-our-clothes-off-as-we-stumble-through-the-front-door sex with my husband?

Once we were on the dance floor, Jake pulled me closer to him and pressed his hips up against mine, keeping one hand on my lower back. I raised my arms and moved to the music, feeling the spin of the alcohol reach my head. I stared at my husband deliberately, intently, and he put his fingers on the curve of my waist, running them up and down my sides, brushing my breasts with his thumbs. He put his head next to my ear and whispered, "God, you're hot."

I smiled, seductively, and we continued to dance until the song was finished and the DJ spun another. "I want another drink," I said, pointing toward the bar, and Jake nodded, leading me back to where we'd stood, before. He ordered us two more, and once they arrived, he sipped at his while I sucked mine down almost immediately. We smiled at each other like idiots.

"I feel like we're doing something wrong," I said, feeling giddy. I glanced at my watch. It was close to eleven o'clock. "We're usually on the couch by now, trying not to fall asleep."

"You're not getting any sleep tonight," Jake said. His blue eyes had darkened, a tell-tale sign he was turned on. I flashed back to the moment years ago, when I found him in bed, in the middle of the day, waiting. Already hard. The same hungry look in his eyes.

"Oh, really?" I said, finishing that last swallow of my drink.

"Really."

I opened my mouth, about to say that he better follow through on his words, when I felt another body bump into me from behind. I turned my head, and saw an attractive blond man who looked to be about our age, maybe a few years older, smiling at me.

"Sorry about that," he said, taking a small step back.

Something about the friendly smirk on his face told me that was a lie. "That's okay," I said, tilting my head toward him so he could hear me over the music. "It's crowded."

"Have you been here before?" the man asked, and I shook my head.

"I'm Will," he continued, holding out his hand.

"Jessica," I said, shaking it. "And this is my husband, Jake." I moved so that Will could see I was there with someone, despite being flattered that he seemed to be into me. He wasn't my normal type—I tended only to like dark haired men—but he had a nice smile and an open, relaxed demeanor. He wore a tailored, white button down and a pair of jeans that fit well enough to make it clear that he spent a good amount of time at the gym.

"Nice to meet you," Jake said, shaking Will's hand, as well.

"I hope you don't mind me saying this," Will said, "but I was watching you two out on the floor. Your wife is sexy as hell."

My breath caught in my chest as I looked at Jake, worried he might be offended and the lighthearted mood of the evening would be ruined. But Jake only sipped his whiskey and smiled. "She is, isn't she?" he said. He leaned over to kiss me on the side of my neck, sending shivers across my skin.

"Would you mind if I asked her to dance?" Will said, and I started to protest, thinking this guy was being way too forward, but then Jake put his mouth next to my ear.

"Do it," he whispered. "I want to watch."

His words caused a rush of arousal between my legs, and I looked at him with wide, questioning eyes.

He nodded. "It's up to her," Jake said, "but I'm fine with it."

"Thanks," Will said. He held out his hand to me and tilted his head, charmingly. "What do you think?"

I glanced at Jake again, whose eyelids had become slightly hooded, and something about that made me follow Will only ten feet or so away from my husband, and let this other man—this total stranger—put his hips against mine and begin to move my body with his.

It was odd, at first. Another man hadn't touched me that way for years. But I felt Jake's gaze on us, unwavering, so after a minute, I started to sway my hips even more sensually than I had with my husband. I let Will's hands roam up and down my back and I gave his well-muscled arms a deliberate stroke with the tips of my fingers. He turned me around to face Jake, and then stood behind me, lifting one of my arms up to rest on his shoulder and putting his forearm across the front of my waist. My husband stared at me with a shade of desire I couldn't remember seeing on his face before. It vibrated in the air between us, a living, breathing thing. He watched me with Will, the two of us keeping rhythm with the music until the song ended, and then Will led me back to the bar. To Jake.

"Do you guys want to get a table?" Will asked. "Get to know each other a bit?"

"I think we're going to head home," Jake said. "But thanks."

"Okay," Will said, reaching into his back pocket and handing me a business card, which I slipped into my small purse. "In case you ever want to get together another time." He smiled. "Thanks for the dance, Jessica. And Jake, for allowing me the pleasure."

"Sure," I said, barely able to tear my eyes away from Jake's face.

"Let's go," he said, in a husky voice. He caught the bartender's eye, threw a few twenties onto the bar, and she lifted her chin in acknowledgment. He grabbed my hand and pulled me through the crowd again until we were outside in the night air, which seemed substantially cooler than it had before we'd entered the overheated club. We hurried toward the parking garage, still hand-in-hand, and when we got to our car, instead of unlocking it, Jake pushed me up against it and kissed me. I snaked my hands up around his neck and pressed my body against his, feeling him already hard as he used his hands on my breasts. Ache and wanting throbbed between my thighs. *This,* I thought. *Oh god, all of* this.

"That was so fucking hot," Jake murmured against my mouth. "Watching him touch you like that. Seeing you touch him."

"Take me home," I said, breathlessly, but he shook his head.

"I can't wait." He glanced around the dimly lit, almost empty garage, and led me behind our black SUV, which was parked in the far corner, away from the entrance. He used his fingers to quickly unbutton my jeans, and then his own. "Turn around," he said, gruffly. He grabbed my long hair at the base of my neck and gave it a gentle pull. "Now."

Surprised by his assertiveness, but too aroused by it to protest, I complied. It didn't matter that we might get caught. All that mattered was getting my husband inside of me as soon as possible. I wriggled my jeans down, and he did the same with his. And when Jake entered me, reaching around and pressing his fingers against my clit at the exact same moment, I couldn't help it, I cried out. He clamped his other hand over my mouth as he moved, muffling the noise I made, thrusting until both of us shuddered.

"Holy shit," I whispered as his body went limp, the weight of him resting upon my back. We both were breathing hard, but we quickly refastened our jeans, and then he kissed me again, this time, softly, with a familiar tenderness.

"I can't believe I did that," he said, giving his head a little shake. His cheeks were flushed.

"It wasn't just you," I said. My legs trembled as I took a couple of steps toward the passenger side door, waiting for him to unlock it. He did, and then held it open for me. Once I was in my seat, he shut me inside, and then went around to climb in, too. We sat in silence a moment, both of us trying to catch our breath. My heart pounded. My head was spinning. I didn't know what to think. Or say.

"Are you okay to drive?" I finally asked him.

"I'm fine," he said. "I barely touched that second drink." He paused, and then looked at me again. "You got his number, right?"

I pressed my lips together and nodded, my gaze fixed on his.

"Good," he said, that one word splitting my thoughts in a hundred different directions. Something between us had shifted.

Two

By eight a.m. the next morning, the parking lots at Marymoor Park fields were already full. Jake and I had arrived at seven to set up, fueled by two Venti, quad shot Americanos we'd picked up from Starbucks on the way over. Ella's game was scheduled to start at eight-fifteen, and Jake was currently leading the girls in warm up exercises on the sidelines, while the head coach spoke with the coach from the opposing team. I, on the other hand, had settled comfortably into my camp chair on the other side of the field, sipping the last of my now-lukewarm coffee as I watched my husband encourage Ella and her teammates to do jumping jacks.

"Better them than us, eh?" a familiar voice behind me said, and I turned around to see my best friend, Charlotte, approaching. She had gorgeous bluntly-cut, shoulder-length auburn hair, the build of a runway model, and the mouth of a trucker. We'd met six years before when her daughter, Bentley, who was seven at the time, told Ella, the same age, to fuck off during soccer practice. After apologizing profusely for her daughter's behavior, Charlotte had looked at me with a twinkle in her brown eyes and murmured, "I don't know where the fuck she learned to talk like that." I'd laughed, and we'd been friends ever since.

"No shit," I said, now, maybe a little too loudly, because two other mothers of girls on the team sitting a few feet away scowled at me. I gave them a cheery, innocent smile and then looked away.

Charlotte set up her own camp chair right next to mine, then plopped down and crossed her ridiculously long legs. "How are you?"

"Good," I said, feeling my cheeks warm as an image from the night before in the parking garage flashed inside my head. It still didn't feel quite real.

"Hold it." Charlotte peered at me, pulling her black sunglasses down to the tip of her nose. "I know that look. You got laid!"

I laughed. "Can you say it a little louder? I don't think everyone on the other side of the park heard you."

She made a dismissive motion with her hand. "Richard and I haven't had sex in three months. I don't think I've even seen him naked since March. I need details."

"It was nothing," I lied. I finished my coffee and set my travel mug on the grass by my feet. "We went out for dinner downtown, and then had a couple of drinks at a club. We danced. We felt young again." I still didn't know how to feel about what had transpired on that dance floor, let alone our behavior in the parking garage, so I wasn't ready to share the details with anyone. Even with Charlotte, who I usually did tell almost everything.

"Shut up. I don't want to hear it." Charlotte was forty-seven, after getting pregnant by an anonymous one night stand when she was thirty-three—"Forgot the condom. Whoops!" she always said—and then met Richard, a corporate attorney, at a library benefit she had organized when she was five months along. To his credit, the idea of raising another man's child didn't faze him. He fell in love with Charlotte's headstrong, brash nature and was ready to settle down, so they got married before Bentley was born. Charlotte liked to complain about their lack of a sex life, but so did a few other moms I knew. More often, though, they complained that their husbands wanted sex too much, too often. "Doesn't he understand how *tired* I am?" they'd whine. I'd nod sympathetically, despite having the opposite problem. Even though Jake complimented me and verbalized his desire to have sex, when he failed to act upon those words, I wondered if something deeper was going on. Over the last year I'd had terrible flashes of insecurity, worried that maybe he wasn't turned on by me anymore.

"Do you feel like we do this enough?" I asked him several months back, not long after the holidays. We were in bed, having just managed a quickie, which I'd initiated by dropping to my knees in the bathroom while he was brushing his teeth. Not giving him a chance to say no.

"Do what?" he replied, rolling over to his side to face me.

"I feel like we're so busy, sex has sort of fallen off our radar."

"That's normal, isn't it?" he said. "We're not newlyweds anymore."

"I know. But I feel like we talk about it more than we do it."

"I *like* talking about it," he said. "Don't you?"

"Yes," I said, feeling like I wasn't doing a good job of getting my point across. I tried again. "I just want to be sure that you're getting enough sex." I paused, and tried to keep my tone lighthearted. Opening myself up, showing vulnerability, even with someone I loved and trusted as much as Jake, was not my strong suit. "You know what they say. If a man isn't fucking you, he's fucking someone else." I'd never been cheated on—at least, not as far as I knew. But what if that pudge of my belly was turning Jake off? What if something about me, about the mundane-quality our daily life together had taken on, had driven him into another woman's arms? I lay totally still, holding my breath, more than a little terrified to hear his reply.

"I would never do that to you," Jake said, vehemently. He moved his hand from my breast to my chin and forced me to look at him. "You know that, right? We're busy, yes. Are we having as much sex as we used to? No. But that doesn't mean I don't want you." His blue eyes searched mine, suddenly concerned. "Do you still want me?"

"Always," I whispered, as a few tears escaped. Not only did I believe him, but I also hadn't considered the possibility that Jake might worry that I wasn't as attracted to him as I used to be. Our dwindling sex life had taken on a self-feeding quality: when Jake stopped initiating sex as much, so had I. There were moments when it would feel like we were becoming my parents—two adults living in the same house, raising children together, but not connecting on a deeper, more meaningful level—and it scared me. Jake was everything my father—and Peter—was not: emotionally present, self-aware, affectionate, and a little goofy. When we met, I thought, *This is what love is supposed to be like.* And yet, here we were, focused on everything except our romantic life.

After that conversation, I told myself that everything was fine: we were still attracted to each other, and the way we talked and flirted was enough to keep us connected and intimate. Sex would happen when time and circumstances allowed. Still, actions meant so much more to me than words, which is why last night at the club had been so thrilling. When we had gotten home, we were barely through the door before Jake was kissing me and leading me up the stairs to our bedroom, where he stripped off my clothes, then his, all while whispering about how Will had touched me, how obvious it was that this other man had wanted to do more with me than dance. Then, we whispered about what we'd done in the parking garage, after that. Replaying how intense it was; how incredibly satisfying. It was the best sex we'd had in years. Maybe ever.

"We did it *twice*," I whispered conspiratorially to Charlotte, now, feeling like I had to give her something or she'd never stop pressing me for details. It was either that or tell her about the contingency mess I managed to sort out for one of my clients yesterday, and I knew she didn't give a shit about real estate. She was an event planner, more interested in appetizers and flower placement than plumbing issues and property line infringements.

"Oh my god!" she said. "I'm so jealous I could scream!"

"Jealous of what?" another voice said, and we both looked up to see Tiffany Mitchell standing next to us, clad in her standard Lululemon uniform. Her straw-blond hair was pulled into a ponytail, high on top of her head, and she wore full make up, including false lashes, to attend her daughter, Lizzy's, soccer game. She was the head of the PTA at the middle school, and wedded to her college sweetheart, Ben, who owned a chain of several successful car dealerships on the Eastside.

"Jessica got lucky last night," Charlotte informed her.

I gave my best friend's forearm a playful smack. This was partially why I hadn't told her about dancing with Will, or the parking garage. She delighted in shock value so much that discretion wasn't always her forte. I also wasn't sure how she'd react to my dancing in front of Jake with another man. Before Charlotte met Richard, the great love of her life was a photo journalist named Alex, whom she'd lived with for several years in her late twenties before finding out that he had been cheating on her almost the entire time they were together. As a result, she was especially touchy when it came to any situation that even hinted around infidelity, and while I'd only danced with Will, I worried it still might upset her. After getting married and having kids so early in my twenties, I'd lost a lot of girlfriends who were on different paths. I treasured what I had with Charlotte; I didn't want to do anything to jeopardize our friendship.

Tiffany made a pinched face. "That's not really something I needed to know."

"Oh, come on," Charlotte said, teasingly, clearly enjoying herself. "Don't you and Ben get crazy on occasion? Maybe a birthday blow job?"

"Charlotte," I said, with a touch of reproach. I loved her, but sometimes, she took things too far. Even though the sun was shining, the wind picked up, so I zipped up my fleece jacket and stuck my hands inside its pockets.

"It's fine," Tiffany said, brightly. "You know what they say people about who talk about sex all the time." She gave Charlotte a pointed look. "They're the ones not having any."

I had to repress a smile. Tiffany might look the part of a dumb blond, but she was far from it.

"Touché," Charlotte said, cheerfully, but I could tell from the way her body had tensed that Tiffany's comment had hit a little too close to home.

"Nice to see you, ladies," Tiffany said. "Hope you'll be at next week's bake sale meeting. Be sure to bring a list of your favorite gluten-free, sugar-free options!"

"Will do," I replied, even though just the thought of attending the meeting made me tired. The last thing I needed was another item on my to-do list. Tiffany, however, seemed to thrive on anything that had to do with helping out at the school. I envied her a little, because she didn't work outside the home, so even with three kids—Lizzy, who was Ella's age, and her twin boys, Isaac and Sam, who were seven—she had time to be involved in all of their extracurricular activities. With my unpredictable work schedule, having to be at the beck and call of my clients and their needs, the most I could usually do was show up at my kids' events and cheer them on. *That's more than your mom did for you*, I reminded myself. I hoped it was enough.

"That woman needs to calm her tits," Charlotte said, after Tiffany had left us to join a small gathering of her PTA friends sitting further down the sideline. "Can you imagine what having sex with her is like? There's probably a two-page, bullet-point agenda, like the ones she does for those damn meetings. 'Kissing, two minutes. Discuss pros and cons of going down on each other, thirty seconds.' Poor Ben."

"You're awful," I laughed. Ben appeared to be much more easy-going than his wife, always laughing and passing around drinks at social events, making sure that everyone was having a good time, while Tiffany was more likely side-eyeing the caterer's choice of entrée and pointing out how she would have picked white roses instead of red—"red is so *tacky!*"

I turned my attention to the other side of the field, where the team was stretching and getting ready for the game to start. My eyes landed on Ella, who waved at me, excitedly. I waved back, overwhelmed by the young woman she was starting to become. At thirteen, she had gotten her period—an event that was "totally gross" according to her—and needed to wear a bra, which Kari, her step-mom, had taken her shopping for at Victoria's Secret without talking with me about it, first. "But she needed it, and she was with us that weekend," Kari said, when I confronted her. "I was trying to help."

"Right, but I'm her mother," I said, attempting to remain calm.

"Taking her shopping for her first official bra is something that she should have done with me." In the long run, I knew it wasn't that big of a deal, but I couldn't shake the disappointment I felt about not being there to help Ella navigate that particular milestone. Kari had apologized, but then I saw her roll her eyes at Peter when she turned around to go back inside their house, annoyed with me, and I had to restrain myself from going after her and giving her another, not-so-diplomatic piece of my mind. She wasn't a bad person, but she also wasn't a very bright one, so I chalked up her mistake to that, and tried to let it go. When your ex marries a woman you don't especially like, that's really all you can do.

"Love you, baby!" I yelled, now, cupping my hands around my mouth. Ella ignored me, this time, and instead, adjusted her ponytail. She had my long brown curls, and her dad's green eyes. Tucker looked more like Peter—a carbon copy of him, really—with a black crew cut, pale skin, and green eyes, as well. Jake and I had talked about having another baby, one of our own, but at the time, right after we'd gotten married, the kids were more than enough for us to handle, so we decided that we would be happiest focusing on them and not having to deal with the diapers and potty-training phase again.

I felt the tiniest sense of relief that Jake hadn't insisted on having a baby with me, because the truth was, I'd missed out on the freedom most other twenty-somethings experience. I'd gone straight from my parent's house to living with Peter, never having the kind of autonomy most young adults have during and after college, living on their own, doing whatever they want, when they want. I never got the chance to know what it was like to focus only on myself—to take no one else's needs into account. After my divorce, especially, I had to grow up quickly, and find a job to help support myself and my toddlers with only a two-year business degree. Real estate turned out to be a good fit—mostly because it allowed me to make my own hours and work from home if one or both of the kids got sick and couldn't go to daycare. But that flexibility didn't transfer to my social life. At the office, fellow agents around my age would ask me to join them for drinks or dinner, and I'd have to decline.

"I need to pick up my kids," I'd tell them. Even on the weekends they were with Peter, I didn't go out, choosing instead to stuff as many hours of kid-free, uninterrupted work into two days as I could handle. Overall, it was difficult for me to connect with my peers. The women I *did* spend time with at the kids' swimming lessons or story time at the library were mostly in their thirties and forties—women who had waited to become mothers. They were nice enough, but it was hard to establish close friendships because of our age difference. Our life experiences simply didn't mesh. I didn't fit in with women in their mid-twenties, either, the few that I knew, because they were mostly unencumbered, able to spend their time however they chose.

"Can't you just get a babysitter?" one of my female coworkers asked me once, when I told her I couldn't take off with her and a few other agents to Vegas for a girls' long weekend. "Or ask your ex to watch them? You work so hard. You deserve a little 'me' time!"

My face burned with embarrassment, because even if I could get a babysitter or ask Peter to take the kids for four days instead of his usual two, I was barely making ends meet as it was and couldn't afford to make the trip. Child support from Peter helped, but in the beginning, my commissions were still sporadic enough that I had to keep to a strict budget in order to pay my bills. The only "me" time I had was in the shower, but even there, more often or not, Ella and Tuck were in the bathroom, too, poking their heads around the curtain. But instead of telling my coworker all of this, I said, "I don't like to be away from them for that long."

"Oh. Okay," she said, with an incredulous look, obviously having no clue what I was talking about. I would have envied her more, if I had the time. I didn't have any family nearby to pitch in—my parents still lived in Boise, where Peter and I had left right after we married. I didn't want to go back home, even though my parents offered to take us in, because I wanted to prove to them—stubbornly—that I could make it on my own. Not to mention the fact that Peter wouldn't have tolerated me taking the kids that far away from him. However poor of a husband he had been, he was a good father, which was one of the qualities that had attracted me to him in the first place—the two of us bonded over our mutual desire to be better, more present and involved parents than the ones we'd had.

I lived like this for two years, working my ass off to build my business and support the kids, going on the occasional date when I was asked, but rarely having sex. In some ways, that desire had been temporarily turned off after I had babies, which had been a point of contention between me and Peter. My need for physical touch was already overloaded by nursing each of them for a year and a half, and, as they got older, after the divorce, their insistence to be *on* me was constant—hugging, snuggling, kissing, crying, or looking for comfort when they didn't get their way. I was all touched-out. It wasn't until they got a little older that that changed—my body started to become mine again. Then I met Jake.

He saw one of my properties online, and called me at the office. "I'm an executive recruiter," he said after he introduced himself. "I have a client moving here in a few weeks who really wants to buy something instead of living in corporate housing. He told me what he's looking for, and I said I'd make a few calls to try and find him an agent."

"That was generous," I said, already liking the deep, but friendly tenor of his voice. While we were still on the phone, I quickly Googled his name and clicked on his company's website, immediately attracted to his easy smile and deep blue eyes. He looked to be about my age, twenty-five, or maybe a bit older.

"I'm a full-service kind of guy," he said, and I wondered if I'd only imagined the flirtatious, implied sexual innuendo. It had been months since my last date, when I uncharacteristically had a one-night stand with a guy I was physically attracted to, but hadn't clicked with on any other level. My body was primed, aching for the kind of satisfaction that my vibrator didn't provide.

"I could show you the house, first," I offered, on a whim. "For your client." It didn't make sense, really, for me to show the property to Jake, but for whatever reason, I felt a spark between us, even in those first moments on the phone. I wanted to see if it carried over in person. I also wanted to get laid.

"That'd be great," he said. We made plans to meet at my listing that evening, and the minute he stood in front of me as I opened the door, my heart skipped a beat. He was tall, over six feet, with broad shoulders but a lean, runner's build. He wore jeans and a navy blue polo, which set off his eyes.

"Nice to meet you," he said. He extended his hand, and I took it.

"You, too," I said. The warmth of his skin on mine flowed through my whole body. It wasn't love at first sight, by any means, but it was definitely lust. He had an energy about him that pulled me in; a quiet confidence and ease in his presence that couldn't be faked. I glanced, surreptitiously, at his hips, wondering how well-endowed he might be. I'd only had sex with one man who wasn't of average size—the man I'd had the one night stand with months before—and the experience left me wanting to do it again.

"Let me show you around," I said, and we spent the next half-hour walking from room-to-room, while I imagined various scenarios of the two of us fucking in each of them. *Should I go for it?* I wondered. *He seems attracted to me. Should I kiss him and see how he reacts?* But something stopped me—something that told me Jake had the potential to be something so much more than a one-night stand. However sexually frustrated I was, the one thing I wanted more than physical release was to find someone to actually share my life with.

So instead of trying to seduce him on the spot, I pointed out the amenities the owner had added: a bar in the den, a pop-up flat screen TV in the master, and a high-end pool table that would be left behind if Jake's client wanted it. When we returned to the entryway, I grabbed my purse and keys and looked at Jake. "So, do you think your client might be interested in making an offer?"

"I have a confession," he said, the corners of his mouth curling upward into an appealing manner. "He already told me he was going to call you tomorrow. He saw the pictures online and decided it's exactly what he wants. He's buying it."

"Oh," I said, surprised, and a little confused. "Did you come to see the house to make sure the pictures were accurate, then?"

"No," Jake said. "I came because I wanted to meet you." His eyes twinkled.

"Oh," I said again, and despite my earlier thoughts of what he and I might do together, I suddenly felt a little uncomfortable being alone, at night, with a complete stranger. *Ted Bundy was handsome, too,* I thought, moving my individual keys between my fingers, like tiny daggers, just in

case. I was usually a pretty good judge of character, but you never could
be totally sure.

Jake glanced down at my hand, seeing what I'd done with the keys.
"Oh god, sorry," he said, quickly. "That came out kind of creepy, didn't
it?" He laughed. "I'm not a weirdo, I swear. I just liked the picture of you
on your listing. I think you're pretty." He held up his hands, palms facing
me, in a gesture of surrender.

Later, we laughed about that moment when we recounted the story
of how we met—how I'd been considering jumping his bones and then
became worried he might be a serial killer who lured unsuspecting real
estate agents to a showing before burying them in his backyard. But that
night, since the kids were with Peter, Jake took me out for a late dinner
at an Italian restaurant near my office.

"Did you grow up in Seattle?" I asked as we sipped at our respective
cocktails—a vodka tonic for me and a Scotch on the rocks for him. My
physical attraction to him had only increased during the short time we'd spent
together, and I hoped that his personality turned out to be just as appealing.

"Florida," he said. "Outside of Tampa, in a shitty trailer park with my
mom and sister. I couldn't wait to get out." He gave me a crooked smile
and leaned against the back of his chair. After spending a few years in
sales, I had learned that peoples' postures and facial expressions often could
tell you more about them than what they said. Jake's body language was
relaxed and open, like he had nothing to hide. I took this as a good sign.

"I felt the same way about Boise," I said, liking that we could
understand that about each other's early life. Every time our eyes met, my
stomach flipped over, and my mind raced with impure thoughts. "My
parents weren't happy when I left."

"My mom couldn't have cared less," he said. "She preferred the company of vodka and random assholes she picks up at the bar to spending time with her kids." A brief darkness clouded Jake's eyes.

"I'm sorry," I said. My heart ached for him, imagining as a little boy, how lonely he must have been, and decided to disclose another, similar bit of my past. "My parents weren't around much, either, though their drug of choice was work."

"What do they do?" Jake asked, appearing sincerely interested.

"My father's an oncologist, and until a couple of years ago, my mom was dean of the physics department at Boise University. She just teaches, now. They're both incredibly practical, and analytical. Not exactly touchy-feely. My brother and I were alone, a lot."

"Leah, my sister, and I were, too." He gave me a wry smile. "Thus you and I became the self-employed, independent types."

"Huh," I said, unaccustomed to feeling a connection with someone so quickly. Most of my first date conversations were more of the awkward, "Hey, this is great weather we've been having, huh?" variety. It was a little unnerving, how easy it was to talk with him; I normally didn't reveal so much about my personal life to a stranger. "I never really thought about it that way, but you're right." I released a short sigh. "If only my mother thought being a real estate agent made me successful."

Jake seemed perplexed. "She doesn't approve?"

I leaned forward and rested my forearms on the table, and Jake did the same, so our heads were closer together. "She doesn't *dis*approve. It's more like she wishes I'd done something more academic. Like Scott."

"Your brother?"

"Yep. He's a biological research scientist for the National Institute of Health."

"That's in Maryland, right? Bethesda?"

I nodded. "He's quite the intellectual." Growing up, my brother and I had never been especially close, and since he elected to settle back east after completing his Master's degree at MIT, that hadn't changed. He occasionally texted to check in on his niece and nephew, but in six years, he'd only met them a handful of times, when he came home for the holidays. He wasn't married, or even dating anyone, as far I knew. Like my parents, it seemed his priority was his career. My career was important to me, too, but being a mother would forever come first. I never wanted Ella or Tuck to feel about me the way I had felt about my parents.

"Well, if you ask me," Jake said, "what you do takes high intellect. Number crunching! Wheeling and dealing to make the sale!"

I smiled, and shrugged. "Yeah, my parents prefer book smarts to people smarts." I paused. "You haven't mentioned your dad."

Jake shrugged. "There's not much to say. He took off when I was eight and we never heard from him again. I told myself every morning that I was going to do whatever it took to get the hell away from Tampa and never look back. I got the best grades I could, and with the help of a few supportive teachers and a good high school counselor, I managed to get a full ride to the University of Florida."

"Impressive."

"Thanks!" he said, flashing me another dazzling smile. "After I graduated, I landed a position as a junior recruiter at Microsoft here in Seattle, but it only took me a couple of years there to realize that I could make way more money as a freelancer, so I went into business for myself."

"That's amazing," I said, with admiration. "I got an Associate's degree, then I met my ex, married him after six weeks of knowing each other, and we decided to move here."

Jake grimaced, but with a smile. "And that didn't work out so well?"

I laughed. "Well, the marriage part, not so much. He grew up without a mom, so he was really anxious to have a family—kids and a wife to take care of them, and I was flattered when he said he wanted that woman to be me. I liked that he wanted a more traditional life, so we just took the plunge, thinking loving each other and both of us wanting a family would be enough."

"And it wasn't," Jake said, solemnly.

"Not for very long. I realized pretty quickly that he was just another version of my father. He was gone all the time, focused on work so he could be the breadwinner. He was pretty controlling, actually. We argued more and more until we realized it wasn't going to work." I paused, and took a deep breath. "The only good thing to come out of it was our two gorgeous kids." I held Jake's gaze, waiting for his energy to change—for him to suddenly "remember" that he had an early morning meeting and make a beeline for the exit. The few men I'd gone out on dates with since my divorce tended to stop calling after I told them I was a mother. I decided to be honest with Jake upfront, in case it would make him run. Better to get it over with, before I got invested.

But his expression didn't change. In fact, he smiled, a crinkled fan of lines appearing at the outside corners of his eyes. "How old are they?" he asked.

"Ella is six, and Tuck is five." I showed him a recent photo of Ella's slender arm wrapped around Tuck's neck in a half-hug, half-headlock. They were sticking out their tongues and crossing their eyes, hamming it up for the camera.

"They're cute," Jake said. "I bet you have your hands full."

I nodded, and put my phone away. "It can be hard," I said, "but I love them to death." I teared up a little as I spoke—my pride in being a mother far surpassed any pleasure I took from my career. The way their eyes lit up when they saw me—the way they threw their bodies at me, knowing I would always be there to catch them—made every minute of stress and hard work since the divorce worth it.

"I'd like to meet them," Jake said.

I gave sort of a half-shrug, feeling protective of my babies, worried that maybe I'd shared too much. Since the divorce, I hadn't dated anyone long enough or seriously enough to introduce them to the kids. It was one thing if I got hurt while dating, but there was no way I'd expose Ella and Tucker to someone if I wasn't certain that the relationship would last.

My hesitation must have shown on my face because Jake reached over and put his hand on top of mine. "No rush," he said. "I get it. We just met. But you should know I do like kids. I've always wanted to be a dad." He rubbed his thumb on the side of my hand, and I shivered. He continued, his eyes riveted on mine. "A lot of women I've dated say they want to get serious with someone—get married, have a family—which is definitely what I want." I imagined with the less-than-stable upbringing he'd endured, having a family, and creating a life for his children that he himself didn't get to have, would be a priority. But it also pressed a panic button inside me, since Peter had claimed to want the same things. What if Jake ended up being just another man who wanted to control me?

"They say it, but don't mean it?" I asked, cautiously.

"Exactly. A lot of them are looking for a man with a bank account to take them out and buy them expensive shit." He shook his head. "That's not my thing. I'm looking for something real. Someone real. A person I can root for and she can do the same for me. A true and equal partner."

I nodded, pressing my lips together, feeling a little overwhelmed by how deep this conversation was getting. But I needed to know how any man I dated felt about possibly becoming a step-father, so I decided it was a good thing Jake and I talked about it sooner rather than later.

We shut the small bar in the restaurant down that night, and when he kissed me at my car, my entire body felt electrified. Everything in me wanted to take him home—to find out if our conversational chemistry carried over to the bedroom. But I forced myself to resist that urge, sensing that I'd found something precious, and rare.

We spent six months dating before he met the kids. The first time we slept together was, quite literally, an eye-opening experience. Jake was a slow, considerate lover, seemingly more focused on my pleasure than his. After I'd had my first orgasm, he got on top of me, elbows bent, bracing himself on his forearms. His face was only inches from mine. "Look at me," he said, hoarsely. The tip of his cock teased between my legs, and I bucked my hips, trying, unsuccessfully, to get him to enter me. But then, I did as he asked, and he finally slid inside. My eyes closed again, reflexively, my head turning to one side, basking in the pleasure I felt, and he immediately stopped moving.

"Please," he said. "*Look* at me, Jess."

A little reluctantly, I fixed my gaze on his, and he began to move inside me again. I felt more naked than I ever had before as I looked into his deep blue eyes; a wall inside me crumbled, seeing the passion and love he felt for me. I trembled, exposed in a way I was not accustomed to, and while it unnerved me, it also made me realize that I'd never let a man that close to me, before—I'd never let my guard down—even when he was inside me. This knowledge—this moment of pure and total connection—solidified my decision that Jake was the right man for me.

Three months after I introduced him to Ella and Tuck, he proposed. They took to him immediately; Tuck, especially, when Jake showed up at our small house with a Spiderman puzzle that he promptly opened, and then sat down on the floor with my son so they could work on it together. Later that day, he accepted an invite to Ella's impromptu princess tea party, happily donning the sparkly crown and pink feather boa she insisted he wore. Seeing Jake with my children only made me fall in love with him more.

We invited his mother and sister to our wedding, even offering to pay their airfare and accommodations, but they both declined, citing "health issues."

"More likely they can't get sober long enough to get through security," Jake said, embittered. His sister had taken both to the bottle and her mother's lifestyle, relying on a constantly revolving roster of boyfriends to support her. Jake's honesty about his emotions—his gift of self-awareness, and his ability to articulate how he felt was refreshing after the few years I spent with Peter, whose only clearly expressed emotions seemed to be hungry or horny. Initially, I'd mistaken my ex-husband's sometimes cocky, strong-but-silent-type personality as strength. In fact, I was attracted to that part of him, thinking it meant he would nurture and protect me and whatever children we had. But as our time together went on and he flat-out refused to communicate about anything that had to do with our relationship, accusing me—as my parents often had—of being overdramatic when I felt upset, I began to shut down, as well. Ultimately, this dynamic led to our undoing, and even as I fell in love with Jake several years later, I was apprehensive about opening up—afraid to have another marriage that might fail. But there was something about him that made me feel safe. Still, the revelations I made to him were more like the intermittent drip of a leaky faucet; I worried if I let loose, if I told him everything about me at once, I'd scare him away.

"They're starting," Charlotte said, now, jerking me back to the present. She nodded toward the other side of the field, where Jake was calling out the roster for the first half of the game.

"You got this, girls!" I yelled, pulling my hands out of my pockets to clap.

At the sound of my voice, Jake looked over, giving me a knowing smile that sparked an instant blaze of excitement. *When had that stopped happening?* I wondered. *When did I stop getting turned on by just* looking *at my husband?* About the same time he stopped getting turned on every time he saw me naked, I decided. During our first few years together, I couldn't get undressed in front of him without him feeling me up, which typically led to something more. I thought back to the night before, how I'd felt when Will had asked me to dance and Jake whispered in my ear—*I want to watch*—and how I felt my spine straighten, overwhelmed by a sensation I couldn't quite name. Knowing that this other man thought I was sexy, and that my husband—the man I loved, the person I'd committed my life to—was excited by watching me be touched by someone else was a foreign, intoxicating thing.

"Hey," Charlotte said, jostling me with her elbow. "Stop ogling Jake. Ella just made the first goal!"

"Shit," I said, as the small crowd of parents cheered around us. "Way to go, honey!" I called out, even though the team had already moved on to the next play.

"You must have had some kind of night," Charlotte observed, raising a single, perfectly plucked eyebrow.

I gave her a small smile and then shrugged, turning my attention back to the game. It had been quite a night. And one thing I knew for sure, Jake and I were going to talk about what it meant when we got home.

Three

"My team *sucks*," Ella said, as I walked with her toward the parking lot, where Kari was supposed to pick her up. Jake was still on the field, gathering soccer balls and taking down the portable team benches, and then would meet me at our car.

"It doesn't suck, honey," I said, reflexively. I put my arm around her shoulder and hugged her to me, but she jerked away.

"Yeah, it does! Sarah was supposed to be passing and clearly she didn't because *duh*, she hogged the ball the whole game and that's why we lost!"

"Well, that's something you can talk with Jake about, and he and the other coaches can bring it up at practice, right? Something to work on?"

"I guess," Ella said, kicking the asphalt with the tip of her black and bright pink cleats.

"Don't do that to your shoes, please. They're expensive." I tried not to sigh. She may have gone from looking like a little girl to a young woman, but there were moments I spent with her when she still acted like an unreasonable toddler, and I understood why parents used to marry girls off at thirteen. "Get this hormonal little psycho out of here!" they probably said to prospective suitors. "I'll even throw in a few goats!"

"Okay! *God!*" She glanced around the parking lot for Kari's red minivan. Peter owned his own construction company, and since having Ruby, Kari had stopped working as a hair dresser at the high-end salon she'd been at since she graduated from cosmetology school—at Peter's request, of course—so she was usually the one to chauffer the kids around. Now that they were a little older, we kept a pretty lax custody arrangement— the kids usually stayed with me and Jake during the week, and then three weekends a month, plus half of their school vacations with their dad. During the summer, we inverted this set up, and they stayed with Jake and me on the weekends, and their dad and Kari during the week. Dealing with Kari more than Peter could be a pain in the ass, but I told myself it could be much, much worse, considering some of the divorce/custody nightmares I heard about from my friends. The kids actually liked Kari, and most of the time, they loved having a little sister to play with. Seeing them dote on Ruby was the only time I felt a tiny twinge of regret that Jake and I hadn't had a child of our own.

"There she is," I said, pointing to the entrance. Kari rolled down her window and waved as she drove toward us.

"Did Tucker win?" Ella asked. Both of my kids were highly competitive, so it was always a challenge when one of them lost a game and the other won.

"I don't know," I said, gently. I'd texted Peter a little while ago to ask how Tucker's game was going, and he'd replied, as usual, with brevity: "Not over yet." Baseball games took much longer than soccer; a bonus of

Peter's decision to coach Tucker's team and Jake doing the same for Ella's.

"Hey!" Kari said as she pulled into a parking spot, and then climbed out of her van. Ella ran over and popped the back open, throwing her gym bag in before scrambling over the back seat to greet Ruby, who I assumed was in her car seat.

"Love you, honey!" I called out. "Bye!"

"Bye!" Ella said, sitting down next to her half-sister.

"Sorry I'm late," Kari said, pushing her long, perfectly straightened, light brown, honey-blond-highlighted hair away from her face. She once told me that her fashion icon was mid-1990's Jennifer Aniston. She wore skinny jeans and a white crop top that showed off her flat stomach and belly button ring. "Ruby is refusing to put clothes on lately. I had to chase her around the house for like, twenty minutes."

I smiled. "Ella did that when she was three, too." As always, I tried not to look at Kari's breast implants, which presented as two overinflated water balloons placed on top of her slender rib cage. When Peter first introduced her to us, Jake had said to me later, after they'd left with the kids, "Well, the good news is that she'll be safe in the event of a water landing."

"Really?" Kari asked, now setting her hands on her hips. "I asked Peter about that, but he said he couldn't remember."

I tried to picture how this conversation had gone between the two of them, with her chatty, "like"-peppered dialogue, and his more serious, laconic communication style, and cringed. They seemed happy enough— Kari had actually been thrilled that Peter wanted her to quit her job and be a stay-at-home mom—so honestly, what made their marriage work was none of my business.

"Mama!" Ruby squealed from the car. "I want to go home!"

"She peed her pants!" Ella called out, helpfully. "It's all over her car seat!"

"Shit," Kari said, frowning. "See you tomorrow night at seven?"

"Yes," I said. "We'll pick them up."

I waited until they drove off to head to our car, where Jake was already waiting for me. "Hey," I said. "Sorry you guys lost."

"Eh." He shrugged. "That little bitch Sarah wasn't passing like she was supposed to."

I laughed, and told him that Ella had basically said the same thing.

"Smart, that girl of ours," he said. As always, my heart warmed when he referred to the kids as "ours." In Jake's mind, Ella and Tucker had four parents, and he was one of them. "I'm starving," he said. "You ready to go?"

Twenty minutes later, I was in our kitchen throwing together turkey sandwiches while Jake took a shower in our bathroom upstairs. I had to show a young couple a few houses around Bellevue at two, but our day was free for the next few hours.

"That looks great," Jake said when he came to stand next to me at the kitchen island. His hair was still wet, and he smelled like soap. He grabbed the sandwich I'd set on the plate for him, and I took a bite of my own before reaching into my small, going-out-for-dinner purse, which I'd tossed on the counter the night before. I pulled out the business card Will had given me, and very deliberately set it on the granite countertop, next to Jake's plate, keeping my index finger on it for a minute.

"Yes?" Jake said, after swallowing the bite of food he had in his mouth.

"We should talk about this."

"About what?" He took another bite, chewed it, swallowed again, and then grinned.

I smacked his arm, playfully. "You know what."

"I do?"

"Jake…."

"What?"

"I'm being serious. What happened last night was…crazy."

"Crazy good or crazy bad?"

"Well, the sex was good. Obviously." I was a little sore, actually, but it was the rare, immensely pleasurable, I-got-laid-the-way-I-need-to kind of tenderness, so I had no complaints. Jake was generally a very gentle lover, focused on lots of foreplay—a "the woman always comes first" kind of guy—which was nice, but sometimes, I wanted him to bend me over and fuck me like he was paying for it, like he had last night.

"Just good?" His tone told me he was teasing and loving every minute of it.

"It was amazing, okay? Is that what your fragile male ego needed to hear?" I smiled, so he'd know I was teasing him, too. I walked around the island and entered the family room, where I sat down on the couch. I was a little nervous to talk about all of this with him. I worried that telling him how much I liked what happened last night would upset him—that it took the attention of another man to get me that turned on.

"You forgot your sandwich," Jake said.

"I'm going to kill you." Normally, I loved the way he injected humor into our conversations, but I wanted to have a serious discussion. "Come sit with me. Please."

He took a minute to gauge the look on my face, nodded, and then walked over to join me, carrying his plate with him. "It was pretty amazing, wasn't it?" he asked, sounding pleased with himself.

I nodded. "I don't think I've ever felt anything like it." I paused, and grabbed a pillow to hug against my chest. "But it felt weird, too. Letting him touch me like that. And seeing how much you liked it." My stomach twisted, remembering.

"Weird, why?" Jake asked.

"Because I'm your wife. Because I'm not supposed to get turned on by anyone but you." I'd never caught Jake checking out other women when we were together, but when he wasn't around, I'd certainly noticed other, attractive men, especially over the last year, as our sexual life had quieted down. *I can look at the menu as long as I eat at home,* I reassured myself when another man caught my eye. I never wanted to cheat on my husband, but I couldn't deny the pangs of physical attraction I sometimes felt. Now, I held my breath, seeing how he would respond.

"Says who?"

"I don't know," I said. "The marriage police? The people who made up the whole 'til death do you part thing? God?"

He laughed. "Honey, I get it. It felt strange to me, too. I didn't know I'd get so turned on watching you dance with some other guy, but damn. When he asked, all I could think was how hot it would be." He set his plate on the coffee table in front of us. "It was a total rush. He wanted you. And that made me want you even more."

"I could tell," I said, unable to keep the flush from my cheeks, recalling the way Jake had pushed me up against our car.

He reached over and took my hand. "Are you okay with it? You don't feel bad, do you?"

"No."

"Guilty?"

"No." I looked at him. "Why did you ask if I got his number?"

"I don't know." He let go of my hand and then sighed. "Okay. That was a lie. I was thinking it might be fun to do it again. See you dance with him."

"Just dance?" I put the words out there between us, hovering, watching my husband's face, waiting for his response. After the sex we'd had last night, I'd pictured Will dancing with both of us, me in between them, their bodies pressing against mine. And then, the next image was of the three of us, together, in bed, naked. Me between them, again. If we did it together it wouldn't be cheating.

"Would you want to do more than that?" Jake asked. His blue eyes darkened, pupils enlarged.

"I don't know," I said. "Would it be awful if I did?" I swallowed hard, thinking back to when I was twelve years old and found a stack of my brother's Penthouse Letters magazines in a drawer in his room. I'd been looking for his fancy calculator so I could use it for my homework, and suddenly found myself reading about people doing things with their clothes off that I'd had no clue could happen. One story, in particular, stood out to me, of two men with one woman. One of the men was the woman's husband. The descriptions of them both kissing her, their hands roaming her body and the pleasure she took from it, had stayed with me. In the years since, my fantasies had often led back to this scenario— being the center of two men's attention, sometimes with both of them touching me, and others, with one watching while I had sex with the other. And now, since last night, I couldn't get those images out of my head. I couldn't stop picturing myself as that woman.

"Not awful," Jake said, softly. "I'd say pretty much the exact opposite of awful."

I felt a flood of relief. "Really?"

"Really." Jake leaned forward, cupped his hand behind my head and pulled me closer so he could kiss me. "I love you, Jess. I want you to be happy. And if this…works for you…for us…if it might make our sex life better, then I think we should talk about it."

I kissed him again, sat back, and took a deep breath before telling him about the story I had read, the one that I kept coming back to. It was strange, but exciting to be sharing something I'd kept private for so long. It made me feel closer to him.

When I was done, he scooted over and put his hand on my thigh. "That's the kind of porn I like. Two men, one woman."

"You're just saying that," I said, not quite believing him.

"No, I'm not. It's what I like."

"You never told me that."

"You never told me, either."

He was right. That fantasy was something I'd been afraid to share with anyone, even Jake, because I never thought it was something I would ever actually do. I also worried if I had told him how much the idea of having sex with two men at the same time turned me on, he would feel like having sex with him alone wasn't enough. I was afraid it would hurt him.

"There would have to be rules," I said, quickly. "If we decide to do this. Lots of them. To make sure nothing bad happened between us. Because people try this open marriage shit and it fucks things up, every time, right? We have to be careful. And smart. And safe."

"Yes," Jake replied. "But I don't think this would be an open marriage, exactly."

"Why not?" My heart was pounding inside my chest as we spoke. I couldn't believe we were having this conversation. I couldn't believe Jake was turned on by the idea of having another man join us in bed.

"Because I'm not interested in having sex with other women. I'm interested in watching you have sex with another man. Both of us having sex with you. Together."

Something about hearing him speak the words out loud made me need to close my eyes. I could hear the blood rushing in my ears. The possibility that this might actually happen was equally thrilling and terrifying. "It's not exactly fair that you don't get to have sex with someone else, too," I said, I opened my eyes and looked into his, searching for any hint of uncertainty. There was none. That was something I loved about Jake—his face almost always clearly expressed what he was feeling, so I never had to wonder if he was hiding something from me. Unlike Peter, who had been, and still was, difficult to read, with Jake, what you saw was what you got.

"It's not about that. The idea of being with another woman doesn't turn me on half as much as the idea of seeing you with Will."

"Are you sure? You wouldn't resent it? You wouldn't be jealous?" I asked, fearful that Jake hadn't yet considered this possibility. "Because there's no *way* I could watch you touch another woman the way Will touched me. I'd want to scratch her goddamn eyes out. I'd want to *kill* her. It's a total double standard."

He gave me a meaningful look. "Did I seem jealous last night?"

I remembered the sheer lust on my husband's face inside the club. The way he took me against our car moments later, and then again, when we got home. No, jealous was not the word I'd use.

"It's still not fair," I said. "Why can't I give you the same freedom you're willing to give me? And why are you okay with that?" It felt selfish, and I was worried that regardless of what Jake said now, if we actually followed through, he might freak out or demand a quid pro quo arrangement. And I just couldn't stomach the thought of another woman in our bed.

"I think it has something to do with the fact that what turns me on most is when you're turned on," Jake said, after a minute. "Nothing gets me hotter than knowing you're excited. Seeing the look on your face last night when Will touched you…." He trailed off for a second before continuing, as though he were picturing exactly that. "I guess that since I know seeing me with another woman wouldn't turn you on—that it would hurt you—there's nothing hot about it." He grinned. "I mean, don't get me wrong. It's not like I haven't thought about what it would be like to have another woman join us—I am a guy—but honestly, I think it would be way too much work, trying to satisfy two women at once. Someone would always be waiting around, tapping her foot." I laughed, and he cocked his head. "But hey, I'd be fine if you're into the idea of having sex with a woman on your own. I'd be more than willing to sit back and watch."

"How generous!" I said, with a wry smile.

"What can I say? I'm a giver." He grinned again.

I shook my head, smiling. "Sorry to disappoint you, but that's not my thing."

"You've never fantasized about it?"

"Nope." I'd never been sexually attracted to women, even when I read the lesbian or bisexual scenes in my brother's magazines. The idea didn't turn me on. But having Jake ask me about it ignited another question in my mind, so I looked at him, a little fearful to verbalize it. "Are *you* into the idea of being with another man?" I held my breath, waiting for his answer, not sure how I would feel if he said yes. It hadn't crossed my mind that part of the reason he might want to bring another man into our bed was because of a desire to explore that specific part of his own sexuality. I felt a twinge of discomfort, not because I had a problem with bisexuality, but because what if he did want to have sex with Will, too, and ended up liking it better than being with me? Maybe this whole thing was a bad idea.

But Jake didn't hesitate. "No, I'm not. The thought of it is kind of kinky, and if it was something you wanted to watch, I would probably give it a try—again, only because it would turn you on, which would turn me on, etc., etc. But I don't feel any need to do it."

I nodded, a little relieved that we could avoid this possible complication, and then was quiet a moment before continuing. "We would have to be really honest with each other. We can't hold anything back about how it makes us feel."

"Agreed," Jake said, solemnly. "We talk about everything. Totally honesty. If one of us wants to stop, we stop. No questions asked."

"Are we really going to do this?" I asked. I was excited and scared out of my mind.

Jake smiled. "Grab his card," he said. "And my laptop."

And just like that, it began.

Four

It turned out that talking about having a threesome with your husband was a lot easier than actually making it happen.

"What if we read him totally wrong?" I asked Jake, after we sent Will a note and he didn't get back to us right away. We chose email—creating an anonymous account—instead of texting or calling him because we weren't sure we felt comfortable having him know our phone numbers. For all we knew, he could have been a psycho. Or married. The last thing we wanted to do was mess with someone else's marriage—that, along with honesty about how we were feeling about the experience and always using condoms, was one of the most important rules we discussed. "What if it was just a dance and we're out of our minds to even consider that he would want to do something like this?"

"We won't know until we ask," Jake said. We had just said good night to the kids, who both had been up until ten doing homework. Now, we were nestled into our king size bed—"plenty of room for three," Jake joked the other day—in the dark as he curled up behind me.

"Back that shit up, woman," he growled, pulling my hips tighter against his.

I laughed, basking in the warmth and strength of my husband's body, thrilled that once again, he had reached out for me. We'd had sex every day—nine times!—since our conversation on the couch, each encounter fueled by the memory of my dancing with Will at the club, and what it had led to in the parking garage. What it might lead to, now. I felt like a lust-crazed teenager, constantly thinking about when we could do it next.

Sex hadn't really been on my radar until I found the stash of magazines in my brother's drawer. I swiped one of them, hoping he wouldn't notice, and took it to my own bedroom, slipping it under my mattress. I brought it out at night, after I was sure my parents had gone to bed. My body responded to the blatant sexual descriptions; my face flushed and the spot between my legs ached with a strange, but pleasurable feeling. At first I confused it with having to use the bathroom—the pressure was similar—but when I squeezed my thighs together, rubbing them back and forth, it took on a whole other level of intensity and instinctually, my hand slipped downward and began to move. My flesh throbbed and my breathing changed. The tension I felt built up and up and then suddenly—surprisingly—released. Waves of bliss coursed through me. I immediately wanted to do it again.

Still, questions sprinted through my mind. *Am I normal? Do other girls do this?* And then, a horrifying thought—does my *mother* do it? I thought about asking Scott, since he was the one who had the magazines in the first place, but I couldn't handle the idea of confessing something so intimate to my older brother. What if he laughed at me? Or worse, what if he told his best friend, Mike, who sometimes smiled at me in a way that made my heart race?

I shoved the magazine under my mattress that night, only to think about it constantly the next day. At school, I looked at Ryan Miller, the boy who sat across from me in AP algebra, and instantly flashed on an image of him naked, with an erection, touching me the way the men in the magazine had touched the woman. My face got hot, and I must have made some kind of sound, or Ryan felt my eyes on him, because he turned his head and frowned.

"What?" he asked, and I shook my head, quickly averting my gaze, grateful that other people couldn't see inside my head.

Later that day, I came home to find my mother in the kitchen, standing next to the counter while she chopped celery, carrots, potatoes, and onions. My mother had about ten recipes she made on regular rotation; it was a Tuesday, so I knew roasted chicken and vegetables was on the menu. She had gone back to her position as professor at the college as soon as she could after I was born, working her way up to her current position as dean, only teaching morning classes so she could be home in the early afternoon to greet us and to make dinner. But then she would usually hole up in her office in the basement, writing lectures, grading papers, or researching complicated physics theory for her next journal article.

"If you bother me," she often reminded us, "one or both of you had better be on fire." Scott didn't seem to mind being kept at a proverbial arm's length; in fact, he thrived on being left to his own devices. But I often envied the kind of mothers some of my friends had—the baking-cookies, snuggling-on-the-couch, going-shopping-at-the-mall-for-no-reason variety. I was pretty certain if my mother had to describe her version of hell, those three activities would be it.

She made it a point to cook our dinner not as a family bonding tactic, but to please my father, a man who thrived on routine. For him, it was always a bowl of oatmeal with flaxseed for breakfast, tuna salad or a BLT for lunch, fish, chicken, or steak with vegetables for dinner—if he was home from the hospital to eat with us—and almonds and apples for any snacks. He rarely ate anything sweet, other than fruit, insisting that processed sugar was the root of all medical-problem evil. "That'll put you in an early grave," he said, sternly, any time he caught me or Scott eating candy.

"I'd rather die younger and happy, eating what I want," my brother usually replied, flippantly, and my dad would laugh. Again, Scott seemed naturally better-equipped to shrug off the pressure to abide by our father's regimented lifestyle choices. Then there was me, who, when faced with the condemnation shooting from my dad's dark eyes, would shuffle obediently to the garbage and throw away whatever treat I had been eating, waiting for him to praise me. My dad worked long hours at Boise General—when a patient of his was in crisis, he might not come home for days at a time—so when he was around, I felt anxious to win his approval. He seemed like a god to me, out there devising treatment plans and performing procedures that saved peoples' lives. The least I could do was not commit the sin of eating a Snicker's bar in front of him.

"How was school?" my mom asked, now, as the lifted the cutting board and carefully scraped the veggies into the roasting pan on the stove. She wore her standard, weekday work outfit: a pair of black slacks and a button-down shirt, not unlike the ones in my father's closet. She sometimes took on a softer look by throwing on a cardigan, but she never strayed from the colors brown, black, and navy blue. Her sandy blond hair was cut in a sensible, chin-length bob, and as usual, the only makeup she had on was a little mascara. When I was sick and couldn't go to school, she took me to work with her, instead of the two of us staying home. I remember those days vividly, because she set me up with blankets and a book on the small, brown leather loveseat in her tiny, book-and-paper-filled office, along with a huge mug of hot tea. One time, when she came back from teaching class, three of the professors she oversaw in her department—all men—entered the room with her. Each of them had on a similar variation of the brown tweed or black pantsuit my mother often wore. With her straight-hipped build and smaller chest, the only difference I saw between her and the men who worked under her was the lack of a tie around her neck. She was unconcerned with the extraneous, as was, it would seem, my father.

"Your mother has the finest mind of anyone I've ever met," he sometimes proclaimed, especially after my mother would talk with him about complicated theories she was exploring in her work. My mother's face would light up at those words, and the look between them was the closest I ever saw to affection being expressed in their marriage. They were sensible people, and rarely argued. When they did, they were reasonable about it, weighing the pros and cons for whatever issue was at hand, never raising their voices or calling each other names, as I had witnessed some of my friends' parents doing. Their discussions seemed more like two lawyers debating two sides of a case until they were able to find common ground and reach a practical resolution. In general, our home was a peaceful one; histrionics were discouraged.

When my best friend, Kara, stopped sitting with me at lunch in fifth grade—when she stuck out her tongue and told her new best friend that I wet the bed until I was six—I came home crying, and that night, my mother came into my bedroom after I'd refused to come downstairs for dinner.

"That's enough, Jessica," she said, sitting on the edge of my bed.

"You're over-reacting."

I sniffled into my pillow and rolled over to look at her through swollen eyes. "I am not!"

"Tell me the facts," my mom said, curtly.

"Kara's a *bitch*," I said, relishing the sharp edges of the curse word in my mouth. Neither of my parents swore often, but they didn't discourage us from doing it. "Words are tools," they said. "If you have reason to cuss, then fine. Do it. But only if the occasion truly calls for it."

"That's a judgment," my mom said, correcting me. "The *facts* are that she didn't sit next to you at lunch and she told someone else one of your secrets. That's it. What she did hurt your feelings, but there's nothing you can do about it, now. The best reaction is no reaction. Don't let her know that she hurt you. Don't stoop to her level by telling one of her secrets. Be the bigger person, Jessica. That's the best revenge."

This was how my mother insisted on helping me or Scott through any type of problem: Identify the facts. Determine if you can change anything about them. If not, move on as if nothing had happened. How we felt about something was usually irrelevant.

A couple of years later, I thought about how to tell her the facts of what had happened after reading one of my brother's magazines as I hung my backpack on the hook by the back door. "School was fine," I said, in response to her inquiry. My stomach was in knots as I tried to come up with a way to broach the subject of what I'd done in my bed last night without ratting on my brother for having the magazines in his room, or admitting that I'd taken one for myself.

"Do you have homework?" my mom asked as she opened the oven.

"Just some reading for English."

She frowned. "They're not doing enough for you in math and

science, if you don't have assignments to bring home. I should talk to the principal about upping the curriculum."

I bobbed my head as my leg jiggled up and down under the table. In seventh grade, I was already in AP algebra, but even that didn't seem like enough for my mom. I took a deep breath, unsure how to articulate the facts of what was on my mind without actually having to talk with her about sex. Hearing how babies were made had been painful enough; my parents had revealed the specifics to me when I had asked several years before, in third grade, after I told them what I'd heard from other kids— that a man had to pee inside a woman in order to get her pregnant.

"That's not how it works," my mom said. Her posture changed, and a strange expression took over her face. She looked to my dad, who was sitting with us at the kitchen table, eating breakfast. His short brown hair had recently been cut, and he sported a well-groomed mustache, as well. Scott had already left for early morning swimming practice, driven there by one of his teammates' parents.

My dad leaned forward, resting his elbows on the table linking his fingers lightly together over his plate. His brow furrowed, and I felt a pit form in my stomach, like I was about to be punished for doing something wrong.

"Babies are made when a man's penis gets hard and he puts it inside a woman's vagina," he said, in the same monotone manner that I'd heard him use on the phone when he gave instructions to the nurses at the hospital on what to do with a patient. "A fluid called semen comes out of the man's penis, and sometimes reaches an egg that a woman has in her uterus, and that egg, fertilized by the sperm, is what grows into a baby."

I pictured my father putting his penis into my mother and cringed. Suddenly, I didn't want to talk about this subject anymore.

"Do you have any more questions?" my dad asked, and I shook my head, feeling uncomfortable.

I had that same feeling that afternoon in the kitchen, when I wanted to ask my mom if what I'd done the night before—the feeling I'd had—was normal. I was afraid that she might tell me to ask my father about it, the way she had when I got my period in sixth grade. If I had problems with math or science, she was more than happy to help—in fact, she often foisted her help upon me when I didn't ask for it—but when it came to my body, she let my father, the doctor, handle my inquiries. And since there was no *way* I was going to tell my dad about the story I'd read, I decided to not tell my mom, either. I didn't talk to anyone about it, at all.

Now, almost twenty-five years later, the one thing the experience at the club with Will had done for my relationship with Jake was make it easier to talk about sex, and our feelings about it. It felt as though we'd stepped into a different world together, where the colors were brighter, the sensations more intense. The volume on our sex life had been turned up, high, and our bodies—and our minds—were overwhelmed by the pleasure of it. We started telling each other more about what really turned us on.

"I love it when you whisper dirty things in my ear," I told him one night, when we were naked in bed—somehow, over the last ten days, we had stopped bothering with pajamas—both of us lying on our sides in the dark, facing each other.

He kissed me, deeply, then moved his mouth and set his lips against my earlobe. "Dirty things," he whispered. "Dusty, muddy, filth."

I laughed and gave his chest a little push. "Idiot," I said, with deep affection.

He smiled and then put his mouth close to my ear again. "I can't wait to see you fuck Will," he said. His breath was hot. "I want to see you ride him."

I released a short, staccato breath of my own, feeling myself get immediately wet.

Jake pulled back so he could look at my face. "Better?"

"Yes," I hissed, and then began to move my lips down his neck.

"Use your teeth," he murmured, something he had never requested before. I complied, grazing his skin, feeling him shudder as he twitched against my leg. He groaned and rolled on top of me, pinning my arms above my head. He moved his hips until they forced my legs apart. The tip of his cock slid back and forth over my slickened clit.

"Put your hand over my mouth," I said. "Like you did against the car."

"Not yet," he said. He shifted the tiniest bit, and then thrust inside me, causing me to cry out. Only then did he clamp his hand over my lips. Still, I moaned, feeling my lips vibrate against his palm. I wanted him to know how much I loved that feeling. How much I wanted to be taken.

"I want the lights on," he said, gruffly. "I need to see your face when you come."

I nodded, and he took his hand off of my mouth to reach over to hit the button on the base of the bedside lamp, illuminating the room with a soft glow. He propped himself up on his elbows and looked down at me with the dark blue eyes I could never resist.

"I need to rub my clit," I said, even though he was still inside me. He gave me a small, wicked smile, then lifted his body off of me just enough for me to slip my arm between us. When my fingers hit the right spot and began to rub in small circles, he pushed his hips forward gently, using only the tip to fuck me, slowly. Teasingly.

"Holy shit," I said, in a ragged breath. "Yes, like that. Fuck me like that." My fingers moved faster, feeling his eyes on my face as my entire body clenched, then spasmed, and went over the edge. "Oh god, I'm coming!" I said, and as though intuiting what I needed, Jake shoved inside me, hard, and to his hilt, over and over again, causing my one orgasm to roll over into another, and then one more before he finished, too, finally collapsing on top of me.

"Mmm," I said, wrapping my arms around him. The weight of his body on mine was perfect—warm and reassuring. "You feel so good."

He rolled off of me onto his back, keeping one hand splayed on my stomach. "I love you," he said.

"I love you, too," I said, lacing my fingers through his, feeling closer to him than I ever had. We lay in companionable silence for a few minutes, basking in the pleasurable afterglow, until I finally spoke.

"When did you start masturbating?" I asked.

He released a short laugh. "Where'd that come from?"

"I'm just curious." I quickly told him the story of my first orgasm, after reading the hot stories in my brother's magazines.

"Honestly," he said when I was finished, "my mom told me I discovered my dick when I was eight months old and treated it like a magic joystick from that moment on."

"Ha. Tucker did that, too. I think he was closer to a year, though."

"Well, he's twelve, now, and I have no doubt he's figured out how to get off."

"Ew." I gave him a playful jab in the stomach with my elbow.

"You asked. I was eleven when I remember having my first real orgasm. Within a couple of years, I was jacking off maybe six or eight times a day."

"What?" I exclaimed, shift my body so I could look at him. "You can't be serious."

"Teenage boys have remarkable recovery time. And are perpetually horny."

"Wow." I turned and snuggled back into our spooning position. "Maybe you should talk to Tuck about it. So he doesn't think anything is wrong with him. Or Peter can."

"You've already told the kids that masturbation is normal. They were like, eight or nine?"

"Yeah, because my parents never talked to me about it so I thought I was a total pervert."

Jake moved his hand so he could gently squeeze one of my breasts and then put his lips on my ear. "My gorgeous, pervy wife."

I moaned a little. "Oh god," I said. "We're not doing this again, are we? I've got four showings tomorrow and two listing appointments! We haven't gotten a good night's sleep in almost two weeks!"

He bit my earlobe, softly. "I don't care," he whispered.

I rolled over to face him, letting his long arms encircle me, and put my hands flat upon his chest. I didn't care, either. In fact, I was thrilled he wanted me again. That he couldn't help himself. "What am I going to do with you?" I said, letting my fingers wander downward.

"Let me show you," Jake replied, and then reached over to turn on another light.

Five

"Tuck!" I hollered my son's name from the kitchen, where I was throwing together his lunch and before-practice snack. "Get your butt down here or we're going to be late!" It was a daily battle, getting my twelve-year-old out of bed and off to school by seven-thirty. Jake had already left with Ella, who popped out of bed like a jack-in-the-box at six a.m., even on the weekends.

"Just a *minute!*" Tucker yelled, in a tone I'd need to have a chat with him about on the drive to school.

"Don't forget your uniform in the dryer!" I replied. Our laundry room was upstairs, one of the features that had sold me, especially, on buying this particular house when Jake and I got married. When we met, I'd been renting a small, two-bedroom bungalow on the outer edges of Queens Ridge. Even with child support from Peter, it was the only thing I could afford on a single-parent, one income budget. Working in the tech industry as a recruiter for companies like Microsoft and Amazon,

Jake made substantially more money than I did at the time, and after he proposed, he was more than happy to sell his one bedroom condo in downtown Bellevue and use the proceeds to put toward a down payment on a house for all four of us to live in together as a family. I'd struggled with this gesture, at first—my pride as a woman who could take care of herself and the kids on her own took a definite hit—but I decided that my discomfort would fuel me to work even harder at becoming one of the top realtors on the Eastside. Two years later, I was awarded highest-selling real estate professional in the area. We had split the bills fifty-fifty ever since, something that when I was a teenager, my mother had told me was essential for a relationship to be successful.

"Never become so reliant on a man that you don't have the ability to take care of yourself," she often said. "Get an education. Make your own money."

Her expectations, and my father's, were that I would do as my brother—who was three years older than me—had done, and enter a four-year university. But unlike Scott, I didn't have a clear idea of what I wanted to do with my life, so much to my parents' disappointment, I enrolled in community college, meeting Peter not long before we both graduated with AAs in business. Six weeks later, he and I took an impromptu trip to Vegas and got married on a whim.

"What are you going to do with your life, now?" my mother demanded when I came home with a thin, gold band on my finger, announcing my plans to move to Seattle with Peter. My father was at the hospital, as usual, leaving my mom to deal with what I had done on her own. Part of me wished that he were there, too, yelling. At least that would have meant that he cared. "What kind of job do you think you'll be able to get?" Her usually pale skin was bright red, and her gray eyes flashed with anger.

"We'll be fine," I said, bolstered by a specific brand of youthful, invincible, self-righteousness. "We'll figure it out."

"'*We*?'" my mother said, with a shrill edge. "What about *you*? *Your* education and *your* life? You have no idea who you even *are*, Jessica! You can't be making these kinds of enormous decisions! You're ruining your life!"

"You were only twenty-three when you met dad," I countered. My mother had been in graduate school, and my father, about to start his residency, when they met. They got married two years later, after my mother had graduated with her master's, and then decided to proceed with her PhD.

My mother gave me another furious look. "It's not the same thing. I'd already spent five years on my own, working and paying for tuition and rent. I didn't have parents to help me." My mother had been a later-in-life, surprise baby, born to her parents when they both were in their mid-forties. Since they were already accustomed to a childless life, my mom said she often felt like a nuisance to her parents—just another one of the animals they took care of on the potato farm she was raised on outside of Idaho Falls. She was sixteen when her father died of a sudden heart attack out in the fields, leaving my grandmother a heavily mortgaged house on 50 acres of land. Bankrupt, my mom and grandmother had to move to Boise in order to live with her mother's sister, where my mom ended up attending the university where eventually, she would become a professor. My grandmother passed away before my mom had Scott and me, so I knew little about her.

"I have Peter, now," I said, fighting off the tight feeling in my throat. "I don't *need* your help!"

I finished packing my bags after she left my room, and a few hours later, Peter and I had filled the back of his beat up Ford truck with as many of our belongings as we could manage. We began our trek west, him in his truck, and me in my ancient Honda Accord, with barely enough money for first and last month's rent on an apartment when we got to the other side of the Cascade Mountains.

We settled in the far outskirts of Redmond where rents were cheaper—me with a job waiting tables in downtown Kirkland and Peter doing scut work for a construction company—going several months without talking to either of my parents. (Peter's mother had died in a car accident when he was a baby, and his father didn't seem to care what Peter did with his life, as long as it didn't interfere with his.) But then I got pregnant, and though I was excited, I was also overwhelmed, and the only thing I could think to do was call my mom.

"Oh, Jessica," she sighed, when I told her I was already four months along. But then her voice brightened. "Are you going to find out if it's a boy or a girl?" Something about the idea of becoming a grandparent changed her—softening some of the harsh edges I'd spent my own childhood butting up against. She sent gifts and came to visit, even staying with us for a week after I gave birth to Ella. "You're the sweetest baby girl ever, aren't you?" she cooed as she held my newborn infant, and while it made me happy to see her be affectionate with my daughter, I wondered why she hadn't been the same way with me; at least, when I'd been old enough to remember it. My father, however, remained as detached with Ella and Tucker as he had been with Scott and me. I tried not to let it bother me, but there were times I couldn't stop myself from shedding a few tears, wishing my dad was a different kind of man. Wishing I knew for sure that he loved me.

When I was ten years old, my class was assigned a short "The Person

I Admire Most" essay, and I'd decided to write about my dad. I'd always been a little in awe of the work he did at the hospital, how he'd hurry out of the house, even in the middle of the night, if one of his patients needed him. I'd hear him get up, and I'd rush to my bedroom window to watch him go down the front steps toward his car, the tails of his black trench coat flapping behind him like a superhero's cape. I'd written about that in my essay, and when he walked through the front door that night after work, I rushed to greet him, the paper in my hand.

"Can you read this for me?" I asked, waving my essay like a white flag as he loosened his tie with one hand and set his briefcase down on the entryway table with the other. He looked groggy, as he always tended to when he got home from a shift, as though he'd been rudely awoken from a long afternoon nap.

"Not now, Jess," he said.

"But it's about you," I said, unwilling to be deterred. I didn't tell him the reason I'd written about him—I wanted that part to be a surprise.

"I've had a long day," he sighed. He walked past me, toward the kitchen, where I knew he would pour himself a glass of red wine— "good for the heart"—from one of the bottles on top of the refrigerator. I followed him, hoping that after he'd had his drink, he would relax and be more open to reading my essay. Scott was upstairs in his room, and my mother was in her office, which was in the basement. She hadn't come upstairs to greet my dad, which wasn't unusual. Oftentimes, I'd have to pound on her door to get her to emerge and eat the dinner she'd prepared before disappearing.

I sat at the kitchen table, legs swinging, as I watched my dad pour the ruby-red liquid into a glass. He took a small sip, and then a longer one. He stared out the long, rectangular window over the kitchen sink at the blossoming pink cherry tree in our side yard, not seeming to register that I was in the same room.

"Dad," I said, a little impatiently. "I really need you to read this. I want to be sure it's good."

"Ask your mother," he said, tiredly.

"She's *working*," I said, feeling a small spot in my throat start to tingle. I didn't ask much of my father—I knew what he did was important. My mother liked to remind me and Scott of that fact, often. But I wanted him to *know* that I knew it. I wanted him to read my essay, pull me into his arms and tell me that it was the best thing he'd ever read.

"Carol died this afternoon," he said. He turned around and rested his hips against the edge of the countertop, crossing his arms over his narrow chest. He was a tall man, but slight. My mom was always trying to convince him that he needed to gain ten pounds.

"One of your patients?" I asked, quietly. He rarely discussed the people he took care of by name—something about patient privacy laws—so I sensed this woman must have been pretty important to him.

"She was only nineteen," he said, and somehow, he looked even more bedraggled. He stared at me, but it seemed like he was looking right through me. "She had bone cancer."

"I'm sorry," I said. I felt helpless, and like I might actually start to cry. I had the crazy thought that maybe *I* should get cancer. Then I could stay at the hospital and he would spend time in my room, playing Scrabble or Uno with me, feeding me green Jell-O and popsicles while I slowly got better, the way I knew some of his other patients had.

"I did everything I could," he said, and I nodded, pretending to understand the magnitude of what that entailed. I looked down at the paper I held, and the words upon it began to blur.

My dad sighed, picked up his wine, and walked past me again, out of the room. Before I realized what I was doing, I took my essay and ripped it into shreds, then stood up and threw the mess into the garbage can, shoving it down as hard as I could. I stormed out of the kitchen and walked past the living room, where my dad had settled into his recliner, glass in hand. I paused at the bottom of the stairs and looked at him.

"I love you, Dad," I said, but my words seemed to fall on deaf ears, because he didn't respond. He didn't move. He didn't say that he loved me, too.

Later, after I became a single mother and experienced days where I was so exhausted I could barely remember my own name, let alone cater to every one of my children's demands, I understood that my dad was grieving that night, unable to be present in the way I needed him. But that wouldn't be the last time I wondered if he loved me, nor was it the first that he'd been too distracted to pay attention to me. Even when Ella and Tucker were born, he made little effort to be a part of their lives, something that grieved me, because I'd hoped he might soften as he got older. I hoped we might connect in a way we never had before.

The most fatherly thing he'd done after I became an adult was to offer to let me, Ella, and Tucker come live with them when Peter and I divorced. And despite my refusal of that offer—at the time, I was still resentful of his lack of involvement in my childhood—and the challenging few years of single parenthood that followed, I never forgot that fight with my mother the day Peter and I left, when she told me I was ruining my life. Even as I built my real estate business, I knew she had wanted more for me, a fancier degree and a more academic career, like hers. I never stopped feeling like I had failed her. I never stopped wishing that my father had shown up that day to beg me not to go.

Now, I had to shake off the memory of that feeling as I threw a bag of smoked almonds, three cheese sticks, and two tangerines into Tucker's snack bag, and then shoved that inside his backpack, which was waiting by the garage door.

"Tucker Jackson Wright!" I hollered again, using his full name so he would know that I was serious. I stood at the base of the stairs that led from the kitchen to the second floor, and pounded my fist on the wall. "If you don't get down here right this instant, I am leaving without you!" I needed to be in the office by eight-thirty to meet with a couple who had flown in last night from LA and wanted to find a six-bedroom, five-bath house with a view of Lake Washington, and I had the perfect property in Mercer Island to show them. I had listed the house, too, so I was in for a double commission if they decided to buy it, which I was pretty certain they would. People responded well to my more laid-back sales style. I was never pushy; I never uttered the phrase: "You *have* to buy this house!" I'd witnessed other agents say exactly that, or lie about having to beat other offers on the property, and their potential buyer's expression would often fade from interest to one of annoyance. Nobody likes being told what they "have" to do, least of all when they're about to dole out a huge portion of their savings for a down payment. Instead, I asked my clients leading questions like, "Can you picture your kids in this playroom?" or "What would you cook for the holidays in this gorgeous kitchen?" Eventually, they reached their own conclusion, and usually, if all the planets aligned with pre-approved financing and my ability to get them to imagine living in a particular house, I'd make the sale. I'd be furious if Tuck made me late and cost me this one.

Less than a minute later, my son stumbled down the steps, his gym bag in tow. "Do I have time for breakfast?" he asked as he pushed past me without so much as a good morning. His black hair was spiked on top of his head with an inordinate amount of gel, and he wore baggy cargo shorts with a blue T-shirt.

"No, you do not." I tossed a granola bar at him, which he managed to catch, even while carrying his bag. "If you had been down here twenty minutes ago, you could have had the eggs and toast I fed your sister. Grab a banana, too."

"'Oh, Ella's so perfect,'" he said, in a voice that I was sure was meant to mimic mine. He put the granola bar into his bag, and then reached for a banana from the bowl on the counter. "'Ella gets good grades and cleans her room and gets up early like an old person.'"

"Stop," I said, trying not to laugh. He actually nailed my voice pretty well. I picked up my laptop bag and my purse, and pushed him playfully out the side door into the garage. He was quiet on the ride to school, even though I tried to ask him how things were going with his friends and in his classes. As was per usual since he turned twelve, he gave me monosyllabic answers like "fine" or "good." Never any details. He was so like his father that way—non-communicative, and hard to reach, at times. I kept hoping that it would just be a phase.

"Bye!" I said as he got out of my car at the school. "Have a good day! I love you!" I didn't care if his friends might be nearby and hear me; I was determined to make sure my children never doubted how I felt about them. He grunted, and gave me a half-wave before trudging toward the front doors. The campus was covered in a sprawling, red brick building that resembled a community college more than a middle school, nothing like the single box-like structure where I'd gone to junior high outside of Boise.

As a realtor, I worked for myself, but also as part of a larger company,

Kendall Properties, which was founded back in the 80's by the woman who was technically my boss. Real estate had long been a man's career, and Nancy Kendall set out to change that. Today, she was a powerful woman in her late fifties who prided herself on maintaining a roster of high-producing, well-respected agents in the Seattle market. She gave me a chance when I was a newbie agent, a single mother, trying to support my two kids—and the best and only way I knew how to repay her was to make enough sales to help keep Kendall Properties rated as one of the top agencies in the Northwest.

I entered the mirror-front building that overlooked the busy I-405 freeway with fifteen minutes to spare before my meeting. Nancy was always here by seven o'clock, without fail, and was usually the last one to leave at night. "Don't ask your staff to do anything you're not willing to do yourself," she once told me was her business model. "Set the example, and the expectation for them to live up to it."

I greeted Nancy's assistant, Tony, and then rapped on her door before entering.

"Come in!" she said, cheerfully, but I only popped my head inside.

"Just wanted to say good morning," I said with a smile. "Jake sends his love." He hadn't, but Nancy adored my husband, and always wanted to hear how he was doing.

"Such a sweet man," she said, looking up at me from her desk. She was a striking woman, not pretty, exactly, with her oddly shaped nose and wide forehead, but she had a powerful aura about her. Her posture was perfect and her suits and smooth, smartly-cut brown bob were always impeccable. I'd always thought she and my mother might get along, but when I'd suggested I might invite Nancy over to join us for a visit the last time my mom had come to our house for the weekend, she had looked at me like I was out of my mind.

"What would I possibly have in common with a woman who sells real estate?" she asked, and the words pinched inside my chest. Did she not realize that *I* was a woman who sells real estate? Did she not hear how condescending she sounded? But I didn't push the issue; I knew from experience that it wasn't worth it to try to explain how I felt.

"How are the kids?" Nancy asked me, now.

"Driving me crazy, as usual, but good." I smiled again. "You should come over for dinner soon." Nancy was twice-divorced from men who both had a hard time dealing with her success and she'd never wanted any children of her own, but she was great with Tucker and Ella, talking to them like they were grown-ups in a way I could always tell they liked.

"I'd love that," she said. "Talk to Tony and let's get a date on the books."

"Done," I said, and then headed to my own office, which was down the hall and around the corner from Nancy's. I didn't have an assistant anymore—I found that I actually stayed on top of my work better if I didn't have to spend the time waiting for someone else to remind me to do it. Or dealing with the aftermath if they failed to do what I had asked.

"I don't know how you manage not knowing when and if you're next paycheck will come," my mom said to me on the phone a few weeks ago, and not for the first time. I'd been telling her about a particularly complicated deal that could lead to substantial commission, hoping that she might see how difficult my job actually was, and, subsequently, how rewarding it could be. Instead, she chose to focus on its unpredictable nature.

"That's what fuels me to work so hard," I said. "The not knowing. The fact that my next deal could be my last keeps me on my toes, making sure it won't be."

She'd made a clucking sound, then, clearly not convinced of the merit of this particular financial dynamic. "I'll take a steady, reliable paycheck, with benefits, any day of the week," she said. As usual, I gave up trying to get her to see my point of view.

Now, I sat down at my desk and opened my laptop. As I waited for it to boot up, I checked my phone, and saw a text from Jake. "He wrote back," it said. "Check our new email." My heartbeat sped up and my chest flushed as I read those words. I dropped my phone into my purse and typed my password to unlock my laptop, immediately logging into the anonymous email account Jake and I had set up in order to reach out to Will. There was only one email in the inbox, a reply to "The couple you met at the Cove." We'd kept the note brief, saying that we'd like to take him up on his offer of getting to know each other better, figuring it would be wiser to save the specifics of what we were thinking for an in person discussion.

"Hey guys!" Will wrote. "Sorry for taking such a long time to respond to your email. It went into my spam folder. I was cleaning it out tonight and saw that you'd reached out. I hope I'm not too late. Yes, absolutely, I would love to get to know you two better. Jessica is an amazingly sexy woman and I loved dancing with her. I like the vibe you two had, which is why I approached you in the first place. The fact that you decided to reach out tells me that you are the kind of couple I need to get to know. Let's meet for a drink, wherever you'd be most comfortable, and we can go from there. Here's to a new and exciting friendship." And then he signed off simply, as "Best, Will."

I re-read his words three times before grabbing my phone and shooting off a text to Jake. "Should we meet him for a drink?"

"I'm game if you are," Jake replied. "Want me to set it up?"

I stared at the screen for a minute, glancing back at Will's email, and then to my husband's message. My breath became shallow. The phone on my desk buzzed; the receptionist informed me that my clients from LA were waiting for me in the lobby.

A powerful burst of excitement vibrated through me. I remembered the way it felt to step out on the dance floor with Will, to let him touch me the way only my husband normally would, and it made *me* want to be the one to email him—to experience that dare-devil thrill of starting something new.

And so, before I could change my mind, I sent Jake another text: "Let me do it," I said, and then I walked down the hall, thinking, *Why not? What do I have to lose?*

Six

J ake stood outside the doorway that led from our bedroom into our walk-in closet, leaning against the wall. His arms were folded across his chest as he watched me try on yet another outfit.

"What about the red one?" he suggested. "The one you wore to Charlotte's birthday party?"

"It makes my ass look big," I said as I pulled off the form-fitting blue shift dress that looked more parent-teacher-conference than woman-maybe-about-to-have-a-threesome. In my fantasies about this situation over the years, I'd always cut straight to the get-naked-with-two-men-part; I never thought about what I would be wearing before that.

"Maybe he likes big butts," Jake said, faking solemnity.

"That's enough, Sir Mix-a-lot." I reached down to the floor, plucked a single high heel, and then chucked it half-heartedly, not really meaning to hit him. It was the Saturday of Memorial Day weekend, three days after we had heard back from Will, and we were meeting him for drinks at a downtown cocktail lounge in about an hour. The kids were with Peter and Kari through Sunday night, but we still thought it was a better idea to pick a spot far outside of Queens Ridge. We didn't want to run into anyone we knew.

"Honey," Jake said, after pretending to duck. "He's not going to care what you're wearing."

"But I do," I said, grabbing a low-cut, sleeveless black jersey dress from a hanger. I pulled it over my head, turned sideways, and then grabbed the swell of my stomach, grimacing at the mirror. "Do I have time for a tummy tuck before we go?"

"Stop it. You're gorgeous," Jake said. "Wear it."

I twisted around to see how I looked from behind. "Are you sure?"

"Baby," Jake said, coming towards me. He turned me to face the mirror as he stood behind me, his hands on my hips. "This is the body Will danced with. The body he wanted to touch. He loved how you look. He called you sexy, remember?"

I nodded, having a hard time looking at myself. The small insecurities about my body, the ones that I carried with me every day but usually managed to ignore, were suddenly magnified. I was terrified that if I ended up naked in front of Will, he'd take one look at my less-than-flat belly and slightly sagging, I-nursed-two-babies-breasts and start muttering excuses about how he had to leave.

"Close your eyes," Jake said.

"Why?"

"Just do it."

I complied, and Jake continued, his mouth next to my ear. "Think about how his hands felt on you. The look on my face when I was watching you with him. How I couldn't control myself long enough to get you home."

As I listened to his words, my face warmed, and my body relaxed. No matter how many times over the last month we'd talked about what happened that night, remembering it never failed to turn me on.

"Now, open your eyes," Jake said.

I did, and when I saw my reflection, the uncertainty I'd felt had faded away. I shifted and gave him a kiss. "Thanks. I'm just…nervous. It feels strange, getting ready to go on a date with my husband and another man."

"Your husband thinks it's *hot*." He winked, grabbed my hand, and made me follow him downstairs and into the garage. He wore dark jeans and a light blue button down with the sleeves rolled up. Casual, but nice, and the shirt color brought out his eyes.

We didn't talk much on the drive, and forty-five minutes later, we parked and walked inside the Blue Moon Lounge, where we saw Will already sitting at a table in the back. He rose to greet us as we approached. It was still fairly early, only eight-thirty, so there weren't too many people in the immediate vicinity, and the music piped through the sound system was low enough for conversation.

"Hey," he said, reaching out to shake Jake's hand, and then pulled me into a quick, firm hug. He smelled amazing, a mix of soap and sweet, light cologne, and looked handsome in jeans and a green shirt. His blond hair was still damp, and seeing him for the first time in the light, I noticed a mischievous sparkle in his brown eyes. "Thanks for reaching out."

"Our pleasure," Jake said. He pulled out a chair for me, and then sat down next to me. Will sat across from us at the small, square table, and a server quickly appeared and took our drink orders.

"So," Jake said. "Tell us more about you." I recognized his business-like, interviewing-a-candidate-voice, and it struck me that maybe my husband wasn't as calm about the situation as he wanted me to believe.

"Well," Will began, "I moved here for work about three months ago from San Diego, and I'm finding it a little hard to meet people because my hours at the office are long."

"What do you do?" Jake asked. "If you don't mind me asking."

"I'm a financial officer for a large corporation. They opened a branch here, and I'm in charge of getting everything up and running. I'll be moving back to San Diego by the end of the year."

"Nice," Jake said, bobbing his head.

"Anyway," Will continued, "My place isn't very far from here, or the Cove, so I've been making myself go out for a little while on the weekends. I don't want to turn into one of those creepy single guys who doesn't have a life." We laughed, and so did he. "I'm forty, and have never been married—"

"Why not?" I asked, cutting him off, instantly curious. In my experience, men of a certain age who have never walked down the aisle came in two varieties: they're either total playboys, who tend to treat sex like a sport, or entrepreneurs, whose genuine loves in life are money and success rather than marriage and family. In Will's case, I was hoping for the latter, because Jake and I had already decided that if Will came across as a player who slept around, we would walk away.

"I never really felt the need," he said. He shrugged. "I've had a few great long-term relationships, but marriage and kids aren't what I'm looking for. I love my job."

"That makes sense," I said, making eye contact with him for what felt like too long of a moment before I had to look away and take a sip of my drink. My heart was pounding, again remembering how his hands felt on me when we had danced. Thinking about Jake's hand over my mouth in the parking garage not long after that.

"I'm an executive recruiter and Jess is in real estate," Jake said. "We've been married seven years."

"Seven years," Will repeated, and then caught my gaze, again. "Feeling itchy, are you?" He raised an eyebrow and smiled.

"A little," I said. And then I winked at him, surprised by my own boldness. Jake reached over and rested his hand on top of my thigh. I was so focused on my connection with Will in that moment, I jumped a little at my husband's touch.

"We've never done anything like this," Jake said, giving Will a look laced with meaning. "Have you?"

"That depends on what you're referring to," Will said, still smiling. "If you mean dance with another man's wife, then yes, I have."

"Have you done more than that?" I asked, making sure I sat up straight so my cleavage wouldn't go unnoticed. "With another man's wife?" Jake's fingers tensed, and I held my breath, trying to slow my racing heartbeat.

"Wow, so we're going to get right down to it, huh?" Will said. He released an easy-going laugh and took a sip of his beer. "All right, then. I like it." He paused, and looked back and forth between me and Jake. "Yes, I've done more than that. Not very often, though, because it can be difficult to find like-minded people, and I'm very particular. I'm not out there going to swinger parties or clubs or anything. I prefer more discreet situations. So occasionally, if I see a couple I like, with a woman as attractive as you, Jessica,"—here, he nodded toward me and smiled— "then I might ask the woman to dance and see what happens. You never know where it might lead. Most of the time, it doesn't lead anywhere, so I'm happy you guys decided to get in touch."

He shifted in his seat, and I felt his foot brush against mine under the table. That small point of physical contact brought back the rush of stimulation I'd felt the night he danced with me. I couldn't believe the intense attraction I felt. I didn't even *know* him. What I felt was more visceral than that—a reaction that came from an entirely different place than what I felt for my husband.

Jake finished the Scotch he'd ordered and motioned for the server to bring one more. "How does it normally work for you?" he said to Will. "If you don't mind us asking."

Will sat forward and rested his forearms on the table. We leaned in closer, too. This was not the kind of discussion we wanted anyone to overhear. "Like I said," he explained, "it's not something I've done a lot, but the few times I have, it works pretty much what we're doing tonight. We meet, we chat, we see if the chemistry is there—"

"It's there," I said. Again, emboldened.

"Yeah, it is," Will said. He looked at me, appreciatively, and then I felt him lift his foot, rubbing the side of his ankle against mine. I grabbed Jake's hand and squeezed it. He gave me a quick look, as though to inquire if everything was okay, but then he must have seen the flush of excitement on my face, because he smiled before turning his attention back to Will.

"And then what?" Jake asked.

"We talk about boundaries. Things you might draw a hard line at doing in a situation like this." He paused. "To be clear, I'm only interested in being with Jessica. I'm not bi."

"Agreed," Jake said.

Will sat back. "It's important for me to be highly respectful of your relationship. That comes first. If things feel weird in the middle and you need to stop, that's fine with me. I don't want to do anything that might damage your marriage."

"I appreciate that," I said, lifting my own foot out of my shoe and using it to touch Will's leg under the table, which made him smile again. The server brought Jake his second drink, but he barely seemed to register it.

"Of course," Will said. "This is an ideal situation for me, because I'm not looking for emotional involvement, and most single women are looking for a husband. But if this is something you've decided to explore as a couple, as an expansion of what you already have, together, then I'm honored to be a part of that. You can trust me not to invade your private life, and I would expect the same consideration from you. In fact, I find it works best if we don't know each other's last names, or specific places of work. It's about sex, pure and simple. And if we click, we reach out when one of us feels like doing it again. I've also been in situations where I'm with the wife alone, and she goes home and tells her husband about it later, which can be super-hot, if you're into it." He shrugged. "Otherwise, it's no strings attached."

Jake and I looked at each other, a silent conversation taking place: *Do we do this? Right now, tonight?*

"The band goes on at nine," Will said, nodding toward the stage closer to the entrance of the bar. "It's less techno than the Cove. I thought I might ask Jessica to dance with me again. Start there, and see how it goes."

"I like that idea," Jake said, turning so he could give me a quick kiss. He took a sip of his drink and then set it back on the table. "Can you give us a minute?"

"Absolutely," Will said. He stood up and excused himself to the restroom.

"Well?" Jake asked, as soon as Will left. "What do you think?"

"He seems normal," I said. My voice shook a little, and so I cleared my throat. "I like him. How he talks about respect, consideration, and discretion." Jake and I had talked about all of these things over the past few weeks as being vital to any situation we decided to explore.

"Me, too," Jake said. "What kind of boundaries do you want to set?"

"I don't really know. I mean, I don't want him to tie me up or spank me or anything. Nothing violent or painful or weird." I paused. "Do we need to say that?"

"I'll say it," Jake said. "Right now. And talk to him about having to use condoms." He stood up.

"Are you sure about this?" I asked. "Totally and completely sure?"

"I am if you are," Jake said. "We can stop any time. If it doesn't feel right, we'll leave. I'll make that clear. Okay?"

"Okay."

He hesitated. "Are *you* sure?"

"Yes." The word felt small, considering the significance of what we were about to do.

He nodded, and then walked in the same direction as Will had gone. I sat alone at the table, finishing my vodka and tonic, thinking how surreal it was that my husband was in the bathroom with another man, talking about what kind of sex they were both going to have with me. My body throbbed with anticipation as images flashed through my mind of what might happen next. I never thought I would be able to indulge this fantasy. I never fathomed I'd have a partner in life who would have it, too.

A few minutes later, Jake and Will returned to the table. The house lights lowered and the band began to play. They had a bluesy, sexy sound—a low, steady drumbeat accompanied by sonorous, aching horns.

"We're good?" I asked, as the two of them sat back down.

"All good," Will said. He stared at me with such open, hungry intensity, I didn't know how to respond. The three of us finished our second round of drinks, keeping our conversation light, but when more people arrived and the music made talking more difficult, Will stood up and offered me his hand. "Will you do me the pleasure?" he asked, and I nodded.

"Wait," Jake said, as I stood up. I looked at him, concerned, thinking that he might have changed his mind—that he'd realized he would be too jealous to let this adventure proceed past anything more than a dance. But then, he pulled me closer and whispered, "Make sure I can see you."

I nodded, and let Will lead me out onto the floor.

Seven

Will's condo was only three blocks away from the lounge, so after an hour of both he and Jake dancing with me, we decided to walk there instead of drive. The two men flanked me as we made our way down the street, no one saying much. We entered his building and walked past the security guard at the front desk. Inside the elevator, Will turned to me and tentatively reached out his hand, pushing a stray strand of hair away from my face. I didn't get my usual blowout, something Jake had requested. "Your curls make you look a little wild, like you've just been fucked," he told me. "It's sexy as hell."

Now, when Will's fingers touched my cheek, I sucked in a quiet breath and looked at him. Before I knew what I was doing, I kissed him. His lips were soft and full, and I sighed as he pulled away too quickly. Dancing with them both for an hour, showing off for my husband— and then, when Jake danced with me, for Will—had revved the level of my arousal to a place where I felt almost breakable, like freshly blown glass.

As we stepped off the elevator and into the hallway, I looked at Jake, whose eyes, once again, were clouded with lust. "Was that okay?" I asked him, still feeling the need to reassure myself that he was comfortable with what we had decided to do. I'd just kissed another man in front of him, and I couldn't help but think of the fury I would have felt seeing him kiss someone else.

"Yes," he said, with enough certainty that I knew it was true.

"Here's me," Will said, using a key to let us into his place. It was a sleek, newer building. Will had told us his company leased his apartment for his stay through the end of the year. He welcomed us into the living room, where I saw a small, but modern kitchen closer to the front door, and a hallway off to the right that led, I presumed, to his bedroom. There was a desk in the living room littered with paperwork and a dual-screen computer, along with a printer and three coffee cups.

"Do either of you want another drink?" he inquired, but both Jake and I shook our heads.

Will smiled. "Okay, then. Let's sit for a bit, maybe?" He gestured to the living room, and Jake and I went to sit while Will picked up a remote control from the counter, turned on some low music, and then joined us on the couch, each of them flanking me, again. The light in the room was dim, with only two lamps on end tables.

"Beautiful view," I said, in a shaky voice. I nodded toward the floor-to-ceiling windows leading out to a small balcony, which overlooked the Seattle waterfront, including the neon-lit Ferris wheel.

"Yeah, it's not too bad for cooperate digs," Will said. He placed a hand on my thigh, moving the hem of my skirt upward about an inch. He leaned over, moved my hair out of the way, and kissed the side of my neck, gently. When I felt Jake do the same, my breath hitched inside my chest. The sensation of both of their mouths on my skin set my nerves on fire.

I turned my head toward Will, and his mouth found mine again easily, like he had been kissing me for years. It began softly, just our lips, and it was me who allowed my tongue to dart out and tease his. Jake moved closer behind me, his hands on my waist, and then upward, cupping my breasts as Will continued to kiss me more intently. Will entwined the fingers of one hand in my hair, and moved his other hand back to my lap, where he began to push up my skirt even further, his fingers slipping along my bare inner thighs, lightly teasing. Acting solely on instinct, I straddled him, kissing him more, grinding my hips against his. Jake squeezed my ass, the way he knew I liked.

"Take me to your bedroom," I said to Will, finally pulling my mouth and tongue away from his. My voice was husky—demanding. I almost didn't recognize it as my own.

Without a word, the three of us stood, and we walked, me in front of both men, Will's hand on my lower back, gently guiding me down the short hallway into a dark room.

"Can we turn on some lights?" Jake asked. His voice, too, was deeper than normal.

Will switched on a bedside lamp, lending enough glow to the room to see each other clearly. I stood by the bed, uncertain, now that I was here, what to do. Questions raced through my mind: *Should I undress myself, or wait for them to do it? Who would go first? Would it be awkward for us? Would Jake see me naked with Will and freak out? Would I freak out?*

But then it didn't matter, because both men moved to stand with me in between them, as I'd pictured they would, with Jake behind me, and Will in front. Jake reached down and pulled my dress off of me, up over my head, and I stood there in the black lace thong and push up bra I'd bought for this specific occasion. Will stepped back and looked me over from head to toe, his eyes moving over my body slowly. Appreciatively.

"Your curves are amazing," he said, moving closer, his hands going immediately to the swell of my breasts as he kissed me again. He pushed his hips against mine and I could feel how hard he was. Behind me, I could hear Jake getting undressed, and then felt him behind me, naked, his excitement evident, too. His fingers were on my waist, and then my hips. His right hand traveled to the spot between my legs he knew better than anyone else ever had.

"Oh god," I moaned against Will's mouth, and he answered by moving the hand in my hair from the side of my head to the nape of my neck, where he gathered my curls in a fist and gave them a slight pull backward, exposing more of my neck. His mouth slipped away from mine, down to my collar bone, kissing and lightly grazing my skin with his teeth as Jake dropped to bended knees and began kissing his way up my back, steadying himself by holding onto my waist. When he reached my bra, he undid the hooks, freeing my breasts, which Will responded to by gently squeezing them both, and using his mouth to go back and forth between my already-stiff nipples.

The heat between my legs was astounding. My heart beat pounded inside my head. I couldn't think; I could only react. When Will stepped back to undress, I turned around and sat down on the side of the bed, looked up at my husband, and then took him in my mouth, all the way to the hilt, causing his head to roll back and his breath to quicken. I took my time, using my lips and tongue and a little bit of my teeth, the way I now knew he loved it, my hands resting on his thighs. Will came closer to us, standing next to Jake, and it felt natural for me to move my mouth from Jake to Will, vaguely noting that they were different, but about the same size. I went back and forth between them, stroking and sucking, getting wetter by the minute, until I finally let them both go and scooted backward far enough so I could lie down.

Both Jake and Will stood naked at the edge of the bed, watching me as I reached between my legs and began moving my fingers so they could see how turned on I was.

"Fuck, you're beautiful," Will murmured, and then he joined me on the bed, lying on his side, putting his hand on top of mine, helping me. Learning how I liked to be touched. Jake continued to stand, watching us, his eyes focused on what was happening. Will's fingers increased their pressure, moving more quickly, more intensely, until I finally had to close my eyes and let go, feeling waves of pleasure ride through my body, my skin peppered with chills, my nipples erect.

"Holy shit," I whispered after the last spasm hit. I opened my eyes and Will was staring at me, his fingers still entangled in mine, and wet. I took his hand and lifted it to my mouth, gently sucking them clean. When I finished, Will kissed me, tasting me on my own tongue.

Jake climbed next to us, then, lying on his side, too, and put his mouth next to my ear. "That was so hot, baby."

"Good," I said, then looked at Will. "I need to get fucked." I'd never said those words to my husband—to any man—but in that moment, they felt right.

Will got up and opened the drawer in the nightstand next to the bed, pulling out a condom, which he quickly donned before climbing on top of me. I kissed him again. I could feel him moving on my thigh, so I opened my legs, and he got up, remaining on his knees, lifting and bending my legs so Jake could look down and see Will as he entered me. But instead of letting that happen, I suddenly shifted my weight and pushed Will over so he landed on his back, surprising him by straddling his body, resting my palms on his chest. He looked up at me and smiled. "All right, then," he said. "If that's how you want it."

"Yeah," I said, firmly, looking at my husband. "That's how I want it." Jake sat up, and I reached over and stroked his erection as Will moved his hips so that I could slide down on top of him. The moment Will slipped inside me, I let Jake go, and my eyes rolled back in my head as I began to move my hips, fucking this other man, this stranger, while my husband watched. Another orgasm built quickly inside me, and I leaned forward to let my nipple graze Will's mouth as I began to fuck him harder, and faster. Jake got on his knees so that his cock was near my face, and I took him inside my mouth again, sucking. I stopped moving my hips, so Will lifted his and began to thrust in a steady rhythm, the motion helping my mouth move on Jake. The tension inside me mounted, until it finally went over the peak and unspooled, sending me into a strong set of muscle spasms that caused me to collapse. Jake slipped from my mouth, and I felt him move again, and get behind me. Will pulled out of me and then my husband entered me, where another man had just been, grabbing my hips. Will shift one of his hands so his fingers were between my legs again, moving them as he'd done before, while Jake fucked me, hard, and I came again, crying out right before Jake did, too. We lay together, unmoving for a moment, until Jake stepped back and it was Will's turn to flip me over onto my back. He spread my legs, moving his eyes up to my face.

"Now it's how I want it," he said, not waiting for me to reply before he slipped his sheathed cock inside me, cupping his hands on the back of my knees and pushing them so he could get inside me more deeply. Jake lay down by my side and kissed me, putting his hands on my breasts and squeezed my nipples, then put his mouth against my ear.

"You have no idea how beautiful you are," he murmured. "You're a fucking goddess."

Will continued to move, speeding up until he tensed and groaned, finishing, and then thrust a few more times before he stepped back, and smiled at us both. "Wow," he said. "That was amazing. For a first time, especially."

"A first time ever, for us," Jake said, keeping his hands on my body. Making me feel safe.

"Are you good, Jessica?" Will asked.

"I'm good," I said, my breath still a little uneven. I looked at Jake. "For now."

Jake smiled, and kissed me, and Will laughed. "My kind of girl," he said. He turned around and head into the bathroom, closing the door behind him. The water ran, and I assumed he was washing up.

"Are you sure you're okay?" Jake asked me, using one hand to push my messy hair out of my face, as Will had in the elevator. "You're not freaked out?"

I shook my head. "It was fantastic. Not that being with you alone isn't." I hurried to add the latter statement, not wanting my husband to think even for a moment that sex with him wasn't enough.

"I didn't think that's what you meant," Jake said. His face was close to mine, so I kissed him again.

"I love you," I said.

"I know you do," Jake said, playfully. "I'm glad you're happy."

"Are you?" I still couldn't quite believe that he wasn't jealous, witnessing another man be so intimate with me.

"Very. I've never seen you like that."

"Like what?"

"I don't know, exactly." Jake moved a little closer to me, so that the lengths of our bodies were pressed up against each other. "Powerful, maybe?"

"Thank you." I liked that Jake saw me as powerful, especially in a situation like this, where it could easily seem like I had been objectified, my body used by two men for their pleasure, alone. But as I lay there with my husband, basking in the afterglow of the most intense and satisfying sexual experience I'd ever had, the truth was, in that moment, it felt more like I had used them for mine.

Eight

As I entered my teenage years, I began to notice how little time my parents actually spent together. We were not a family who took trips to Disneyland or Hawaii, nor did my father whisk my mother away for impromptu romantic weekends. Their social life together consisted mostly of occasionally going out for dinner together, usually to celebrate one of my mother's journal articles being published or one of my father's patients going into remission.

"We'll be back in a few hours," my mom told me one Saturday evening, when I was fourteen. Her latest research article was being lauded as "a revolutionary theory in the field of quantum mechanics" in her scholarly circles, so my father had made reservations at their favorite steakhouse. My mother wore a black cocktail dress, and had even swiped on a little red lipstick along with her usual mascara. "Be good."

I gave her a dutiful nod, but my heart bounced against my ribcage as I thought about how, unbeknownst to my parents, Ryan, the boy I'd pictured naked after I found my brother's magazines, was coming over to "study." Scott was away for the weekend at a swim meet, so Ryan and I would have the house to ourselves. He wasn't my boyfriend, nor did I really want him to be. All I knew was that he was cute, and I couldn't stop thinking about touching him the way the women did the men in the magazine I still kept stashed under my mattress. Reading about sex no longer felt like enough; I wanted to know what it felt like. I wanted more.

"Let's go, Sheila," my dad said, impatiently. He stood at the front door, dressed in a black suit, his hand on the knob. He was not a person who allowed himself, or anyone else in our family, to be late.

I watched out our front window as they got into my dad's Mercedes and backed out of the driveway. When I was sure they'd gone, I raced upstairs to change into the low-cut top I'd borrowed from my friend, Wendy, for just this occasion. I tucked it into my tight jeans and then quickly applied two coats of mascara, pink blush, and some lip gloss. Looking in the mirror, I puckered my shimmering lips, hoping that Ryan's eyes would be drawn to them and he wouldn't be able to resist kissing me. But even if he didn't take the hint, if he didn't make the first move, I'd already decided that I would.

He knocked on the front door a few minutes later, and I opened it, feeling like my heart was beating in my throat. "Hey," I said.

"Hey." His voice squeaked a little, but I ignored it, choosing instead to focus on his long lashes that framed his dark brown eyes. He had braces, and I wondered if they would hurt my lips when we kissed, but I wasn't going to let that discourage me.

"Come on in," I said, moving aside so he could enter. As he walked past me, I looked at his body, wondering what his penis would feel like in my hand. Would it move around, or just lay there while it got hard? My body twitched in anticipation.

"Where do you want to study?" he asked, and I gestured to the living room, which was to the right of the entryway.

We sat down on the couch and he opened his math book on his lap. "What part were you having trouble with?" he asked.

"Um, the formulas," I lied. My mom taught physics; I'd learned the Pythagorean Theorem in sixth grade. But Ryan didn't need to know that.

"Like, quadratic, or....?" he asked, looking at me with raised eyebrows. He licked his lips and I took it as a sign.

I lunged toward him, knocking his book off of his lap and kissed him. He startled, but didn't push me away. He slipped his tongue inside my mouth and rolled it around, which felt weird, but kind of good, too. I put my hand on his thigh, and moved it toward his crotch, wanting him to do the same to me. But instead he grunted, and sort of shoved his hips in my general direction, so that my hand shifted on its own and landed on his erection. I began to rub him, in a similar motion to the one I used on myself when I was alone in my room. I was about to undo his zipper when the front door opened.

"Jessica!" my mother voice struck me like lightning.

I whipped around to see her standing in entryway, fury etched across her face. Ryan stood up, quickly, grabbed his book and started toward the door, where he ran past her and was gone. I wished I could follow him.

"What are you doing home?" I asked, my voice trembling. I glanced at the clock on the mantle over the fireplace. They'd only been gone half an hour.

"I didn't feel well," she said, impatiently, resting a hand flat against her stomach. She was pale, a little green around the edges, like she might soon throw up.

"We were just *studying!*" I said, anticipating her next question. My cheeks were hot, flaming with the embarrassment of being found in a compromising position, not to mention getting caught having lied, by omission, to my parents.

"You were doing more than that!" she said, as my father appeared in the doorway behind her.

"What the hell is going on?" he demanded. His dark eyes flashed. "Who was that boy?" He must have seen Ryan dart down the front steps and across the lawn.

"Ask your daughter," my mom said, accusingly.

"His name is Ryan," I said, stuttering out the words. "He came over to study. I forgot to tell you." I dropped my eyes to the floor, unable to ignore that I was still turned on by the little Ryan and I had done. I felt frustrated we didn't get to do more.

"Don't lie to us, Jessica," my father said, sternly. "You know perfectly well you need to ask permission to have anyone over when we're not here."

"But you're *never* here!" I said, feeling tears well in my eyes. "Mom's on campus, and you're always at the hospital! How am I supposed to have a *life* if I can't have *friends* over?"

"That boy was not just a friend," my dad said, in a thundering voice. "What were you doing with him?"

"Nothing!" I said, throwing my back against the couch and crossing my arms over my chest.

"You're smarter than that, Jessica," my mom said in a harsh voice. "You don't want to be that kind of girl. You don't want to be *easy*. Do you understand me?"

I remained silent, feeling their judgment pour over me like hot, black tar. I'd taken a required health class the first part of my freshman year, so I knew that masturbation was perfectly normal, but my gym teacher, who taught the human sexuality portion, had stammered and blushed his way through that section of our book, and seemed relieved that no one raised their hand when he asked if there were any questions. All I'd taken away from the class was that, yes, sex was something everyone did but it wasn't something most people talked about.

"Answer your mother," my dad said, now, in a firm voice.

"Yeah, I understand," I muttered, and then stood up in order to run up the stairs to my room. I slammed the door behind me, and threw myself on my bed. The sound of their voices floated up the stairs, but I couldn't hear what they were saying. All I knew was how embarrassed I felt, and how anything I did with a boy after that was something my parents could never know about.

I thought about that night, now, the Friday night after Memorial Day weekend, when Jake and I were going over a list of things that needed to get done around the house. The lawn needed mowing, the deck had to be power-washed, and the paint on all of the shutters was peeling, so they were in need of sanding down and a fresh coat of Queens Ridge homeowner's association–approved, Bright Lights white. We would have tackled the list last weekend, but after our night with Will, Jake and I had spent most of Sunday in bed, sipping coffee, reading the paper, and replaying what had happened the night before. The kids got home after dinner, and the four of us decided to spend Monday at a Queens Ridge community picnic that Tiffany had organized.

"You're looking gorgeous," Charlotte had said when we arrived at the park. She kissed my cheek and gave me a quick hug. "All happy and glowing."

"Thanks," I said, glancing down at the blue sundress I'd chosen to

wear. It showed a little more cleavage than I normally would have been
comfortable with for a family event, but after Will had complimented me
on my curves, I felt more confident showing them off. I wished I could
tell Charlotte that having a threesome with your husband was better than
a trip to the dermatologist for Botox and a chemical peel, but I was
still worried she'd think what we had done was simply a way to justify
cheating. I didn't feel prepared to face that kind of judgment.

"Babe," Jake said, now, jerking me back to the present. "Did you hear
me?" We sat at the kitchen island, the household to-do list and two glasses
of white wine in front of us. The kids were upstairs in the family room,
eating pizza and watching TV. "I think we should hire someone to take
care of the shutters. Do you agree?"

"Did you like the first girl you had sex with?" I said, totally ignoring
his question. I quickly summarized my experience with Ryan that night
when my parents walked in on us, a story I'd never told him before. "I
was thinking about it, and I realized that I wasn't upset that he might not
like me, I was pissed that I didn't get to do what I wanted with him." I
paused. "Is that weird?"

"I don't think so," Jake said, setting the pen he held down on the
piece of paper in front of him. "I wasn't in love with the first girl I messed
around with. I guess I liked her because she was pretty, but mostly, I
wanted to touch her boobs."

"Exactly!" I exclaimed, getting up from my stool. I spun him around
so that I could stand between his legs, putting my arms up around his
neck. "I just wanted to get my hands on Ryan's cock!" I kissed him and
let one hand drop downward to his lap. "Like this." I moved my hand,
feeling my husband twitch under the thin fabric of his shorts.

"Mmm," Jake murmured against my lips. "God, I wish I would have known you in high school. We could have gotten into all sorts of trouble."

"I can get you in even more trouble, now." I tugged at his waistband, and slipped my hand behind it, feeling the jerk of him growing hard, knowing I would have to stop if I heard one or both of the kids' footsteps. This wasn't something we normally did, making out in the kitchen, especially when the kids were still awake, but I couldn't help myself; I liked the sense of daring, the idea that we might get caught.

I moved my mouth to his ear and said, "Remember how I looked with my hand on Will's cock?" I bit his earlobe lightly. "My mouth?"

Jake groaned, and I withdrew my hand, stepping away from him in order to sit back down.

"Hey!" he said, smiling, his blue eyes filled with lust. "It's not fair to start something you're not going to finish!"

"Who said I'm not going to finish it?" I said, playfully. "But we need to get the chores sorted out. I think you're right. We should definitely hire someone to do the shutters."

"You are an *evil* woman," Jake chuckled. I relished the feeling that he saw me in an entirely different light, now—something separate from the woman I was as his wife and a mother—a woman who wielded words like "cock" like verbal Viagra, who didn't hesitate to stroke him in the middle of the kitchen even though the kids might walk in. I liked this version of myself; I felt more honest, more authentic, somehow. I was more comfortable in my own skin.

"So, Tuck can mow the lawn after his baseball game tomorrow," Jake said, "and I'll handle the power washing. What about Ella?"

"The flower beds need weeding," I said. "She and I can do that together."

"She's going to *love* that," Jake said, and I laughed. Ella didn't mind getting dirty when she was doing something fun, like playing soccer, but she tended to pitch a fit whenever we asked her to do anything that required garden gloves or bathroom-cleaning products. It was always a struggle to get her to do her chores, but Jake and I were sticklers about making sure our kids knew the value of hard work, even if we could afford to hire a cleaner. Most of their friends' families had housekeepers; some even had drivers who would bring them to and from their activities and school.

"Bentley actually *has* a Bentley," Ella bemoaned to me a few weeks ago, when work was too busy for Jake or I to take the kids school, so they had to take the bus.

"No," I corrected her. "*Charlotte* has a Bentley, because Charlotte built her own event planning business from the ground up. She started when she was twenty-one, as a bartender for another company. Then she catered kids' birthday parties, and busted her butt for *years* to get the point where now, she plans Bill and Melinda Gates' fundraisers. She *worked* to afford that car. Bentley only gets to ride in it." I'd actually tried to talk Charlotte out of buying a car with the same name as her daughter, but she refused to listen.

"I've had a picture of a silver Bentley on my vision board for twenty years," she said. "I love it so much I named my daughter after it. I'm buying the fucking car."

Now, Jake's phone buzzed on the countertop in front of him, next to the to-do list. He picked it up and checked the message. "It's Will," he said.

My breathing changed, instantly, my head suddenly swimming with images from the previous Saturday night.

Jake handed me his phone and I read the short email: "Hey guys. Just wanted to say hello, and tell you again how much fun I had last week. Let me know when you're up to playing again. Or Jessica, if you're interested, I'd love to get the chance to spend some time with you alone so you can tell Jake all about it, later. Totally up to you guys. Take care."

I handed the phone back to Jake. "What do you think about that?"

"You mean being with him without me?"

I nodded, pressing my lips together. We had yet to discuss this particular possibility, but I had thought about it, and was intrigued by how it might play out. Having a threesome was hot, but the idea of Jake *not* being there with me and Will—knowing my husband would be at home, thinking about what I was doing—amped up my excitement even more. He'd be watching me, in a sense, the way I'd always fantasized a man might do, but only *after* the fact, through my description, alone.

Jake reached over and took my hand. "How do you feel about it?"

"I don't know." I squeezed his fingers. "I mean, you trust him, right?"

"Yeah. Do you?"

"Yeah. He's not creepy or weird about the whole thing, like I was worried he might be."

"So you feel comfortable with him."

"I do."

"And I know you liked fucking him." Jake kept his tone low, too. His eyes fixed on mine.

"I did." My breath immediately hitched, remembering how it felt to have Will touch and kiss my body. To feel him slide inside me.

Jake and I were quiet for a moment, staring at each other. "If you want to, I'm fine with it," he said, breaking the silence. "I have to admit, it's a huge turn on, knowing another man wants to fuck my wife."

I gave him a coy smile. "Strokes your ego a little, baby?" I hadn't given much thought to that side of things, how this dynamic put Jake in the position of alpha male—leader of the pack. He might not only be turned on by watching me have sex with another man—he might get off on the power *he* felt, giving his "permission" for it to happen.

He nodded. "I also like that it seems that you can't help yourself. Or at least, you don't *want* to help yourself." Again, his eyes fixed on mine. "You want to fuck him, too. Don't you?"

"I do want to fuck him," I said, slowly. I watched his face respond to my words. He licked his lips and released a quick, hard breath. This kind of talk was different than the playful, innuendo-laced flirting we used to do before we met Will. It was raw, visceral, and direct; more affecting because it wasn't only talk—it was something we were actually going to do.

"Then you should," he said. "As long as you feel safe." He waited a beat, and then gave a slight frown. "And as long as you don't think you might develop feelings for him." He looked at me with questioning blue eyes.

"Oh god, honey, not at all," I said, surprising myself by how true this was. I liked Will, I thought he was funny and smart and attractive, but when I thought about him, it was only in terms of sex. I didn't picture us going out on dates or snuggling together on the couch. I wasn't interested in learning about his childhood, or whether or not we liked the same kind of food. The only person I cared about those kind of things was my husband. Again, my mind flickered to that night all those years ago, on the couch with Ryan, when all I'd wanted was to know what his cock would feel like in my hand. I didn't have a crush on him; I didn't want him to be my boyfriend. Later, even as I fumbled my way through two high school relationships—one in which I would lose my virginity to at the beginning of junior year; a less than sixty-second event that left me orgasm-less and deeply disappointed—my mother's words never left my mind: "You don't want to be *that* kind of girl; you don't want to be *easy*." I couldn't help but feel that there was something wrong with me, because what if I *did* want to be that girl? I thought about sex a lot. When I was at school, I liked how it felt when I caught a boy staring at my cleavage, knowing that he might be wondering what it was like to have sex with me. I liked knowing that my body could influence his thoughts. Besides my threesome fantasy, I often pictured myself in a room with a large group of men—ten or more— waiting their turn to fuck me. This was my favorite fantasy actually, the idea of so many men standing in line, stroking their hard cocks, me on the bed, legs open, taking on as many of them as I could.

Still, as I got older, I never actually considered acting on my fantasies. Save a few one-night stands in college (before I met Peter), and after my divorce, I'd only had sex with men I cared about. But now, what I felt about Will had *nothing* to do with love and everything to do with lust. It was casual, based on physical chemistry. Like he had said, no strings attached.

"Are you sure?" Jake asked, and I loved him all the more for the question. It showed me he had a few insecurities, too. That he wasn't pushing me into this possible scenario with Will purely for his own satisfaction. He wanted to be sure that my heart still belonged to him, and only to him. Which it did.

"Completely, totally sure," I said. I stood up and wrapped my arms around his neck again, hugging him to me. His arms encircled my waist, his hands resting on my ass, and we stood there, kissing. I thought about telling him about my fantasy of having a roomful of men waiting to fuck me, but something made me hold back. Because even though he'd been open to having a threesome, and now, to the idea of me having sex with Will on my own, I was afraid he might judge me for the sheer depravity of wanting to be fucked by so many different men at one time. That experience was probably one better left to be lived out in private, and only inside my mind.

We were still kissing when Ella came tromping down the back stairs and into the kitchen. She was in pajamas, a pair of blue shorts and a matching top. Her curls were pulled into a messy bun.

"Oh my god, *gross!*" she said. "Seriously, guys. Get a room, okay? Nobody needs to see that."

"What, *this*?" I said, teasing her. I gave Jake another full-on kiss, making fake groaning noises as I did. Jake laughed against my mouth, but joined in on putting on the show for Ella.

"Oh, baby," he said in a fake, swoony voice. "Kiss me *harder!*"

"*Ewwww!*" Ella said as she opened the fridge and grabbed a raspberry seltzer. "Stop!"

"Stop what?" Tucker asked, as he entered the kitchen, too. He was wearing sweatpants and a red T-shirt. His normally gel-spiked black hair was soft and flat after taking a shower.

"They were making out," Ella said. She screwed up her face.

"Gross," Tucker commented.

"That's what *I* said!" Ella laughed, and the rest of us did, too. Jake and I had never purposely shied away from kissing or hugging in front of the kids, but thinking it about, now, I realized that Jake had often pulled away from me, almost reflexively, when they would walk in the room, in order to focus on what they needed. But tonight, he hadn't. It felt good to show them what a healthy, loving, adult relationship looked like in terms of physical affection. I never wanted them to feel the same kind of shame I did the night my parents walked in on Ryan and me.

Jake released me from his embrace. "Is the pizza all gone?" he asked, grabbing my hand and pulling me around the island toward the stairs.

"There are a few pieces left," Tucker said.

"Dibs!" Jake said. He let go of me and raced up the stairs.

"Not if I get there first!" Tucker yelled. He spun around and chased after his step-dad.

Ella and I grabbed a bag of cheddar popcorn and a package of cookies from the pantry. A few minutes later, we were all settled on the large sectional couch in the family room, eating junk food and watching some mindless teenage melodrama the kids had picked out. My thoughts raced with images from our experience with Will, from the subsequent encounters Jake and I had had since that night, and I shivered.

Jake put his arm over my shoulders to pull me closer, and nuzzled my ear. "You good, baby?" he asked.

I turned to look him straight in the eye. I felt more than good. "I want to do it," I said, under my breath, so the kids wouldn't hear. "Alone."

THE weekend went by quickly, with Saturday morning games and afternoon chores. I spent Sunday morning preparing for an open house, and then the afternoon chatting up potential buyers as they strolled through to check out the property. Half of them were looky-loos— occupants of nearby houses taking advantage of the opportunity to snoop through their neighbor's home—but at least three agents confirmed that they would send me an offer by the end of the day.

The next morning, after the offers were in and the highest had been accepted by my clients, I decided to do a little research on this new development in our sex life. I had my suspicions, but wanted to know more about what it meant to experience this kind of intense arousal from a clearly non-traditional behavior. Were there a lot of other people out there who enjoyed this? Or was there something twisted about our reaction, about our relationship, about us?

I opened a search engine, and posed my fingers over my keyboard, unsure of what to type. I could search for information about threesomes, and I was sure a ton of links—most of them porn—would come up, but it was more the dynamic of me being with Will alone and telling Jake about it later that I was anxious to know more about. That, I couldn't name.

After a moment, I typed in the only thing I could think of: "Men who like to hear about their wives having sex with another man," and a long list of articles and blog posts came up, most of them including one of two terms: "hot wife" or "cuckoldry." I clicked on the first one that caught my eye, entitled, "The Psychology of the Hot Wife," and began to read, relieved to learn that it was fairly common for a man to fantasize about his wife having sex with another man. The author, a sex therapist, stated that most people expect that a husband would feel threatened by and jealous of such an experience, and wouldn't get why he was aroused by it. The article explained that heightened arousal from this particular sexual dynamic was due to the "sperm competition reaction." Basically, if another man puts his sperm into a man's wife, one very straightforward method of trying to ensure that the other man's sperm doesn't impregnate her would be to fill her with his own. The human penis, the article said, was designed to work as a suction pump when thrust in and out of a vagina, the glans around the penis basically scraping another man's sperm out of a woman's body.

"Holy shit," I murmured, finding it fascinating that at least for Jake, biology was at least part of the reason he was so turned on by watching me with Will.

I copied the link and emailed it to Jake, with the subject line: YOU HAVE TO READ THIS, and then clicked on one of the recommended articles about cuckoldry at the bottom of the post. But as soon as I read that most women in a cuckold dynamic got off on humiliating their husbands by sleeping with other men and then telling their spouse how much better a sex partner the other man was, I went back to the first article, because nothing about what I experienced with Jake and Will had to do with humiliation. Nor did I want it to. Even if I slept with Will on my own and came back home to tell Jake every little detail, it would be for pleasure to be experienced *together*, not about making Jake feel like he wasn't enough.

As I was about to click on another link, I got a return email from Jake. "Interesting. So, I guess you're a hot wife." The words were followed by a devil-horned emoji. "Isn't that what I've been telling you all these years?"

I smiled, and wrote back: "Flattery will get you everywhere." His compliments meant more to me, now that he was backing them up. For the most part, since our night with Will, I'd stopped keeping track of who had initiated sex, because it no longer seemed to matter who reached out first. What mattered was that we didn't seem to be able to get enough of each other.

My phone rang, then, and I had to stop reading, but I bookmarked the article. "Hi, this is Jessica," I said, absentmindedly as I put my cell to my ear.

"Jessica! It's Tiffany!"

"Oh, hi, Tiff," I said, part of me wishing I'd checked my caller ID. She tended to be chatty, and I'd already wasted enough time online. I needed to get to work.

"What are you up to?" she said, brightly.

I paused. *I'm doing research about why it's so hot to fuck a man other than my husband, Tiff. What about you?*

"I'm at the office," I said, instead. "Can I help you with something?"

"Well, I know you weren't at the bake sale planning meeting—"

I coughed. "Yeah. Sorry about that. I had to show a property in Issaquah that night." What I'd actually had was an extra glass of wine with dinner so driving wasn't an option. Not to mention the fact that if I'd shown up with booze on my breath, a few of the moms of Queens Ridge—possibly including Tiffany—would be buzzing about my need for rehab within the week.

"That's fine. But I wanted to keep you in the loop, in case you still wanted to be part of it."

"When is it, again?" I asked, tucking my phone between my shoulder and ear so I could use my right hand to navigate to my online calendar. With the inordinate number of social events the kids' middle school had throughout the year, they needed a calendar all their own.

"Day after tomorrow," she said. "We still need two gluten and sugar-free batches of cookies. Do you think you can handle that for me?"

I grit my teeth at the slight condescension in her tone—I wasn't her bake-sale-bitch. Still, with my years of practice dealing with sometimes-snippy clientele, I managed to remain polite. "Sure, I'd be happy to."

"I'd do it, but my mom fell and broke her wrist last night, so I'm swamped helping her out."

"That's awful," I said, feeling bad for how I'd reacted to the way she'd worded her request. She was probably just stressed. "Is she okay?"

"Other than complaining a lot, yeah," Tiffany said, in a tired voice. "I've ordered a meal delivery service for her for the next couple of months, and a cleaning company to come take care of the house, but nothing I do seems to be good enough. It's like she forgets I've done anything, at all."

"I can relate," I said, feeling an unexpected thread of connection form between us. "Your dad's not around?"

"He's out of the picture," she said, in a way that made it clear the subject wasn't one she wanted to discuss. I didn't know much about Tiffany's upbringing, but that was only because I'd never bothered to ask. I made a mental note to make a better effort to actually talk with her at school functions, maybe even ask her to coffee.

"I'll bring the cookies with me when I drop off the kids on Wednesday morning," I said. "If I can rearrange a few meetings, I'll try to stay a while and help out."

"That would be great," she said, in a softer tone. "And oh, while I have you, have you heard about this new app everyone's talking about? It's called 'Neighbors.' Everyone in Queens Ridge is signing up. It's used to discuss community issues and events. There's also a want-ads section, so you could use it to post about the houses you're selling, too. My girlfriend in West Seattle told me about it. It sends notifications when someone posts something, and you can respond publicly or privately. It's a fab way for everyone to stay connected."

"Sounds great," I said, actually intrigued by the want ad section. I was always looking for another way to market properties or find new clientele. "Can you send me the link?"

"You can look it up in the app store on your phone and create a log in. I'm the moderator for Queens Ridge, so I'll approve you right away!"

I thanked her, and we hung up, and as the app downloaded, I texted Charlotte. "Tiffany needs me to bring two batches of gluten-free, sugar free cookies to the bake sale Wednesday. HELP?!?"

She wrote back almost instantly. "I got you, girl. My baker will knock them out for you along with the vegan brownies she's making for me!"

"Thanks, lady!" One of the benefits to being best friends with an event planner was her unlimited access to vendors who were willing to help her out in a pinch. I liked to bake, but I didn't have time to fuss over the dietary requirements. "Cocktail date later this week?"

"Yes, please!" she replied, followed by a long line of x's and o's.

I had a stack of forms in my inbox that I needed to get through before I met new clients for lunch at noon. But I kept going back to everything I'd read about the "hot wife" practice, cycling through the facts over and over again, looking at them from different angles. Having learned even a little bit about why Jake and I both might be reacting so strongly to this dynamic, I started to feel more excited about fucking Will without Jake there. We weren't freaks; we weren't mindlessly responding to our more primal impulses. Jake and I didn't *have* to indulge this particular fantasy. In fact, I imagined many might say that indulging it was wrong—that once a couple got married, they should only have sex with each other. But since we both *wanted* to explore this experience, why shouldn't we? We weren't religious, and because Will was single, we weren't breaking up anyone else's relationship. As long as we were thoughtful and safe, if we continued to communicate and check in about our feelings, playing out this fantasy might actually be *good* for our marriage. It felt like it already was.

I picked up my phone again, staring at Charlotte's text. Everything in me was burning to talk with her about Will, about how incredibly empowered and sexy and strong I'd felt after what I'd done with him and Jake. It was a high like I'd never felt before, and I wanted to tell my best friend every detail. But I still worried that my having sex with Will— especially now that I was planning to do it without Jake there—might strike too close to the idea of infidelity for Charlotte, triggering painful memories of Alex. She'd worked too hard to put those behind her; I wasn't going to be the one to bring them back up.

No, I couldn't tell her. Talking about it with anyone would be too much of a risk.

Nine

I walked into the Tipsy Sailor at quarter past eight on Friday night, hoping that Charlotte hadn't been waiting for me too long. It was rare for her to not be working an event on a Friday, but she'd recently hired a manager whom she said was more than capable of handling the 75-guest wedding her company had been hired to plan.

"The bride is fifty," she'd texted me. "The groom is twenty-eight. Robbing the cradle, much? And can you imagine the sex? Lucky bitch."

Now, I scanned the nautically-themed bar, which was a tad cheesy, but the only non-national chain establishment in Queens Ridge that served a decent vodka martini. It was the place Jake and I would have stopped if we hadn't made the impulsive decision to have a drink at the Cove last month. I couldn't believe it had already been six weeks since we met Will, and two since we went back with him to his apartment. I'd emailed him to set up a time for just the two of us to get together, and we had decided on Saturday night, since the kids would be at Peter's, but then my mother called and said my dad had back-to-back surgeries at the hospital all weekend so she wanted to fly in from Boise and see her grandchildren. I couldn't exactly tell her she wasn't welcome because I had plans to have sex with another man and then come home and tell Jake all about it. Instead, Will and I rescheduled for the following Saturday, and for the rest of the week, when I wasn't working, I cleaned the house and snapped at the kids to pick up their shit in preparation for my mother's scrutiny.

I heard my name called out behind me, and turned to see Charlotte already sitting at a table in the corner of the bar. I smiled and waved, then made my way over to her, teetering a bit on the heels I'd decided to wear, having eschewed the sensible flats and two inch pumps I'd taken to several years back for practicality and comfort. I liked the way the higher heels made my hips sway when I moved; it reminded me of the short walk I'd taken down the hallway to Will's bedroom, the way I'd been acutely conscious of his and Jake's eyes on my ass.

"Hello, gorgeous," a man said to me, as I passed by his table, where he sat alone. He was older, probably in his early sixties, with silver hair and tan skin etched with lines, but he had an irresistible twinkle in his blue eyes, which he used to quickly look me over from head to toe. "Buy you a drink?"

I smiled, and shook my head, flattered by the compliment. Other than Will, I couldn't remember the last time a stranger had hit on me out of the blue like that. "Thank you, though."

He lifted his drink. "My loss."

"Oh no," I said. "I'm positive it's mine."

He smiled, and my cheeks flushed as I made my way to the corner. Where had that come from? "Sorry I'm late," I said, dropping into the chair across from Charlotte. "Ella forgot her laptop so I had to run it down to Peter's house. She needs to do her homework tonight, before her grandma gets here." Peter and I had agreed to swap weekends so the kids could spend time with my mom, but he still wanted them to spend Friday with him. However mismatched he and I had been as a couple, I couldn't fault his commitment as a father. He was never late on his child support payments, nor did he flinch when I asked him to pitch in on things that fell outside of normal costs, like summer camp or medical bills. He had followed through on his vow to be a more present, involved parent than either of us had had, both of us ever-focused on what was best for our kids.

"No worries," Charlotte said, taking a sip of her drink. She waved for the server, and I ordered a top-shelf vodka martini. "Loving the curls, by the way." She gestured toward my head. Her top was dark green, and her shock of red hair was, as usual, straight and smooth.

"Thanks," I said, reaching up to touch my hair. "Jake says they make me look like I just got fucked." I laughed, and Charlotte did, too.

Our server arrived with my drink, and Charlotte waited for him to leave before giving me a pointed look. "Okay. You two are obviously having way more sex than you used to. What gives? Are you sneaking Viagra into his coffee?"

I was in the middle of taking a sip of my drink when she said this, and I almost spit it out. "Uh, no. No Viagra. But yeah. Lots of sex." I grinned, unable to keep the gleam from my eyes.

"I'm so jealous! You said he'd been spending more time with the kids than between your legs. What changed?"

I shrugged, having to bite my tongue to keep from telling her the truth. "We just…started talking more."

"About what?"

"Our sex life. What really turns us on."

"Like what?"

"I'm not telling you that."

"Why not? Is it weird shit? Does he like things up his butt or something?"

I laughed, loudly enough that the people at the table a few feet away from us turned to look at me. "Jesus, Charlotte!"

"What?" she said, innocently. "It's not like I'd judge him if he did."

I shook my head, still chuckling. "He likes the idea of having a threesome," I said, deciding I could trust her with at least that. If it remained a hypothetical, maybe it wouldn't upset her.

Charlotte rolled her brown eyes. "Please. Every man on the planet has that fantasy. Two women, pretending to be lipstick lesbians for their enjoyment. Live-action porn."

"No," I said. I took a measured breath. "Two men, and me."

"So, like a bi thing?" Charlotte tilted her head. "He wants to play with another guy's dick?"

I laughed again. "No!"

"What? I had a boyfriend in my twenties who was straight, but told me he occasionally liked to trade oral with other guys for the kink of it," Charlotte said. "Not when we were together, of course." Her expression changed, and I knew she was thinking about Alex, of the many women he'd been with while professing his loyalty and love to her.

"That's not what Jake is into." I hesitated, worried that getting more specific might be too much. But then I decided to take a chance, leaving out a few key details, to see how she reacted. "He likes the idea of watching me with the other guy, and me having sex with them both. So we've been...talking about it a lot, as foreplay." I paused. "Is that weird? Or wrong?"

Charlotte tensed, and again, I knew she had to be thinking about Alex, but then she made a dismissive noise as she sipped her drink. "Not weird. Or wrong. As long as it's just a fantasy." She set her glass back on the table between us. "Fucking someone else with your husband might sound hot in theory, but I would bet you a million bucks that if you actually followed through, it would end badly. It might not be technically cheating, but there's no way a guy wouldn't be jealous once he sees another man touch you."

"Of course," I said, not making eye contact with her. The truth was that I believed Jake when he claimed not to feel jealous of Will—he wasn't demeaned or humiliated by seeing me fuck someone else. He was turned on by it as much as I was. But how could I explain that to her? How could I make her believe me? I looked back at Charlotte. "But talking about it has really heated things up."

"Clearly. You look amazing."

"Stop."

"You do," she insisted. "You're wearing that vampy red lipstick and *eyeliner*, for Christ's sake. I haven't seen you put on liner since my holiday party!" Every December, Charlotte's company put on a gorgeous, formal event at the Bellevue Hilton, inviting pretty much all of her high-end clients, along with everyone we knew from Queens Ridge. It was the event of the season. But since our night with Will, I'd begun putting on a full face of makeup each day, realizing that I'd fallen into the same mascara-only rut that my mother lived when I was growing up. It felt good to glam up a little. I'd underestimated how powerful a thing it was to make an effort to *feel* pretty—I automatically felt more confident when

I looked in the mirror. I appreciated the shape of my lips and brightness of my complexion, the wicked sparkle in my eyes. I saw myself the way I imagined Jake and Will had seen me on the night we shared.

"I got a Brazilian, too," I said, lowering my voice. I'd gotten it done in anticipation of being alone with Will, showing it off to Jake the minute I got home from a later showing that night. I barely greeted the kids, who were doing homework at the kitchen table, instead, leading Jake upstairs to our bedroom. I locked the door behind us.

"What're we doing?" Jake asked, but instead of answering him, I quickly stripped naked, leaving on my heels. I took my fingers and fluttered them between my legs.

His eyes widened and he immediately dropped to his knees, grasping my ass with his hands and putting his mouth on me. I shuddered as he flicked the tip of his tongue over my newly bare skin.

"Hey, Jake!" Tuck's voice called out from the hallway. "Want to play catch before it gets dark?"

"Not now," Jake replied. He looked up at me and muttered, "Can't a man eat his wife's pussy in *peace* around here?"

I giggled, quietly.

"But I need to practice before the game this weekend!" Tuck argued. "I can't do it without your help!"

"I said, *not now*, Tuck," Jake repeated, louder this time. "Go downstairs. I'll be there in a bit."

"And don't bother us unless one of you is on fire!" I said, stealing my mother's favorite line, albeit for an entirely different reason.

"Yeah!" Jake said as he unbuttoned his shirt. Twenty minutes later, he'd given me two orgasms, and I'd straddled him the way I knew he loved, moving my hips until he came, too.

"So, I take it you like the wax job," I said, afterward, as we lay together on the bed, catching our breath.

"I like everything about you, no matter what," he said, ever the diplomat. "But yeah. It feels different. I like it. A lot."

"I think Will will, too," I said, wickedly. My fingertips glided over his cock, and it twitched.

"Don't get me started again," Jake groaned. "I really should go help Tuck."

"Go on, then," I said, smacking his bare butt as he stood up. "Thanks for being such a great step-dad."

He grinned. "Thanks for being such a great lay."

I smiled as he threw on a pair of shorts and a T-shirt, realizing that this was the first time for as long as I could remember that he'd chosen sex with me over doing something for one of the kids.

"Holy shit!" Charlotte exclaimed, now, snapping me back to the present. "What have you done with my bush-loving Jessica?"

"I never had a *bush*! Everything was trimmed!" Charlotte and I had changed clothes together at the Queens Ridge community pool last summer, and it just happened to be after a couple of weeks of neglecting my bikini line. She'd never let me live it down.

"And now it's gone." She sniffled and pretended to wipe away a tear from her eye. "My baby girl is growing up."

"How is Bentley?" I asked, using her "baby girl" reference as a segue from the subject of my sex life with Jake. I was a little worried if we kept talking about it I wouldn't be able to keep myself from telling her everything. "Ready for the game tomorrow morning?"

"I think so," Charlotte said. "What time is your mom getting in tonight?"

"Eleven. Jake's picking her up at the airport."

"I couldn't get Richard to do anything for my mom if I paid him."

"Your mom doesn't *want* him to do anything for her." I loved hearing stories about Helen, Charlotte's mother, who, while they were both independent, was so different from mine. Helen was in her mid-seventies, still a hippie of sorts, and had never married Charlotte's father. Or anyone else for that matter. She had worked for Planned Parenthood as a counselor for years, and now, in retirement, she regularly showed up for marches against women's healthcare care defunding, holding a sign that said, "I can't believe I still have to protest this shit!" She was the kind of woman who refused to let men open doors or pull out a chair for her. "I can to it my own damn self!" she had yelled at Richard the first time she met him and he'd tried to help her out of her coat. "I didn't burn my fucking bra for you to come try and save me with your toxic masculinity!" Richard had basically refused to have anything to do with Charlotte's mother after that. And while I found her hyper-feminism reactions amusing, I couldn't say that I blamed him.

"So, do *you* like the idea?" Charlotte said as she finished her drink and signaled the bartender for another.

"Of doing something for your mom?" I asked, confused.

"Of a threesome."

"Oh," I said. I gave a short laugh that came out sounding high-pitched and strangled. "I mean, yeah, I guess. Like you said, in theory. It's fun to talk about."

"But you wouldn't do it." Charlotte's gaze was sharp; I couldn't escape it.

"I doubt it." I looked away, pretending to cough. I hated lying to her, but it felt like the only thing to do.

She sighed. "Right now I'd settle for Richard being able to get a hard-on that lasted more than ten minutes."

I laughed again, genuinely this time. "Maybe you should sneak *him* some Viagra."

"Don't think I haven't considered it, sister." Charlotte's drink arrived and she raised her glass for a second time. "To Viagra!" she said. "And the threesomes we'll never have."

"To Viagra!" I hoped she wouldn't notice that I didn't repeat the second half of her toast.

LATER that night, I was already half-asleep when Jake crawled into bed after picking up my mom from the airport. "She get in okay?" I murmured as he curled up behind me.

"Yep. All set up in the guest room. She wants to go to Ella's game first, and then the last half of Tuck's."

"Any bets on how long it takes her to start hinting we should hire a maid?" Every time my mom visited she found a way to suggest that perhaps I would be better off hiring a professional to clean the house, as she and my dad always had. I managed to laugh it off, but the implied criticism still got under my skin.

"Don't let her get to you," Jake said. He gave me a quick kiss on the side of my neck. "At least she's here." I knew he was thinking about his own mother, who had never even met Ella and Tuck. He was right—I should be grateful mine at least made an effort.

The next morning, I tried to utilize a positive attitude toward my mom when I entered my kitchen a little after six and found her already up, clad in yellow rubber gloves as she scrubbed down my stove.

"Did you bring those from home?" I asked, as playfully as I could without having had my normal influx of caffeine. I wanted us to start out on the right foot.

"Good morning," she said, ignoring my question. She was dressed in jeans and a short sleeved, blue knit top. Her no-nonsense, stick-straight silver bob was tucked behind both of her ears. "Are you working today?"

"I have a few showings this afternoon." My internal guard shot up— the one built, brick-by-brick, by years of living with my mom, knowing this seemingly innocuous inquiry was a set up.

"You'd think being self-employed would give you the freedom to take a couple of days off when your mother is here," she said.

And there it was. I took a deep breath before responding. "Being self-employed means catering to my clients' needs, accommodating their schedules," I said, lightly, though my jaw clenched. However much value my mother had placed on her own career—however many weekend hours she spent holed up in her office when I was a kid—somehow, she still found a way to criticize the kind of work I did and how many hours I spent doing it. My mother was accustomed to others doing her bidding—both her students and the professors who worked under her. She couldn't fathom the demands of a client-based business like mine.

"I don't know how you do it," she said, scrubbing at some invisible spot on the counter next to the stove.

There was no right way to answer, so instead, I walked over and hugged her, trying not to choke on the lemon-masked scent of chemical cleaning agents. We were the same height and build, though my chest was more substantial than hers, and I had my father's hair color and curls. I was still the one who had to initiate any kind of physical affection between us.

"How long have you been up?" I inquired.

"About an hour." She pulled away from our stiff embrace and removed her gloves, setting them on the counter. "I don't sleep more than five hours a night anymore."

"How's Dad?" I poured a cup of coffee from the pot my mother had already brewed, and then sat on one of the stools on the opposite side of the island. I hadn't seen my father for almost six months, when Jake, me and the kids had spent four days before Christmas at my parents' house, playing in the Boise snow. As usual, my dad was at the hospital almost the entire time.

"Cancer doesn't know it's Christmas," he was fond of saying when I was a kid and asked him if he could take at least a few days off around the holiday so we could go sledding or snowmobiling like my friends' families did during the break from school. That was one of the few benefits to growing up in Boise—we almost always had a white Christmas. Later, my dad would repeat those same words to his grandchildren, who this year, looked at me with incredulous eyes.

"Aren't *we* your family?" Tuck asked, and Jake and I gave each other pointed looks.

"It's generous of your grandpa to work so other people can be with their families," my mom said, jumping, as always, to her husband's defense.

"Out of the mouths of babes," Jake said, later that day, as we drove home on Christmas Eve so the kids could spend Christmas morning with Peter and Kari. Since then, I'd texted with my dad a bit—his preferred method of communication, because it was brief and didn't require him to respond right away, as a phone call would—but our conversations only skimmed the surface of what was going on in our lives.

"Kids are good?" he'd ask.

"Yes. How's work?" I'd reply.

"The same. Good days and bad. Some more than the other. The circle of life."

"I can only imagine." It was frustrating, how little I knew about what it was like for him to deal with life or death situations on a daily basis. My mother said he didn't like to talk about it, but as time passed, I concluded that he didn't *want* to talk about it, or maybe he didn't know how. I told myself that because he was a surgeon, he had to maintain a certain amount of emotional distance from his patients—that opening himself up to feeling everything that went along with telling someone about swollen and angry, malignant tumors in their bodies, and subsequently, having to slice into their fragile bodies to cut the cancer out—was simply too much of a burden to bear.

"Busy with work, as usual," my mom said, now. She sighed and shook her head. "He could have retired last year, but no. He says his patients need him too much." Since she had stepped down as dean of the physics department, she had spent her time writing articles on advanced quantum theories and teaching part-time as a tenured professor. But without the more strenuous demands of heading up the department, a few months ago, she confessed to me that she had too much time on her hands. My father was working as much as he ever had, if not more.

I made a neutral sound, not wanting to insert myself into the middle of issues my parents might be having.

"It's not like we need the money," my mom continued. "I don't understand why he doesn't want to relax after spending so many years running around the hospital."

"It's never been about the money for him." I imagined my dad would sit behind his desk, helping people through one of the most painful and devastating diagnoses a person can endure, until the day he died.

"I know," she sighed. "It's about helping people. It's not like I don't understand that. I guess I just wish that once in a while, your father could make his life about me."

You're not the only one, I thought, feeling a lump form in my throat. I scanned her face, saddened by the pain I saw in her steel-gray eyes. That was the thing about my mother. She came across as stoic, even cold, but then there were rare moments like these when she dropped her guard and showed how vulnerable she really was. As a woman born in the fifties, and the daughter of conservative parents, she had been taught that the only important roles she would play in her life were those of wife and mother. After I had my children—especially after my divorce and a couple of years of single-parenthood—I realized what a feat it had been for her to reject those limiting, traditional expectations and pursue a male-dominated field of study; in fact, to become an often-cited researcher and highly-esteemed professor. Sometimes I wondered why she and my father decided to have children in the first place, but never worked up the courage to ask. I was too afraid she might say she regretted becoming a mother, and no matter how old you are, that's something no child wants to hear.

"I'm sorry," I said to her, now.

She gave a quick shake of her head. "Enough about me. We have a soccer game to get to!" She clapped her hands once, and I smiled at this rare show of enthusiasm. However much she had lacked as a mother, she really did make up for in how she treated her grandchildren. And while it stung a little to see her lavish the kind of attention I used to crave from her onto Ella and Tuck instead of me, I told myself that it was better late than never.

A little over an hour later, the three of us arrived at Marymoor Park, where Peter was already waiting for us in the parking lot. My ex-husband drove an enormous white truck with a double cab and his construction company's bright red logo, "Mr. Wright General Contractors," emblazoned upon both sides. Like Jake, Peter had worked for other companies doing grunt work until he realized that the real money was in going into business for himself, using his last name as a play on words for his endeavor.

"Hey there," I said to him as Jake, my mom, and I climbed out of Jake's SUV. Ella was already on the field with her teammates and other coach, and Peter stood on the sidewalk in front of his truck. "Aren't you supposed to be at Tuck's game?"

"Ella asked me to bring her," Peter said. "We got donuts." His voice was low and gruff, something I'd found sexy when we first met, and later came to despise when our brief marriage started to fall apart. He was dressed in jeans, a blue and white baseball jersey, and wore a matching baseball cap on his head. At five-foot-ten, he was a few inches shorter than Jake, and after years of too many fast food meals on job-sites, his build had become stockier, too.

"Hello, Peter," my mom said. She smiled, but didn't show any teeth. She'd never liked him very much, especially after we'd eloped. She was always cordial with him, though, for the sake of her grandchildren, even after we divorced.

"Sheila," Peter said, bobbing his head once, in her general direction. He wasn't the president of her fan club, either.

"Good to see you," Jake said, reaching out to shake Peter's hand. The two were friendly enough with each other, but Jake told me that he found Peter's less-than-amiable personality too much like the men his mother used to bring home. "She was an asshole magnet," he said. Not that Peter was an asshole, Jake hastened to add, but I knew that when things didn't go my ex's way, he certainly possessed the potential.

Jake and my mother headed across the field to where Ella was, leaving me alone with Peter. "Everything good?" I asked him. "The kids get their homework done?"

"Yeah." He shoved his hands into his front pockets and thrust his shoulders back. "Tuck says his algebra teacher doesn't like him so that's why he's getting a C."

"Bullshit. He's getting a C because he keeps turning in his assignments late. I told him he needs to ask for extra credit to make up for it, but he hasn't." Tuck, especially, liked to try and play Peter and me off of each other. If his complaining about school didn't work with one of us, he'd try the same approach with the other, seeming to forget that for the most part, as long as we kept it about the kids, Peter and I did a pretty good job of maintaining a united front.

Peter raised his thick, dark eyebrows, which lifted his baseball cap. "He didn't tell me that part."

"Shocking," I said, and Peter gave a short, rough laugh.

"Does he need a tutor?"

I shook my head. "He understands the work, he just doesn't want to do it." I paused. "Maybe I'll have my mom help him, while she's here."

"No way," Peter said. "Did you forget the flashcard torture she put you through?"

I laughed, feeling a brief flicker of connection with my ex—a fond memory in our shared history. We'd been at an on-campus coffee shop a few weeks after meeting, having a conversation about our childhoods, when I told him a story about my mom.

"She made me multiplication flashcards when I was *six*," I said.

"When other kids were playing with Barbie dolls and learning to read, she sat me down at the kitchen table and ran math drills."

"That's nuts," Peter said.

"Right?" I shook my head, remembering. She'd done the same thing with me to learn addition and subtraction when I was four. "She was dead set on me knowing that shit before anyone else," I told Peter. "She'd say, 'What's two times two Jessica? Come on, that's an *easy* one!'" My throat swelled a little, thinking about how scared I'd been to disappoint her by giving her the wrong answer. "She wanted me to be exactly like her, and I'm just not." I'd done fine in my math and science classes throughout my formative years, but never loved them the way I knew my mother wanted me to. I wasn't passionate about any subject, really, and chose to get a business degree because I figured it was general enough in scope to qualify me for a variety of jobs.

"Fuck your mom," he said, firmly. We were sitting together on a couch in front of a warm fire, holding hands. "You can do whatever you want."

He'd kissed me, then, right there, amid the sound of coffee grinders and the chatter of other customers, and I felt like he was the kind of man I wanted to spend my life with, someone who would encourage me to be my own person. He seemed resolute, at ease with defiance in a way I found sexy. It wasn't until later, a year or so into our marriage, that it dawned on me that the characteristics that first drew me to him—his strength, the decisions he made about what he wanted his life to look like, and what role he expected me to play in it as his stay-at-home wife—was a tool he used to keep me at arm's length. It felt too similar to how I felt in my relationship with my father—a realization that had made me cringe. I knew the marriage wouldn't last.

"Good point," I said, now. "Maybe you can talk with him? Jake and

I have already tried."

"Yeah. Of course." He glanced at his phone, which had just buzzed. "I gotta go. Kari's heading to Tuck's game with Ruby."

"Okay. I'll bring my mom by in a couple of hours and take him home after. Thanks again for being flexible, so she can see the kids."

"No problem," he said. "Tell Ella to kick some ass." I watched him pull out of the parking lot, imagining how he would have reacted if another man had asked me to dance, the way that Will had. Certainly not the way Jake did. Peter had been more possessive than that, instantly jealous if another man even looked my way. I was sure if I'd worked up the courage to tell him about my fantasy of having a threesome with another guy, he would have freaked out. When we were together, if I mentioned a male coworker or customer at my waitressing job—the only job I could find when we first moved to Seattle, before I got pregnant— he would ask me if I thought the guy was good-looking, his tone already an accusation. Usually, I'd reply "no," because any other answer would have started a fight. But there were times when I'd say "yes" for the sole purpose of pushing his buttons, tired of being punished for something I wasn't doing, knowing it would piss him off.

I made my way across the grass to join my mom, who was busy chatting with Charlotte on the sidelines. I looked at the other men on the field—the fathers and coaches—and my eyes landed on a tall, dark-haired man I didn't recognize. We made eye contact, and I felt myself give him a slow smile. He smiled, too, then, in a way that suggested if I asked him too, if I walked up and began flirting with him, if I touched his arm and held his gaze in a certain kind of way, there was no doubt I could get him to fuck me. I could probably even sneak him into the park's bathroom, lock us in a stall, and then let him take me up against the wall. It would be quick, physical, and satisfying. I wouldn't even have to know his name.

I looked over at Jake, then, only to find him watching the way I'd been looking at the other man. I felt a sharp stitch of panic, worried that I'd upset my husband—that I'd crossed some kind of unspoken line—but then he raised a single, suggestive eyebrow, and I realized from the look on his face that it turned him on to have caught me looking at someone else that way. He might even have been imagining a similar scenario, or the same one, with him out on the field, watching our daughter play soccer while I fucked a stranger in the bathroom, knowing he'd hear every detail about it, later. The idea of that sent a rush of pleasure through my body, and I had to force myself to ignore it. I hadn't thought about sex this much, so blatantly and with such fervor since I was a teenager. It felt like I was tapping into something that had been too long-suppressed, unleashing a part of me that had been yearning to be freed. It felt like I was becoming a new person—like a brand new world was about to open up.

Ten

My mom spent the entire weekend spoiling her grandchildren, ignoring my request to avoid doing exactly that. When they returned from a shopping trip on Sunday afternoon—yes, she would even spend time at the mall for her grandchildren, something she had loathed when I was a kid—Ella carried two bags from Forever 21 and Tuck, an elaborate Star Wars set from the Lego store, one Jake and I had deemed too expensive to buy for his twelfth birthday the previous month.

"Look!" Tuck said, showing off the box to me and Jake. We were in the kitchen, getting dinner ready before Jake would drive my mom to the airport. He hugged and kissed my mom before racing upstairs. "Thanks again, Grandma! I love you!"

"You're welcome," my mom said, beaming with self-satisfaction.

"Grandma bought me *six* outfits!" Ella said, lifting her bags for me to see. "I *love* them!"

"I'm glad, sweetie," my mom said.

"I'm going to try it all on again!" Ella said, and in a flash, she was gone, too.

"Mom," I said, but she cut me off.

"I know what you're going to say." She held up a single hand. "And I don't care. I don't get to see them often enough and when I do, I'm going to buy them what I want. It's more for me than for them."

I glanced at Jake, who was over by the sink, suddenly very studiously chopping romaine for a Caesar salad, purposely avoiding looking at me. He knew better than to get involved in a discussion like this. I sighed. "Fine. But *only* because you don't get to see them very often." I'd explained to my mom more than once how important it was to me and Jake—and Peter and Kari—to teach the kids that they needed to work to afford extravagances, but seeing the joy on all three of their faces allowed me to make an exception. It wasn't like my mom did this every weekend. It suddenly struck me that in doing these kinds of things for them, maybe she was, in her own way, attempting to make up for the fact that she'd never done them with me.

"They're such good kids," my mom said. "You're doing a great job."

"Thank you," I said, feeling the kind of internal glow that only praise from a parent can ignite.

The next morning, after a Sunday night, family dinner and a fashion show where Ella modeled the new pieces of her wardrobe—including a pair of Daisy Duke short-shorts that would be promptly returned as soon as my mom had left—Jake carried my mom's suitcase out to his car. He had just returned from dropping the kids off at school; they'd said goodbye to their grandmother before they left.

"I'm happy I came," my mom said as I hugged her goodbye. "I need to do it more often."

"Sure," I said, despite a flicker of apprehension. The only reason my mom and I were able to get along as well as we did, now, was because she *didn't* visit very often. It was better when we went to them, so we could control when it was time to leave.

A few hours later, after Jake had dropped her at the airport and both of us were at work, I was in the middle of showing a property in the far outskirts of Woodinville when Ella called from the nurse's office, saying she had thrown up in gym class.

"Oh, sweetie, I'm sorry. Can you hang in there for an hour for me to finish up with one of my clients and then I'll come grab you?"

"No, Mom," she said in a tiny voice. She was on the verge of tears. "I'm really sick."

"Okay, baby," I said, knowing she had to really not be feeling well to drop her normal sassy tone. "I'll be there as soon as I can." I would have called Jake or Peter to see if they could pick her up, but my husband was at Amazon headquarters in Seattle for the day, meeting with the HR team to better understand the newly-created executive management positions he'd be recruiting for, and Peter was working a construction site way out in Maple Valley for the next couple of weeks, where cell phone coverage was spotty, at best. And with Ella sick, I was sure Kari wouldn't want her around Ruby.

Thirty minutes later, I had rescheduled with my client and pulled into the parking lot at the school. But as I was about to head toward the building, I heard my name called. I turned to see Tiffany charging toward me, wearing neon-green yoga capris and a matching tank top; I felt a twinge of envy of her stay-at-home mom status—the freedom she had to go to the gym in the middle of the day. "Hey, Tiff," I said. "How's your mom?"

She flinched. "The pain meds make her sick and forgetful, and it looks like she's going to need surgery to get a few screws put in so her wrist will heal properly."

"I'm sorry to hear that." I glanced toward the entrance of the school, then back at her. "I don't mean to cut this short, but Ella threw up in gym, so I need to get to get her home."

"Oh, poor thing!" Tiffany said. "Wait. Which class is she in?"

"Ms. Kelly's."

Tiffany frowned.

"What?"

"Well, I hate to tell you, but Lizzy said that Skylar Woo is bulimic, and apparently, she's been showing other girls how to throw up their lunch."

"Hmm," I said, unsure if this was true. From what Ella had told me, Tiffany's daughter, Lizzy, had a reputation for starting rumors. "That's terrible. But Ella's actually sick."

"Are you *sure*?" Tiffany asked, lifting a blond brow. "Lizzy told me that she watched *six girls* do it yesterday in the locker room. That's why I'm here, to talk with Principal Martinez. I'm positive he doesn't know what's happening." Her face brightened. "Maybe you and Ella can come with me?"

"There's no way Ella's doing it on purpose." Ella had loathed throwing up since she was seven and chugged three cans of root beer, then ate a King-size bag of Skittles in less than an hour. She spent the night over the toilet, crying as I rubbed her back and held her hair. Ever since, if she even felt a hint of nausea, she would start to cry, terrified she might end up vomiting. She had also never touched another root beer or bag of Skittles.

"Can I talk to her?" Tiffany asked. "Maybe alone? If you're not there, she might tell the truth."

"I don't think that's a good idea." My jaw clenched, irritated by her implication that my daughter was lying. Moments like this with Tiffany made it difficult to want to know her better. When she wanted something, when she was convinced she was right, she had a tendency to push, which only made me want to shove back, harder. I turned to walk away. She called out after me again.

"I haven't seen your request for me to approve you on the Neighbors app!" she said.

I gave a half-hearted wave, but kept moving. I'd downloaded the app, but had been so distracted by our time spent with Will, I had forgotten to create a login. I'd try to remember to do it later, if anything, for the possibility of more advertising for my current listings.

I got Ella home—the poor thing was hollow-eyed and pale when I found her in the nurse's office—and set her up in front of the TV in the family room upstairs, placing a giant bowl next to her on the couch in case she had to throw up again and couldn't make it to the bathroom in time. When I returned a few minutes later with ginger ale and a sleeve of Saltines, I set them on the coffee table and plopped down beside my daughter.

"Back tickle?" I asked, and she nodded, shifting onto her side so she could lay her head in my lap. I lightly ran the tips of my fingers in circles around her slender back, over and over again, as I had since she was a baby. Slowly, she began to relax, and her breathing became deep and regular.

"Thanks, Mama," she whispered. She only called me "mama" when she didn't feel well, or when she was upset. She'd changed to calling me "Mom" when she was around eight, and I'd been saddened by the transition. For whatever reason, "mama" felt more intimate to me. Like she needed me, still.

"You're welcome, sweet girl," I said. I had to fight to not tear up. I stroked her curls away from her face. "I'm sorry you feel sick." I checked her forehead, but as the nurse had told me, Ella didn't have a fever.

"Barfing is the *worst*."

"I ran into Lizzy's mom on my way in to get you," I said. "She told me that Skylar has been showing other girls how to throw up their lunches."

Ella turned her head and looked at me. "What? It's *Lizzy* who's doing that! It's so gross." She settled her gaze back at the TV, where she was streaming an episode of Grey's Anatomy. "I mean, who would do that on *purpose*?" She shuddered.

"Lizzy's doing it?"

"Yeah. For like, six months."

"Why didn't you tell me?"

Ella shrugged. "I was pretty sure Lizzy didn't want anyone to know. So it's weird that she told her mom it's Skylar." She paused. "Why would she lie?"

I thought for a moment. "Well," I finally said. "Maybe she's trying to ask for help, in her own way. She might not have the courage to tell her mom what's happening with her, but by saying that someone else is doing it, she might be hoping that Tiffany somehow realizes what's really going on. Or at least asks her about it."

"That's stupid," Ella said. "Why wouldn't she just tell her mom the truth?"

"Maybe they don't have a close relationship," I said, as diplomatically as possible, even as I wondered about how Tiffany might react to this kind of information. I didn't know her well enough to know for sure, but I imagined she might not automatically believe what Lizzy had to say.

"Maybe she's scared her mom will get mad. Not all moms and daughters know how to really talk to each other."

"Did you and Grandma talk to each other when you were my age?"

"Not the way you and I do," I said. "She was pretty focused on her job."

"Like Grandpa?" Ella asked. "Grandma told us this weekend that he should get his mail at the hospital instead of their house."

"Your grandma can exaggerate a little bit," I said, again, watching how I worded my thoughts. "He probably could spend more time with her, but his work is important to him."

"Well, yeah," Ella said. "He like, saves people with cancer!"

"Yes, he does. But like I said, Grandma's work is important to her, too. That was what they talked about with each other, more than anything else. It's what they had in common. Now that she isn't dean of the department anymore, she has more time on her hands, so I think she wishes he would cut down on his work, too."

"They should talk about spending more time together," Ella said, sagely.

"You're right, they should." But try as I might, I couldn't imagine that conversation resolving anything. Though I never saw my parents discuss it outright, it had always been clear that the crux of their marriage was centered on each other's intellect, and the loneliness my mother seemed to be experiencing fell outside of those bounds. I doubted that either of them knew how to work through something so emotionally complicated.

We were quiet for a few minutes, watching the drama at the fictional Seattle Grace hospital unfold as I continued to tickle Ella's back. After a while, she sat up and ate a few crackers, then took a couple of sips of ginger ale.

"Feeling better?"

"A little bit."

"Good. Hopefully, it's only a 24-hour bug."

She nodded, and then looked like she was thinking about saying more. "Lizzy does something else, too," she finally said. The words were hesitant. "Or at least, she *says* she's doing it."

"Really?" I said, trying to sound casual, despite the fact that my motherly warning bells had sounded. "What?"

Ella dropped her eyes to the couch. "She's giving Conner Hendrickson blow jobs. But she says it's no big deal, because it's not really sex."

"Wow," I said, as evenly as I could. "What do you think about that?" Despite my resolution to be as open about sex with my kids as possible so they didn't experience the same confusion and shame that I had, it was still a bit disturbing to hear the phrase "blow job" come out of my thirteen-year-old daughter's mouth.

She widened her round, green eyes, looking a little fearful. "I don't know."

I reached over and squeezed her hand. "It's okay to talk with me about this kind of stuff, honey. I'm glad you brought it up. It can be really confusing." I didn't want her to shut down, so I had to force myself not to launch into am immediate lecture about condoms and how blow jobs aren't actually in some mystical, "not really sex" category. I waited for her to speak again.

"I feel like she's being sort of slutty," Ella said, quietly. "I mean, putting a boy's penis in your mouth *is* sex. Right?"

I nodded. "Yep. But more than that, it's a pretty intimate thing to do with another person."

"So gross," Ella said. "I am *not* putting a penis in my mouth, like, ever!"

I laughed, thinking about what I'd done with Jake and Will a few weeks ago, and how much I'd liked it. "You might change your mind about that, but I'm glad you feel that way, now." I paused, trying to think of the right thing to say. "The thing is, when you have sex with someone, even if it's 'just' a blow job, you're sharing a piece of yourself. When you're in a loving, committed relationship, sex is, hopefully, more of a give and take situation that you both agree upon." Ella watched me, intently, so I continued. "But especially when you're younger, that give and take is tough to navigate. It sounds like Conner is taking a blow job from Lizzy, and maybe not giving anything back. It's also really easy to confuse having sex with a boy with being loved by him. Physical intimacy definitely isn't the same as emotional intimacy, and you can't exchange one for the other. Does that make sense?"

I thought about Will, then, feeling somewhat strange talking to my daughter about confusing sex with love when my connection with him had nothing to do with that particular emotion. A brief flash of guilt nipped at me—a faint shadow of the shame I'd felt when my parents walked in on me and Ryan when I was fourteen—but then I reminded myself that I was a grown woman, and clearly, after what I'd done with my husband—and was about to do, alone—with Will, I had the ability to have sex without linking it to emotion. I couldn't have done something like a threesome when I was younger and riddled with insecurities about whether I was thin or pretty enough, or whether or not a boy liked me. I wouldn't have had the confidence, or more importantly, a true understanding of what my sexual desires were so I could take control of an encounter, or at the very least, ask for what I needed. Peter never gave me an orgasm because even though we were married, I couldn't work up the courage to tell him how I wanted to be touched; I was too afraid that if I told him that what he was doing wasn't working—that kissing me a little and then fucking me wasn't enough to make me come. In fact, by the time it was my turn for an orgasm, he was already in the kitchen, making a sandwich. But he never knew it, because I used to fake satisfaction so he wouldn't get his ego bruised. Of the many ways that Jake differed from my first husband, one of the most significant was how from the start, he wanted to know what I liked, checking in as he used his hands or mouth on me. "Is that good?" he'd ask, and because he cared so much, I felt comfortable saying "a little faster," or "slower," or "a little more to the right." He made me feel safe.

But now, in talking with Ella, I had to remember that she and Lizzy were barely teenagers, and had much to learn about themselves and the intricacies of having sex. "Ella?" I said, when she didn't answer my question right away.

"Yeah," she said. "I get it."

"And do me a favor," I said. "Don't call her a slut. It's a really mean word. She's young to be doing this, but being curious about sex is a totally normal thing, and she shouldn't be made to feel ashamed of herself."

Ella gave me a worried look. "You're not going to tell her mom, are you?"

I shook my head. "It's not my place. But *you* might be able to say something to Lizzy about it. Maybe let her know, sort of casually, especially if she brings it up, that you're there for her if she wants to talk."

Ella thought about that for a moment, and then lay back down, resting her head in my lap again. I wanted to say more, to ask her if *she* had done anything close to what Lizzy was doing, but I knew if I pushed the subject, she'd clam up. Better to leave the door open for her to come to me later. Meanwhile, I'd have to decide if it was a good idea to talk to

Tiffany about Lizzy being the purge ring leader after all.

"You're a good mom," Ella murmured, then, snuggling her head against the pillow in my lap.

"Thanks, honey," I replied, thinking for the first time how *she'd* feel if she knew about what I'd been exploring, sexually, with her step-dad and Will. I imagined her disgust in discovering that I not only enjoyed giving a blow job to one man, but two, and the thought of her revulsion made me a little sick.

Whatever happened on Saturday, my children could never find out.

Eleven

I stood in front of Will's building alone, trying to work up the courage to enter. It was almost seven, and I'd left Jake at our house about an hour before, kissing him passionately in the garage as we said our goodbyes. The kids were with Peter for the weekend, and not scheduled to come back until Sunday night.

"Have fun, baby," Jake said as we stood next to my car. "Be safe. Text me when you get there, and when you're about to leave, so I know you're okay."

I nodded, searching his face for any hint that he might be hesitant to let me go through with this experience. But his expression revealed nothing but excitement and the beginnings of lust, so I kissed him again. "I love you so much."

"Love you, too, gorgeous."

I'd texted him in the garage across the street from Will's building, as I told him I would. Now, my knees shook as the security guard confirmed with Will that he was, indeed, expecting a visitor. I held my breath in the elevator; my nerves were on high-alert, drunk on adrenaline. My heart felt as though it might pound right out of my chest. I glanced at my reflection in the mirrored wall, happy that I'd shopped for a new dress and lingerie. It felt strangely intoxicating, selecting something so intimate for another man's enjoyment, but I'd modeled what I'd chosen for Jake the minute I brought it home, so really, it was for him, first. He'd had a hard time not stripping it off of me. I'd spent the last couple of days feeling constantly stimulated, thinking about what it would be like to be alone with Will. At night, Jake and I had whispered to each other about it, too—how excited he was for me to come home and relay every detail.

Will answered his door almost immediately. He was dressed casually, in jeans and a black, V-neck T-shirt. His feet were bare. "Hey, you," he said, welcoming me inside.

"Hey," I said, a little breathlessly. When the door closed behind me, I dropped my purse on the small table in the narrow entryway. I was about to say more, but before I could, Will pulled me into his arms, and kissed me, passionately. I could feel him, already hard, against my leg, and I tensed, only for a second. He immediately let me go and stepped back.

"Shit, sorry," he said, giving me a worried look. "I've just been thinking about doing that for two weeks."

"No, that's okay," I said, with a shaky smile. What woman *wouldn't* like to hear that? "I liked it. I guess I didn't really know what to expect."

"Let's have a drink," Will said. He motioned toward his living room. "Ease into things. And if you're not feeling it, I'm totally okay if you want to leave."

I looked at the couch, then shook my head. I appreciated how considerate he was being, but I didn't want to make small talk with Will.

I had come there for one thing. "This isn't a date," I said, boldly. "I don't need you to seduce me."

"All right, then." He stepped toward me and pressed me up against the wall. His hands roamed my body. When they reached my breasts, he moved his lips down my neck, nipping my skin with his teeth. I kept my eyes closed, focusing on the ripples of pleasure moving through me, surprised at how easy it was to be alone with him. To give this man, who I barely knew, full access to my body.

My mind strayed to snippets of what my husband and I had done with Will the last time we were here. I thought about Jake, at home, now, knowing that another man was touching me—knowing that he was likely reliving the night the three of us had been together, too. Picturing me doing the same things, again, without him, waiting for me to come home. The headiness of these thoughts only fueled my desire.

Will's hands moved over my hips to the outsides of my thighs, where he used them to push up my dress. When his fingers found my lingerie, he gripped my flesh. "God, I love a woman in stockings," he muttered.

I set my hands against his chest, then, shoving him away from me. I began to pull my dress off over my head, slowly, and with deliberation, revealing the royal blue and black corset I'd chosen to go with a black lace garter and seamed thigh-highs. I stood there, my shoulders back and my chin slightly lifted, letting his eyes roam over me. After a moment, I took his hand and led him down the hall to his bedroom. I felt like a Victoria's Secret model, gliding down the runway, or a high-class call girl about to do her job.

Once we were in his room, Will stripped off his shirt, and I stood in front of him, trying to undo his belt. It stuck, and I yanked on it a couple of times, until finally giving up. "Help!" I said, laughing.

He laughed, too, and immediately obliged, undoing the top button of his jeans for me. I was about to unzip them, but Will surprised me by taking me into his arms and walking me backward until I had no choice but to fall onto the bed, my legs bent and hanging over the side. He dropped to his knees, spread my legs, and then ran his hands up and down the silky fabric that encased them. "So fucking beautiful," he murmured, and then his lips were on my inner thighs, nipping lightly, the same way they had on my neck. He nuzzled between my legs, barely brushing over the fire there. I moaned a little, reaching down to touch his head, trying to urge him to do more.

"Not yet," he said. Once again, his lips moved over the skin of my thighs, his hands continuing to stroke my stockings. One of my heels fell off and he took a moment to put it back. "Those stay on." He stood up, and then lay on top of me, kissing me, the heft and pressure of his body different than Jake's, but just as reassuring. I reached down and touched him through his jeans, struggling to get them unzipped.

"Those come off," I said, mischievously, and he laughed again, helping me with the zipper and then shimmying until he was naked. I couldn't believe how comfortable I felt with him so quickly. I had worried that I would freeze up and have to leave—that perhaps this fantasy should remain only that. But here I was, as full of aching and longing as I had been the last time, more confident than ever that I wanted to do this. In that bedroom, I wasn't a mother or a wife. I was simply a woman. I was Jessica. All I wanted from this man was sex.

"Put your mouth on me," I said. As an adult, I'd never been assertive like that about what I wanted; at least, not until recently. But there was a new boldness rising up inside me. And when Will complied, when he gently moved my lacy black thong to the side and used his tongue to tease me, I closed my eyes again, tensing my muscles, slowly letting the pleasure build, and when Will's fingers joined his mouth, I knew release was only moments away.

"Oh god, yes, like that," I moaned, and so he moved his hand a bit faster, increasing the pressure of his tongue, and then I was coming, wave after wave of sparks exploding through my body, white lights flashing behind my eyes. He curled his fingers inside me, keeping his tongue moving, gently, leading me to tense again, almost immediately, and another spasm rippled through me.

"Fuck yes," he muttered. He continued his movements until I came again, and then once more, until I finally laughed a bit and pushed him away.

"Jesus," I said, breathing hard. I'd had more than one orgasm during sex with Jake, but never one on top of the next like that, rolling together. I felt a flicker of guilt, thinking that if anyone should be giving me new sexual experiences, it should be my husband, but then I realized that Jake was part of *this* experience, even if he wasn't here to witness it. I would go home and tell him what Will had done, and I imagined Jake between my legs, determined to recreate it.

"That was amazing," Will said, joining me on the bed. We kissed, and I felt him begin to undo the top few hooks on my corset, revealing my breasts. He shifted and got on top of me again, but quickly moved so that he was straddling me, his hips just under my chest. He held my breasts together with his hands and slipped himself between them, his thumbs flicking my nipples as he moved slowly, forward and back, coming close enough to my mouth so I could lick and suck the tip of him. He looked down at me, watching, so I made sure to make eye contact when he was in my mouth.

After a minute or two, he stopped, and flipped me over onto my stomach. "Get on all fours," he said. I did, hearing him rustle in the side drawer. I glanced over and saw him pull out a condom. He tore the package open, and put it on before slipping inside me in one swift movement, grabbing the flesh of my ass as he did. I groaned, feeling him filling me up, pushing back against him. We began to move in sync, then, slowly at first, and then faster, until I felt another orgasm begin to build. I adjust my body so I could put my own hand between my legs, finding the spot I knew would send me over the edge.

"Yes," Will said, thrusting with intent. "Come with me."

"Fuck me harder," I hissed. I closed my eyes, moving my fingers, picturing my husband's face, thinking about how the last time I was in this bed, in this exact position, I had his cock inside my mouth, and the memory of that was all it took. My body began to convulse, and I cried out. Will's hips slapped against my ass in a heated motion, moving faster and faster until he stiffened and cried out, too, and then collapsed onto my back.

We remained like that for a few seconds, until he rolled off of me and shifted so that I could roll over, too. We lay on our backs, staring at the ceiling, our breathing slowly returning to normal, not saying a word until I turned my head and looked at him.

"That was fun," I said, and he grinned.

"Hell yeah, it was." His cheeks were flushed and his blond hair was messy, flopping over one side of his forehead. His brown eyes sparkled. "*You're* fun."

"Thanks," I said, basking in the pleasurable afterglow of my orgasms and his compliment. I did sort of an internal, emotional check-in: Was I attracted to him? Was I having any kind of romantic feelings? Did I want to be with him more than my husband? The answer to the first question was yes: I was attracted to Will, but only physically. I liked him, but not in a starry-eyed, gee-I-get-a-funny-feeling-in-my-stomach kind of way. He was smart, handsome, and an excellent lover. But the only thing I could really think about was how much I couldn't wait to get home and see Jake. I didn't want to cuddle with Will, the way I always did with my husband after we had sex. The only thing I wanted from Will was what he had just given me. The only longing I felt was for the man I already loved.

"You doing okay with all this?" he asked, and once again, I appreciated that his consideration for my feelings. "Not too weirded out?"

"Surprisingly, no," I said. "I was worried I might be."

"Yeah, I can imagine it's pretty strange to be here, doing this, for the first time." He rolled over onto his side and propped up his head with his hand, his arm bent at the elbow. "I've never been someone's first before."

"Really?"

He nodded. "Yeah, the few other couples I've done this with were more experienced than me. The women were great, actually. They kind of taught me how it all worked. What my role is, and how to play it."

"Interesting," I said. I told him about the few articles I'd read online about the hot-wife dynamic.

"Wow," he said, when I'd finished. "I never gave much thought to *why* the whole thing is such a turn on. But it makes sense, what you said about biology." He paused. "For me, though, it's more about seeing the woman really embrace herself as a sexual being, shedding her inhibitions. There's something really powerful about that."

"It's been powerful for me, too," I said, thinking about how much more confident I'd felt over the last several weeks. I wondered if this was what it would have been like for me if I hadn't gotten married and become a mother so young; if I'd spent my twenties having sex with men purely for pleasure's sake, and I felt a stab of regret for not having granted myself that kind of freedom. But that feeling was quickly erased by the realization of how lucky I was to be experiencing something similar to it, now.

"Did you meet all of the couples you've been with the same way you met us?" I asked Will.

"Hold that thought," he said, and then popped up and walked across the room to the bathroom, closing the door behind him. The water ran, and a couple of minutes later, he returned and joined me on the bed. "Okay. So, I met two couples the same way, but the one other I actually found online. There are all sorts of websites you can peruse for this kind of thing."

"Like, dating websites?" I asked, unsure of what he meant. "Hot-wife, match-dot-com?"

"No," he said, laughing. "Just for sex sites. Adult Fun-dot-com, Craigslist."

"Craigslist?" I repeated, with disbelief. "The same place people post about their garage sales?"

Will laughed. "Well, yeah, but it's in a different section. There are lots of sketchy people on there—a lot of hookers and spam accounts trying to get you to sign up for porn sites—but there are also some normal, intelligent, sexually adventurous people. That's how I met my last couple. I posted an ad, and they answered it."

"That's crazy," I said, trying to imagine going online to look for what Will, Jake, and I had come to somewhat naturally.

"A little bit, yeah." Will reached over and set his hand on my stomach. Normally, I would have felt self-conscious about my not-so-six-pack-abs and found a way to shift on the bed so he wasn't touching me there anymore. Instead, I let him gently stroke the bulge of soft flesh that peeked out from under my corset, enjoying the way it felt. "You look gorgeous, by the way," he said. "So hot."

"Thanks," I said. "Not too hooker-ish, with the heels?"

"Just the right amount of hooker-ish."

I laughed, and then sat up. "I should probably get going."

"Oh no," Will said. "I'm not done with you, yet."

"Is that so?" I glanced at the clock on his nightstand. It was a little after eight. "I told Jake I'd be home by nine."

"Then I'd better be quick," Will said, wickedly. He grabbed my hips and pulled me down, into a prone position.

Fifteen minutes later, we were done, and I'd had two more orgasms, in quick succession. Five minutes after that, I walked to my car, headed home to my husband, the scent of another man still on my skin. I'd left Will's place after a brief conversation, in which we decided that we would let some time pass before we saw each other again, something he told me he had learned was a good way to keep things casual. "Seeing each other too often can lead to emotional attachment, which I know neither of us wants."

"Where the clitoris goes, the heart soon follows?" I said, lifting my eyebrows, and he laughed.

"Something like that."

As I drove east, across the 520 bridge, I kept replaying what I'd just done. It felt surreal, trying to process it, even though my body still ached pleasantly from its recent exertion. I'd texted Jake before I left, letting him know that I was safe and on my way home to him.

"I'll be ready," was all his return text said, and the words caused a twinge of renewed excitement between my legs. When I pulled into our garage, the door shutting behind me, he was already standing at the bottom of the steps that led into the kitchen, waiting, clad only in a pair of black, silky pajama pants. His erection was evident. His blue eyes were dark; his gaze, unrelenting.

I climbed out of my car, my curls still a mess from being in Will's bed, my cleavage practically popping out of the top of my dress. Jake strode over to meet me. He took me into his arms and set his mouth against my ear. "Tell me everything," he said, huskily. "Don't leave anything out."

Three Years Later

Twelve

It was Friday night, after nine, and for the third time that week, and my husband was working late.

"I'm sorry, babe," he said when he called me earlier that evening, after Ella and Tuck had already left for Peter's house. Ella turned sixteen five months ago, back in January, but I was still getting used to her being able to drive on her own; I made her text me when she arrived safely at her destination, especially if it involved the freeway. "I know it sucks," Jake continued, "but there are three candidates in Beijing who can't interview any other time. Microsoft's HR department has been breathing down my neck to get this position filled."

"I thought you hired Justine so she could *cover* shit like this," I said. It had been almost a year since Jake decided to expand his business by bringing on more recruiters, a change that necessitated an actual office for him and his employees to work out of. I'd expected this when he first brought up the idea; what I hadn't expected was how the hours he spent at said-office—training his new hires, monitoring their work, taking care of benefits and payroll and other staffing issues that presented themselves—would almost double compared to when he worked solo, from home.

"I did," he said, sharply. "But she's only been working for me a few weeks, and I can't risk her fucking up the interviews. I need to be here."

"Parker or Trevor can't do it?" Those were his other employees, two perky, hungry-for-success young men in their mid-twenties whom he'd hired within the first month of his decision to expand.

"Training her is my responsibility, not theirs." I could picture him on the other end of our call, at his newly-installed, adjustable, standing desk, his strong jaw clenched in annoyance. He'd cut down shaving to twice a week, resulting in a rough, salt-and-peppered stubble I found sexy, and had grown out his previously buzz-cut hair a couple of inches, giving me something to grab onto with my fingers when we had sex. Not that that was happening very often.

"Fine," I said before hanging up on him, not waiting for his reply. Unbeknownst to Jake, I had made reservations at the same Thai place we'd gone to the night we met Will almost exactly three years ago. I also went shopping for new lingerie, a sexy, low-cut little black dress, was freshly waxed, and even got a spray tan. I had planned for us to finish out the night at the Cove, dancing and remembering the fun we'd had there, hoping that reliving those moments might lead us to end our date with the two of us tearing off each other's clothes. With how much Jake had been working, and how much more the kids' had going on now that they were both in high school—as a junior, Ella was an officer on the dance team, as well as class president, and also worked part-time at Olive Garden; and Tucker, who was a sophomore, was such a talented pitcher, he'd been selected to play the position on the varsity team—our family was busier than ever. Tonight was supposed to be just about me and Jake. It was supposed to be special.

I paced the kitchen, opened the fridge, and then slammed it closed, my resentment toward Jake's absence mounting. I tried to remain rational as I made my way to into the family room and dropped down onto the couch. It wasn't just Jake who was working more—the real estate market in the Pacific Northwest was booming—record numbers of people were moving to Seattle on a daily basis—so my hours spent at the office or out showing properties had increased, too, though not as much as my husband's, making it difficult for our downtime to mesh. The truth was I wasn't only angry at him; I was angry at *us* for letting our romantic life slip down on our list of priorities again.

My thoughts turned to the six months Will stayed in Seattle—the once-a-month, intensely hot encounters we'd had. Jake joined us again for one of those times, but the others I was with Will alone, and then went home to relive each experience with my husband. There were a few instances when Jake might be too busy for us to have sex immediately after I'd return from Will's place, but the next morning, all it took was a few words from me to get things going.

"I love how Will's cock feels inside me," I'd murmur, after kissing my husband awake.

"Dirty girl," he'd reply. His breathing changed and his body tensed. Nothing got him hard as quickly as hearing me whisper in his ear about how much I loved being fucked by another man.

After Will returned to San Diego, Jake and I decided to write a profile and put it up on AdultFun.com, the site Will had recommended. (I couldn't bring myself to put it on Craigslist, alongside garage sales, and where I sometimes advertised the properties I was trying to sell.) But as soon as we posted it, we were overwhelmed by the emails that flooded our inbox, many from men immediately ruled out as a potential partner by their one sentence, poorly punctuated, and/or outright offensive responses. Some expressed their desire for incestuous, father/daughter roleplay—ugh—or they referred to me in a demeaning manner as their "cock slut" or "whore-hot-wife"—so we took our profile down and decided to live off the memory of the times we'd had with Will—and as a result, each other. The excitement stemming from those experiences lasted a few months, until the thrill of repeating the same story began to wear off, and I started hinting that it might be fun to find someone to create new memories with. We put the profile up again, determined to take our time before meeting anyone. Eventually, that led us to Tim, a single, attractive, and successful estate attorney who had never been with a couple or participated in a hot-wife dynamic, but was highly interested in the indulging this fantasy. When we met him for drinks, our comfort level and instant chemistry reminded us so much of how we'd felt with Will, we went to his house that night.

Over the next year, I met Tim on my own once a month, always on a weekend when the kids were with Peter and Kari, and always telling Jake every detail of what I'd done. Tim was smart, charismatic, and fun in bed, but when he told me that he'd met a woman, and it looked like it might get serious, I ended things, and we amicably parted ways. After another break—a shorter one, this time—we met Vincent, a divorced advertising executive who I ended up seeing every six weeks or so, as our schedules allowed, but again, he ended up meeting a woman he wanted to date, so our dalliance ceased.

That was a year ago, when Jake decided to expand his company. We had put our profile up a few more times since then, but were turned off by the majority of responses we received. Many of the men were more interested in a cuckold dynamic, wanting to come in to our relationship as a "bull"—which we learned was a man who thought he had more sexual prowess or larger cock than the husband of the woman he's fucking, who gets off on humiliation; or, they wanted a one-time encounter, which wasn't something Jake or I were comfortable with doing. We suspected that those men were likely married or otherwise attached, looking to get away with something once—while their wife was out of town, perhaps— but unable to meet on a regular basis. We preferred something ongoing, where trust, and the resultant eroticism, could grow. It was discouraging when we couldn't find another match, and, coupled with our increasingly busy schedule, it had been several months since we'd even discussed the possibility of finding someone new.

Now, I shot a quick text to Charlotte. "What time will you be done?" She had told me earlier in the day that she had a thirty-person anniversary dinner that night for a couple celebrating fifty years together. "*Fifty* years," she'd exclaimed. "Can you believe that shit? Who *stays* with someone that long?"

"I'm just wrapping up," she responded, now, almost immediately. "Apparently the happy couple is itching to get home and celebrate in a way that doesn't involve canapes and champagne.".

"Jake bailed on date night," I said. "Drinks at the Sailor?"

"Hell, yes!" she said. "Wait. Drinks, or DRAAANKS???"

I laughed as I typed. "I think we'd better stick with drinks." The distinction was one made not long after we first met, when the two of us ended up knocking back four martinis each on what was supposed to be a casual, "Let's-sip-a-single-cocktail-and-get-to-know-each-other-better" girls' night out. When Jake showed up at last call to drive us home—Richard was out of town for work, Bentley was at a sleepover, and my kids were with Peter and Kari—he practically had to drag me and Charlotte out of the bar.

I didn't remember much from that night, but I did recall my best friend yelling, "I want another DRAAANK!" as we stumbled across the small dance floor toward the door, and then me, chiming in, "DRAAANKS! We want DRAAANKS!"

It became our inside joke; "DRAAANKS," loosely translated, meant we weren't just looking to take the edge off. We were going to get wasted. It wasn't something we actually did very often—quite rarely, in fact—but it still made us laugh.

I ran upstairs, quickly, fussed with my hair, and was about to head out the door in my jeans and T-shirt when instead, decided to wear the same dress I'd bought for my night out with Jake. I changed, briefly glancing at myself in the full length mirror we had on the back of our closet door. The dress was sleeveless, had a deep V-neck, accentuating my cleavage, and otherwise fit me perfectly, skimming the hourglass of my figure before it ended right above my knees. The black fabric set off the lightly bronzed, fake glow of my skin, and I swiped on a slash of blackberry lipstick and a second coat of mascara to complete the look. Just because Jake and I didn't get to have date night, didn't mean my prep work for it had to go to waste.

I entered the Tipsy Sailor ten minutes later, and Charlotte waved at me from a table by the front window, looking like a springtime Pippy Longstocking with her red hair pulled into two ponytails on either side of her neck. She wore a boat-necked, bright lime green sheath, a color only a toddler or someone with her porcelain complexion and auburn locks could successfully pull off.

I scanned the room as I made my way over to her, pleased to notice a few men giving me an appreciative once-over look as I walked by. Maybe I'd tell Jake about that. Maybe knowing that I'd thought about picking up a stranger at a bar—or at least, realizing that I felt confident enough that I *could*—would turn him on and end our sexual dry spell.

"Hey," I said, dropped down in the chair across from my friend. Our server arrived and we both ordered margaritas, with a side shot of Patron.

"So, how mad are we at Jake?" Charlotte asked, pointedly.

I sighed. "Not very. I'm just frustrated."

"Here," she said, picking up her phone from the table. She unlocked the screen, and shoved it toward me. "This will cheer you up."

I looked down to see the Neighbors app open to the Queens Ridge page. Tiffany was still the moderator for the discussions that went on there, and I'd finally signed up after Nancy told all of the agents at Kendal Properties that they should be using the app to advertise properties and our services. There was a spot for general commentary about what was going on in our community, a classified section, crime and safety, along with a few other categories, including a recommendation list, where I was happy to know that over the past two years, I was the most-mentioned real estate professional in Queens Ridge. There were at least ten new posts a day, ranging from event announcements to people reporting when their cars had been broken into, so others could be on the lookout. Charlotte had the app open to the general commentary area, to one of Tiffany's posts.

"Fellow Queens Ridge residents," she had written, "I need your help in identifying the person whose dog is constantly pooping on our front lawn. I have gone to every effort I can think of to catch this inconsiderate pet owner, including posting a polite sign requesting that the person cease and desist their animal's rude behavior, and sitting outside on my porch for hours at a time in an attempt to catch them in the act, to no avail. I cannot believe the size of the excrement this animal leaves on our grass. Does someone have a PET HORSE in the neighborhood that I don't know about? And what kind of person thinks it's appropriate to allow their animal to desecrate my property on almost a daily basis? I am INFURIATED!!

If you are the offender, know if someone doesn't turn you in, I'm having security cameras installed. I WILL find you."

I glanced at the picture included in the post—an exceptionally large pile of excrement—and then shoved Charlotte's phone back over to her. "Gross."

"She's out of control," Charlotte said. "She actually used the word 'desecrate,' like her yard is some kind of holy land this dog is taking a shit on." She paused, as our server delivered our drinks. "'I *will* find you,'" she said, in a mock, deep voice, and then rolled her eyes. "Who does she think she is, the Liam Neeson of Queens Ridge?"

I gave a short laugh, but then felt a little guilty for being amused. It turned out that Tiffany's mother's forgetfulness after breaking her wrist wasn't due to the pain pills she was taking—she actually had been in the beginning stages of Alzheimer's, and soon after, moved in with Tiffany and her family. Dealing with all of that, plus the fact that according to Ella, Lizzy had continued to be the girl who offered up blow jobs and whatever else boys wanted from her, I had a hard time understanding how Tiffany had time to worry about whose dog was crapping on her lawn, let alone post about it to the entire community.

"People deal with stress in different ways, I guess," I said to Charlotte, now. "I feel bad for her, though, with her mom being sick, and the way Lizzy is acting up."

"You're right," Charlotte said as she picked up her margarita and took a hefty swallow. She puckered her lips, and then frowned. "Wow. Sorry. I'm an asshole."

I laughed. "A real asshole would never admit it." That was what I loved about Charlotte—she could sometimes cross the line with her sharp wit, but she also owned up to it and apologized when she went too far.

"Do you think she knows? About Lizzy?"

"I'm not sure." I took a swallow of my drink, too. "I'd like to think that if it were Ella, I'd sense something was going on." At least, I hoped this were true. But then I thought about the fact that I'd managed to hide what Jake and I had been doing in our sex life from Charlotte—and everyone else we knew—for the last three years, and it struck me that you could never really know for sure what the people in your life—even the ones you were closest to—were doing behind closed doors.

"Bentley has been giving me the play-by-play about her shenanigans with Riley." Charlotte rolled her eyes. Riley was Bentley's first real boyfriend; Ella had told me about him a few weeks ago. "Sometimes I regret raising her to be able to tell me anything." She shuddered. "I did *not* need to hear that her panties were soaked after they were kissing at the movies last week."

"What?" I sputtered, spraying the table with the bit of margarita I'd had in my mouth. I looked at Charlotte, aghast. "She did not say that to you."

"She sure did," Charlotte said, cheerfully. She grabbed the shot glass next to her drink and bobbed her head toward mine, indicating that I should do the same. We clinked them together over the center of our small table, and then both knocked back the Patron in one swallow.

"Ugh!" I said, as the alcohol burned my throat and warmed my stomach. "Why do we *do* that to ourselves?" I couldn't remember the last time I'd done a shot of straight anything, let alone tequila.

"Because it makes the bullshit misery in life more bearable," Charlotte said, and her brown eyes clouded.

I frowned, intuiting what she meant. "What's going on with Richard?" A few months after I joked that Charlotte should sneak Viagra into her husband's coffee, she confided that Richard had problems getting an erection.

She shook her head. "I keep trying to get him to go to the doctor, in case there's something physical going on—it could be something like an enlarged prostate—but he won't. It's been nine months since we even tried having sex. He won't even *talk* about it anymore. He's totally shut down."

"Oh, honey," I said. I reached over and squeezed her hand.

"He's only fifty-three. I can't spend the rest of my life like this," Charlotte pressed her lips together, clearly fighting back tears.

"I wouldn't be able to, either," I said, thinking about my own, currently less than satisfying sex life. "Have you thought about seeing a marriage counselor?"

"That's not going to get his dick hard."

I laughed. "Okay. But if what's going on is more in his head, talking about it with you and someone who can help him figure out where this all stems from could be a first step? Or they could help you get him in to see the doctor."

Charlotte sighed. "He *hates* talking about his feelings. He seems perfectly content with the way things are. He walked in on me using my vibrator last night and didn't say a *word*. He just turned around and *left*."

"Wow," I said. "I'm sorry."

"I've been talking with someone," she said quietly, keeping her eyes on the table.

"Like a therapist?" I asked, confused.

"No." She looked up at me, guiltily. "A guy I met at an event I did for the Bill and Melinda Gates' Foundation. Bryan. He's divorced. He and his wife didn't have sex for almost five years before he finally threw in the towel. He wishes he didn't wait that long."

"How often are you talking with him?" I asked, keeping my voice as even as possible. I was shocked to hear that Charlotte, who was usually so vehemently against anything that even tip-toed around the issue of infidelity, was talking about intimate issues in her marriage with another man.

"We're just friends," Charlotte said, with more than a touch of defensiveness. "I'm not spending time with him. We're just texting. He gets what I'm going through, you know? I can tell him how I'm feeling—how lonely I've been. It really helps to talk with someone who's been there."

"Sure," I said, in a neutral tone. "I get that." I paused, and swallowed a bit more of my drink. "Are you thinking about leaving Richard?"

"I'm not cheating," Charlotte declared, instead of answering my question. Her cheeks were flushed pink, either from the alcohol or self-righteous indignation. Probably a little of both. I made it a point to not talk too much or too often with the men I'd slept with—there was no texting or phone calls in between seeing each other, except for the ones necessary to set up our next meeting. But while Charlotte wasn't sleeping with this man—at least, she wasn't, yet—she was opening up, sharing with him about the problems she and Richard had. *Which is worse?* I wondered. *Which creates more of a risk?*

"Honey, you know I'd never judge you, even if you had. You can tell me anything." I felt a little sad, knowing that I couldn't do the same; at least, not when it came to my sex life.

Her expression softened. "Jesus, I'm sorry." She shook her head. "After everything that happened with Alex…." She trailed off, and looked down at the table, again, picking at the edge of her cocktail napkin, tearing off tiny shreds. "I never thought I'd be capable of even *thinking* about cheating."

"But you are."

"I don't know," she said. Her eyes filled with tears. "I really like having him to talk to."

"Maybe you need to *tell* Richard that. Maybe it will help him realize how serious this is for you. For you marriage."

"I love him," Charlotte said, blinking fast, as she carefully wiped beneath her eyes with the tips of her fingers. "Richard, not Bryan," she added, quickly.

"I know," I said, gently. "I wish I could fix it for you."

"You know what I hate most?" she continued. "That Bentley sees us like this. Richard doesn't even hold my hand anymore, or kiss me when he leaves the house. He doesn't *touch* me. We just…exist. We co-parent. Bentley's almost seventeen and I'm afraid we've completely fucked her up."

"I'm sure you haven't," I said. "Teenagers are so self-involved, I swear most of what we say or do around them doesn't even register." Even I spoke these words, they rang hollow. "You and Richard do need to work this out, though" I said, instead. "*Make* him get counseling with you. Tell him your marriage is at stake. That you really can't keep living without some kind of sex life. Be clear that you're at the end of your rope."

"Easier said than done." She gave me a lopsided smile. "Why can't every man be more like Jake? Can't you clone him or something? Or at least have him teach some how-to-be-a-good-husband classes at the rec center?"

"Jake isn't perfect. We have our issues, too. Tonight, for example."

"What else?"

"He always leaves clothes in the dryer when he does a load of laundry. He never folds or puts anything away. It drives me nuts."

"Oh no!" Charlotte said, with mock horror. "*Divorce* his ass, immediately!"

"He also says he 'cleans' the kitchen, but really all he does in put the dishes in the dishwasher. I still have to sweep and mop the floor and wipe down the appliances."

"So hire a maid," Charlotte said, with a snap of her fingers. "Problem solved."

"That would make my mom *way* too happy."

"At least your mom doesn't tell your kids inappropriate stories about how she spent the Summer of Love."

"Yuck." I didn't care how old a person was, it was never a good thing to think about your parent having sex.

"No kidding." Charlotte paused as the server stopped by and asked if we wanted another drink. After we told him we were fine, and would take the check, she went on. "We should have a get together the next time your parents are here."

"They'll actually coming in a few weeks, when school gets out." It would be a rare occasion when my dad agreed to take a few days off—at my mother's insistence, of course. My mother had continued to teach part-time over the last few years, but had also joined a local senior activities center. There, she'd met a few other women who were either single, widowed, or simply looking for reasons to get out of their house.

They went out for dinners, formed a book club, and played Bunco every Sunday afternoon. They'd even taken a couple of trips together, one to New York and another to London—this year, they were discussing spending week in Mexico, or possibly taking a Caribbean cruise. It was heartening, to hear about my mother's connection with this group. The majority of her colleagues in the physics department had been male, and she had little time—or desire, as far as I could tell—to forge friendships with other women. (She had not, suffice to say, been active on the PTA.) But now, whenever we spoke, she no longer complained about how little my dad was at home; instead, she told me about the conversations and adventures she had with her new friends.

Unfortunately, she had never managed to bond with Charlotte's mother the same way. The last time they saw each other, at Easter, Helen had spent the entire meal regaling us with tales of her latest protest march, repeating the phrase "fuck the patriarchy" enough times I was worried she had developed a verbal tick. My mother had nodded and smiled politely while Helen spoke, despite what I recognized as her distaste for Helen's profanity and overtly unbridled breasts. Though they both had challenged the stereotypical role of what a woman "should" be or do with her life, they expressed their defiance in decidedly different ways.

"Perfect," Charlotte said, now, with a huge smile. She was always happier when she had a gathering to plan, more so if it was for her personal life, instead of work. "I'll put something together for the Sunday after school gets out. I'll invite Tiffany!"

"I'm sure she'd appreciate that." I kept making half-hearted promises to myself to get to know Tiffany better, but hadn't done a very good job at following through. I never did tell her that Lizzy had been the one teaching other girls how to purge in the locker room, since Ella informed me that Lizzy had stopped doing it right after Tiffany spoke to the principal, probably worried that she would get caught. And while I'd been tempted a few times to find a way to express my concern over Lizzy's alleged promiscuity, I honestly didn't know how I would have that conversation with Tiffany. It didn't seem like something I'd want to hear about from another mother, unless it was someone like Charlotte, who knew and loved my daughter as much as I did, so I kept my mouth shut.

We finished our drinks, paid the bill, and then ended up chatting for another hour about less serious subjects than the ones we'd begun our evening with. After Charlotte and I hugged in the parking lot, I climbed in my car and checked my phone. I'd missed a text from Jake. "Where are you?" he asked. I hadn't bothered letting him know that I was going out with Charlotte, thinking that he would still be at the office by the time I got home.

"Drinks with Charlotte," I replied. "On my way, now." He didn't answer, which could mean he was irritated with me for worrying him, or already asleep. I hoped for the latter. It was almost one in the morning, and both of us needed a good night's rest instead of trying to hash everything out when he was exhausted from a sixteen hour work day and I was still the tiniest bit annoyed. Those circumstances seemed more like a recipe for disaster than resolution. Regardless, I knew we needed to talk, so we didn't end up like Charlotte and Richard or my parents— married, raising children, living in the same house, but leading separate lives.

Thirteen

Jake finally stumbled into the kitchen around ten the next morning, as the sun streamed in through the French doors that led out onto our deck, highlighting the fact that window washing was not high on anyone in this family's to-do list. He made his way over to the Keurig machine. I'd already had my coffee when I got up at eight, but then put in another pod and set out his mug, so all he would have to do was press the brew button. It was a silent mea culpa—my small way of saying "sorry for being a bitch" the night before.

I watched him from my spot on the couch in the family room, legs crossed. My foot bounced as he added a splash of cream and a teaspoon of sugar to his mug. He wore dark gray gym shorts and a black T-shirt, and when he turned around, I saw that his face was lined and puffy; the tender skin under his blue eyes almost looked like he'd been punched.

He took a swallow of coffee and gave a quiet sigh of relief. "Are you still mad?" he asked, warily.

"No," I said, though that wasn't entirely true. I was emotionally-hungover from the frustration I'd felt last night, despite knowing it wasn't fair for me to hold it against Jake when he had no choice but to work. But it wasn't the first time *knowing* something to be true didn't change how I *felt* about it. Sometimes it took a while for my heart to catch up to my head. "I'm sorry I hung up on you, though. That was shitty."

"It's okay," Jake said. "You were looking forward to going out. I was, too. I really am sorry."

"I know," I said, the tension I felt starting to diminish. "How did the interviews go? Did Justine do okay?" When he hired her, Jake told me that Justine, a woman in her fifties, had worked in HR for almost twenty years, so she had recruiting experience, but not at the executive level, and not in the technology field, Jake's area of expertise. She would require some serious hand-holding through the training process.

"She has a lot to learn before she'd totally up to speed," Jake said, now, as he came over to join me, sitting on the opposite end of the couch. He scratched at his chin—the stubble that was bordering on looking like the beginnings of a deliberate beard. "But overall, she did well. I think we found the right person for the job."

"That's good." It felt like we were making small talk on an uncomfortable first date, instead of a husband and wife of twelve years, and I hated it. I looked at Jake and unexpectedly, my bottom lip trembled and tears filled my eyes. "I miss you, baby."

Jake put down his coffee on the table in front of us and scooted closer. "Me, too," he said, as he took my hand. He leaned over and gave me a soft, lingering kiss, and I tasted coffee and the slight, familiar funk of his morning breath. He set his forehead against mine. "We're too damn busy."

I nodded, blinking my tears away, but didn't speak. Despite how open we'd become with each other about our sexual desires, talking about my deeper emotions, showing him any sign of possible weakness, still didn't come naturally to me.

"Tell me your feelings, Jess," he said, which only made me want to cry more. About a year ago, I'd shared how my mom used to say, "Tell me the facts" about a situation, so now, when Jake sensed I was upset about something, he made a point to ask me the opposite question. And every time he did, a few more bricks would crumble away from the wall I'd built to protect my heart.

I forced myself to answer. "I'm just so damn afraid if we don't start making our relationship more of a priority, we're going to turn into my parents. I can't live like they did. I *refuse* to. I feel like we're right back where we were three years ago, and I hate it." Just saying the words, being honest with my husband, lifted an enormous weight that had been sitting on my chest. I released a small sigh of relief.

"I know," Jake said. He shifted back, searching my face with tired blue eyes. "I've been thinking about that, too. I don't want to live like that, either. But we talked about this. I'm expanding the company so eventually, I can work less. It's going to take some time for everything to balance out." He reached over and used the side of his thumb to wipe a bit of wetness from my cheek. "You've been working a lot, too." He said this with concern, not as an accusation.

"I know." I sighed. "It's hard to say no to new clients right now. I get so panicky that my current deals might be it for a while, because you never know when the housing bubble is going to burst again." I'd just been starting out in real estate when the recession hit, fighting for every listing, every potential commission that would keep a roof over my children's heads. There were some months where I didn't make a single penny, scraping by on the child support Peter gave me, paying for gas and my utilities with my credit cards, and eating macaroni and cheese or bowls of cereal for dinner every night of the week. Now, with the huge influx of growth Seattle was experiencing—people flocking to the area faster than construction companies like Peter's could build places to house them—I couldn't help but work more, taking on as much, if not more business, than I could handle. For every one iron in the fire, I felt like I needed at least six more. That kind of uncertainty in my career was a double-edged sword: Nancy had told me to let it drive me to land the next listing or sale, which it did, but it also created the constant feeling that no matter how hard I worked—how many deals I made, or commissions I earned—it would never be enough.

"I totally get it," Jake said, and I knew this was true. But he didn't struggle with the same insecurity that I did. He was human, of course, and had moments of self-doubt in his work, but fear of not doing enough—especially in my career—was a cloud that hung over me, even on my sunniest, most successful days.

"You know what else I miss?" I asked, wanting to lighten the mood. "Sex. Dirty, kinky, *fun* sex."

Jake laughed. "It's been a while, hasn't it?"

"A month and two days," I said. "Not that I'm counting."

"Of course not," he said, smiling. "I'm sorry, babe. My brain's on total overload. I just haven't been thinking about it."

I quickly relayed what I'd had planned for us the night before.

"Well, shit," Jake said, frowning. "That would have been awesome. No wonder you were pissed."

"It's my fault. I should have told you instead of making it a surprise." I had to remind myself that the only way Jake could understand my feelings or meet my needs was for me to vocalize what they were. Realizing this, more than anything else, had been the most beneficial result of deciding to explore a more adventurous sex life. Talking openly about what turned me on ended up being a gateway into talking about other things.

"We haven't put our profile up for a while," I said, cautiously. I didn't want him to think that my go-to solution to a challenging situation was having sex with someone else. But I also couldn't deny the desire I had to spice things up again—to feel that wild, heart-hammering thrill of a strange man touching me.

"We weren't having the best luck finding someone," he said. "I wasn't sure you still wanted to do it."

"Do *you* still want to?" I asked. *What if he said he doesn't?* I wondered, feeling a stitch of concern in my chest. *And I still do?*

But then I didn't have to worry, because he nodded. "I think it was good for us." He paused. "And not just in bed."

I reached out and rubbed his forearm, giving it a quick, affectionate squeeze. Our eyes met, and it seemed like a hundred words were spoken in a language that only Jake and I understood.

"The last few times," Jake began, "it seemed like a lot of the guys were more into the idea of being with you alone instead of having me involved." That was true—along with the men who wanted to be "bulls" or have me call them "'Daddy," several men said they'd be interested in fucking me alone and having me tell Jake about it later, but not in having Jake there to take part.

"Yeah, but the whole point is that we're doing this together," I said. I gave him a questioning look. "Right?"

"You fucked the other guys without me there," Jake said. "So, not together in *person*, every time we did it." The rise and fall of his chest sped up, slightly, and his cheeks flushed.

I held his gaze, watching as his pupils expanded, almost obliterating the blue of his irises. "Are you saying you don't want to have a threesome, first?"

"I'm saying," Jake began, releasing a breath he'd apparently been holding, "that maybe you should pick a guy out on your own."

"What?" I asked, thinking I'd heard him wrong.

Jake didn't flinch. "You could post our profile, but leave out the stuff about me joining in. Just say I like to hear about it. You pick out the guy, decide if you like him, and then fuck him. Alone."

The blunt, raw nature of his words struck a chord in me that hadn't been played in far too long. Our energies instantly shifted, and the heat between us became its own being—a living, breathing entity. I loved it when Jake spoke to me with such blatant eroticism. My throat went dry, so I swallowed, and licked my lips. "You wouldn't go with me to meet him?"

"No. I think you should meet him on your own."

"Really?" His suggestion surprised me, even though the times we had put our profile up, it was me who sifted through the rubble of responses to find the few men that actually met our standards. We preferred someone single, of course, easy-going and smart, with a healthy sense of humor, but didn't have any particular requirements when it came to looks. (Privately, I preferred well-endowed men with dark hair, but I kept this bit of information to myself, not wanting Jake to ever feel like his more average sized cock wasn't enough for me. It was, but I also couldn't deny the pleasure of being stretched further, being filled up more than I was with him.) Jake was only interested in reading the emails from the men I wanted us to meet. With both Tim and Vincent, we'd kept to the same process as we had with Will: we all had drinks together, checked to see if the chemistry was there, and then embarked on a threesome, after which I would have monthly encounters alone with the men, and come home to tell Jake all about it. There was something reassuring about Jake's involvement at the start, so that a potential lover saw him as a real person, not only some theoretical husband I went home to. It was clear that I belonged to someone else.

"Yeah, really," Jake said, now. "I trust you. And I like the idea of you choosing him on your own. Fucking him only because you want to, without any input from me."

"And then you'd join us," I said, wanting to be sure I fully understood what he was saying. "Another time, after that."

"No," Jake said. He held out his hand and I laced my fingers through his. "You fuck him. Without me. Always. I never meet him."

The air caught in my lungs, imagining this scenario. The idea of Jake knowing my lover only through my descriptions of the time I spent with him was a dizzying concept. I thought about the men who had looked at me at the bar the night before, and realized if Jake and I agreed to indulge in this new dynamic, and if they had fit our general parameters, I could have gone home with any one of them. That sort of unfettered freedom was even more enticing than what we'd already explored.

I caressed the side of Jake's hand with my thumb. "Why?" I asked. As thrilling as this prospect was, I felt like I needed to be totally sure he would be okay with it actually happening, because suddenly, I wanted nothing more than to do it.

"Well," he said, "seeing you fuck other men is incredibly hot. Watching you take both of us on."

"I sense a 'but' coming on," I interrupted.

"*But,*" he said, with a mischievous grin, "when you came home and told me what you'd done with him alone, I always had a clear visual of what he looked like...exactly how he touched you and fucked you, because we did the threesome, first." He took a deep breath, and then released it. "I don't know. It just seems like it would be even hotter if I had no idea what he looks like...what he does to you and how you react to it...except for being forced to *imagine* the details when you describe them."

"Upping the ante," I said, realizing that I'd been holding my own breath, listening to him. All I could think about was how my body was reacting to the simple suggestion of trying something new. My pulse raced and my hands shook. The warmth between my legs ached.

"Yes," Jake said. Again, he searched my face. "Does it turn you on to think about doing it?" His voice was low, a little graveled. "Does it make you wet?"

Instead of speaking, I surprised him by straddling his lap in one swift movement, lifting my nightie so my ass rested on top of his thighs. His coffee sat untouched, likely lukewarm, by now, on the table in front of the couch.

"Well, hello there," he said, sliding his hands onto my hips at the same moment I wrapped my arms around his neck, crossing my wrists at the base of his skull. He kissed me, then, and I answered by grinding against him.

"It could be fun," I murmured against his lips.

"Just fun?" Jake leaned forward, and nuzzled my neck so he could gently kiss my collarbone.

"Super fun?"

He laughed, a low, rumbling sound; its vibration passed from his body into mine. Jake's fingers wandered up and down the curve of my sides, teasing. "You want to fuck a stranger, totally on your own?"

"Yes." I shivered with pleasure.

"Do you want him to do this to you?" One of Jake's hands moved, his fingers brushing lightly over the outside of my panties, and he paused, raising an eyebrow. "Hmm…I guess that answers my question about it getting you wet."

"Shut up and fuck me," I said, playfully biting his bottom lip. I bucked my hips, trying to get my husband to press harder. Every cell in my body begged for satisfaction; I felt like I was drowning in a pool of need.

Jake shifted, and suddenly, we were laying down, me on my back, him on top of me. I liked the feeling of being trapped, unable to move; even though it was only for a moment, I liked it when he took control. Our ruined date night was forgotten, the months of too much work and not enough sex vanished from my thoughts. The only thing that mattered was that we'd found a new room to explore in the house of our marriage.

Who knew how many more we might discover after that.

Fourteen

He was late.

I sat alone at a Starbucks in downtown Bellevue, nervously waiting for Andrew, one of the men who had responded to the profile I had edited—removing our usual reference of having a threesome—and posted on AdultFun.com:

Are you looking for zero emotional involvement, but something more satisfying than a one-time hook up with an intelligent, discreet partner? Me, too.

I'm married, in a hot-wife relationship with my husband—he gets off on hearing about me playing with another man, and I'm turned on telling him about it. Definitely not something I do a lot, and I am very particular. Discretion is paramount.

To be exceptionally clear—I am only interested in an ongoing situation with a single, available man. NO MARRIED OR OTHERWISE ATTACHED MEN. I'm not looking to be wooed or taken on dates or to fall in love—this is about sexual pleasure, pure and simple.

I tend not to send pictures until we have a vibe going, for privacy's sake. But I am curvy and pretty—says the stranger on the internet who isn't sending you a picture—with long, brown curls, gray eyes, and a wicked smile. No smokers, heavy drinkers, or men into heavy drugs. Open to any race, age range between 35 and 50-ish. We are drug and disease free. You should be, too. Condoms required.

I'd put the profile up the same morning as Jake and I had decided to pursue me meeting someone on my own, thinking there was no reason to put it off, especially because it had always taken us a while to find someone. But I was immediately flooded with responses, and Andrew had been one of the first I read.

Now, as I sat in Starbucks, my pulse jittering, I impatiently checked the email account Jake and I still used to communicate with our "friends," I wondered if I'd made a mistake in choosing to meet Andrew for my first time doing this without Jake, even though and the tone of his email had been appealing:

Hey there. My name is Andrew and I'm in my early 40's, looking for this kind of fun. I've had some experience, yet I wouldn't say it's a regular part of my life. I'm a very open-minded and non-judgmental guy.

Professionally, I'm an IT executive and business owner with roots in programming (yes, I'm a bit of a geek, but a cute one—ha!). I've got quite a lust for life. I'm laid-back, love to laugh and see where a moment takes me. Stat wise I'm 5'10", 170lbs., fit, dark hair and eyes.

I have a keen understanding of your need for discretion. What you and your husband have worked out is incredible, and I have the utmost respect for you both. It's so important to know your partner, what makes them tick, and to be open to their fantasies and desires. I'm recently single, coming out of an 8 year, exclusive relationship, so I'm very safe. Happy to get tested if you'd feel more comfortable seeing those results.

I work in downtown Bellevue and live in Kirkland. I can host, and have a somewhat flexible schedule.

Let's meet, soon. You won't regret it.

It was the confidence in that last line that convinced me to write him back, and his willingness to get tested for possible STDs. (We'd done this with Will, Tim, and Vincent, as well, just to be sure we were all healthy, despite my insistence that we continue to use condoms. I was on the Pill, but the last thing I needed was to get pregnant and not know who the father was.) Andrew and I discussed our general boundaries and expectations, eventually exchanging pictures, and then decided to meet for an in-person chemistry check. It was strange, at first, not showing the emails or pictures to Jake, discussing the pros and cons of a particular man, as I had with Tim and Vincent, but also exhilarating, more empowered than I'd ever felt before.

"I think I found someone," I told my husband, after Andrew and

I had emailed a couple of times. "We're going to meet for coffee on Thursday. If that's okay." I knew it was possible that Jake might change his mind about my going through with this set-up, alone, so I felt compelled to continue to check in on how he was feeling.

"Of course it's okay," Jake said. "Just make sure I know where you'll be."

I nodded, feeling a deep, overwhelming sensation of adoration for my husband. The level of trust he had in me, when I really stopped to think about it, was astounding. Part of me still wondered how he was able to allow me this kind of freedom when I couldn't do the same for him.

"Where does that kind of confidence *come* from?" I asked him, later that night, when we were discussing how most people would think that having this kind of sexual openness in our marriage was a sign of its dysfunction rather than its strength. "I mean, honestly. You don't have a single jealous thought about me doing all of this on my own?"

He shook his head. "You already have the most amazing man in the world. You'd have to be a serious idiot to fuck things up with me."

I laughed, because he was right. Being with Will, and later, Tim, and then Vincent, made me fall a little more in love with my husband. I would come home, still a little drunk with lust, feeling confident and sexy in a way that was new to me—feeling desired by another man, and then having sex with him, leaving almost immediately after that, was a potent experience. Walking to my car, knowing what I'd just done was the most delicious secret I'd ever had. When I got home, Jake would take me into his arms and reinforce everything I was feeling about myself, saying how beautiful and strong and sexy I was. How much he loved watching me embrace this side of myself.

But now, waiting for Andrew, my stomach twisted, as I considered the horror stories of women disappearing after meeting a man they'd found online. Maybe that was part of the thrill—the not knowing what to expect, the illicit nature of what I was doing. Jake had the address of where I was, and I'd already texted him to let him know that I'd arrived, and would do the same when I left. Still, my heartbeat thudded inside my ribcage as I waited for Andrew to appear; I had to take a few deep breaths in order to slow my sprinting pulse. When I was single, and before I met Jake, I'd been on a few first dates after having met someone online, but the stakes in this situation with Andrew were higher. This wasn't a casual get together to see if we'd want to go out again—we were meeting solely to see if we wanted to fuck.

I glanced at the coffee shop's entrance, hoping to see Andrew walking through it. The pictures he'd sent bore out the general stats he provided in his first email, even though the images were taken at angles and with shadowy lighting that didn't reveal his entire face. In some, he had on a baseball cap and a pair of sunglasses; in others, the shot was taken from behind, so I could only see the back of his body. I understood why he'd chosen those particular images—the ones Jake and I used were similarly discreet, so if anyone saw them other than the person we'd sent them to, it would be difficult to be absolutely certain that it was us. But taking a bit from each of Andrew's pictures, I could see that he had black, somewhat wavy and longish hair, olive skin, and dark brown eyes. He had a nice body, but no sculpted, gym-rat muscles, which was fine with me. Neither Tim nor Vincent had possessed six-pack abs, but both were handsome enough, and more importantly, highly invested in making sure our encounters were filled with steamy details that I could pass on to Jake. They understood that my husband was as much a part of this dynamic as I was.

"You're pretty exceptional," Tim told me once. "I swear every other girl I've had sex with immediately wants to discuss wedding venues." We were lying in his bed after having sex, and I was thinking about how long I would need to lay there before I could leave. Usually, I gave it ten minutes, just so I wouldn't seem rude. He rolled over onto his side to look at me. "How do you manage to keep everything so separate?"

"You mean why am able to fuck you and not stalk you?" I said, remaining on my back as I considered his question.

"Exactly."

I shrugged. "To me, sex and love are two completely different things. I love Jake, but not you." This was the easiest explanation I could come up with when it came to describing how I was able to indulge in casual sex. I understood that it was generally assumed that women weren't supposed to be *able* to engage in sex without becoming emotionally involved, but clearly, at least in my case, that wasn't true.

Tim laughed. "Be honest with me, now. Don't hold anything back or worry about my ego."

"Sorry," I said, laughing, too. "Here's the thing. My emotional connection to sex is with Jake. He meets those needs, so there's no risk of expecting you to do the same. There's nothing missing in my marriage that I'm trying to compensate for by being here—it just adds to what we already have." I waited a beat. "Also, I have sex with him all the time, which only reinforces how we feel about each other, while you and I only get together what, once a month? That's by design."

When I first met Tim, Jake and I were so enticed by the renewed intensity that another man brought to our sex life that we got a little greedy. Tim and I started seeing each other every other weekend, every time the kids were with Peter and Kari, which turned out to be too often. I found myself constantly thinking about the next time Tim and I would be together, instead of focusing solely on Jake, which scared me, so I told Tim I was too busy with work to meet more than once a month. My off-hand comment to Will the first time we'd been together alone—"where the clitoris goes, the heart soon follows"—wasn't too far off the mark. Controlling the frequency of my encounters with someone else, as I had with Will, was the best and most efficient way to protect my marriage.

"Jessica?" a man's voice said, snapping me out of my thoughts.

I looked up and saw Andrew standing next to me, feeling like I'd swallowed something sharp. Now that he was there in person, I instantly suspected that I'd seen him before. *Did I sell him a property? Or maybe he strolled through one of my open houses?* "Andrew?"

"That's me." He flashed a smile, showing off a set of straight, white teeth. "Really sorry I'm late. I got stuck in traffic."

"No worries," I said, deciding that it wasn't that big of a deal. Traffic on I-405 was insane pretty much any time of day, despite the toll lanes the residents of King county had voted for. I always factored in at least an extra half-an-hour when I used the freeway to meet clients.

"Can I get you something to drink?" he offered, glancing at the long line leading up to the counter. The buzz of the coffee grinders and other peoples' conversations filled the air. Being in the midst of this normalcy and knowing I was there to decide if I was going to fuck the man I was sitting with added an extra kick of adrenaline.

"I'm good, thanks," I said, hoping my voice wasn't as wobbly as my body felt. "I've only got about half an hour." He was twenty minutes late, and I had a property to show that afternoon. Normally, Jake and I liked to spend at least an hour with a potential match, even though I usually knew in the first five or ten minutes whether or not I wanted to sleep with him, the same way I could tell if a client was going to make an offer on a house. I read the energy in both situations, the subtle signs a person gave away about themselves that they weren't necessarily aware of. In this case, checking for chemistry meant I looked for a certain set of characteristics. I wanted to fuck men who made and maintained eye contact with me when they spoke. I wanted to fuck men who possessed a good mix of confidence and playfulness—who knew how to be funny and insert clever, not crude, sexual innuendo into our conversation. I liked men who told me I was beautiful—because really, what woman didn't want to hear that? I liked men who bantered with me, men with a quick wit, like Jake. It was an immediate turn off if a man walked into our meeting already assuming that he was the "chosen one," simply because we'd asked him out for coffee or drink. I automatically rejected men who thought that just because I was sexually adventurous—that I'd posted an ad with my husband, looking for sex, or, "shopping for cock," as one man we'd met crudely put it—he didn't have to work a little to seduce me. A desire to explore outside the bounds of my marriage didn't automatically make me a sure thing.

Andrew grimaced as he sat down across from me. "God, sorry again. Did I just take myself out of the running? I'm usually very punctual. *And on time.*" He leaned back against his chair, rested the tips of his fingers on the edge of the table, and gave me a charming smile. He had full lips, and I immediately wondered what it would feel like to kiss them. I did a quick check of his left hand—no ring on the fourth finger, nor any tan lines or indentations that would indicate he was married and pretending that he wasn't. He'd said he was recently out of a relationship, but I always checked for physical confirmation, just in case.

"Not necessarily." I smiled, and took a moment to appraise him. His wavy hair was shorter than it had been in his pictures, cut haphazardly, but in an appealing, he-might-be-an-artist-who-doesn't-bother-with-a-comb kind of way. His skin was tanned, and his brown eyes were dark enough that it was difficult to decipher iris from pupil. He wore black slacks and a pin-striped, blue button down that was rolled up at the sleeves, exposing an expensive-looking silver watch on his left wrist. "You look a little familiar," I said. "Have we met?"

"Possibly," he said, cocking his head. "I feel like I've see you before, too." He paused. "Sorry for the half-assed pics I sent. I know they weren't exactly clear."

"That's okay," I said. "Discretion is a good thing." I felt sure I recognized his voice. "Did we go on a date, and I don't remember it?"

He laughed—a low and appealing sound. It made me want to say something funny, again. "Oh, I think I would have remembered you," he said, with a lively edge. "I don't often forget a date with a smart, beautiful woman." Suddenly, he sat forward, resting his forearms on the table. "Wait. Did you ever work at a restaurant in Kirkland?"

"Yes," I said, instantly set on guard. *Oh shit. He might know my last name.* And then it hit me. "Okay, hold on. Are you *Andy* the bartender, from the Lakeside Grill?" When I was twenty-one, almost eighteen years ago, a restaurant on Lake Washington was the only place I'd been able to find a job when Peter and I first moved from Boise. It was a busy spot, especially during the summer months, and they employed a lot of bartenders, but there was one, in particular, that I was always happy to have on my shift, and that was Andy. He was a cute and funny guy that the other female servers tended to overlook because he wore thick, nerdy glasses and carried a little extra weight around the middle, but I had always liked his smile and the way he made me laugh every time I picked up a drink order from the bar. Now, the bulge of his stomach and his glasses were gone, and instead of a crew cut, his hair was grown out. He looked like a totally different person.

"Um, yeah," Andrew said, now. "I've been using my full name since I started my company." He peered at me. "Why can't I place you?"

"I wasn't there very long," I said. "Only six months or so." I had been four months along when I realized I was pregnant with Ella—at the time, I wasn't in the habit of tracking my periods, or reliably taking the Pill— and Peter had insisted that I quit my job and let him pay all of our bills. Only one among many bad decisions I'd made during our relationship.

"Wow," Andrew said, smiling. "Small world, huh?"

"No kidding." I took a deep breath and frowned. "Unfortunately, it means that this isn't going to work."

"Why not? Please don't tell me you're traumatized by my previous, not-so-hot geek-factor. I have contacts, now! And I'm not wearing a Star Trek T-shirt!"

I laughed. "Oh god, I *forgot* about that! It was red, right?"

"No *way*. Anyone in a red shirt always died on Star Trek. I'm strictly a blue shirt. Like Spock."

I shook my head, smiling. "Still a little bit of a geek, then."

He palmed his forehead. "Shit! You're on to me!" He smiled, too, and his dark eyes twinkled. "Come on. Don't write me off, yet."

I looked at him, taking in his newly chiseled jawline and bedroom eyes. Back when we worked together, I was drawn to his sense of humor, but especially to how talkative he was—at least, compared to Peter. I had never thought about Andy-the-bartender in a romantic sense, but I'd liked him. I remember thinking he would make a great husband someday.

"I'm sorry," I finally said. "I really shouldn't do this it with anyone I know." While Jake and I had never specifically discussed whether or not it would be a good idea to engage in this experience with someone we knew, I assumed it went without saying that anonymity was the most important element of maintaining discretion.

"You don't know me," Andrew countered. "You *knew* me. Briefly. For like, six hours at a time eighteen years ago. I'm not the same guy I was at twenty-five, and I'm sure you're not the same person you were back then, either, because like I said, I would have remembered someone as beautiful as you." He reached across the table and touched the back of my hand with his fingertips. An undeniable bolt of excitement shot through me.

"Well," I said, "you definitely have more game than you used to." I couldn't deny the attraction I felt—he was funny, smart, and physically, definitely my type. But a little voice inside my head told me I needed to walk away.

"Oh, I'm just getting started," he said. "Geeky boys do *everything* better."

"Is that so?" *So much for walking away*, I thought. I was having too much fun talking with him.

"Absolutely," Andrew said. "We're *very* interested in how things work. Including a woman's body. We like to push buttons. And then push them again." He stroked my hand again with a single finger. "Let me push your buttons, Jessica." His voice dropped as he spoke this last sentence, and my breath hitched inside my chest. I'd been attracted to the other men I'd slept with as part of this experience, but this was different. The way he was talking to me, using words as seductive weapons, it was as though he'd climbed inside my head and targeted the one thing that made a man impossible for me to resist.

"I'm sorry," I said, again. I stood up and grabbed by purse. "I have to go."

He stood up, too. "Okay," he said. "Let me at least walk you to your car? To make up for being late?"

I hesitated only a moment before agreeing, and a few minutes later, Andrew stood next to me in a parking garage not unlike the one where Jake had taken me up against our car after watching me dance with Will. But thankfully, unlike that night, there were several people in the immediate vicinity to keep me from doing something I might regret with Andrew. I kept looking at his lips, wondering what they might feel like on my skin; what kind of buttons of mine he'd be able to find and push. I worried that with the attraction I felt and the way he made me laugh, he'd already found a few.

"Are you sure about this?" Andrew asked. "I can keep things casual. Totally discreet. Scout's honor." He held up the index and middle fingers on his right hand.

"Were you actually a Scout, or are you just really trying to get yourself laid?" I teased.

"An Eagle Scout," he said, solemnly. We were standing a couple of feet away from each other, but then he leaned in closer and put his lips right below my ear. "I used to be a good boy, but I've changed." His breath was hot, and tickled. It took everything in me to fight the overwhelming impulse to turn my head and kiss him.

Instead, I took a step back. I held out my hand. "It was nice to see you. Sorry it couldn't work out."

"Me, too," he said, taking my hand in his. His skin was soft, save a few calluses, and his grip was firm. His eyes bored into mine. "You know how to reach me, if you change your mind."

"I won't," I said. But even as I spoke the words, I found myself wondering whether they were true.

"SO, how'd it go?" Jake asked me later that night, as we stood in our bathroom, getting ready for bed. I'd texted him, after my meeting with Andrew, to let him know I was safe, but between showing my clients six houses and then having to get dinner on the table while Jake helped the kids with their homework, we had been too busy to discuss the details. "Did you like him?"

"He was nice enough," I said, as casually as I could. "But I think I'm going to keep looking." I'd wrestled all afternoon with the idea of telling Jake that I had recognized Andrew, and how that felt like a line we shouldn't cross. But if I was being honest, the bigger line was about how Andrew had *talked* to me—and how attracted to him I'd been. Ultimately, I decided that it would be better to keep that information to myself. The way Jake spoke to me about sex since we met Will had become *our* thing—it wasn't something I shared with other men. There were times when I was alone with Will or Alex or Vincent, and they might talk dirty to me while we were in bed, but none of them had used it as foreplay to the extent that Jake did. None of them understood the extent to which words had a certain kind of power over me. My reaction to Andrew was unnerving, because he seemed to so quickly get inside my head. I wasn't sure how that had happened. The sense of vulnerability I felt—that Andrew saw more about me than I had wanted him to—was the real reason I couldn't see him again.

"No spark, huh?" Jake said. He set his toothbrush back in the holder and then came over to stand behind me, slipping his arms around my waist. He nuzzled my neck, and then set his lips in the same spot Andrew's had been, on my ear. "You need someone who makes you wet, right baby?" he whispered. He grazed my earlobe with his teeth, and a chill shot across my skin.

I closed my eyes. "Right," I said, telling myself this was only a little white lie. My clit ached after Andrew and I parted ways; I probably would have given myself an orgasm, if I had had the time.

"I want you to find someone," Jake continued. "I want to hear how you fuck him." His words created vivid images, but in that moment, instead of focusing on my husband's words, all I could think about were Andrew's.

All I wanted was his deep voice inside my head, telling me exactly what I needed to hear.

Fifteen

The next afternoon, a little after one, I stepped inside Kendall Properties' front door. The receptionist, Kimberly, who was a slightly chubby, middle-aged woman with fluffy, bleached blonde hair and a penchant for bedazzled tops, greeted me. I had floor time, which meant if anyone happened to call or show up and needed to speak with an agent about one of our properties, Kimberly would direct them to me. Most agents hated being chained to a desk for four hours, but I actually relished the opportunity to catch up on paperwork, and the possibility that whoever might call or show up could end up as my client.

I spent a couple of hours in my office, making calls and sifting through the messy stack of paper on my desk. Around three-thirty, Kimberly buzzed me from the front desk.

"I have someone on the line for you," she said.

"Great," I said. "Put them through." I hoped whoever was calling might be looking to buy, and would be interested in the Falls, a new construction development about five miles outside of Queens Ridge. I had an ongoing relationship with the investors and general contractor, so I listed every house in the project. I'd pre-sold almost all of them, but had two left. If the person calling ended up buying one, I'd be in for a double commission.

I smiled as I picked up the phone, knowing that it was possible for someone to pick up on my expression based on how I answered. "This is Jessica," I said, cheerfully. "What can I sell you today?" This was my standard, doing-floor-time greeting, and while it sounded cheesy, I found that if my tone was earnest and warm, it actually won people over.

"A second chance?" a man's voice said, and I instantly recognized it as Andrew's. I stiffened.

"How did you find me?" I asked, lowering my voice. My heart raced. I got up and shut my office door. My last name was Wright when I worked with Andrew at the Lakeside Grill; I'd left him yesterday feeling confident that despite our connection the past, he wouldn't know how to find out more about me, now. I couldn't decide if I was thrilled or terrified that I'd been wrong.

"Please don't freak out."

"You didn't answer my question," I said, tightly.

"Facebook. You commented on a friend of mine's post. Chelsea Wallace?"

I felt a flicker of panic. Chelsea was a client—an older woman who ran a successful online jewelry company called Frost. She had purchased an eight-bedroom house on Lake Washington from me several years ago, and sent me a friend request when I was working with her, as many of my clients do. Last night, while I was scrolling through Facebook— I mostly used social media as a way to maintain contact with my clients, in the hopes that if they needed to buy or sell property again, they'd automatically think of me—I'd liked her picture of the lake in front of her house, blue and glittering in the afternoon sun, and commented, "Gorgeous!"

"How do you know Chelsea?" I asked, still wary that Andrew had contacted me at work.

"I designed her website. My company manages the tech side of Frost's e-commerce." He coughed, and then cleared his throat. "I saw your comment on her post, recognized your picture, and felt like it was some sort of weird sign, since we literally just saw each other. I was hoping you'd be flattered. I can't stop thinking about you."

The way he said it—the way his voice shifted into something that sounded the way I imagined warm honey might feel—loosened the tension in my neck. After all, this was Andy-the-bartender—the sweet, funny, nerdy guy I'd known almost twenty years ago. He loved computers and Star Trek. He made up limericks about customers' drink orders and walked me to my car when we both had a closing shift. He was harmless.

"Are you still there?" he asked. "I'm truly sorry if I crossed a line. I just…felt something when we saw each other." He paused. "Didn't you?"

"Yes," I said, before I could stop myself. "But that doesn't change the fact that I can't do anything with you."

"Even if I swear I won't mess with your real life?"

"You're calling me at my office," I said, unable to keep the accusation from my tone. "That's pretty much the opposite of being discreet." He knew my last name, now. He could look me up online, find out where my kids went to school. Jake and I never mentioned that we had children to any of the three men we'd been with, simply as an extra measure of protection. Saying I was "in real estate" always felt general enough—I could have been a real estate developer or investor, not necessarily an agent. I also never mentioned Queens Ridge as specifically where Jake and I lived—another level of precaution. No one had found out who I was before, nor had they tried, as far as I knew. And even though it seemed to be a coincidence that Andrew had found me on Facebook, I felt the tiniest bit sick.

"My last name is Rochester," Andrew said. "I own a company called Lightning Web Design. My address is 42 Lost Lake Road in Kirkland. Google me, if you want. Run a background search. I don't have anything to hide."

I was silent. Having him offer me offer me as much, if not more, information about him than he knew about me was reassuring, but still, I was hesitant. It was an entirely different thing for a guy like Andrew, a single man with no entanglements, to be involved in something like this. If it somehow got out that he had sought out this kind of arrangement, I doubted that he would face the same kind of judgment I would as a married woman—a *mother*—with a public, fairly high profile job. However often I reminded myself that I was a grown woman, now, capable of making her own choices, not only when it came to sex, but everything else in my life, the faint whisper of my mother's voice still drifted inside my head: "You don't want to be *that* kind of girl."

"Jessica?" Andrew said. "What are you thinking?"

"A lot."

"Are you angry?"

"Not exactly. More…conflicted." I *had* felt something when we saw each other—that all-important, hard-to-define flash of chemistry that I suspected would translate into scintillating sex.

"I'm sorry," he said again. "I was too impulsive. I should have emailed, instead. I wasn't thinking. I just…" He trailed off, and this time, I finished his sentence.

"Felt something."

"Yeah." I closed my eyes and remembered his lips against my ear as we stood together next to my car, how he'd murmured, "I used to be a good boy, but I've changed"—how those words carved my thoughts into a thousand different images of the things the two of us might do together. I shivered, feeling a familiar ache, low in my belly. I imagined what might have happened if I'd kissed him, then. How he would have tasted. How he might have pressed himself against me. What his fingers might have felt like tangled in my hair.

"Let me think about it," I said.

"Okay," he said. "That's fair. If I don't hear from you, I'll assume your decision is made and leave you alone. But I promise you won't regret giving a reformed geek a chance to show you his wicked-hot moves."

I laughed, he gave me his number, which I put into my cell, and we hung up. I sat in my office alone, my mind whirling. I considered how Andrew had found me, the very next day after we had coffee. Maybe it *was* some kind of a sign that we were supposed to connect. Maybe the sex would be so amazing, it would turn Jake on to hear about it like nothing had before. Maybe I was making a big deal out of nothing.

Or maybe, I was about to talk myself into something I really shouldn't do.

IN the days that followed Andrew's call to my office, there were end-of-the-year banquets for Ella's dance and Tuck's baseball teams, as well as preparations for my parents' upcoming visit. Jake was at the new office more than ever, still working on getting Justine up to speed, and I ended up receiving offers on both of the remaining houses in the Falls development, so I didn't have much time to think about Andrew. But when I did, I kept going back to how differently he carried himself than he had when we'd worked together. Back then, he'd seemed goofy and kind—a good person to have as a friend. Now, he came across as mysterious—a bit of a bad boy, really—a good person to have hot, casual sex with. What caused this transition? It made me think about the other guys I had known in my twenties, the ones who had seemed more like boys than men at the time, and wondered who they'd become. *All the paths not taken*, I thought wistfully, fleetingly, before reminding myself that no man could compare to Jake. But it was that niggling question that drove me to want to see Andrew again.

I wished I could talk with Charlotte about Andrew, but she seemed to only want to talk about Bryan. "He just *gets* me," she said during one of our daily text conversations. "He totally understands my feelings, and he makes me laugh like crazy."

Be careful, I wanted to say, though who was I to warn her about the perils of talking with another man when I'd had sex with three men in as many years. It seemed hypocritical—how could conversation with a man be more intimate than getting naked with him, letting him *inside* your body? But I hadn't allowed myself to become emotionally attached to anyone the way she seemed to be doing with Bryan. If I'd learned anything over the last few years, it was that having sex with someone was a multifaceted experience, involving your mind, body, and soul. When I was with Jake, we connected on all three of those levels. His words crawled into my mind, stimulated my body, and amplified the love I had for him even more. My experiences with Will, Tim, and Vincent were purely physical—my mind and my heart belonged only to my husband— which is what kept my relationship sacred and safe.

But simply speaking with Andrew had pushed my body into a spiral of want. It was tempting to see if adding the mental aspect would heighten my experience—and subsequently, Jake's, when I told him about it—even more. Isn't that what he had suggested we needed to do—up the ante? Push our boundaries? Jake was intensifying his side of this arrangement by not being involved in choosing who I slept with, forcing himself to only imagine the things I did with another man. As long as I reserved my heart for my husband, didn't it make sense that I escalate what I did in the experience, as well?

"So, I'm thinking I might talk to Andrew again," I told Jake, casually, in the late evening, on the kids' last day of school. Ella was at work, and Tuck was over at Peter and Kari's house, getting ready to head to eastern Washington for a baseball tournament. Jake and I were sitting on our back deck, enjoying a majestic, glowing-embers sunset, each of us sipping at a glass of wine. Since our failed date night, he'd made absolutely sure that he was home by seven on Fridays, so we could enjoy at least a few hours together, whether or not we went out.

"Changed your mind, did you?" Jake asked, raising a single eyebrow.

"I never really decided against him." *This is true,* I thought even though my heart was pounding inside my chest. I wasn't lying to Jake; I just wasn't sharing how profoundly my first meeting with Andrew had affected me. A lie of omission, committed only to protect my husband's feelings. And he didn't *really* need to know that I'd known Andrew briefly, in the past. It was so long ago, and besides, it automatically added an extra layer of security to what otherwise could be a risky situation. "I wanted to give it a little more time," I told Jake, "since he was one of the first replies I got. It always took us longer to find someone."

"You don't feel like you're settling, do you?" He ran his fingertip around the rim of his glass, making it sing.

"Not at all," I said.

"When are you going to see him?" He stopped moving his hand, though his fingers lingered on the edge of the glass.

"Not this weekend, obviously," I said. My parents were due to arrive the next day, and we had the barbeque Charlotte had ended up inviting half of Queens Ridge to on Sunday.

"But soon, though."

I nodded.

"Good," he said, and the air between us suddenly felt like it had in his car, after we had met Will at the club—full of possibility, longing, and excitement. Everything a good marriage is supposed to have.

Sixteen

I sent a text to Andrew the next morning, asking if he was still interested in getting together, even though I knew that he was. I told him that my parents were visiting for the weekend, so we wouldn't be able to get together until the following one, which he said he understood. "Real life comes first," he wrote. "Literally."

Jake laughed when I told him Andrew's last remark. "I see why you like him," he commented, and I instantly felt guilty for not telling him the entire truth. But I wasn't *technically* breaking any of the rules we'd set in place to protect us. He knew our last name and where I worked, but he'd also given me all of his personal information, which I'd confirmed by doing as he had suggested—I Googled him. He was, indeed, the founder and CEO of Lightning Design, a sizable internet design and tech services company. He was also single, according to the King county public records I reviewed online, and his house really was on the street in Kirkland that he'd named. If he'd been lying about any of it, I would have cut things off immediately. But since he'd been honest, I decided to trust him.

"What time are Grandma and Grandpa coming?" Ella asked me when she finally woke up, around noon. Her shift at Olive Garden had ended after ten the night before, but she always spent a few hours scrolling through Instagram while Snap Chatting with her friends when she got home from work, so gone were the days when she used to leap out of bed before the sun came up. Two years ago, as a freshman, she'd abandoned soccer to join the highly competitive Queens Ridge Raiders dance team, so instead of spending my Saturday mornings at short games, once or twice a month during competition season, I endured eight to ten hours sitting on uncomfortable bleachers. Dance demanded a lot of time, energy, and long hours of practice, but it was something Ella truly loved. I'd watched her self-confidence soar since joining the team—so much that she nabbed the position of junior class president without putting much effort into a campaign. Luckily, Bentley had also joined the team, so unless she had an event the same day, Charlotte joined me on those rock-hard bleachers, and we cheered our daughters on, together.

"They should be here around four," I told Ella, now. Despite being dressed to meet clients, in a knee-length black shift dress covered in a tiny, white-flowered print, I was in the middle of doing an extra wipe-down of the kitchen in preparation for my mother's critical eye. "How does your room look?"

"Meh." Ella shrugged as she gathered her long curls into a messy bun on top of her head, securing it with a black elastic tie she almost always wore around her wrist. I marveled as the beautiful young woman she had morphed into over the last few years: she'd grown three inches, and long hours of dancing had carved her body into a lithe, well-sculpted piece of biological art. Her skin was smooth and clear, her green eyes sparkled, and her stomach was flatter than mine had ever been. Unlike Bentley, she had yet to have a boyfriend, but being single didn't seem to faze her. There were boys at school she thought were cute, but too immature, or they spent too much time partying. "I'm *so* not going to date a pothead," she had declared to me at the beginning of her junior year. "I hate the smell of pot, and I *definitely* hate the smell of stupid." For her to be so self-assured at such a young age thrilled me. Tucker, on the other hand, still tended toward impulsive, silly decisions, like spending all his fifteenth birthday money on an expensive skateboard that he'd insisted he "needed" and we'd refused to buy him as a gift, and then proceeded to ride it exactly two times before letting it gather dust in the garage. I kept telling myself that boys mature slower than girls, and that Tuck would eventually start to grow up.

"What does 'meh' mean?" I asked Ella. "Is your room clean or not?"

"It's fine, Mom. God." She opened the fridge and grabbed a Greek yogurt, along with a package of fresh raspberries.

"Fine isn't any clearer than 'meh,'" I said, lightly. I normally didn't bother to force the kids to clean up their rooms; as long as they did their own laundry and didn't leave food on their desks to rot, I figured it was their mess to tolerate—I could always close their doors so I didn't have to look at it. But it was a different story when my mother came to visit; she wouldn't ride the kids about the state of their room, she'd ride me. "Can you at least see the floor?"

"Yes!" Ella said. She walked into the family room, set her breakfast on the coffee table, and flopped onto the couch. "You totally freak out whenever Grandma's here. You need to chill. Tell her it's your house and you'll keep it as filthy as you want, then not give a shit if it bothers her."

"Easier said than done," I told her, choosing to ignore her language. I swore enough that it was a little hypocritical to expect her not to. "Please make sure the bathrooms are clean, too, okay? Especially the guest bath." I paused. "And double check that I put the right soap in there. You know Grandpa needs his Irish Spring."

Ella laughed. "That's so weird. Like some other soap isn't going to clean his skin just as well."

"Grandpa is a creature of habit." Just as he stuck to the same meals almost every day, he insisted on using the same soap. When it went on sale, my mom would fill an entire shelf in the bathroom cabinet with the shiny green boxes it came in so he wouldn't unexpectedly run out. He said his regimented ways helped keep him focused on his work: "Any energy I waste thinking about what kind of soap to use or what I should eat takes away from my ability to think about how to save one of my patients," he told me once, and I'd never forgotten it. I'd admired this level of self-discipline, but never embraced it as my own. I was a fan of variety, in my beauty products, the food I ate, and, as I had discovered, my sex life.

"Oh my god, Mom," Ella said, snapping me out of that thought. "I forgot to tell you about Lizzy!"

"What happened this time?" I asked. Lizzy was generally too snappish and bitchy for she and Ella to be friends, but she was on the dance team with her, so my daughter, at my prompting, tried not to participate in spreading the rumors about what Lizzy did with boys under the bleachers or in the back seats of their cars. She did, however, like to talk to me about it.

Ella swallowed the bite of yogurt and popped a few raspberries in her mouth before answering me. "Ryder Hanson had a party last weekend because his parents were out of town and Lizzy went into a bedroom with him and some random dude she didn't even *know*. They were in there for like, an hour, and when she came out, her hair was all messed up and everyone else could see that the guys were still getting dressed."

I frowned. "I wonder if they were drinking." I knew Ryder and his parents, Chuck and Christine; I had sold them their house. When they first moved here about eight years ago, Ryder had been a sweet ten-year-old, obsessed with Legos and still holding his mother's hand. Now, he was a senior, and quarterback on the football team, with a reputation for having a new girl on his arm every few weeks.

Ella snorted. "Um, they totally were. Ryder's always bragging about how his parents don't even notice how much booze he steals from their bar. They just replace it. He's such a douche."

I couldn't help but feel a touch of pride that Ella had disdain for boys like Ryder. "I feel bad for Lizzy," I said.

"She has a ho account on Instagram, too."

"A *what*?" I asked, stopping mid-swipe as I cleaned the counter. I gave my daughter a baffled look.

"A ho account. 'Ho' is short for 'whore.' It's where a girl posts sexy pictures of herself, separate from her regular account. She calls it Lizzy_the_Ho. If I had one it would be Ella_the_Ho. They do it so people will tell them they're hot." She rolled her eyes.

"Tell me you're joking." I felt sick thinking of this sixteen-year-old girl plastering intimate pictures of herself on the Internet. It reeked of desperation and lack of self-esteem. Not to mention that the images, if they were as sexy as Ella indicated, could be considered pornographic. Lizzy was under eighteen; what she was doing was illegal, though I doubted she realized that.

Ella shook her head and popped a few more raspberries. "Nope. A couple of other girls on the team have them, too. They don't post their faces, but everyone knows who they are."

"You don't have one, right?" I couldn't help but ask.

"God, Mom! *No!* I'm not that dumb."

"I know. Sorry. I just needed to be sure." I paused. "Does Lacy know?" Lacy Sullivan was a former Seahawk cheerleader who had been the dance team's coach at Queens Ridge High School for the last twelve years. She held the girls to a high standard when it came to their behavior, both on and off the dance floor. I couldn't imagine she'd be okay with something like this.

Ella shook her head. "You can't tell her."

"Oh yes, I can." I might not have felt comfortable talking directly to Tiffany about her daughter's behavior with boys, but there was no way I could let something like this go. Sexual exploration was normal, but this crossed a line.

"No, Mom! Then everyone will know I told you! They'll *hate* me!"

"No, they won't," I said. "And even if they do, you can tell them you told me because you're concerned about their safety. Who knows how many perverted men are following their accounts, looking at their pictures? What if they or someone else gives away what high school they go to? They could be kidnapped...or worse." I gave her a sharp look, and she nodded, reluctantly.

"I didn't think about that," she relented.

I quickly made a note in my calendar to call Lacy, and then, a few hours later, I returned from meeting with clients to find that my parents had arrived early. A rented blue sedan—my dad always insisted on having his own vehicle in case there was an emergency with one of his patients and he needed to get to the airport quickly—was in the driveway, blocking me from going into the garage, so I parked on the street. Walking up the winding pathway that led to our door, I noted that Jake had placed a few pots of cheerful red geraniums—my mother's favorite—on our front porch.

I entered the house to the sound of voices coming from the family room. "Hello?" I called out as I walked down the hall that led past the living room into the kitchen. Jake, Ella, and my mom and dad were all seated on the sectional sofa.

"Hello, Jessica," my dad said. He looked so much older than when I'd last seen him, at Christmas, when we'd gone to stay with them a few days. His previously brown and silver curls had gone entirely white and the dark circles under his eyes were more pronounced than ever. He looked like an emaciated Albert Einstein.

"You're here early," I said.

"We took an earlier flight," she said. "Thought we'd surprise you. But then you weren't here."

"I had to work," I told her. My voice was tight, even though I forced myself to smile. It was still hard for me to deal with my mother's admonishments about my working too much when she'd spent most of her life doing the same. It took everything in me to not point that out. "I wasn't expecting you to be here until four." I glanced at the clock over the mantle. "It's only three-thirty."

"Oh, I know," my mom said. "I just figured you'd manage to be here the day your parents are scheduled to arrive."

"I have to get ready for work," Ella said, rising from the couch before I could respond, which was probably a good thing. She'd showered since I'd seen her earlier; her damp curls hung halfway down her back, and she wore fitted black dance shorts with a red t-shirt.

"You, too?" my mom said, making a sour face.

"I have to work Friday and Saturday nights, Grandma," Ella said. "That's when I get the best tips from the servers." Not waiting for my mother's reply, she headed upstairs, and I envied her ability to not get drawn into—or even be aware of—my mom's passive-aggressive games.

"She's coming with us to Charlotte's for the barbeque tomorrow," I said after she was gone. I thought about pouring myself a glass of wine to take the edge off the irritation I felt, but didn't want to deal with my mother's inevitable raised eyebrows and commentary: "You're *drinking*? Before five o'clock?" Instead, I went to sit next to Jake.

"Hi babe," he said, giving me a quick kiss. He took my hand and gave it a reassuring squeeze. *I'm here,* the gesture said. *Don't worry. I've got your back.*

"The yard looks great," I told him. "Thank you."

"Of course," he said.

"How's business?" my dad asked, directing the question at Jake as he returned to the couch.

"Couldn't be better," Jake said. "There's a hiring boom around here, so I'm busier than ever trying to find the right candidates to fill all the positions. I can barely keep up."

"Good, good," my dad said, bobbing his head.

"I'm busy, too," I said, though he hadn't bothered to ask. Like my mother, he wished I had chosen a more intellectually illustrious career. But I wondered if even *that* would be enough to bring us closer, since his relationship with my brother Scott, who worked as a biological engineer, was just as distant as the one I had with my dad. Still, I wanted both of my parents to understand how hard I worked. "All of those new hires need somewhere to live," I went on. "House prices are sky-rocketing. It's a total seller's market. If a property goes up for sale, it almost always ends up in a bidding war." I looked at my mom, who didn't seem to be listening. "That's why I had to meet clients, today. They've been renting forever, waiting for the right house to buy, and finally the perfect one went on the market. We couldn't hesitate."

"Did they get it?" Jake asked. He knew how long I'd been trying to find a house for the Clarks, a sweet young couple with eighteen-month-old twin girls.

"Yep," I said, giving him a smile. "It took an all cash offer, twenty thousand over the asking price, but it's theirs."

"That's awesome, babe," my husband said. "Isn't that awesome, Mom?" He smiled at my mother, who had insisted from the minute we married that he should call her "Mom," too.

"Wonderful," she replied, but I could tell she was distracted and didn't really care that I'd managed to find my clients a home. "Is Tuck at Peter's?" she asked, looking around the room, as though he might magically appear.

"No," I said. "They're over in eastern Washington this weekend for a baseball tournament. I thought I told you that." I didn't "think" I'd told her; I knew I did. We'd had a conversation about it the day before, while she was packing for the trip.

"Our grandson isn't even going to *be* here for our visit?" my mother exclaimed. "We come all this way and Ella is working and we don't get to see Tuck?"

"Sheila, it's fine," my dad said. There was a sharp edge to the words.

"I *told* you he had the tournament," I said.

"And I told you that this was the only weekend your father could be away from the hospital," my mom said. "I thought the least you could do was have Tuck stay home."

"She's being ridiculous," my dad said sharply, as though my mother wasn't there. "Ignore her. We're just happy to be here."

My mother's gray eyes were glossed with tears, which shocked me; I couldn't ever remember it happening before. Everyone was silent for a moment, and it felt as though a thick fog had crept over the room. I glanced at Jake, who was very studiously looking at the fingernails on his free hand.

"Hey, Mom," I finally said. "I thought you and I could make a dessert to bring to the barbeque." Charlotte was having the gathering catered—she loved to eat, but didn't like to cook—but my mother and I tended to do better if we had a project to work on together instead of simply sitting around, so I told Charlotte we'd make something.

"Okay," she said. Her tears were gone so quickly, I wondered if I had imagined them.

"Peter sent us a video of Tuck's games today," Jake said. "Want to watch them with me upstairs, Dad?"

"Sure!" my dad boomed, a little too cheerfully. He'd never gone to any of Scott's swim meets in high school, so I knew Tuck's baseball game likely didn't interest him, but he looked happy to have an excuse to leave the room. He didn't look at my mom as he passed her by, deliberately giving her a wide berth. I gave Jake a grateful look.

"Is everything all right?" I asked her, when we were finally alone. "I've never heard Dad snap at you like that."

"You know how your father is."

"He's never made you cry."

"I had something in my eye. Maybe it's the dust."

I decided to ignore that particular jab. "Mom. What's going on? Tell me."

She sighed, and looked at me. "He's not very happy with all the time I've been spending with my friends. He thinks I'm wasting my time socializing and taking trips when I could still be teaching full-time or doing more research."

"That seems strange. He doesn't want you to have friends?" I knew my father's admiration for my mother's intellect was a huge part of what he loved about her, but it never crossed my mind that he might resent the way she'd cut down on her time at the college.

"He's just used to our life being a certain way," my mom said, sounding resigned. "He's not good with change."

I nodded, thinking about his regimented behavior through the years, and it struck me how something I'd admired about him might actually be an impediment. Life was messy—constantly shifting, taking you down unexpected paths. If you weren't willing to bend, to go with the flow of opportunities as they appeared, you could become stubborn, paralyzed—unable to grow.

"He deals with so much chaos every day," my mom continued. "Patients in crisis, people in terrible pain and dying. His routine gives him some sense of control." She shrugged, and gave me a wan smile. "We've been together so long, what I do has become *part* of that routine, and now that I'm doing something different…well, it's been a struggle for him to adjust. Nothing I do seems like enough."

Welcome to the club, sister, was the first thing that popped into my head, but as this was a rare instance when my mother was talking *with* me instead of *at* me—treating me like an equal—I managed to bite my tongue. "That must feel terrible," I said, instead. "I'm sorry."

"Thank you," she said, sincerely. And then, she grabbed my hand in an uncommon gesture of affection. I felt a swell of love in my chest. "Can

I tell you something?" she asked.

"Sure." I held my breath, having no clue what she might say. *Is she thinking about divorcing my dad? Have things between them gotten that bad?*

"I want you to know that when I see you with Jake, when I see how both of you light up when you look at each other, the way he's affectionate with you, and always seems so present and aware of what you and the kids need—well, it makes me *so* very happy for you." She paused, and squeezed my fingers, blinking away tears once more. "I'm so happy you have that kind of relationship."

For a moment, I was too shocked to speak. This outpouring was so out of character for my mother, it hit me that my vision of my parents' marriage—my interpretation of it as a child, and even now, as an adult— was limited, because clearly, there was an entirely different world going on between them than what I had been privy to growing up. Just as my children didn't understand the full scope of my relationship with Jake, the story I'd told myself about my parents was composed only of footnotes— the brief flashes I was there to witness, and the conclusions I'd reached as a result. For every one of those moments, there must have been a thousand others that only happened between them. Only they knew the full scope of what they were to each other. As much as I hated it when I felt like my mother judged me, it also wasn't my place to judge her, either, as I had so often over the years. Maybe it was time for that to change.

"I appreciate it that, Mom," I said, my voice breaking. "I really do." I leaned over and hugged her, pressing my face into her shoulder. At first, her body was stiff, but she quickly relaxed and hugged me back, with fierce strength.

"Take care of your marriage," she whispered, and I nodded, wondering how she would react if she knew what I had done with men other than Jake, and what I would soon do with Andrew, but then forced the thought from my head.

There were some things that other people—your mother, especially—just didn't need to know.

Seventeen

I got a text from Andrew around noon the next day, as we were all getting ready to head over to Charlotte's house for the barbeque. "I can't stop thinking about you," he said. "What your body is going to feel like under mine."

My cheeks flushed; I was flattered—and instantly aroused—as I read his words. I'd only texted with the other men I'd been with to confirm the places and times we were going to meet. Talking with Andrew now, a kind of mental foreplay, felt marvelously forbidden—and a little dangerous. "Me, too," I quickly texted back. "Can't talk now." I deleted both messages, and then threw my phone in my purse before we headed out the front door, feeling our communication burning like a secret, hot flame inside my chest.

"Who else is going to be here?" my mom asked, as we pulled up in front of Charlotte's house ten minutes later. Charlotte and Richard lived in a similar, but bigger house than we did, and it was set upon a full acre that butted up to a lush, tree-lined green belt. It was a sunny day, and both sides of the street were packed with parked cars, with no less than ten people making their way across the lawn, heading toward the side gate that led into Charlotte and Richard's back yard.

"Bentley just Snapped me and said that there were at least fifty people in their backyard," Ella said from the back seat, where she was sandwiched between her grandparents.

"Why would she snap at you about that?" my dad asked.

"Snap *Chat,* Grandpa," Ella explained, laughing. "It's sort of like texting."

"Looks like more than fifty," Jake said, as he finally found a parking spot for our SUV, more than a block past the party. After getting out of the car, we walked along the sidewalk, my dad striding at least five feet in front of all of us—after years of rushing down the halls in the hospital, he didn't know how to walk at a leisurely pace. As we approached Charlotte's house, my phone buzzed inside my purse.

"Here," Jake said, taking the rectangular baking pan filled with the coconut cream cake my mother and I had made the night before. He nodded toward my purse, which was slung over my shoulder. "You'd better take it, in case it's work. We'll meet you there."

"Thanks honey." I grabbed my phone as the rest of my family headed toward the back yard. A glance at the screen told me it was Charlotte. "Hey. I'm right outside."

"I invited Bryan, last minute, last night," she said, sounding panicked. "Am I out of my fucking mind?"

"Holy shit," I said. "Maybe." But then I thought if it didn't faze Richard to walk in on his wife using a vibrator—if he didn't realize that something was going wrong in his marriage when they hadn't had sex in nine months—then maybe he wasn't observant enough to pick up on any vibes between Charlotte and Bryan. Or worse, maybe he wouldn't care.

"I just *really* wanted to see him," she said. "We talk all the time, but we haven't seen each other since the fundraiser where we met. I thought the party would be a good excuse."

"I'll be there in a minute," I said. "Are you drinking yet?"

"I've had two. You need to catch up."

I laughed, and hung up, only to see that I'd received another text from Andrew while I was chatting with Charlotte: "I know you can't talk, but you can read. I keep thinking about your red lips. How they're going to feel on my skin. And your body. Your beautiful curves. I want to explore every inch of you."

I read his note three more times, feeling my heartbeat flutter in response, and then I deleted it, as well. But I still felt like I'd been lulled into a trance, and before I could stop myself I texted him back. "It's your eyes that do it for me. And how you whispered right next to my ear. I love that."

I stood on Charlotte's lawn, waiting to see if he'd respond right away. It only took a moment for my phone to buzz again. "I thought you couldn't talk?" he said, adding a smiley face at the end of his words. "I guess I'll have to show you what not talking actually is when I put my hand over your mouth while I'm fucking you."

A zing of arousal pinched between my thighs as I imagined him doing just that. *Jesus,* I thought as I deleted that message, too. *Next weekend can't come soon enough.* I had to force myself to turn off the sound on my phone and return it to my purse. With a deep breath, I went through the side gate and entered the back yard, where people were either milling around with drinks in their hands, or sitting on the spacious deck in the two enormous outside living sets I'd helped Charlotte pick out at Costco the previous year. The sun was shining, but there was still a slight cool quality in the air, which was pretty standard for June in the Pacific Northwest. True summer, when it stopped raining and the temperature actually went higher than seventy degrees, didn't usually hit until the middle of July.

I glanced around, spotting Charlotte through the kitchen window, standing in front of her sink, so I headed inside.

"It's crazy, right?" she asked. "*I'm* crazy."

I knew she was talking about inviting Bryan, so I shook my head, hoping this was the answer she wanted. I didn't think it was necessarily the smartest thing she could do, but she'd already done it, so my pointing that out wouldn't help.

"You look cute," I said. She was wearing a dark purple sundress with white polka dots, and her red hair was pulled into a loose bun on top of her head, with long, straight wisps framing her face. Her brown eyes were highlighted with smoky gray shadow and a couple of coats of black mascara; her lips painted a soft, pale pink.

"Thanks," she said.

"Which one is he?" I asked, peering through the window until my eyes landed on Tiffany. She stood next to her husband, Ben, talking with two other couples. I moved my gaze again, and found Jake sitting with my parents on the deck, all three of them already with a beer in hand. Charlotte's mother, Helen, stood next to them, wearing a rainbow tie-dyed T-shirt and an ankle-length, blue and billowy skirt. Her hair was more strawberry blond than her daughter's, streaked with silver, and she wore it in long, loose braid, down her back. She gestured emphatically as she spoke to my parents and Jake, probably in the middle of a story about her latest protest adventure. My mother's mouth was frozen in a small-mouthed smile and my dad was staring at the bottle he held

as though it were trying to memorize the label. The younger kids ran
around the large back yard, squealing as they chased each other, while the
teenagers, including Ella, Bentley, and Lizzy, sat together in the shade of
a large maple tree in a far corner of the yard, their attention not on each
other, but instead, riveted on their phones. I thought about Lizzy's "ho"
account, and cringed, reminding myself that I needed to talk to Lacy
this week about what was going on with some of the girls on the team.
I'd texted Charlotte about it last night, but Bentley had already told her
about it, and she agreed it was right to bring it to their coach's attention.

"He's over by the grill," Charlotte said, grabbing a half-empty glass of
white wine from the messy counter. "Talking to my husband. Jesus. I'm
an idiot." She knocked back the remainder of her drink.

I moved my gaze again and saw Richard, in his standard party outfit
of green plaid shorts and a matching t-shirt, standing by the built-in
grill wearing a white apron and a wide black belt that held his large
silver spatula and a giant, meat-piercing fork. (Charlotte's caterer took
care of most of the food for the parties she threw, but Richard always
insisted on being in charge of the barbeque, itself.) Smoke rose from the
grill as he moved chicken breasts out of the way in order to make room
for the platter of uncooked hamburgers a man, who I assumed must be
Bryan, held. He was tall, about six-two, and a little pudgy, like a former
athlete gone soft. He had short light brown hair and what looked to be
an easy smile. He wore khakis and a pale blue, short sleeved polo and
an expensive-looking gold watch. The two men were laughing about
something, so as far as I could tell, Richard had no idea that Bryan was
Charlotte's confidant.

"He looks nice," I said. "I'm sure it'll be fine."

"I hope so," Charlotte said. "Me and my big mouth."

"Is there anything I can help with?" I asked.

"Go make sure my mom isn't traumatizing your parents. I'll be out there, soon."

I nodded, then headed outside, first pouring myself a vodka tonic from the bar Charlotte had set up by the French doors that led out to the deck. *I will not check my phone,* I chanted silently, inside my head. *I will not, I will* not. But again, I couldn't help myself. I set my drink down and reached inside my purse. Sure enough, the green notification light was blinking.

"I'm hard right now," Andrew's text said, and I felt my entire body tighten. "I'm thinking about what you're going to taste like. How it's going to feel the first time I push inside you."

I shoved my phone back in my purse, mad at myself for looking in the first place, but also unable to deny how much more reading them made me ache to see him. I picked up my drink, put a smile on my face, and went to join my husband and parents on the deck.

"Jessica!" Helen exclaimed when she saw me. "You look amazing! What have you been doing with yourself?"

Jake raised his eyebrow at me and smirked, and I felt a little sick, thinking about Andrew's texts. really, they weren't that big of a deal. It was all part of me ultimately coming home to my husband and telling him all the fun, sexy things Andrew and I did.

"Nothing new," I lied. "Drinking a little more water."

"From the fountain of youth?" Helen said, smacking her palm against her own leg as she chortled at her own joke.

"Dad," Jake said, standing up from his chair. "Why don't we go see if we can help Richard man the grill?"

I shot him a grateful look. I'd told him last night, as we lay in bed, what my mother had told me about the tension in their marriage, and the subsequent moment of connection we'd shared, but he'd agreed that it wasn't our place to try to fix the problem. We could only try to run interference while they were here.

Tiffany and Ben approached us on the deck, along with a woman I could only assume was her mother, whom I'd never met before. At a dance competition last year, Tiffany told me that they hired someone part-time take care of her mom when they couldn't be home with her, but there were times when the aide wasn't available and Tiffany would have to miss one of Lizzy's performances on the team. Now, Tiffany looked more tired than usual—gone were her previously standard hair extensions, fake tan and lashes. She wore minimal make up and had on a pair of jeans and a thin, red sweater; her hair was in a simply ponytail. Tiffany's mother, a petite woman with a short, silver-blond bob, not too unlike my mom's hairstyle, had on a pink and white floral dress and a white cardigan. Her mouth was open, slightly, and she seemed to be looking off over the top of the house, at something in the distance.

"Hi Tiff," I said. I gestured toward my mother. "This is my mom, Sheila."

"Hello," Tiffany said, bobbing her head. Her smile seemed strained, and I felt sorry for her situation, more than ever. "This is my mom, Theresa." She touched her mother's shoulder. "Say hi to everyone, Mom."

Theresa looked at her daughter, clearly confused. "Where's Joseph?" she asked. "He said he would be here. We're supposed to talk about going to prom."

"Your husband died ten years ago, Mom," Ben said, in too loud a voice, as though his mother-in-law was deaf instead of suffering from memory loss.

My heart ached, watching this moment unfold. I couldn't imagine how painful it was for Tiffany, having to watch her mother struggle like this, watching her fade away. It made me wish that I didn't have to tell Lacy about what Lizzy had been up to with her inappropriate account on Instagram; more stress was the last thing Tiffany needed.

"Benjamin," Tiffany said, tightly, and under her breath. "The doctor said it's less confusing if we play along."

"Please, call me Ben!" Ben said, addressing us as a group instead of responding to his wife's comment. He had on tan cargo shorts and a white Tommy Bahamas shirt, his beer belly causing it to strain at the buttons. His brown hair was slicked back and heavy with gel; I could see where his comb had gone through it. "Nobody wants to buy a car from Benjamin. But Ben, Ben's your buddy, Ben's your pal. A guy you can trust!" He chuckled, and then glanced around our immediate circle. "I need a drink. Can I get anyone a refill?"

"Thank you," my mom said, lifting her empty beer bottle. "I'd love one."

"My pleasure," Ben said, taking it from her. "Anyone else? I'm here to serve!"

"I think everyone's fine," Tiffany said, giving her husband a weary look. I imagined dealing with her mother's medical issues—having her live with them—wasn't easy on their marriage, either.

"Classic car salesman schtick," Helen muttered, after Ben walked away.

"I don't think so," I said, not wanting to add to Tiffany's emotional load.

"No, Helen's right," Tiffany said, stiffly. "My husband doesn't know how to turn that side of him off. He's all salesman, all the time."

"Your husband's an asshole," Theresa said. Her blue eyes suddenly looked more focused, like the part of her that had drifted off had snapped back in place.

Helen snorted, Tiffany looked horrified, but before anyone could say another word, Isaac, one of Tiffany's ten-year-old twins, started screaming for her from across the yard. Another boy stood next to him, holding a red ball up over his head, clearly taunting Isaac with it.

"Excuse me," Tiffany said, taking her mother's hand and leading her back across the lawn, in Isaac's direction.

"That poor woman," Helen said, shaking her head.

"Dementia?" my mom inquired, looking at me, and I nodded.

My mom shuddered. "If that ever happens to me, put me in a home, immediately," she said. "I don't want to be a burden."

"The minute I start to really lose it, I'm taking a bottle of pills and putting myself out of misery," Helen said. "I say let me die with dignity."

My mother nodded. "Maybe I'll do that, instead of a home. End things on my own terms." It was a rare for her and Helen to agree with each other, but I knew my mother, a woman whose intellect was the major focus of her life, wouldn't be able to stand the idea of losing that part of her.

"Can we change the subject, please?" I asked, lightly. "This is supposed to be a party."

My mom smiled, and Helen laughed, and then asked my mother if she had any fun plans for the summer. As my mother launched into a description of the cruise she and her friends were hoping to take in the fall, I searched the yard for Jake and my dad, and found them standing in front of the bar, with Ben, listening to Tiffany's husband. My dad had his phone in his hand, rudely reading something, probably a report about one of his patients or an email from a colleague. Even when he left the hospital, he never really *left* it.

I looked over to the grill, and saw that Charlotte had joined Richard and Bryan there. She stood between them, holding another glass of wine, smiling, nervously, as the three of them talked. Richard began making animated gestures to go along with whatever he was saying, and Bryan's eyes flickered from Richard's face to Charlotte's—the subtlest of movements, but I caught it, though possibly only because I knew what was going on between them. I saw the way she returned his glance, too, with a flash of fondness in her dark eyes that spoke of so much more than a simple friendship. Was Richard really so dense as not to pick up on what was happening right in front of him? And how could Charlotte, who claimed to love Richard, not be honest with him about the fine line she was walking by sharing her intimate feelings about her marriage with another man?

But then, I thought about the texts Andrew had sent, how much I enjoyed having this tiny bit of pleasure that I could keep entirely to myself, and I imagined that Charlotte felt much the same way about her interactions with Bryan. I imagined Jake discovering my texts with Andrew, and flushed with shame and guilt. But how could it be worse than other men kissing me, undressing me, slipping inside me and making me come? If *that* didn't make him jealous, a few innocent texts certainly wouldn't, either.

"Excuse me," I said to my mom and Helen, who were so engaged in conversation with each other they didn't respond. I wound my way back inside the house, my phone in hand, heading toward the guest bathroom, anxious to see what Andrew had to say to me next.

Eighteen

My parents flew out late Monday afternoon, and not long after that, Peter dropped Tucker off at our house, exhausted, but happy that his team had taken second place at the tournament.

"What do we have to eat?" Tuck asked, dropping his gym bag and baseball bat in the entryway. Peter stood behind him, looking sunburned and tired, too. When he took off his baseball cap, his short black hair stood out from his scalp like chicken fluff, and it looked as though he had sprouted a few more lines around his green eyes.

"Barbeque chicken in the fridge," I said as my son passed me by without a hug. "Hey. You're welcome!"

"Thanks, Mom!" he called out, rushing back to throw his arms around me. He smelled of dirt, and slightly musty, teenage boy sweat; I wondered if he'd showered at all over the past two days. "You're the best."

"Uh-huh," I said, with a shake of my head. He took off toward the kitchen, and I smiled at Peter. "Thanks for taking him."

"No problem. He played great." Peter shifted his feet, and shoved his hands in his pockets, dropping his eyes to the floor. "So, Kari's pregnant. I thought you should know."

"Oh," I said, feeling a surprising pang of discomfort. It was a strange thing, watching a person you used to be married to build a family with someone else. I felt a brief sense of wistfulness for what we *could* have given our kids—a life not affected by divorce, without the back and forth between two houses. Even though I knew it never would have worked long term with Peter, I sometimes felt guilty that the kids didn't have their biological parents in one home. "Congrats."

"Yeah." Peter sighed. "It was a surprise."

"Ah." I didn't know what else to say. *Sorry you knocked up your wife?*

"Is Ella home?" he asked, peeking over my shoulder into the house.

"She's working," I said. "I told her she needs to save up at least a thousand dollars this summer if she wants to go to Nationals next year." Ella's dance team had placed high enough at the state level in spring to qualify to attend Nationals the following winter, but it cost almost two thousand dollars per girl to make the trip, and Jake and I had agreed that if she wanted to go, she needed to pay for half of it herself.

Peter nodded. "She told me. She wasn't happy."

"Too bad," I said, with a short laugh. "You agree with me, right?"

"Yep. She needs to have some skin in the game."

My phone buzzed, then. I glanced at the screen, and sure enough, it was a text from Andrew.

"I'll let you go," Peter said.

"Tell Kari I said congrats, too," I told him as he turned to walk away. He waved in acknowledgement, and after I shut the door behind him, I eagerly looked at my phone. Andrew had sent me a picture of him lounging in bed, showing off his chest and arms, and the chiseled "V" of muscles that pointed below his waist. It was a black and white image, and one of his hands was resting flat on his stomach, his long fingers splayed. "I'm thinking about you," his text said. "It's making me hard."

I smiled, feeling a stab of daring excitement in my chest. "Show me," I quickly typed, and my breath quickened when less than a few seconds later, the picture I'd requested came through.

"Honey?" Jake called out from the kitchen. "Is there any more chicken? Tuck doesn't want to share."

"Coming!" I said, but before I went to join them, I sent Andrew a text: "I can't wait to feel you in my mouth." This was foreplay of the most exhilarating variety. All of this mental build up, Andrew's provocative words flying around inside my head for days before we planned to meet. It was different than simply showing up at his house to have sex, as I had with the others. This man had to touch himself at the very thought of me and wasn't afraid to say it. It made me desperate to want to see him.

It made me want to do things I'd never done.

THE week seemed to go by more slowly than usual, even though my days were peppered with text exchanges with Andrew, distracting me from the listing agreements and contingency forms that littered my desk. I went home every night, every cell in my body stimulated from the way he spoke to me. It was different, somehow, than when Jake whispered suggestive words in my ear. He'd seen me when I was tired and cranky, when I was sick with the flu and throwing up in a bucket next to our bed. He'd been with me almost every day for almost thirteen years, seeing me with makeup and without, on the days when I remembered to shave my legs and the winter months when I turned into a sasquatch, reasoning that I could get away with it because I mostly wore pants. He knew the ugliest things about me. He'd dealt with my PMS, and on more than one occasion, listened to me rant and complain about my parents or a deal at work that wasn't going my way. I wasn't only one thing to Jake; I was a million things, good and bad, rolled up into one. All of that was inside his head when he touched my body or said something sexual simply to get me wet. But with Andrew, I was only *one* thing—the woman he wanted to fuck. There was nothing else clouding how he saw me, no lingering disagreements or hard decisions we had to make about parenting. So the things he said to me, the *way* that he said them, felt more pure—and so much more intense. My body ached with longing, every nerve beneath my skin on high alert.

"Before I let you come tomorrow night," Andrew texted me on Thursday afternoon, "I'm going to take my time getting to know your body, how it tastes. How it smells. How it reacts to my touch. I'm going to work you into an unbridled need to be fucked."

I was with clients when this showed up on my phone, so I couldn't text him back. But my body responded—blood rushed to the cleft between my thighs; my breath became shallow—and I hoped my face didn't give away the nature of what I'd just read. And then, as my clients and I got into my car, more words came: "I always wondered what you'd be like in bed," Andrew said. "That sweet, pretty, curvy little twenty-one year old girl who got married too young. I used to jack off thinking about what your tight little pussy would feel like around my thick cock. I used to wonder if you're the kind of girl who would take it the ass."

I wasn't that kind of girl—at least, I hadn't been so far—but suddenly, I imagined myself doing exactly that. Not with my husband. With Andrew.

The debauchery of his suggestion permeated any previous boundary I had. Anything felt possible; there were no limits to what we might do.

Haunted by his words later that night, once the kids had disappeared into their rooms for the night, I dragged Jake into our bedroom and tore off his clothes. I dropped to my knees, took him in my mouth, and then, after a moment, I pulled him down to the floor straddled him right there, riding him until we both came.

"Someone's excited about tomorrow night," Jake said after we were spent, and lay together with our legs still entwined. My head rested on his chest, and I could hear his heartbeat thudding away.

"Mmm-hmm," I said, feeling a nip of guilt that he didn't know how, exactly, that excitement had been fueled. *Just tell him about the texts*, I thought, as we climbed into bed, turned off the lights, and he curled behind me, as he always did, before we went to sleep. *Tell him and get it over with. Make it sexy. Make him part of it.*

But I held my tongue, again reasoning that I was simply doing what Jake had suggested in the first place—making the experience more exciting. What did it matter if he didn't know about the texts, if in the end, I still came home to him and told him every detail of what I'd done?

The next day, I barely got through two meetings with clients at the office and three showings before I rushed home to make sure the kids left for Peter and Kari's house by four. When Jake came home from work at five-thirty, I was starting to feel jittery, which was normal before I would go to see a new lover on my own, but this was the first time I'd done it without Jake being part of the process. More significantly, perhaps, it was the first time I was going to be with a man I'd allowed access to not only my body, but my mind.

"You're sure you're okay with this?" I asked my husband, after I'd showered. It was part of our ritual, Jake watching me get ready to go be with another man. He liked to see me do my hair and makeup, and help me pick out what I should wear. He would end up touching and kissing, but nothing more than that, driving me crazy with want. Tonight was no different. He sat on the toilet with his hands resting in his lap, his blue eyes skating over my body, taking in every inch of me.

"I'm sure," he said. "Are you?"

I stared at him a moment, my mind flashing to the litany of texts Andrew had sent me. *Jake* wants *me to do this.* "Yeah," I told my husband. "Maybe a little nervous. It's the first time you haven't met someone I'm going to be with."

He got up and came over to where I stood, in front of our long, double vanity. He cupped my face in his hands, kissing me tenderly before pulling back and dropping his hands to my waist. "You're amazing, you know that?" he said. "You're so fucking sexy. You have no idea how hot it is for me to know what you're about to do."

I reached a hand between his legs. "I have *some* idea."

He groaned. For him, the anticipation, the self-denial, was all part of the thrill. This time, because we were doing something so different, I imagined these feelings were amplified.

He's enjoying this as much as I am, I told myself as I stood on my tip-toes and put my mouth next to his ear. "I want you to send me a picture of you stroking while I'm gone." I bit the side of his neck.

"Jesus," he muttered, and he shivered.

"I want you to think about his hands on me," I continued, enjoying his reaction. "How his mouth will be between my legs, tasting me. How I'm going to use my mouth on him."

"Baby, you need to stop, or I'm not going to let you go," he said. He kissed me again, quickly, and then stepped away. "Look at you, with that smirk on your face. You're still a fucking goddess, you know that?"

I nodded, still smiling, thinking about the time a couple of years back, when we'd just met Vincent, that Jake and I had another conversation about why he was so turned on by me fucking other men.

"Did you ever think about doing this with any of the other women you dated before you met me?" I asked.

"Sure," Jake said, "but I never brought it up."

"Not even to Carmen?" Jake had only had one long term relationship before we met, and that was back in Florida, when he was still in college. He was with Carmen for three years, and they only broke up because he moved to Seattle. She was his first love, something that used to bother me to hear about when he and I first began dating. I knew everyone had a past—I'd been married to Peter and had two kids, for god's sake—but I couldn't help but be a little envious that I didn't get to have Jake's love and devotion, first.

He laughed. "Carmen would have tried to beat the *shit* out of me if I suggested we have a threesome, let alone that she should have sex with someone else and tell me about it, later. Colombian women are a little crazy when it comes to fidelity."

I nodded, immediately picturing Carmen—Jake had shown me a picture of her once, after which I'd tried, and failed, not to compare myself to her exotic features and petite, but somehow also perfectly curvy frame. I imagined her shouting expletives at Jake in automatic weapon-speed-Spanish, pounding on him with her small fists, and then the two of them ending up in bed for hot makeup sex.

Jake must have seen the shadow cross my face as I pictured this, because he put his arms around me and pulled me to him so that my cheek was pressed up against his chest. "I've always been attracted to strong women," he said. "But you, Jessica, are by far the *strongest* woman I've ever known. When I met you, I loved how you knew your own mind. The way you stood your ground with your parents, and even when things didn't work out with Peter, you made a life for you and the kids with not much help from anyone else." He took a deep breath, and then continued. "After watching my mom manipulate every guy she was with into taking care of her, I admired that about you more than I can say." I nodded, my head still against his chest, listening to the reassuring thump of his heartbeat. "Seeing you have sex with someone else, or even just hearing about it, reinforces the strength I've seen in you from the start. That's part of what turns me on...the way you aren't afraid to do what you want...fuck someone, right in front of me...or even without me. There's something phenomenally sexy about a woman confident enough to do that."

I reminded myself of that conversation as I finished getting ready to meet Andrew, putting on a blood-red corset and black garters and stockings to wear under my dress. My husband loved me, more than he'd loved anyone else, and I felt the same way about him. It was the only way we were able to do something as exciting as this—it was the thing that made me believe that whatever happened with Andrew, nothing between Jake and I would change.

"Be safe," he said as I climbed into my car, and I told him that I would.

After backing out of the driveway, I punched Andrew's address into my GPS, and then shot him a text, letting him know that I was on my way.

"I'm ready," he responded. "The front door's unlocked."

I felt my cheeks flush and my breathing become more erratic as I thought more about what it would be like to see him. What if it didn't live up to the anticipation? What if he was a terrible lover, and I immediately regretted agreeing to be with him? I told myself I could leave, if I wanted to, that I was under no obligation to go through with what we had planned. We'd discussed that, briefly, in a few texts, and he'd made it clear that if I didn't feel comfortable or safe, that he would be totally fine if I decided to go home.

"You won't want to, though," he'd added.

"Cocky, much?" I replied, but I was smiling.

"You fucking love it."

He was right, even though part of me wished I wasn't so drawn to that side of him. I was used to taking the lead, and I was curious to find out if Andrew would try to wrangle it from me.

Thirty minutes later, I pulled up in front of his house—a modern, sleek, three-story structure with tall, rectangular windows and a large roof deck that I imagined had views of Lake Washington, even parts of downtown Seattle. The yard was well-manicured, and lined with bountiful, silver-edged, variegated dogwoods. It was a large house for one man, but I knew from my online research about Andrew's company that it was extraordinarily successful.

After texting Jake to let him know I'd arrived, I locked my car and knocked on the front door. I took a couple of deep breaths as I waited. I heard the patter of bare feet, and then, there he was, standing before me, wearing only a soft-looking pair of black, drawstring pajama pants, and nothing else.

"Hey," he said, in a low voice. "Come on in." He moved to the side, and I entered through the threshold, marveling at the vaulted ceilings of the entryway and the lavish, but still contemporary, crystal chandelier hanging above us.

I set my purse down on the glass-topped table next to the door, and then turned around to take him in. He was as handsome as I remembered from our brief in-person meeting—his black hair was wet and tousled. His skin was olive-toned and his eyes were as dark as coal, burning with an intensity that matched what I felt inside my own body.

"Hi," I said. I took a step toward him and rested a single hand on his bare chest. He was warm to the touch, and his cologne smelled of something spicy and sweet. I looked up at his face, feeling the rapid rise and fall of his chest, and I suspected I wasn't the only one dealing with a case of nerves.

"You look amazing," he said, as his eyes traveled over my face. He reached up and let the backside of his fingers trail down the side of my cheek, giving me chills. "I can't tell you how many times I imagined doing this."

I moved to kiss him, but he leaned back to avoid it.

"Not so fast," he said. He took my hand and led me toward the staircase at the other end of the hallway. As we ascended, my heartbeat pounded inside my chest. I wasn't accustomed to having a lover move so slowly when I arrived; typically, they would ravish me the minute I entered their home, their desperate desire exciting me all the more. Their need of me, the immediacy with which we began, helped set the mood and reinforced the idea that my being there was about sex, pure and simple. There was no small talk, no discussion of the other person's day. But Andrew took his time leading me to his bedroom—a huge master that took up the entirety of the third floor. The bed was enormous and covered in stacks of fluffy pillows and a lush, white down comforter, while the rest of the furniture—two long, low burled wood dressers and a simple gray couch—was straight-lined and spare, reflecting a quiet, architectural elegance.

Andrew and I stood in the middle of the room as I took it all in. "Your house is beautiful," I said. My voice trembled.

"Are you here to discuss real estate?" he asked, with a small, playful smile. "Or are you here to fuck me?"

A burst of arousal shot through me. Texting with him had been different. I'd had time to think about and formulate a properly intelligent, flirtatious and sexy response. Standing in front of him, now, hearing him speak the words instead of just reading them on my phone, I felt overwhelmed, and a little vulnerable. I wasn't entirely sure that I liked it.

But I didn't have much time to think, or respond to his question, because Andrew moved, taking a few steps so that he was standing behind me. He moved my hair out of the way and put his lips against my ear. "Stay still," he murmured. "Don't make a sound."

I sucked in a breath, conflicted over doing as he asked, or responding the way I normally would—by taking control of the situation. Watching a man squirm because of how I touched him or how I spoke was my default; I rarely allowed myself to let anyone have that same kind of control over me.

"Wait," I said, as I started to turn around to face him. But he surprised me by grabbing my wrists and pinning them together, firmly, at the small of my back. I couldn't see his face.

"I said, *stay still.*" His fingers were strong, almost pinching my skin. I could have easily broken free, if I'd wanted to. Instead, I did as he asked; I stopped moving. My entire body trembled.

"Good," he said, releasing his grasp. He tangled the fingers of his right hand in my curls, at the base of my neck, and pulled backward as he placed the palm of his left over my larynx. "You're so powerful, aren't you, Jessica? Strong and sensual and in control. It's sexy as hell." He gave my throat a gentle squeeze, and I panicked for a moment, wondering if doing this without Jake here was the stupidest decision I'd ever made. What if Andrew was violent? If he decided to hurt me, there was no way I could fight him off.

But then he removed his hand and yanked my hair, just hard enough to cause the fire between my legs to throb. "Fuck," I muttered, and he spun me around and clamped his hand over my mouth.

"No sounds," he said, locking his dark eyes on mine. There was a hint of a smile in them, so I sensed that this was all part of the fun he wanted us to have together.

I nodded, indicating my compliance, and then he removed his hand. The tip of his tongue darted out and licked his upper lip as he moved his gaze around my face. "So beautiful," he said. He stepped back and slowly lowered his pants, revealing his erection. He was larger than any of the other men I'd been with—larger than Jake—and I was anxious to feel him inside me. I wanted to strip off my clothes and push him onto the bed. I wanted to stroke and suck him, taking him to the edge, and then back him down again, making him wait. But another part of me was curious to experience what it would be like to let him call the shots. So I forced myself to remain still as he walked around me, letting his fingers drift over my still-covered breasts, waist, and ass.

When he stopped, he stood in front of me again, and finally leaned in to kiss me. His lips touched mine and I began to quiver, fighting to keep from dropping to my knees. The kiss was both tender and intense, and it seemed to go on forever. I wanted to touch him, too, but I kept my hands at my sides, my fingers curling into fists. And then it was him who dropped to his knees in front of me. He pushed up my dress and nuzzled his face between my legs, using the tip of his tongue to tease me over my black lace panties.

I moaned, trying not to buck my hips and grab the back of his head in order to press his mouth harder against me. I felt him smile, and then pull back. He looked up at me. "You think you need all this fancy lingerie to be sexy?" he asked. "You don't. Sexy is how you looked at me when we met for coffee. Sexy is the spark in your pretty gray eyes and the way that you laugh. The way you've been texting with me, letting my words crawl inside your head to fuck your mind before I came anywhere close to your body." He stood up then, and kept talking. "Such a successful, strong woman. No one would guess what a slut you are, would they?"

The word was said with clear admiration—I loved it.

He undid my garters, then, and pulled my stockings down, slowly, removing them, along with my heels. "I want the real Jessica," he said. "Not the Playboy, male fantasy version. I want the only girl who used to be nice to me when I worked the bar." He stood up again, and looked me in the eye. "Give me *that* Jessica."

I hesitated, unsure exactly what he wanted me to do. But then he stepped back, and I decided to take off my dress, and then my corset. I undid the hooks one-by-one, with deliberation, never breaking eye contact with him. Lingerie was my armor, a uniform I wore to enhance the role I played. I rarely got totally nude with any of the other men I'd been with. But here, now, in front of Andrew, I stood naked, my slightly sagging breasts and pudgy belly exposed. My body quaked, waiting for his expression to shift—for the lust he felt for me to fade away—but instead, his eyes skimmed over my skin appreciatively, and then I watched as he walked into the bathroom, returning with a dampened washcloth, which he used to gently wipe off my lipstick, my blush, and some of my eye makeup.

"There she is," he said, when he stepped back.

"I'm not that girl anymore," I said, deciding to break his insistence that I remain silent. "Any more than you're a geek."

He gave me a slow, knowing smile. "Oh, I'm still a geek," he said. "I'm just a few other things, too."

"Have you really thought about doing this with me, all of these years?" His texts had hinted at fantasizing about me when we worked together, but I wasn't sure if it was true, or if he was saying it only to add to the excitement of our foreplay. I'd changed over the years, for sure, but if he'd had a crush on me, wouldn't he have recognized me right away when we met for coffee?

"Yes," he said, and in that instant, I saw a flash of the boy he used to be in his face—the sweet, funny, vulnerable nerd—instead of the confident, in-control, erotic man who stood in front of me, now. For a moment, I worried that he might be in love with me—that living out this fantasy with him was too dangerous a game. But then he spoke again. "I knew you were married, and I was insecure, so I never told you how I felt. Not that you would have let me, but I didn't have it in me back then to simply fuck you and not fall in love with you, too." He must have seen the panic in my eyes, because he smirked. "Don't worry, Jessica. I'm not that insecure boy anymore. I want your mind and I want your body. Your husband can keep the rest."

He could not have given me a more perfect answer. I took a step toward him, pressing my entire body against his, feeling his flesh melt into mine. We kissed, and this time I slipped my fingers into the hair at the back of his head and gave it a tug. His cock twitched on my thigh and we stumbled backward, onto his bed, limbs entangled.

I couldn't get enough of him. His mouth moved over my skin, his fingers teased, and then sunk inside me with intent. I used both hands on him, stroking, feeling the tension between my legs ramp up and up and up as he increased the pressure of his touch, and then I was coming, my eyes squeezed shut. Waves of pleasure shot through me, and before they ended, I pushed him over onto his back.

"Condom," I said, using my own fingers between my legs, making sure he could see what I was doing.

He rolled over, opened the drawer of his nightstand, and pulled out a square foil package, which he quickly opened and put on.

I climbed on top of him again, but instead of doing what he expected, I moved upward, and straddled his face. He grabbed my ass and pushed me onto his mouth. My head snapped backward when his tongue found the right spot. He sucked and licked and used his hands to shift my hips back and forth, working me up again, quickly.

"Fuck, yes, don't stop," I said, and suddenly, my body began to spasm, setting off shooting stars behind my eyelids. I went a little limp, but recovered enough to shift downward, across his hips, then, and slipped him inside me. He felt bigger than anyone else I'd been with—I groaned from the pleasure of it. I set my palms flat on his smooth chest and rode him, rolling my hips, eyes closed, focusing every sensation. His hands grasped my breasts, helping to hold me up.

"That's right," he said. "Make me come."

I moved more intently then, with purpose, unable to control how loudly I moaned as he filled me again and again.

"Look at me, Jessica," Andrew demanded. "Open your eyes."

I didn't even hesitate. Our gazes locked and as he watched me. I felt wild, a little feral, like he could see right through to the very core of me, the place where I had no secrets, where I was about to come undone.

Finally, Andrew's back arched and my own body went stiff, and in that moment, nothing else mattered. I didn't think about anything or anyone.

Not even Jake.

Nineteen

Afterward, Andrew and I lay on our backs on his bed, each of us trying to catch our breath. My mind whirled as I thought about what had just happened. With my other lovers, the sex was always satisfying, but there was still a wall between us—it was one of the ways that sex with Jake felt different. But with Andrew, with so much mental foreplay between us before I stepped into his house, he was right—he was already inside my mind, making our connection more intense and intimate than if I had only allowed him access to my body.

"Well," I said, "you're definitely more than a geek."

"Told you," he said, laughing.

I gave him a half-hearted smack. "Careful, now. We've discussed this. There's a fine line between cocky and confident."

"Here's the line," he said, extending his right arm and marking an imaginary spot in the air, "and there's me." He used his left hand to point to the other side of the room.

"I'm not sure that's something you should advertise." I rolled over onto my side, tucked a pillow under my head, and looked at him. "I have a question."

He rolled over to face me, as well. His brown eyes twinkled. "I have an answer."

"You said you have some experience with this kind of thing, but we never really talked about it."

"That's more of a statement than a question."

"I was leading up to it. Be patient."

"Oh, sorry," he said. His closed-lipped smile turned into a ridiculously charming grin that caused a flutter inside my chest. "Please, continue."

"How many women have you done this with?"

He raised his dark eyebrows. "How many have I had sex with?"

"No," I said, drawing out the word. "How many *married* women have you had sex with? Where their husband knew what they were doing?"

"Oh," he said. "None, actually."

"So you lied?" A jolt of concern shot through me.

"Not at all. My ex and I had an open relationship. We could sleep with other people as long as we were safe, and didn't tell each other about it. Don't ask, don't tell. Some of the women I slept with were married, but their husband definitely didn't know about it."

"Oh," I said, feeling slightly uncomfortable with his cavalier attitude toward being with a woman betraying her husband. Still, I wanted to know more. "That must have been hard with your ex," I continued. "Not knowing if when she was going out with the girls if she might really be with another guy."

He made a noncommittal noise. "Or girl. She was bi. And it was what we agreed to, so it worked for us for a long time. But then she met someone she wanted to be with more than me, so that was that."

"Ouch," I said, cringing. "When did that happen?"

"About a year ago. I took some time alone, and then thought it might be kind of fun to try something different."

"And you saw our ad."

"Yep. Which, I have to say, is kismet. A previously geeky, now somewhat okay-to-look-at successful dude getting to live out his fantasy with the hot girl he had a crush on? Come *on*! They make movies about that shit." I laughed, and he reached over to push a strand of hair out of my face. "How long have you and your husband been doing this?"

I gave him a shortened version of how we met Will, and eventually Tim, and Vincent.

"Ever run into anyone else you know?" he asked.

"Sort of," I said. "This married guy who lives near us in Queens Ridge answered one of our ads a couple of years ago. Which was awkward as hell, because his son plays baseball with mine. Every time Jake and I see him, it's like, 'Okay, buddy. I guess we know what *you're* into. But your wife probably doesn't.'" I paused, again, panic-stricken, because I'd never mentioned to any of my other lovers the name of our community, or the fact that Jake and I had kids. But with Andrew, these details simply tumbled out. I worried I'd said too much.

"You didn't out him?"

"Of course not!" I said. "We didn't even respond to his email. We *did* joke about what would happen if we put it up on the Neighbors app, anonymously, just because it kind of sucks that he's cheating on his wife, but we weren't actually serious about doing it."

"The what app?"

"Neighbors." I took a minute to describe what the social media platform consisted of. "You probably have one for your neighborhood, too."

"Let's see!" he said, grabbing his phone from the nightstand. He did a quick search, tapped on the screen for a minute or so, and then looked at me. "Success! I have just submitted my request to become a part of the North Rose Hill, Neighbors online community!" He set his cell back down.

"Careful there, buddy. Your geekiness is showing."

"Um, hashtag geeky-and-proud!"

We lay in companionable silence for a bit, and I told myself that I should leave. I'd already talked with him more than I should; normally, I'd be gone by now. *Maybe he'll want to have more sex,* I thought. *Or maybe, I'm just enjoying myself too much to want the night to end.*

"So," Andrew said, interrupting my thoughts. "Have you told your husband that we used to work together?"

I shook my head, and felt a flash of regret.

"But you're still here." Andrew fixed his eyes on mine, and for a long moment, neither of us spoke. "I hope I was worth it," he finally said.

"You were adequate," I said, teasingly. I didn't want to think too much about the fact that I was keeping things from Jake.

"Is that so?" He grabbed me and pulled me against him, already hard, again. "Do you normally come like that when a guy is only *adequate*?" He kissed me, passionately, moving one hand to my breasts and the other, between my legs.

"It was actually pretty terrible," I murmured against his lips. "You'd better do it again, immediately. See if you can improve."

"You asked for it," he said, and I closed my eyes and let myself go.

I came home around eleven, having spent two hours more with Andrew than I normally had with anyone else. I'd texted Jake around nine, letting him know that I was staying longer, and he'd replied that I should stay as long as I wanted, as long as I knew that he would be waiting to ravage me the minute I walked through the door.

Good to his word, he did exactly that. I entered the kitchen through the garage door, and he grabbed me, pushing me up against the wall, lifting my dress.

"Did you like fucking him?" he asked, reaching between my legs to yank down my panties.

"Yes," I hissed.

"How many times did you come?"

"I don't know…I lost count." I paused our kiss, and pulled back to stare at my husband. "I love you so much, you know that?"

"I love you, too, baby," he said, and then he turned me around, bent me over on the countertop, groping my breasts and pushing his pelvis against my ass.

"Fuck me," I said, and he groaned, pushing his shorts down. He shoved inside me without hesitation, moving his hands to my shoulders to pull me back against him. I was already so swollen and wet and had come so many times I didn't think I could do it again, but he reached around to move his fingers between my legs, and a moment later I convulsed, quick and hard, crying out his name.

"I couldn't stop thinking about what you were doing," Jake said, continuing to thrust. "Picturing you fucking him. This stranger. Someone I've never met. Knowing you would come home to me."

"Always," I said. Except I hadn't thought much about my husband when I was with Andrew. I usually talked about him in the midst of things, telling my lover how I would describe it to Jake later. It heightened the experience for me, and kept Jake a part of it, but with Andrew, I'd been so swept up by so many of his words already etched inside my brain—the only time I'd talked about Jake was afterward.

"He was so big," I said, wanting to make up for my lack of involving him earlier by engaging him in what had happened, now. "So thick and throbbing and hard."

Jake moaned. "You liked it, didn't you? How big he was."

"Yes," I said. He began to move faster inside me, and I knew that he was about to finish. I shoved back against him, meeting his thrusts, intensifying them, and then he said my name, too, as his body stiffened and shook.

He fell over and lay on top of my back, both of us breathing hard. "So you had fun," he said, and I could hear his smile in his voice.

"I did." I shifted, and he straightened so that I could stand.

"You've never stayed that long with someone."

He said it casually, and without accusation, but I searched his face for any hint that he was upset. "Was that not okay? I didn't have to…"

"It's fine, baby," he said. He took my hand and squeezed it. "I trust you."

I nodded, pushing down a swell of remorse in my throat. As Jake and I got ready for bed, I told myself that being with Andrew wasn't that different than anyone else. *He's just like Will was, or Tim or Vincent,* I told myself again in the shower, as I washed away the scent of him from my skin, trying to combat the sinking feeling that while I might not technically be lying to Jake, I also wasn't being honest with myself.

I woke up late the next morning, and had to scramble to get ready for the open house I needed to be at by noon. My muscles were stiff and sore, but in a pleasurable way. After I kissed Jake goodbye, leaving him to lounge on the couch watching a Mariners game, I drove to the house I had listed last week. I opened all the curtains and blinds, then preheated the oven to bake the two frozen apple pies I'd brought with me. "Nothing sells a house like the aroma of fresh baked pastry," Nancy had told me years ago, when I was just starting out, and she was right. The expression on potential buyers' faces changed the minute they walked through the front door and smelled the pies or cookies I'd made; in that instant, the property went from simply being a house to their possible home.

I lit candles in the living room and master bath, and then opened French doors that led to the outside living space, which was decked out with a large grill and smoker, as well as an elaborate bar. When I returned to the kitchen, I found the green notification light blinking on my phone. My stomach twisted in anticipation, thinking it might be a text from Andrew. But instead, I saw that I'd missed a call from my mother. I glanced at the clock, and since I still had half an hour before any prospective buyers might show up, I decided to call her back.

"I need to come stay with you," she said the minute she answered, not bothering to greet me. "I'm flying in late tonight. I'll take an Uber from the airport, so you don't have to come and get me. Your father and I need some time apart."

"What happened?" I asked, feeling a pit form in my stomach. *Are my parents going to get a divorce?*

"We had an argument that didn't end well," she said. "I'd prefer not to get into the details."

"How long do you think you'll be staying?" I asked, and then instantly regretted it. I didn't want her to feel unwelcome, but my knee-jerk reaction to the idea of having her in my house for any extended length of time was panic. I also couldn't help but think that her staying with us meant no more impromptu, bend-me-over-the kitchen-counter sex with Jake when the kids weren't there.

"I don't know," she said. "I suppose I can go to a hotel, if it's too much of a bother."

"That's not what I meant. Sorry. I was just thinking out loud."

"Thinking that you don't want me to come." She sounded hurt.

"No, Mom," I said, with a hint of exasperation. For someone who wasn't good with emotions, she was excellent at manipulating mine. "I'm just surprised. I know you two have been having some issues, but…"

"He needs a little time to experience everything I still do for him, by me not being there to do it," she said. "Okay? Is that a good enough reason?"

"Of course," I said, gently. I imagined it took a lot of courage on my mother's part to not only make the decision to take some time away from my dad, but to ask to stay with my family. "We're happy to have you," I said. "Text me your flight info so that Jake or I can pick you up. I don't want you in an Uber that time of night."

She thanked me, we hung up, and I quickly sent a text to Jake, telling him what was going on. "I'm sorry, babe," was his response. "I'll get the guest room ready. And pick your mom up tonight."

The muscles in my throat thickened, thinking what a good man he was. And then, as though on cue, a text from Andrew came through.

"I just woke up," he said. "You done wore me out, woman!"

I posed my fingers over the keyboard on my phone, about to type a reply, but something stopped me. This was nonsense. I needed to stop interacting with him so much. I could go to his house, I could fuck him, but I had to stop letting him inside my head.

I put my phone away, just as a young couple knocked on the front door, which I'd left open for people to easily enter the house. I looked up and smiled at them as they moved through the entryway into the living room, where they stopped and looked around.

"Beautiful, isn't it?" I said, cheerfully. "I'm Jessica, the listing agent."

They both smiled, nodding in acknowledgement, but stopped short of giving me their names. This wasn't unusual. People were always wary of anyone who worked in sales, and real estate was no exception. The trick was to give them enough space that they ended up coming to me, instead of me having to chase them.

"Look around," I said. "Let me know if you have any questions." I waved, and then sat down on one of the stools next to the breakfast bar in the kitchen. The sun shone through the large picture windows that overlooked the well-manicured backyard, creating rainbows that danced on the smooth white countertops. I stared outside, thinking about my parents. Thinking about Andrew and whether or not I should tell my husband the truth about the level of interaction I'd been having with my former co-worker. I worried how hurt Jake would be hearing what I'd kept from him. I couldn't do that to him. I couldn't do that to us.

Before I could stop myself, I grabbed my phone. "We need to talk," I texted Andrew. "I'm not sure seeing you is such a good idea."

"It seemed like a pretty amazing idea last night," he said. "What changed?"

"Can you meet me tomorrow?" I asked, thinking it would better to have this particular discussion in person.

"I've got a busy day," he replied. "But if you can come to my office, we can talk there. Around noon?"

He shot me the address, and I told him I'd be there. More people began to arrive, and for the next several hours, I busied myself by talking about the excellent Queens Ridge school district and the benefits of joining the homeowner's association. By four o'clock, I'd already received two offers on the house and I was both mentally and physically exhausted. After everyone had left, and the owners returned, I presented the offers, and then left them to consider which one they wanted to accept.

I climbed into my car and sat in their driveway a moment, not quite ready to head home. The kids would get back from Peter and Kari's around eight, which left me a few hours on my own, if I wanted it. I decided to send a quick text to Charlotte. "What are you up to?"

"Rough day," she said. "Want to meet for a drink?"

"YESSS!" I'd had enough of thinking about the men in my life. What I needed was some time with my best friend.

Twenty

Charlotte breezed through the door of the Tipsy Sailor and immediately spotted me at the table I'd gotten for us. It was warm for mid-June, and she wore a loosely cut, light blue linen dress that would have made me look as shapeless as the sky. It swirled around her lithe body as she made her way toward me, and I took another sip of the lemon drop martini I'd ordered.

"That looks good," she said, eyeing my drink. Her usually smooth hair was a little wild around her face, full of fly-aways she would normally tame with a flat iron. Her pale cheeks were flushed pink, and her brown eyes looked as long she'd been crying.

"Are you okay?" I asked, with concern, as she sat down.

She pressed her lips together and shook her head. "I finally talked with Richard. I told him that I was so desperate that sleeping with another man was starting to look good, and he didn't *do* anything! He didn't call his doctor or tell me he'd go insane if someone else fucked me. He just stood there, with this stupid blank look on his face."

"Did you mention Bryan?"

"No." Charlotte dropped her eyes to the table. Our server approached, and I quickly asked for a drink for her.

"Did *he* mention Bryan?" I asked when we were alone again. "Does he have any clue about him, at all?"

"I don't think so," Charlotte said, looking up at me, again. "He *liked* him, after they met at the barbeque, if you can believe it. He said he thinks they'd be good *golfing* buddies!" She released a half-hysterical laugh. "Can you picture it? The two of them out on the course, while Bryan and I send each other secret texts. Ugh."

Yes, actually, I wanted to say. *I can picture it, because I've been "secret" texting with Andrew in front of my husband, too.* Jake and I were both already on our phones so much for our jobs, he had no reason to think I was doing anything but dealing with clients or other agents, hammering out the details of a sale.

"Do you think I'm a horrible person?" Charlotte asked, her forehead creasing with worry. "Be honest."

"No," I said, emphatically. "I do not." I was more tempted than ever, in that moment, to tell her about Andrew—about *all* of it—but what was the point, really, of her knowing? Was I looking for absolution? For her to tell me that I should go ahead and keeping seeing him? Because if she asked me, outright, if I thought she should keep talking with Bryan, my answer would be no. Her connection with him was clearly an emotional one—he gave her the kind of attention Richard hadn't for several years—and had the potential to ruin her marriage. Wasn't *that* more dangerous than what I had done? I considered asking her if she was thinking about divorce, that it might be for the best. Maybe she was trying to keep something alive with Richard that had died a long time ago. But regardless of what she ultimately decided to do with her relationship, she still hadn't *slept* with Bryan, and because of that, I felt fairly certain that she, considering her history with Alex, would judge what I'd been doing as a worse offense than hers. And besides, I'd already decided that when I saw Andrew tomorrow, I would end things. If I told Charlotte everything, now, it might damage our friendship beyond repair.

"Thank you," she said, looking relieved. She waved a hand in the air, as though brushing the issue away, as the server delivered her drink. "What's going on with you?"

I quickly gave her the rundown of the call I'd received from my mom, and she clucked with sympathy. "That sucks," she said. "Do you think they'll be okay?"

"I don't know," I said. "I really don't want to be in the middle of it."

"God, I don't blame you." She took a sip of her martini and puckered. "Wow. That's strong!"

"I got a double." I lifted my glass and she clinked hers against it.

"To marriage," she said. "The most fucked-up, complicated relationship a person can have." We both sipped our drinks, and she cocked her head to one side, as though she had just remembered something. "Hey, have you talked with Lacy about the whole 'ho' account thing, yet?"

"Shit," I said. I'd been so distracted by thoughts of Andrew, I'd forgotten to reach out to Ella's coach to let her know what was going on with Lizzy, and apparently a couple of other girls on the team. "Let me text her right now, before I forget."

"Good idea," Charlotte said. "Do you want me to come with you, when you see her?"

"I should be fine," I said. "But I'll let you know if I need you to back me up." I pulled my phone out of my purse and found Lacy's contact info, shooting her a quick note that I wanted to chat in person the next day, if possible. She responded immediately, and said she was available in the morning, around eleven. After a quick check of my calendar to confirm that I could make that time work, we decided to meet for coffee at Starbucks on Main Street. I should have no problem getting to Andrew's office at noon. I frowned as I thought about the conversation I would have to have with him.

"What's wrong?" Charlotte asked. "You look bummed."

"Just my parents," I said, quickly. "I'm not looking forward to dealing with my mom."

"I could send mine over as backup," she offered. "Did you see how they bonded at my barbeque?"

I nodded. "I couldn't believe it."

She glanced down at the menu on the table in front of her. "I think I need to eat my feelings. Want to split some nachos?"

"Absolutely," I said, motioning for our server to come to our table. I looked at my best friend and smiled. "Let's get some mozzarella sticks, too!"

"Yes!" she said, and as she motioned to our server to come back, I reminded myself that I'd had my fun with Andrew, but that's all it was. It couldn't be more than that—I wouldn't let it. It was time to end it, before I did something I couldn't take back.

JAKE picked my mother up from the airport, as he promised he would, and she was still in bed when I was getting ready to leave for the office the next morning. "Be nice to Grandma," I told Ella and Tucker, who were plopped on the couch in the family room upstairs, eating cereal and streaming some weird YouTube channel on the T.V. "Maybe you guys could go do something with her while I'm at work."

"Like what?" Tuck asked, with his mouth full. Milk dribbled down his chin, and he lifted the hem of his T-shirt to wipe it away.

"I don't know," I said. "Take her for a walk in the arboretum, or out for ice cream. Or both." Now that school was out, the two of them hadn't done much other than laze around the house, so I figured it wouldn't kill them to help out by entertaining their grandmother.

"Why's she here again so soon?" Ella asked, looking at me with her inquisitive green eyes. Nothing much got past my daughter; she could sense something was up.

"She missed you guys," I said, not wanting to go into details with them about what was happening between their grandparents, especially because I didn't know all the details. "She doesn't feel like she gets to see enough of you."

Ella appeared skeptical, but didn't push the subject. Instead, she said, "Do you *really* have to meet with Lacy today?"

I'd told her my plans the night before, after I got home from drinks with Charlotte, and Ella had tried, unsuccessfully, to talk me out of it. I made her show me the Instagram account Lizzy had, along with three other girls Ella knew on the team who also had them. I was shocked when I saw the images of their young, practically naked bodies clad in thong and push up bras, posed provocatively, bending over to show off their ass or cleavage, with headings like, "TBH," which was a sort of social media game that Ella had to explain to me.

"It stands for 'Truth Be Had,'" she said, reluctantly. "And people are supposed to comment what they think, truthfully, of the picture. Of you."

"Oh," I said, as my eyes ran over some of the comments on one of

Lizzy's "TBH" pictures. There were lots of compliments, mostly from what appeared to be other girls, but someone had written, anonymously: "TBH...you're hot as fuck, but prolly have an STD," and another, "TBH...my brother said you suck enough dick, your nickname should be Hoover."

I looked at Ella in disbelief. "This is *horrible*," I said. "Can you imagine how this makes Lizzy feel?"

Ella shrugged. "Yeah, I guess, but she put the pictures up there, so...."

"That's victim-blaming, honey," I said, forcing myself to keep the lecture I wanted to give her short. "Lizzy doesn't even realize what's she's doing, or why she's doing it. You can't blame her."

Ella didn't appear convinced, but I let it go, for the moment.

"Yes," I told her now, the next morning. "I really have to tell Lacy what's going on."

"Tell Lacy what?" Tucker asked.

"That you stink!" Ella shot back.

Tucker gave a half-hearted kick in her direction, barely touching the side of her leg.

"Mom! He *kicked* me!"

"You're not Ruby's age, anymore," I said. "Work it out." The two of them bickered so much, unless there was the danger of bloodshed, I tended to stay out of it. I kissed both of them on top of their heads, and said I'd be home as soon as I could be that afternoon. Jake was already gone for the day, in Issaquah to meet with several candidates for positions at a new start-up firm that had hired him as a headhunter, taking Justine along with him to help train her. My plan was to meet with Lacy, fill her in, and then head to Andrew's office for a quick, to-the-point discussion, and then head back to work.

I spent a little over an hour at the office, and then headed to meet Lacy right before eleven. I spotted her as I entered the coffee shop, standing at the counter, taking what looked like a tall, black, iced coffee from the barista. She turned and I waved, and then pointed to a table over by the window, where we both headed.

"Hi!" she said, brightly as she bounced up to the table, which I had reached, first. *Once a cheerleader, always a cheerleader,* I thought. Lacy was Japanese, with a sheet of long, black straight hair that she usually wore in ponytail for practices or competitions. Today, it was loose, hanging down to the middle of her back. She had a delicate, but also somewhat muscular build, and a booming voice that seemed more suited for a much larger person. While other coaches had to use megaphones to project what they said, Lacy simply spoke with her normal tenor.

"Good morning," I said. We sat down, and I smiled. "Thanks for meeting with me on such short notice."

"Of course!" she said. She glanced toward the counter. "Do you want some coffee?" She held up her cup. "This is my fifth one today!"

No kidding, I wanted to say, but managed not to. I liked Lacy. "I'm good," I said.

"Is Ella okay?" she asked, crossing her short legs under the table. "Can she still go to dance camp?"

"Oh, she's fine," I said. "And yes, of course. We're all paid up, ready to go in a few weeks."

"Great." Lacy looked relieved. "She is such an inspiration to our younger team members. You're raising quite the leader."

I smiled again, wider this time, feeling proud of my daughter. "Thank you. Are you sure you don't mean bossy?" I laughed.

"Ha!" Lacy said. "Same thing. I love it!" She paused. "Is there something else going on with her I should be aware of?"

"Well, no, not with her." I took a several minutes to explain to Lacy everything Ella had told me about the "ho" accounts on Instagram, including Lizzy's. I showed her the few examples Ella had shown me, and I watched as Lacy's cheery, pleasant expression faded away.

"This is *totally* unacceptable," she said, her dark eyes flashing. "How can they possibly think this is okay?"

"That's what I thought, too," I said, frowning. "I'm concerned for them. For Lizzy, especially, to be honest. I don't know if you know, but she has a bit of a reputation."

"Oh, I know," Lacy sighed. "I've talked with her about it several times, but it doesn't seem to get through. It's like she *needs* the attention, and she's going to get it whatever form it takes. Even if it's something like this." She gestured toward my phone, which was still open to Lizzy's inappropriate account.

"I felt strange bringing it up to Tiffany, directly," I said. "I thought it might be better, coming from you."

Lacy nodded, her lips pursed. "Definitely. I have no problem reaching out to her, or the other parents. They need to know."

"And of course, if you somehow find out that Ella has an account, too, I'd want to know right away." After my daughter had shown me the accounts of the offending girls last night, I'd done a search for several iterations of "Ella_the_Ho" moniker on Instagram, in case she'd been lying to me about not participating in this behavior, but luckily, found nothing. Still, it was possible she was doing it under a different name to protect herself from getting caught, and to keep me from finding out. I trusted my daughter, as much as I could trust any sixteen-year-old, but I knew it wasn't out of the realm of possibility that she would hide this from me.

"I don't think Ella would do it," Lacy said. "But yes, if I find out she did, you'll be the first to know."

"Thanks," I said. "She's afraid the other girls will be mad at her for turning them in."

"They won't know it was her," Lacy said. "I'll say I got an anonymous tip, and confront the team as a whole. I want to give the girls a chance to come forward and be honest with me. I'm big on teaching them to take ownership."

"And if no one comes forward?" I asked. I couldn't imagine any of the girls wanting to admit to their coach what they were doing online, knowing that it would mean their parents would be told.

"Then I'll confront the ones you showed me, personally, and squeeze it out of them." She lifted her arms off the table and turned her hands into fists. "Can you text me the girls' names that you're aware of have the accounts, so I can take screen shots as evidence? I'll take it from there."

"Sure," I said. "And thanks, again."

"Thank *you* for filling me in," Lacy said. "Trust me, we're going to be having some frank discussions about self-esteem, and the dangers of social media."

Lacy and I parted ways at eleven-thirty, and I headed to Andrew's office. I was dreading what I had to say to him, especially since he'd admitted that he'd had a crush on me in the past. Even though he proclaimed he was only interested in casual sex, I worried I might hurt his feelings. All the more reason why I shouldn't have been messing around with someone I knew, let alone allowing him the kind of access to my mind that I'd only ever given my husband. I'd also realized that I'd let myself make eye contact with him when he was inside me and he told me to—again, something I'd only ever done with Jake, something that took our intimacy to a much deeper level than I'd ever shared with anyone else. I felt so guilty for letting that happen; thinking about it on the drive over to see him, I was more resolute than ever to make it clear that was never going to happen again.

I parked in the building's underground garage a few minutes before noon, not wanting to get there early and seem too eager. I'd dressed conservatively, in a fitted lavender high-necked sheath dress, drawing my curls into a tight bun at the base of my neck with a few wisps hanging around my face, and threw on a pair of black patent flats.

I rode the elevator to the seventeenth floor, and told the exquisitely beautiful, ebony-skinned young receptionist at his front desk that Andrew was expecting me. "Can I bring you something to drink?" she asked. The multitude of her long, thin braids shifted as she tilted her head. "Coffee, water, or an energy shot?"

I squinted at her. "Energy shot?"

She nodded. "It has the same amount of caffeine as five cups of coffee. Andrew insists we keep the kitchen stocked with it at all times. I drink, like, three a day."

"Wow," I said, smiling. "I'd better pass." *Is speed-balling caffeine a thing for people in their twenties?* I wondered, as I thought about Lacy's confession of her fifth coffee, earlier. Maybe I should tell her about this energy shot; she'd get the same pay off and not have to pee as often.

The receptionist gave me an indulgent look that I interpreted to mean, "Of course you'll pass, old woman," and then pushed a button on her phone, telling Andrew that I'd arrived.

While I waited, I looked around the small reception area at the multiple matted and framed clippings from newspapers and online journals touting

Lightning Design's rapid rise to the top. "Andrew Rochester Rocks the Tech World!" one headline exclaimed, and again, I felt myself wondering how he had gone from chubby bartender to industry mogul. I'd been so caught up in the whirlwind of our verbal foreplay, and then later, blissful afterglow, I'd forgotten to ask.

I was about to take a seat on one of the plush leather chairs when Andrew approached me. "Jessica," he said, warmly. His low voice immediately set off a spark of excitement in my body. "Come on back." He wore dark jeans and an expensive-looking, slim-fit periwinkle sweater. His black-framed glasses made him seem smarter and sexier than I knew he already was.

I followed him down a long hallway, past a large area filled with desks, occupied by at least fifty young men and women who didn't look much older than Ella and her friends. They were all hunched over their keyboards, wearing headphones and staring at their enormous computer screens with glazed-over eyes. We entered Andrew's office, and as he shut the enormous wooden door behind us, I quickly took in the floor-to-ceilings windows that looked out over the rest of Bellevue, along with his huge glass-topped desk and multiple computer screens that rested upon it.

"Please, sit," he said, gesturing toward the two overstuffed brown leather couches that sat in a far corner of the room. "I assume Jayla offered you something to drink."

"She offered me a shot of something that would give me a heart attack," I said. My voice shook a bit, and I coughed, not wanting to seem nervous. But my insides squirmed as he smiled at me, remembering what that mouth was capable of doing.

He laughed, and we both took a seat, opposite each other, a small table in between us.

"You're quite the mogul, it seems," I said.

"Well, I don't know about that," he said. "I do okay. We have four floors in this building, and another location in near Lake Union. I'm thinking about building something bigger outside of the city limits, a new headquarters, so people won't have to commute as far or deal with traffic." He tilted his head. "Maybe you can help me find the right property."

I made a non-committal noise. The last thing I needed was to find a reason to spend *more* time with Andrew. "How did you go from bartender to all of this?" I made a sweeping gesture, in the general direction of the work area we'd just made our way through.

He shrugged. "I've always been into computers, even in high school. I had a two year degree in basic programming when I was bartending, not really doing anything with it, because I preferred fucking around, eating pizza and playing video games with my friends to holding down a nine-to-five job. But after you left the restaurant, I told myself something needed to change if I was ever going to land a girl like you, so I decided to go back to school and get my Master's in Digital Solutions Development."

"You're joking," I said.

"I'm not," he said, and the look on his face told me he was telling the truth. "I did have a crush on you, Jessica. And when you left, well, I started fiddling around, building websites for my friends, and then word of mouth started to spread, so I hired a few employees, even as I was finishing up school. I also put the nightly pizzas down and started going to the gym." He grinned, and again, I saw the shadow of the sweet boy I'd known. "When I made enough money, I hired a stylist, took some dancing lessons, and that's when I met my ex-girlfriend. We were together for quite a while." He gave me a long, hungry look. "But she honestly didn't hold a candle to you."

"I doubt that," I said, dropping my gaze to the floor. It was flattering to know that he had thought about me all of those years, but also made me feel a little uncomfortable. *Does he still have feelings for me, now? How could he, after it had been so long? He doesn't even* know *me.* But then again, what were the odds of the two of us meeting again, especially in the way that we had? Didn't it mean *something*—that we had a story that required an ending?

"You don't give yourself enough credit," Andrew said.

"So, if all of that is true, when we met for coffee that first day, did you recognize me right away?" I gave him a stern look. "Be honest."

"You got me." He held his hands up in mock surrender and then dropped them back to his lap. "I didn't know it was you when I responded to your profile, but as soon as I saw you in person, I knew it was you."

"But you pretended you didn't." I felt an uncomfortable pit form in my stomach, knowing that he was capable of that brief deception. And that I hadn't picked up on it; I was usually a better read of people than that.

"I wanted to see if you recognized me, considering I look so different," he said. "My vanity got the better of me. Forgive me?" He gave me the same charming smile that made my heart flutter when I'd been in his bed.

"It's fine." None of this mattered, anyway. I was here to tell him we wouldn't be seeing each other again.

"So," he said. "You're having regrets?" He leaned forward to rest his elbows on his knees, linking his long fingers together, loosely.

"Not exactly," I said, feeling my cheeks warm as I looked at him again. "I mean, we had an amazing time."

"We did." His dark eyes remained fixed on mine, and I tried not to look away.

"I'm struggling with not being totally honest with my husband." I took in a breath, and released it, hoping to steady my rapidly stuttering pulse. "I know you and your girlfriend didn't tell each other everything, but he and I always have. That's why this has worked for us. We don't have any secrets. That's our most important rule."

He reclined, then, spreading his long arms along the back of the couch. "Did you go home and tell him what we did together?"

"Yes, but—" I began, but he cut me off.

"Did he like hearing about it? Did it make him want to fuck you?"

I nodded, then, trying to ignore the ache growing between my thighs. This wasn't supposed to be happening. I'd come there to call things off.

"He bent me over the kitchen counter," I said, in a still voice.

"I bet he didn't even wait to take your clothes off," Andrew eyes hadn't left my face. He was reading me, looking for every muscle that twitched. Gauging my reactions to what he said. It felt like I had nowhere to hide.

"He didn't," I said, unable to resist being drawn in by what he was saying. His words pin-balled around inside my head, electrifying every synapse I had.

We were silent a moment, the air in the room thick with desire.

"Here's what I think," he finally said. "I think you're a little unnerved by how much you liked fucking me. I think you're used to being the one in control of everything and now you're afraid that I might take some of that control away."

"I'm not afraid." I lifted my chin the slightest bit, and pulled my shoulders back.

"Prove it." He stood up, took a few steps, and then sat down next to me. He leaned in and put his lips right up against my ear. "Fuck me right now. Here in my office."

I held completely still. This was not why I came. This was crazy. And despite that, I turned my head and kissed him anyway.

His hands reached behind my head and pulled at the clip that held up my hair, allowing it to cascade down. His phone rang on his desk, but he ignored it . He tickled the insides of my thighs as he pushed up my dress.

"Is the door locked?" I asked, breathlessly.

"Do you really care?" he replied, and moved his mouth down my neck to my collarbone, nipping at my skin.

"Someone could come in," I said, closing my eyes as waves of pleasure blasted through me. What I was doing was wrong. But I couldn't stop. I didn't want to.

"They won't," he assured me, but then he got up and turned the latch above the doorknob. "Better?"

"Yes." I stood up, too, and he came back over to me.

"This is what you want, isn't it?" he said, sliding his hands over my hips. "You came here dressed in your sensible business-best, wearing your hair up, thinking that would keep me from wanting to fuck you?" He chuckled under his breath. "What did I tell you on Saturday? I want the *real* Jessica. Not the shiny, made-up version you've given to other men. You came here thinking you were going to end things with me and instead, you're going to let me fuck you."

I sucked in a breath through my teeth, his words affecting me in a way I couldn't deny. My head was spinning. My body was crying out for his touch. I knew better than to let this keep going, but I felt powerless.

He squeezed the ample flesh of my ass and pulled me against him. He kissed me, again, our tongues teasing, and I reached for his waist and tried to unzip his jeans. His right hand shot up and grabbed me by the hair, yanking it hard enough to bring tears to my eyes.

"Stop trying to control me," he said, sharply. "I know it's what you're used to. I know most men crumple and submit in the presence of a powerful woman, but I don't. I see who you are, Jessica. And I know exactly what you need."

He turned me around, then, both of his hands roaming up and down the front of my body, squeezing my breasts as he walked me over to his desk. We were high enough up and far enough away from any other buildings that no one could see us, and there weren't any internal windows looking into his office. No one would know.

"Tell me the filthiest thing you've ever done," he instructed as he bent me over his desk and shimmied up my dress. "Or want to do, but haven't. Something you've never told anyone else."

I pressed my lips together, and pushed my hips back against him, yearning to be fucked, but instead, he slapped my bare ass with his open palm. It burned like a thousand bee stings piercing my skin, but was oddly exciting, too. Before I realized what I was doing, I told him what he wanted to hear. Something even Jake didn't know. "A roomful of men," I said, through gritted teeth. "In line, stroking their hard cocks, waiting to fuck me." I'd never spoken those words out loud; I'd never opened myself up that far.

"Yes," he said. I heard him unbuckle his belt and the quick zing of his zipper being pulled down. "You want to be used a little, don't you, Jessica?" I heard the rustle of a condom package being torn open. The slick and swollen warmth between my legs throbbed. "You also don't want this to be over, do you?" he continued as he jerked my panties out of the way, not bothering to take them off. His fingers probed at me, and he chuckled again, a low, appealing sound. "You wouldn't get this wet for a man you didn't come here wanting to fuck."

But before I could respond, he slipped inside me in one quick motion, and I couldn't help it, I cried out. He leaned over and clamped one hand over my mouth, plunging inside me again and again, until he stopped, suddenly, and pulled out. He rubbed his cock in between my buttocks, the tip of it pressing at the opening no other man had ever touched. "You never told me if you're the kind of girl who takes in the ass."

"No," I said, tense, but panting. "I'm not." I was motionless, waiting, afraid that he might take what he wanted without my permission. But maybe, on a deeper level, hoping that he wouldn't bother to ask.

"I don't believe you," he said. And then, it happened. He slipped inside me, just a little, and I gasped. He stood unmoving, letting me get used to the feeling of him there, inside my most vulnerable spot. "Do you want me to stop?"

I closed my eyes and shook my head. The sensation was exquisite, drawing the thinnest of lines between pleasure and pain. My clit ached, and I moved one hand to rub it, frantically, as he began to move, slowly, in and out. It didn't take long for me to cry out again, my body jerking as he continued to fuck me, gently, slowly and deliberately, until he let out a low moan and finished, too.

He lay on top of my back, the same way Jake had on Saturday night, and I closed my eyes. *What are you doing, Jess?* I thought. I'd never been with another man without telling my husband I was going to do it, first. Not to mention how I had so easily revealed my deepest, most depraved fantasy with Andrew, but never shared it with Jake, who I'd also told that I wasn't interested in anal sex—I worried it would hurt too much. Of course he, being Jake—being the husband who would never want to do anything to cause pain to the woman he loved—respected my feelings and never brought it up again. *Why did I let Andrew do this to me, and not Jake?* I felt a little sick, realizing what I'd done. The lines I'd crossed.

Andrew straightened, allowing me to, as well. I pulled up my panties, and then walked over, on wobbling legs, to the couches, where I found my clip on one of the cushions and proceeded to put my hair back up. I didn't know what to say.

"Not what you expected, I take it," Andrew said as he threw away the condom and quickly zipped up his pants.

"No," I said. I smoothed out my dress and frowned.

"Are you angry with me?" He sounded legitimately concerned.

"I wouldn't say that." I hesitated, trying to find the right words. "I'm just...."

"Conflicted," he said, finishing my sentence for me.

"Yes. This is not how I've done things." I still couldn't believe the fantasy I'd shared with him. *I'm supposed to open myself up to Jake,* I thought. *Not you.*

"Go home and tell your husband about it," Andrew suggested. "I bet you he'll think it's hot. Tell him you planned it. That you wanted it to be a surprise."

I considered this possibility. Jake had said he wanted us to up the ante, but I wasn't sure he'd classify what just happened as me pushing "our" boundaries, or as me, betraying his trust.

"I don't know," I said, feeling a tremor in my throat. This was yet another thing I would have to keep from Jake. That was the things with lies—once you told one, you inevitably ended up having to tell more.

"Oh shit," he said. "Please don't cry. You'll make me feel like an asshole."

"Maybe you are an asshole," I said, but I did so with a small smile. "And I'm not crying. I'm just trying to figure out how I feel about all of this."

"I'm sorry if I made things worse," he said, coming over to stand next to me again. "I couldn't help myself. You *do* something to me. I lose my senses."

You and me both, buddy, I thought. But Andrew didn't have anything at stake the way I did. My guess was that there wouldn't be any consequences for him if people found out. People expected men to have casual sex with women they barely knew. They didn't expect the same of women like me.

"I've been thinking about you pretty much constantly since Saturday night," he said.

"I can only see you once a month." *What am I saying?* I thought. I was supposed to tell him that I couldn't see him at all.

"That's how you've done it before?" He was only a few inches from me, and I looked up into his dark brown eyes, searching them for something I could use to reject him. Some hint that he wasn't a person I should spend more time with. But there was only kindness there, and concern.

I nodded.

"I'm not sure I can only see you once a month," he said.

"I'm not sure, either," I whispered. What I felt in that moment wasn't romantic, exactly. My stomach wasn't filled with butterflies and my head wasn't swimming with images of us holding hands or taking walks on the beach. Instead, what I saw was the two of us in his bedroom again. His naked body pressed against mine. His fingers entwined in my hair.

"It's just sex," I told him. "Nothing more than that."

"Whatever you say," he replied, and then, before I left, I kissed him again.

Twenty One

For the next few days, I didn't answer any of Andrew's texts. I tried to talk myself into blocking his number from my phone, but couldn't convince myself to go that far. Instead, I focused on work, and spending time with my mom, who, surprisingly, had been hanging out with Helen during the day when I was at the office or busy with showings, helping Charlotte's mom organize her next protest march.

"It's pretty amazing what she's done for women's rights," my mom told me, on Thursday night. She was lounging on the couch in the family room with a glass of white wine, while I stood at the island in the kitchen getting dinner ready.

"Well, I think it's amazing you're spending so much time with her," I said, as I used a pair of tongs to toss the sesame chicken salad I'd made. Jake was working late, wooing a couple of out-of-town, high level executive candidates with a Microsoft expense-account dinner at Daniel's Broiler in Bellevue. Ella was at the movies with Bentley, and Tuck was upstairs in his room.

My phone buzzed, then, and even though I tried to ignore it, I couldn't. I worried that in avoiding Andrew, I would miss a client trying to get in touch with me.

"I'm thinking about the taste of your skin," Andrew's text said. "The sweet sound you made when I flicked my tongue against your clit."

My breath hitched, remembering his touch, and I slammed my phone upside down onto the counter. *Fuck, this man is getting to me.* I hadn't told Jake that I'd gone to see Andrew in his office, let alone what had happened when I was there, and the secret felt like a giant splinter lodged inside my chest. It was starting to fester.

Tucker sauntered into the kitchen, then.

"Hi honey!" my mom said to him, brightly.

"Hey, Grandma," he said. "How are you?"

"I'm good," my mom said. "What are you up to?"

"Nothing," he said. He put his hands on the edge of the island countertop and knocked out a few pushups. His arms were thin and wiry, but strong; he reminded me so much of Peter, the two of them could be twins. "Can I spend the night at Sawyer's?" he asked me.

"Sure," I said. Sawyer was his best friend from the baseball team, and lived only a few houses down. "After we eat." I gestured toward the big bowl of chopped cabbage, shredded carrots, and grilled chicken in front of me. *Thank god for Costco prepackaged meals.*

"Salad?" he said, wrinkling up his slightly up-turned, freckled nose. "Really, Mom?"

"Really." Unlike many of the other parents Jake and I knew who allowed their kids to dictate the household menu, our rule was that the kids had to eat whatever we prepared.

He gave me a dubious look. "I'll eat at Sawyer's."

"I don't think so," I said, with growing irritation. My phone buzzed again, and I grabbed it, quickly, ready to tell Andrew to leave me alone, but this time, the text was from Jake.

"Both of these guys are idiots," he said. "One of them just bragged that he spent the summer playing 'sport pussy.' What a pig."

"Oh, let the boy go to his friend's house," my mom said. "You and I can have salad."

"Thanks, Grandma!" Tuck said, and then dashed back up the stairs.

"Please don't do that," I said to my mom, after he had left.

"Do what?"

"Interfere with the kids."

My mom drew her pointed chin into her neck and raised her eyebrows. "You're obviously upset about something, but I don't think it's that. Or what Tuck's having for dinner."

I didn't say anything, silently seething over the fact that however self-involved my mom could be, she could also read me like no one else. I *was* upset—with myself. Because all I could think about was how I could find a way to get back to Andrew's house. Not in a month, *tonight*. It had only been three days since I'd seen him at his office and my body vibrated with need. The pull to see him again was magnetic. Jake and I hadn't had sex since I came back from Andrew's house the first time, and the tension inside me was so extreme that earlier today, I'd even snuck into the bathroom at work and quietly gave myself a few orgasms. It wasn't enough.

"Bye, Mom! Bye Grandma!" Tuck said, as he pounded down the stairs, past us, and toward the front door. His backpack was slung over his shoulder, and he carried his Xbox controller.

"I love you!" I called out, deciding that trying to get him to stay home and eat salad wasn't a battle worth fighting.

He slammed the front door behind him, and my mom and I sat down at the table to eat. I put enough salad in a bowl for each of us, and then poured us both a little more wine. I took a hefty swallow before I picked up a fork.

"Have you talked to dad at all?" I asked my mom, feeling the warm alcohol instantly smooth my sharp, internal edges.

"No. He's called a couple of times, but only to lecture me about how dramatic I'm being."

"Ha. That's what you used to say to me."

Her fork stopped in mid-air. "I did?"

"Oh my *god*, Mom. Are you kidding me? You said it *all* the time! Whenever I was upset."

"Hmm," she said, setting her fork on her napkin. "I don't remember that. I *do* remember trying to get you to focus on the facts of a situation, so you wouldn't feel so bad about whatever was going on. It was a technique I learned from a psychology professor, to help people with anxiety. Identify the facts, so you can let go of the things you can't control. It's supposed to be soothing."

"Yeah, well, it wasn't." I felt shaky, talking to my mother about this particular issue. We normally kept our discussions on the surface. But since we'd had that brief moment of emotional connection when she told me she was happy that I had such a loving relationship with Jake, I needed to try to be more open. Keeping that in mind, I kept talking. "It pretty much made me feel more anxious, because I had to push everything down. I felt like I couldn't talk to you about anything that had to do with my feelings."

My mother frowned, and her thin, silvery-brown eyebrows furrowed. "I honestly thought I was helping you develop better coping mechanisms." She took a swallow of her wine. "Why haven't you told me this before?"

I laughed, and shook my head. "That's my point, Mom. I couldn't. You and Dad were so logical and practical all the time. Scott, too, actually. I felt like something was wrong with me." My voice broke, and I cleared my throat, not wanting to cry.

"Well, shit," my mom said, and because she rarely swore, it made me laugh. She smiled at me, fondly. "I never meant for you to feel that way. I'm sorry."

"Thank you," I said, a little shocked that she'd apologized.

"Your father and brother are definitely cut from the same cloth," my mother remarked after she took another bite of her salad.

"Have you talked to Scott, lately?" However comforting it was to connect on a new level with my mother, I was happy for the change in subject. "I texted him a few weeks ago, but never heard back." This wasn't unusual for my brother; the only way I knew he was alive was from his occasional Facebook posts, which were usually only links to articles he'd either written or contributed to in the field of biological engineering.

"Your brother's not a talker," my mom said. "That's what I have always loved about you, Jessica. You speak your mind. Even when I disagreed with your choices, I was proud of you for making them."

"Thank you," I said, again, quietly glowing on the inside. I wished I had known she felt like this, sooner. I looked down at my salad, suddenly not hungry any more. It had been a long day. "I'm feeling pretty tired," I told my mom. "I think I'm going to go upstairs and lie down. Maybe watch some Netflix. Will you be all right?"

"Of course," she said, waving me away. "Don't worry. I'll clean up."

I headed for the stairs, my phone in one hand and my glass of wine in the other.

Once inside my bedroom, I closed and locked the door behind me. I took off my work clothes and lay down on the bed, staring up at the ceiling, thinking about Andrew. About what I'd let him do to me in his office. I was still a little sore, there, in my most tender, previously untouched, spot, but it wasn't an unpleasant feeling. I'd thought about it more since the last time I saw him, and realized that what had turned me on the most was the way Andrew planted the seed of this particular act as a possibility in one of his texts—*I always wondered if you were the kind of girl who took it in the ass*—so when that moment came, part of me had already decided that I wanted to let him do it. It hadn't been a conscious decision; it happened somewhere deep in my psyche that Andrew seemed to have direct access to. No one had ever read me that easily—not even Jake.

I rolled over, feeling twitchy, desperate to find some sort of relief from the mounting tension in my body. The orgasms I'd had at the office that morning only seemed to increase my longing instead of taking it away. Every time I thought about Andrew, my nerves shot off sparks, recalling the unspeakable pleasure of his exceptional girth filling me. How I couldn't wait to fuck him again.

I grabbed my phone from the nightstand and read through a few of the texts he'd sent me over the past few days:

"You need to be held down and fucked. Your wrists pinned over your head. Your legs spread-eagle. Your body completely exposed. Totally powerless."

"I want you to smother my face again. I want to feel you come on my mouth."

"Your pussy is mine, now. You know that, right?"

I groaned, astonishingly titillated by the way he talked to me. Every fiber in my being told me to go see him. But every inch of my heart screamed that I should never speak with him again.

I looked at the clock. It was only six-thirty, and I knew from experience that Jake's business dinner would last at least until ten o'clock. That didn't leave me enough time to get to Andrew's house and back, and besides, my mother would ask where I was going. If I lied to her, she'd likely be able to tell. The last thing I needed was to have her mention to Jake that I'd disappeared for a couple of hours to some undisclosed place, and then come home with flushed cheeks, messy hair, and a satisfied smile on my face. There was no doubt he'd know what I'd done.

I stood up, and went to stand in front of the full length mirror that hung on the back of the bathroom door. I stared hard at my reflection, noting how my face started to look less like me the longer I looked at it. I reached my hands up and gently pinched my nipples, feeling a resultant, pleasant shock in my clit. My head rolled back as I used my fingertips to lightly brush over the outline of my curves, the same way Andrew had the first night we'd been together. I thought about his mouth, the wet swell of his tongue as it pressed against mine, the delectable softness of his lips brushing over the thin skin of my neck. I thought about his words in my ear: *My cock. Your pussy. That's all that matters. Understand?*

I never knew I could be so aroused by the dominant nature of his words. What did that say about me? Why hadn't I ever had these same feelings come up with Jake? I wasn't a submissive woman, by any means. My husband loved that I was a strong woman—I knew that side of me was much of why seeing and hearing about me having sex with another man turned him on. He admired my strength, my willingness to explore the depths of my desires—to be comfortable of satisfying my urges. But did that mean that I was weak, then, because of how much I liked the way Andrew had been more dominant? Or was it more that it was a relief to not *have* to be so strong and in control all of the time?

Yes, I thought. *That's it.* With the other men I'd been with—even with Jake—I took the lead. I was used to doing that, and not just in the bedroom. I'd been raised to be independent—to never solely rely on a man for anything. So when I thought about all the ways Andrew touched and had spoken to me that first night, it struck me that the most intimate act he performed was wiping off my makeup. I remembered how exposed I'd felt in that moment, and again, when he was fucking me, and demanded that I open my eyes. He took away my armor; his words broke down my walls. He saw *into* me in a way no other man had before.

My phone buzzed on the nightstand, next to my half-full wine glass, where I'd left it. I walked over and looked at the screen through slightly hooded eyes, my heart banging like a drum. Andrew had sent me a close up of his hand wrapped around the base of his thick, beautiful cock, along with the words, "What you do to me."

I'd always scoffed at the idea of "sexting" with someone. Jake and I sent each other fun, flirty texts throughout the day, but it had never risen to the level that Andrew was taking it. *It wasn't just him,* I reminded myself. He wouldn't have anything to work with if I didn't respond.

"I'm naked right now," I told him. "Alone, in my bedroom. That picture made me wet."

"I need to see you," he responded. "All of you."

I returned to my spot in front of the full length mirror, and held my phone so that I could take a picture for him. I ended up taking several, cropping it and adding a flattering filter before I liked one enough to send. I added the words, "Your cock is mine. Understand?" He wasn't the only one who knew how to garner a reaction.

My phone rang almost immediately after that, his name showing up on the caller ID. I hesitated only a moment before answering.

"Your body is amazing," Andrew said. His voice ached with lust. "Get on your bed."

"Where are you?" I said, doing as he asked. I yearned for release; I *needed* what I suspected would happen next. I felt a little nervous, worried that Jake might finish with his dinner early, but not worried enough to hang up the phone. He normally texted when he was on his way home, so I figured I was safe. I'd hear the notification, even if I was on the phone.

"In my bedroom. Naked. My hand on my cock. I'm stroking, slowly, picturing your red lips slipping over the top of me, gently sucking and swirling your tongue around the tip."

I settled back on my pillow and closed my eyes, my right hand skating downward, landing between my legs, while I used my left to keep my phone next to my ear. "My fingers are on my pussy," I told him in a hoarse voice. "I'm already so fucking wet."

"Mmm," he murmured. "I remember how you taste. So perfectly tangy and sweet. I want to roll my tongue around your clit. I want to suck it while I use my fingers on your G-spot."

"That makes me want to come," I said, moving my fingers a little faster as my muscles began to tense.

"Not yet," he instructed. "I want to see your pussy."

I stopped moving my hand and opened my eyes. "I can't." Sending him the naked picture was different. What he had requested crossed a line. It was too intimate. Too much.

"Yes, you can," he said. "Please, Jessica. Show me how wet you are."

It was the "please" that did it, and the way my name rolled off his tongue. I positioned my phone between my spread legs and again, did as he asked. After I sent it, I put the phone next to my ear and waited, taking ragged breaths.

"Jesus," he muttered. "Such a perfect, beautiful pussy. My mouth is watering."

"I need to fuck you again," I said, strangely flattered by his compliment. No one, not even Jake, had said that to me. "It's all I can think about."

"Come over right now," Andrew urged. "I'm so fucking hard. I would love to slip inside that tight little cunt of yours."

Again, his choice of words shot delicious shivers across my skin. I put my fingers between my legs once more. "I can't," I said, quietly. "I have to be quick. Tell me what you're doing. Make me come."

He began to speak, his words painting a picture inside my head. I let myself get lost in what he described—lost in pure, erotic sensation—thinking only of what it felt like to fuck him, until the moment that he told me he was about to finish, and I couldn't take another moment of my fingers rubbing my clit. "Oh, fuck," I muttered as I lifted my hips and let pleasure take over, washing over me in all-encompassing waves, pretending that what had happened was completely normal, that it was all part of what Jake and I had agreed to.

That I wasn't doing anything wrong.

"HAVE you seen Tiffany's latest post on the Neighbor's app?" Jake asked me on Saturday, a couple of days later. It was July 4th, and we were in our bedroom. I had just gotten off the phone with clients who were ready to put in an offer on a one-acre property with a spacious, split-level home in Woodinville, and I wasn't looking forward to sacrificing my lazy weekend morning in order to head into the office and get the paperwork started.

Jake sat bare-chested, his back against our thickly padded headboard, his long legs still under the covers. Now that Justine had had a few more weeks of training, Jake had actually been able to take some time off on the weekends.

"No," I said. I was perched on the edge of our bed, trying to convince myself to get up and take a shower. "I turned the notification option off." It was getting ridiculous, how often people spouted off publicly about HOA lawn-cutting violations—"No more than two inches of growth allowed, people!" one chastised—or how many people had been caught speeding on Main Street in a given week. If I hadn't been referred so many new clients via the app, I would have deleted it from my phone altogether.

Jake held his phone in one hand and began to read. "'Fellow Queen's Ridge residents, we have a thief in our midst!!!'" Here, he looked at me and raised his dark eyebrows. "'I am missing three of my eight garden gnomes from my flower beds. I will not rest until the culprits are named.'"

"That could be difficult," I said. "The thief might go by a gnome-de-plume."

Jake snorted and dropped his phone into his lap. "Funny girl."

I shook my head. "How does she have time for that kind of shit with her mother to take care of, *and* deal with Lizzy?" Lacy had called a team-wide meeting a few days after I'd informed her about the inappropriate Instagram accounts, confronting the group of girls as a whole, asking that the guilty parties to come forward and confess to her, privately. "I have screen shots of everyone who's done it," Lacy had said, according to Ella. "If you don't fess up, you're off the team. Period." (Ella was relieved that her coach had done as promised, saying that she'd found out about the issue via an anonymous tip.) By the end of the day, Lacy had received tearful confessions by not only the girls she knew for certain had an account, but also four others. According to Ella, Lacy had meetings with all of the girls' parents, individually, and told them that if the accounts weren't deleted, or if Lacy discovered that they simply put up another one under a different name, they'd be kicked off the team. No exceptions. So I had to wonder how Tiffany, who clearly knew what Lizzy had been up to, possessed any extra bandwidth to post to all of Queens Ridge about missing lawn ornaments.

"I don't know," Jake said. "Maybe it's a good distraction. I imagine she doesn't get much of a break. Ben doesn't strike me as a guy who spends a ton of time at home."

I sighed. "That's a good point. You're a much kinder person than me." I paused, thinking for a moment. "I should take her a casserole or something. Or offer to help with her mom, so she can have some one-on-one time with Lizzy."

"See, now?" Jake said, smiling. "You're kind, too. That thought wouldn't even cross your mind if you weren't."

Andrew's face popped into my head, then, reminding me how unkind it was to keep things from my husband. I shook my head, as though to erase the thought. "You'll be okay with my mom this morning?"

"Of course," Jake said. "You won't be gone too long, right?"

"I hope not." When I realized that I'd have to go into the office, I had toyed with the idea of texting Andrew and asking if I could come over after I'd finished working, but I managed to fight off the urge. I absolutely could not make a habit of seeing him without Jake knowing about it. The one time I had weighed heavily on my heart.

"What time are Charlotte and Richard coming over tonight?"

"Around six, I think." We celebrated Independence Day with them almost every year, unless Charlotte had an event planned that she couldn't miss. This year, she was relying on her staff to handle the three parties she'd been hired to organize, and we were going to have dinner, then head to Gasworks Park in Seattle to watch the fireworks with the kids, as was our tradition.

There was a sudden, sharp rap on our bedroom door that startled us both. "My iPad stopped working," my mother's voice said. "The screen went black. Is Jake up, yet?" For a smart woman, my mom was hopeless when it came to technology.

Jake and I held each other's gaze and I sighed. "Sorry," I whispered, with a shrug, before heading into the bathroom.

"I'm up, Sheila," Jake called out. "I'll meet you in the kitchen in a few, okay?"

"Okay!" my mom said. "Thank you!"

I stood in front of the sink and reached for my toothbrush. But before I could, Jake came through the threshold and grabbed me. He spun me around and lifted me up onto the long counter, his hands squeezing the flesh of my hips.

"Well, hello there," I said, smiling. "You know I have to get ready, right? My clients are going to be at the office in an hour."

"I know," he said. He leaned down and nuzzled my neck with his lips. "Mmm. You feel so good." He pressed his hips between my legs. He was already hard. Instantly, I flashed on how Andrew had felt inside me. I tried to push the memory down. I wanted to focus on Jake.

I reached for him and jerked down his boxers. His skin was hot, and his cock twitched at my touch. I'd come with Andrew on the phone the other night, but Jake and I hadn't had sex after that. The orgasm I'd had while Andrew whispered in my ear had been good, but I still craved the ever-so-satisfying sensation of being filled up and fucked.

"I want you to fuck Andrew again," Jake murmured as he moved his fingers between my legs. "Jesus, you're already wet."

I grabbed his hand and brought his fingers to my mouth, staring into his blue eyes as I sucked them clean. "You do that to me," I said, when I was done. *You, and not Andrew,* I thought. *My husband.* I didn't want to talk about Andrew. I didn't want to think about him.

And then, as though to prove this to myself, I shifted so that Jake could enter me. I wrapped my legs around his waist. "Fuck me," I said, linking my fingers behind his strong neck. "Make me come." I tried to ignore the fact that I'd said those last words to Andrew a couple of days ago. I tried to ignore the feeling that I wished Jake didn't allow me to always tell him what to do. I wanted him to defy me—to take what he wanted without asking. Like Andrew had.

Jake lifted my hips and held them, moving me up and down on top of him.

"Fuck, yes, just like that," I hissed, and only a few moments later I closed my eyes and shuddered, and then we both lost control.

Jake set me back onto the countertop, his face buried in my neck. "Way better pick me up than coffee," he mumbled through his ragged breath.

"Blasphemy," I said, running my fingernails gently up and down his naked back. He smelled of sweat and sleep; when I kissed his chest, I tasted salt. I pushed him away, but with a smile. "Now, get out of here. I need to get ready."

Jake stepped back, and then over to the sink next to mine. "Have you heard from him at all?" he asked as he turned on the faucet and began to clean himself up, and I knew he was referring to Andrew.

"I haven't checked our email," I said, simply. It was true, I hadn't. But I didn't mention the texts. He was aware that I occasionally communicated with the other men we'd been with via text, but only to set up a time to meet.

"Maybe you should reach out to him," Jake suggested as he grabbed his toothbrush. "Let him know your mom is here, so you can't see him, but you want to again soon."

"I'm not worried about it," I said, as lightly as I could. But I *was* worried about Andrew. I was worried about how much I thought about him. How many times a day I imagined fucking him.

Jake hesitated, looking at me in the mirror, searching my face. "I thought you had fun."

"I did." I looked away from his observant gaze. "I think I'm just distracted by having my mom here. I'm not really in the mood."

He lifted a single eyebrow. "You certainly seemed in the mood a few minutes ago." His blue eyes sparkled, and I smiled.

"Only for you," I told him, and the sharp squeeze of remorse that I felt inside my chest quelled any lingering doubts. That was it. I couldn't keep hiding the truth from my husband. There was no way I could keep seeing Andrew. I needed to do what I'd meant to when I went to his office. I needed to end it. And soon.

Twenty Two

I managed to fend off Andrew's texts over the holiday weekend, claiming that work and family kept me too busy to talk with him.

"When can I see you again?" he kept asking, often enough that I began to feel a little annoyed. *This* was exactly why I couldn't continue anything with him—he wanted something that I couldn't give.

"Friday afternoon," I finally told him. "Three-thirty. At your office." I had to meet clients at four-fifteen; I wasn't going to give him enough time to try and talk me out of my decision. And I definitely wasn't going to wear a skirt.

"You want to fuck in my office again," he texted back. "I knew that you would."

I didn't respond. Now that I'd made up my mind to end things, his bordering-on-cocky speech had become more of an irritant, like he was trying too hard. He was a bit of an ass, really. He didn't seem to possess

an ounce of the kindness Jake had shown me over the years. I deleted the
most recent string of texts between us—the last thing I needed was for
Jake to pick up my phone when the screen was still open and read them.

I made it through the rest of the week, keeping myself occupied with
work, and ferrying Tucker around to the various places he wanted to go.
He would start driver's ed in the fall, and I couldn't wait for him to have
the same ability that Ella did, now, to get herself where she needed to
be on her own. So far, this summer, that had included working at Olive
Garden at night, sleeping in, and then spending most of the day at the
Queen's Ridge community pool with Bentley to "work on their tans,"
a.k.a., check out and flirt with cute boys. (Bentley's relationship with
Riley had been short-lived, as high school romances usually are, so she
and Ella were both single.)

"When's Grandma going home?" Tuck asked me on Friday around
two, as I drove him to one of Peter's job sites in Maple Valley, where he
was getting paid to pick up scrap lumber and sheetrock. Jake, Peter and I
had all agreed that Tuck, like Ella, would need to pay a thousand dollars
toward his first car, so he was spending the summer working for his dad,
making as much money as possible so he could afford the older, but
sporty, two-door Acura he had his eye on.

"I'm not sure, kiddo," I said. "Don't you like having her around?"

"I guess," Tuck said. "I mean, I love her and everything, but she's
never stayed with us so long."

"She's going through a hard time," I said. "It's not always easy being
a grown up."

Tuck made a non-committal noise and was silent for the rest of the
ride, staring out the window at the lush, green birch trees that lined the
winding road we drove upon. We rounded a sharp, hairpin corner, and I

pulled into the driveway that led to the massive residential development Peter was in charge of building. My eyes darted around, searching for signs posted by the realtor responsible for listing the properties, but saw none. Tuck and I got out of the car and headed toward Peter's truck, where he was standing alone, looking over a set of blueprints.

"Hey," he said when he saw us approach. He wore Carhartt overalls and a white hard hat, the latter that he took off and set on the open tailgate. "Ready to work, son?" he asked Tuck, who nodded. Peter pointed at a man standing in front of a half-built house about a hundred feet from us. "Go talk to Mateo. He'll get you started."

Tuck nodded again and took off down the street.

"Bye, honey!" I called out, and he gave me a half-assed wave, but kept going. I smiled at Peter. "He's such a respectful boy. So kind and considerate of his mother."

Peter let loose a laugh, almost choking as he took a sip of water from a two-liter bottle. When we were together, and he had to work long days for someone else during the hot summer, I used to fill those bottles for him at night and put them in the freezer, so the water would slowly melt, staying cool throughout the day for him to drink. I felt a twinge of nostalgia for how innocent we'd been back then. How little we'd known about each other, or ourselves.

I made a visor out of my hand and looked around the development. The houses were in various stages of completion, their wooden skeletons illuminated by the midday sun. "Who's the listing agent?"

"I was actually going to talk to you about that," Peter said, wiping away the sweat from his forehead. It was unusually warm for early July in Seattle, already over eighty degrees. I was happy Tuck had dressed appropriately in shorts and a tank top, even if I couldn't convince him to wear sunscreen. "The developer dumped the guy he was working with," Peter continued. "I gave him your name yesterday."

"Wow," I said. "Thanks. That was nice of you."

He shrugged. "You sell a lot of houses. And it's good for me if he ends up being happy."

I cringed, internally, at his reasoning, but managed to keep smiling. "I hope it works out. This is going to be a huge neighborhood."

"Yeah."

"How's Kari feeling?" It was always a little awkward making small talk with my ex, but I felt like it was important for our kids for us to be able to converse. And if I remembered right, Kari had suffered from some pretty intense morning sickness when she was pregnant with Ruby.

"Puking a lot," Peter said, frowning. "Cranky as hell."

"Sorry to hear it." I paused. "Are you sure it's okay for Tuck to be there this weekend?"

"He helps her with Ruby," Peter said. "It's a good thing." He glanced over to where Tuck now stood. Our son looked like he was in the middle of telling Mateo an animated story, waving his hands and acting out some kind of dance. "I'd better go make sure he gets to work."

"Okay," I said, handing him Tuck's backpack. "You'll drop him back at our house Monday afternoon?"

"Yep."

"Have a good one," I said, and then made my way to my car. An hour later, I was following Andrew to his office, after being offered a heart attack shot of caffeine by the strikingly beautiful Jayla. He grabbed the silver handle on the door and moved to close it, but I stopped him.

"Leave it open," I said. "This won't take long."

He smiled, a slow, sly thing. "Whatever you say." He gestured toward the couches. "Have a seat."

"I'm fine right here." I straightened my posture and looked him square in his dark, moody brown eyes. "I can't see you anymore. I'm not comfortable with what we've done."

"You seemed pretty comfortable when you were doing it," he said. His eyes traveled over my body, taking in my plain black capris and short-sleeved, white eyelet blouse. "You look gorgeous."

"You need to understand what I'm telling you," I said, unwilling to be deterred by his compliment, or the sexual energy that emanated from him. "I made a mistake. One I won't be repeating. I need you to respect that, and leave me alone."

"You're incredibly sexy when you're trying to be the boss," Andrew replied. He took a step toward me, then, standing only inches away. I could smell his sweet, slightly spicy cologne. I could feel his breath on my face. My pulse sped up. "I know that's what you're used to, Jess. Bossing men around. But you like it when you don't have to. You get wet when I take control."

My breath rattled inside my chest as I felt myself begin to soften. It was a chemical reaction, the desire I felt for him, nothing more, but it was strong and difficult to fend off.

"You never should have called me at my office," I said, determined not to waver in my stance. "You crossed a line, and you know it. I know it. And I should have known better than to see you after that. It was wrong. I told you I needed discretion, and you said you would give it. You lied."

"So did you," he said, still looking at me, intently. "You lied to your husband so you could fuck me. You wrote me things that I'm sure he would be broken-hearted to read."

My heart stuttered, and my face went hot. "Are you threatening me?" *God, I've been so stupid. How did I let things get this out of control? What if he called Jake? What if he had kept our texts and sent them to my husband?* My stomach clenched.

He took a step back, holding up his hands in mock surrender. "I'm just stating the facts."

"This is over," I said, gritting my teeth. "Don't text me. Don't call. I wish you the best, Andrew, but I don't ever want to see you again."

He smirked. "You could have told me that over the phone. Or in a text. But here you are."

"I wanted you to see that I'm serious," I said, starting to feel angry. I wanted to smack that smug look off of his face. Yes, I was attracted to him, and the sex had been fantastic. He saw a need in me, and filled it. But I had changed my mind, and he seemed unable to respect that. However briefly enamored with him I had been, I realized he was not what I needed. He was nothing to me, at all.

"I need you to say that you understand," I said, forcefully.

"I understand," he said, solemnly, and once again, he lifted two fingers on his right hand, as he had when we met for coffee, and he walked me to my car. "Scout's honor."

"Thank you," I said. "I wish you well, Andrew, but this wasn't meant to be." I stepped around him, and made my way quickly out of his office and down the hall to the elevators. *I did it,* I thought. *It's finally done.*

I grabbed my phone from my purse and tapped the screen a few times, blocking Andrew's number and then deleting altogether, as I had all of our text conversations. I couldn't change the fact that I'd slept with him, or that I'd been dishonest with Jake. But I could change how I behaved from now on. I would talk with my husband, opening up to him about my desire to let go of the reins in bed. It would be a new experience for us, a different way of pushing our sexual boundaries. My focus would stay where it should—on the man I loved.

The man I swore to myself I'd never keep anything from, ever again.

JAKE and I spent that evening alone, sitting on the back deck, watching the sunset as we sipped at the mojitos I'd made for us to go along with his favorite meal: chorizo and chicken tacos. Ella was at work, Tuck was at Peter's, and my mother had gone out for dinner with Helen.

"Can you believe how much they're hanging out together?" Charlotte had texted me earlier.

"I think it's kind of great," I replied, not only because my mother's new friendship kept her busy enough that I didn't have to worry about keeping her entertained. More importantly, it seemed like spending time with Helen—and possibly the new friends she had made back in Boise—had softened my mom in some way, changing how she saw women who had followed different paths in their lives. Helen didn't have a fancy degree—she never went to college—but she was passionate about women's rights, and spent her life using her very loud, but well-informed, voice to advocate for those who couldn't.

"She's a pioneer," my mom said to me the other day, after spending the day in downtown Seattle, helping Helen pass out fliers about Planned Parenthood, encouraging those who passed by to take the time to educate themselves about what services the organization provided instead of relying on inflammatory political rhetoric to make their decisions. "I had to fight against so much blatant sexism from the moment I stepped into my first advanced physics lab in college. It was such a lonely road to walk on my own." She looked at me, almost wistfully. "Helen understands that, but your father *saw* it," she continued. "And encouraged me to keep walking. I loved him because he was a man ahead of the times."

"He admires you so much," I said. "I knew that, even when I was a kid." I knew that they had spoken a several times over the last few days, and I hoped that for the sake of their marriage, this meant that she might be headed home, soon.

"He did," my mom agreed. "But Helen and I were talking, and I realized I made the mistake of letting him be my only support system. I didn't let other women close to me—I assumed that they wouldn't understand me. I'm beginning to see now that I missed out. Especially in my relationship with you. I focused way too much on my work instead of just being there. Being your mom." She paused, and her gray eyes shone with tears. "I'm sorry for that."

"It's okay," I said, feeling an ache in the back of my throat.

We were both quiet for a moment, letting that subtle, but monumental moment of love and forgiveness settle into our bones, allowing it to become a part of us, of the story we shared.

"I talked to your dad the other night," she finally said. "I'm going home after this weekend."

"That's great," I said. "Although it's been so nice to have you here." I was surprised to realize that I'd meant it.

Now, as I sat on the deck with Jake, staring out at the quickly darkening sky, enjoying the streaked, thick ribbons of pink, orange, and lavender hues, I told him everything my mother had said, and her plans to go back to Boise.

"Well, that's good news," he said.

I laughed. "How so?" I thought perhaps he had tired of having her around.

"You got an email from Andrew."

Jake had made a point of not logging in to our anonymous account since we decided that I would find a new lover without him, so I worried that he'd chosen to look at it now because he sensed how much I had been thinking about Andrew. "Oh," I said, trying to sound nonchalant. "Why did you check it?"

He gave me a sheepish look. "Curiosity got the better of me," he admitted. "I wanted to see what you two talked about. Why you picked him."

I felt a jolt of panic, trying to remember if I'd said anything in my brief email exchange with Andrew in the beginning that would give Jake cause to suspect something wasn't quite right. But then I realized that I'd only ever texted Andrew after we met for coffee. Everything we spoke about before that was mostly logistical.

"And?" I said, again, trying to keep my tone light.

"I get it. He seemed intelligent, and laid-back, at least on the page. Very much your type."

"*You're* my type," I said, lightheartedly, despite the way my heart jack-rabbited inside my chest. "The only type that matters."

"He had an interesting suggestion."

"What was that?" *Shit,* I thought. *I'm not going to get out of talking about this.* I'd considered telling Jake that I didn't want to see Andrew anymore because he'd tried to force me to have anal sex with him, but didn't want to add another lie on top of the ones I'd already told. I wasn't sure how I was going to communicate that I wasn't going to see Andrew again; part of me hoped I could say that he wasn't interested—that he'd ghosted on us, totally disappeared—so I wouldn't have to explain why I didn't want to continue fucking a man who I'd had incredibly chemistry with.

"See for yourself," Jake said, handing me his phone.

I took it from him, and held my breath as I began to read:

"Hello, Jessica. I've been thinking about you and your husband a lot this week. About you, especially. How hot it was to have you in my bed. I hope you told Jake how you let me pin your arms behind your back and told you not to speak. I hope you made it clear just how wet and swollen you were for me. Fucking you was the best sex I've ever had. I'm dying to see you again. Maybe this time you can bring your husband, so he can watch how incredibly turned on his wife gets when I fuck her?

Let me know."

He didn't sign his name, but there was a picture of him attached, the same one of him holding his hard cock that he'd sent me the other night, when we were sexting.

"He's got a huge dick," Jake said, as I handed him his phone. "You weren't kidding." His words were teasing, so at least I knew he wasn't mad or jealous about that, specifically.

Still, I couldn't ignore the twisting sensation in my gut. After the conversation I'd had with Andrew earlier that day, sending this email was a blatant, unmistakable fuck-you to my request to leave me alone. I was infuriated, but I couldn't let Jake see this, so I gave him a coy smile, instead.

"It's not the size of your pencil," I said, forcing a smile. "It's the signature you leave."

Jake groaned, but he was laughing. "Hey, now. *I'm* supposed to make the stupid jokes around here." He raised his eyebrows. "Do you like knowing you were the best sex he's ever had?"

"*You're* the best sex I've ever had," I said, evading his question. I didn't want to think about Andrew, or what I felt like when I was with him. The entire experience was tainted, and the last thing I wanted to do was go into detail about it with Jake. I felt disappointed and afraid—disappointed in myself for letting things with Andrew get so out of control, and afraid that if he was capable of sending this email so soon after I'd told him we were over, that he might do something more, something worse. Something that could make me regret that I'd ever known him at all.

Twenty Three

After that weekend and my mother packed up and went home, I struggled as the days passed, trying to decide whether or not I should tell Jake what happened with Andrew—that I'd been keeping the full truth from my husband for weeks. Part of me ached to come clean, knowing that I would feel so much better not having to carry around the knowledge of what I'd done, but another part, perhaps a wiser one, worried that the truth would hurt Jake more than it would give me relief.

This advice, at least, is what I gave Charlotte about her own situation, when she informed me that Richard had finally broken down about the state of their marriage. She and I had met for lunch the day after Andrew sent the email, and while I wished I could talk to her about the situation, I kept my mouth shut, listening as she told me the story about Richard's emotional outburst.

"I walked in on him in the bathroom," she told me in a low voice, so the people seated near us in the restaurant wouldn't hear. "He was naked, and *crying*. Like, serious, shoulder-shaking sobs."

"Wow," I said. I had a hard time picturing Charlotte's husband, who was a high powered, corporate attorney, losing it like that. "What did you do?"

"I shut the door behind me—Bentley was at the pool with Ella, thank god—and I went over to him and got down on my knees, asking what was wrong." She shook her head. "He told me that he was terrified that I was going to leave him. That I was probably already fucking someone else, and he didn't blame me. He said the more he tried to get an erection, the more it didn't happen. Which stressed him out, which made it harder—pardon the pun—for him to want to even *try* to have sex because he was so worried about not being able to perform. He also said he was terrified of going to the doctor and finding out he has prostate cancer or something, because of what it would do to Bentley and me. So he ignored the whole situation, hoping it would get better on its own."

"Holy shit," I said. "The poor guy."

She sighed. "I know. That's when I started crying, too, because of how I've been carrying on this emotional affair with Bryan. Because that's what it was, right?" She didn't wait for me to answer. "I mean, Alex fucking around on me was terrible—it gutted me—but I'm pretty sure in his mind, it was simply physical with all those other women, and he still only loved me, which is how he justified it when I found out. And I've been justifying having all these feelings for Bryan as being okay because I'm not fucking him, but really, it's almost *worse* to emotionally betray the man I'm in love with. I should have tried harder to get Richard to a counselor or the doctor."

"You did try," I said. "A *lot*. Don't beat yourself up."

"Yeah, but clearly it wasn't enough. He told me about all this underlying anxiety he deals with, and how he has to constantly push it down so he can deal with his huge clients or get up in front of judge and argue his cases. I had no idea that was going on with him, Jess. I'm his *wife*. I'm supposed to know him better than anyone else. How could I not *see* it?" Her brown eyes teared up, and I handed her my napkin.

"I think it's more complicated than that," I said, wanting to comfort her. "Especially when they don't want you to see it." I thought about my own struggles with opening up on a deeper level, even with Jake, how most of the time I didn't even realize I was hiding how I was feeling. It takes courage to reveal our innermost selves, to be vulnerable, when too many times, it can be used against you. But that was the risk, I supposed, in loving someone, and letting them love you. There was the chance they might hurt you, and yet, the brilliant, beautiful possibility that they won't.

"I need to tell him about Bryan," Charlotte said. "Right? He was so open and honest with me, I owe him the same thing."

I shook my head. "No way," I said. "I think the best thing to do is cut off your communication with Bryan. End it. And then focus everything you have on Richard. Be there for him. Help him feel safe again."

Charlotte gave me a dubious look. "Are you sure? I'm not just letting myself off the hook?"

"You're sparing him pain when he's already struggling. If you did tell him, my guess is that it would be only to alleviate your own guilt."

I told myself that the same logic applied to my situation with Andrew. If I told Jake everything, it would only hurt him. And for what? I wasn't going to talk with or see Andrew ever again. The email he sent was probably a one-time thing—a childish, knee jerk reaction to me cutting him off. He'd had a crush on me when we were younger, so I imagined my rejecting him, now, wasn't totally painless. But he'd also told me that he'd engaged in casual hook ups before, when he was with his ex-girlfriend, so he had to know that sometimes, things didn't work out. I told myself it was a good sign that he hadn't called me at work, which he could easily do, and since I'd blocked him on my phone, he couldn't send me any texts. I hoped that after not hearing from him for a while, I could tell Jake he must have lost interest.

"I think maybe I want to take a break from all of the hot wife stuff," I told him one night, a few days after my lunch with Charlotte, when he and I were in bed, about to go to sleep. "I know we thought upping the ante would be good for us, and it was, but I think we can do that even *more* by exploring some kinky things on our own. Maybe you can dominate me a little. Make me serve you." I winked at him, trying to be sexy and playful, but also, to gauge his reaction to that particular suggestion.

"Did something happen with Andrew that makes you not want to see him again?" Jake asked, furrowing his brows. "Did he do something to hurt you or freak you out?"

"Not at all," I said, quickly. "I just want to focus on us for a while." I paused. "Is that okay?"

"Of course," Jake said, raking the fingers of his free hand through his hair. "But are you sure nothing happened? Did he make you uncomfortable?"

"No," I said. "It's not about him." Andrew *had* made me uncomfortable, but it was because of my own reaction to being with him. The intense, automatic excitement I felt in his presence was treacherous. Even if it wasn't emotional—even if I didn't see stars and hearts and imagine spending time outside of the bedroom with him—the connection we had was undeniable, and I suspected that if I had allowed it to continue, it wouldn't have ended well.

"Okay," Jake said. "Are you going to send him an email, letting him know, or should I?"

"Do we even have to?" I sounded like a petulant child, but I wanted the conversation to end. "This is all supposed to be no strings attached."

"Yeah, but it's sort of rude to not let him know. Remember all the guys who basically ghosted on us?"

I nodded. Whenever we'd put up an ad looking for someone new to play with, there were always the men who would respond with enthusiasm, sending excited emails expressing their intense desire to make something happen, and then would disappear without warning. Jake pulled his phone out of the pocket of his black cargo shorts and tapped on the screen. "Let's take care of it, now." He spent a few minutes typing, and then let me read it.

"Hey Andrew," he'd written. "Jess and I appreciate your reaching out, and she had fun with you, but unfortunately, we've had some circumstances come up that have made it so she can't see you anymore. Please know that it's not about you, just real life getting in the way. Thanks for understanding, and we hope you find what you're looking for with someone else."

I looked at him and nodded. "Perfect," I said. I hoped that Andrew would take what Jake had written seriously, and not contact us again. That he wouldn't contact *me*.

"With a dick that big, he shouldn't have any trouble getting laid," Jake said, smiling.

I forced a laugh. *Please let this be the last time we talk about Andrew,* I thought. I worried if he kept coming him up, I might cave and tell Jake everything.

My phone vibrated on the nightstand, and even though it was late, I grabbed it, reflexively, and checked the notification, expecting for it to be from another agent or one of my clients. Instead, I saw a text from a number I didn't recognize, but instantly knew who had sent it. A chill shot up my spine.

"You'll be back for more," it said. "It's only a matter of time."

I swallowed hard, and my stomach suddenly felt full of twisting, slithering snakes. I deleted the text, and blocked that number, too, wondering if Andrew had a second cell phone or if he had picked up a disposable one for the express purpose of contacting me, since I'd blocked him. Either way, his behavior was frightening. *Goddamn it,* I thought. *How am I going to get him to leave me alone?* I'd need to remember to block his email address so he wouldn't keep reaching out to me, there, too. Or maybe I should delete that account all together, to be safe. I could tell Jake it was better to not leave it active, if we weren't going to use it.

"What's up?" Jake asked.

"Nothing," I said, as lightly as I could as I set my phone back down. I rolled over and smiled at him. "Work stuff." *Shit, shit, shit!* I hated lying to him.

"We need a vacation."

"I wish," I replied. Our current work schedules made taking time off together almost impossible.

"How about a mini-vaca, tomorrow?" Jake asked. "We can work a few hours, but spend most of the day at the pool with the kids?"

"Just what teenagers want, to hang out with their parents!"

"Tough," Jake said. "I say we do it. Whether they like it or not."

But in the morning, when we told the kids our plan, Tucker informed me that Peter was picking him up at ten o'clock to head to the jobsite. He also said he didn't have any clean clothes.

"Huh," I said, ruffling his dark hair. "I guess you're wearing dirty ones, then." He'd gotten spoiled with my mom around—when she wasn't with Helen, she'd kept herself busy with cleaning the house and taking care of both of her grandchildren's dirty clothes. The clean house I'd enjoyed, but I knew that once she was gone, it would be a struggle to get Tucker, especially, back in the habit of doing his chores.

"You're such a slacker," Ella said, tossing her long brown curls over one shoulder.

"Shut up, *Elf*-a," Tuck said, using the nickname he'd come up with for his sister when he was seven. Her ears actually were a little pointed at the tips, so of course she hated it.

"*You* shut up, *Smelly*," Ella said. Even at the tail end of fifteen, we still had to prod Tuck to take a daily shower and wash his bed sheets on a regular basis. He didn't seem to mind his own stink.

"Okay, you two," Jake said. "Knock it off." He looked at me. "What's on your schedule today? I already arranged to let Justine manage the office."

"I have to start entering the new development properties on the MLS, but I can do that from here." Earlier in the week, I'd met with the developer Peter had recommended me to—a stout, dark-haired woman in her fifties named Diane, who lived in the ritziest section of the Queens Ridge area with her husband, Chris. She had made her fortune by first flipping houses, and then eventually, used that capital to provide financial backing for new construction developments. She wasn't the warmest person I'd ever met—she seemed a little rigid, actually, and clearly disappointed that I graciously turned down her invitation for me and my family to come visit her church. But ultimately, my professional track record was enough for her to list all of the houses in the development with me. It was a huge win, so I'd sent Peter a case of his favorite Scotch as a thank you, as well as hiring a maid service for the rest of the summer for Kari, since her pregnancy was making her so sick. The commissions I stood to earn from the sales were astronomical, so I figured these gestures were the absolute least I could do.

"When are we going to the pool?" Ella said. "I Snapped Bentley and told her she and her mom should meet us there."

"Oh, good," I said, thinking it would be nice to have my friend to hang out with, too. She and Jake always got along. "I think we'll probably head over around noon? It's going to be a hot one." It was the third Saturday in July, and the temperature was supposed to reach ninety-seven.

"You just want to go so you can flirt with *Carter*," Tuck said. He grasped his hands together and put them next to his cheek, batting his long, dark lashes. "'Oh, Carter is so *hot*. I wish he would come over and *rub lotion* on my back!'"

Ella's arm shot out and punched her brother's shoulder. "Shut up!"

"Ow!" Tuck howled, grabbing his arm.

"Who's Carter?" I asked, choosing to ignore their bickering.

"Yeah," Jake said, smiling. "Who's *Carter*?"

"Don't say anything!" Ella warned her brother, shooting him a dirty look.

Tucker smirked. "He's a life guard. He's in *college*."

"I'm going to *kill* you, Tuck!" Ella screeched, but her brother only laughed and jumped out of her reach.

"How old is this boy?" I asked my daughter, but she was too busy charging at Tuck, who ran for the safety of the stairs, heading up to his bedroom. She chased him, still threatening to kill him. I looked at Jake, deciding that getting the listings into the system could wait. "I guess we'd better get to the pool."

THE community center's parking lot was packed by the time we got there, so we had to walk quite a ways to get to the entrance, where we showed our season passes and then headed inside. Charlotte had texted and said that she and Bentley had saved us a few lounge chairs at the far end of the pool, so once we spotted her, we made our way over.

"Hey," Charlotte said, using her hand as a visor to look up at us. She wore a hot pink string bikini and huge, black movie-star sunglasses. Her red hair was in a tight bun on top of her head. "About time you got here."

"Sorry," I said as I dropped my bag to the ground. "Peter was late picking up Tuck." I kept my eyes on Ella, already sitting next to Bentley, who was lounging about four chairs down from us. Charlotte had put down towels and her beach bag on the chairs so no one else would take them. I watched as my daughter's gaze landed on a tan, handsome blond boy sitting in an elevated lifeguard's chair. When his eyes skimmed over the busy pool in her general direction, she threw her shoulders back and stuck out her chest. *Uh-oh.*

"She *was* going to work," Jake chimed in, as he spread his towel out over the chaise lounge next to me. He had on blue swim trunks and nothing else. "But we talked her out of it. Had to come check out this Carter character."

Charlotte laughed. "Oh yeah. He's *all* I've heard about for the last three weeks. He's a sophomore at Wazzu, home for the summer, and the reason our girls have been hanging out here practically seven days a week." She nodded her head in his general direction, and Jake's gaze landed on the boy both Bentley and Ella were currently smiling at.

"Hmm," Jake said. "Maybe he and I should have a talk."

"You should!" Charlotte said, cackling. "I could use the entertainment."

Jake gave me a quick kiss on the cheek, and then walked over to the edge of the pool, close to where Carter was sitting. Ella and Bentley watched him get closer to their crush, looking at Jake with wide eyes— horrified, I was sure, that he might say something embarrassing about them. Jake wiggled his fingers at the girls with a mischievous grin on his face, and then proceeded to jump in the deep end, which was full of bodies trying to cool off from the early afternoon sun. When he popped up again, he waved and got Carter's attention, saying something that made the boy frown. The girls scowled and picked up their phones— probably Snap-Chatting each other even though they were sitting right next to each other—and Jake continued to bob around in the pool.

Charlotte and I laughed as we watched this unfold. "I fucking *love* your husband," my friend said as she settled back against her lounge chair.

"Me, too," I said. "How are things with yours?" I kept my voice low, so our daughters wouldn't hear.

"Better," Charlotte said. "His doctor referred us to a urologist, and a couples' counselor who specializes in this kind of thing. Who knew there were such people?"

"Dick doctors?" I said, and Charlotte laughed again.

"We've been cuddling at night, though," she said, "which has been really nice. Talking, too."

"And Bryan?"

"Done," she said. "Over with. Kaput. The end. Thankfully, he understood. He wished us the best."

"I'm glad," I said. *Maybe he could have a talk with Andrew,* I thought, with more than a little bitterness.

"Me, too." Charlotte smiled. "We're nowhere near a hundred percent yet, but I feel like we're finally on the right track."

"That's great." I scanned the other side of the pool, my eyes landing on Tiffany and Lizzy lying next to each other. Tiffany wore a surprisingly sensible black one-piece—she was usually known for picking out bikinis that were better suited to girls our daughters' age—and Lizzy wore a blue and white polka dotted bikini; her blond, wavy hair hung loose around her shoulders. She was thinner than her mother—which was saying a lot, since Tiffany was, at most, a size 2. I watched as Lizzy sat up, and began to roam the perimeter of the pool, and when her eyes landed on a group of teenage boys standing together by the snack bar, she headed their way. Tiffany sat up and said something to her, but Lizzy flipped her off, lazily, and kept walking.

"Uh oh," I said to Charlotte, nodding toward them. "Are you seeing this?"

"What?" Charlotte asked, and then her gaze followed mine. We watched as Lizzy approached the group of boys, inserting herself into the middle of the small circle of their young and lightly muscular, tan bodies, smiling and tilting her head flirtatiously as she spoke to them. One of the boys hugged her, reaching down to grab her ass. My eyes flew back to Tiffany, who leapt from her chaise lounge, and marched over to the group. She grabbed Lizzy by her thin arm, but Lizzy yanked away, her face in a snarl er. The boys backed off and scattered, leaving Tiffany and Lizzy standing together, alone, arguing. Once again, Tiffany reached for Lizzy's arm, but Lizzy stepped backward, out of her mother's reach, and then ran off to the bathrooms.

"Lacy talked with Tiffany and Ben, right?" Charlotte asked.

"As far as I know, she talked to the parents of all the girls who had those accounts." I wondered how Tiffany and Ben had handled the issue with their daughter. From the looks of what just happened, it hadn't gone over well with Lizzy.

"Did you hear about Tiffany's mom?" Charlotte asked. "She got out of the house in the middle of the night and they had to call the police to find her. A silver alert, I guess it's called, when someone with dementia wanders off. Tiff posted on the Neighbors app when it happened, asking everyone to keep an eye out."

"No!" I said. I'd been so busy with talking to Andrew, I hadn't been paying much attention to the posts on the app. "That's so sad. They found her, I take it?"

"Yeah, but Tiffany decided to put her in a home so she'll safer." Charlotte shook her head. "Please shoot me if I start to lose my mind."

"That's basically what both of our moms said." The sun beat down on my bare shoulders, so I reached into my bag for the lotion I'd packed; I didn't want to get burned. But after a thorough search, I couldn't find the familiar bottle. "Shit," I said. "I forgot sunscreen. Can I use yours?"

"I didn't bring any," Charlotte said. Despite possessing a generally pale complexion, my best friend tended to tan instead of burn, something she attributed to the unknown ancestry of her father. I warned her all of the time that her blatant disregard for her skin put her at high risk for developing cancer, but she reasoned the that sun came out so little in Seattle, it wasn't that big of a deal. As with most decisions my best friend made, it was pointless to try to convince her to change her mind.

"Does Bentley have any?" I asked, as I leaned over and waded through the bag Jake had brought, too, but came up empty. I usually packed it for us both.

"I doubt it," Charlotte said. "She likes to tan, too."

I swung my legs over the side of the chaise, frustrated. "I swore I put in my bag," I said. "Maybe it fell out in the car."

"Oh, live a little!" Charlotte said, but I ignored her. The last thing I wanted was to deal with the itchy, biting sting of a sunburn.

"I'll be right back," I said, and then I headed toward the exit with my car keys in hand. My trajectory took me past Tiffany, and seeing the despondent look on her face, I hesitated, and then decided to approach her. "Hey, Tiff," I said.

She looked at me with tears in her blue eyes. "Hi!" she said, with a forced smile. She wiped her cheeks with the tips of her fingers. "Beautiful day, isn't it?"

"Are you okay?" I asked, ignoring her attempt at small talk.

"I'm fine," she said, blinking fast. "Is Ella here, too? Maybe she and Lizzy can hang out."

Ella and Lizzy were not friends, but I smiled and nodded. "Sure."

Tiffany put her hand over her eyes, looking in the direction of the snack bar. "I think she went to get an ice cream."

"I saw you guys arguing," I ventured. "After that boy grabbed her."

"Oh, that was nothing," Tiffany said. "They were messing around." But her eyes told a different story. Clearly, she was aware of what Lizzy was doing, and had no idea how to handle it. I couldn't imagine that Ben would be of much help when it came to something like that. He was an affable guy, but as Jake had pointed out, I couldn't remember him ever doing anything parental with their kids.

Deciding to take a chance, I reached out and put my hand on her forearm. Her skin was warm, and felt paper-thin. "You can always talk to me, if you need to, Tiff. Teenagers can be hard to deal with."

"I appreciate that, but I'm fine," Tiffany said.

"I'm sorry to hear about your mom, too."

"Thank you," she said, and her shiny façade finally cracked. I noticed the dark circles under her eyes, and the fan of crow's feet at the corner of her blue eyes. She clearly hadn't been getting enough sleep. "It's the worst thing I've ever had to do."

"I can only imagine. I'm around, if you need a shoulder, okay? I mean it. Call or text me, anytime."

She pressed her lips together and nodded.

"Okay," I said. "I'll talk with you later."

She nodded again, and I quickly made my way to our car. But as I approached, I noticed a small piece of paper under the driver's side windshield wiper. I grabbed it, unfolding it with a sense of dread.

"I miss you already," the note said, and I had no doubt who it was from. My body went rigid, and I swiftly glanced around the lot, wondering how the hell Andrew knew that we were here. I didn't know what kind of car he drove, and it didn't make sense to walk around looking for him, but I did, anyway. He was nowhere to be found.

I felt sick as I crumpled up the note and tossed it in a garbage can near my car. I popped open the trunk and sure enough, the spray can of sunscreen was in the corner. I grabbed it, locked the car, and looked around again to see if Andrew was watching me. He must have followed us here, and the thought of that instantly made me want to call the police and report him as a stalker. But what would I say? That I'd fucked this man a few times while keeping the full truth about my interactions with him from my husband, and now he'd left a note on my car? It wasn't like he wasn't making overt threats toward me or my family. They'd probably laugh me out of the station.

On my walk back to the pool, I thought about how Andrew had insisted, the day he first called me at my office, that he *wasn't* a stalker, and I felt ill. Don't the things that we joke about tend to possess slivers of truth? I found myself wondering if it was a coincidence that he had found me on Facebook, or if he had set out, purposefully, to track me down after our first meeting. With his technical prowess, he may have been able to snoop through public records to find my divorce from Peter and subsequent remarriage to Jake. He'd pretended not to recognize me when we met for coffee—what else could he have lied about?

I considered going to confront him, but decided that giving him the attention he craved would only encourage his behavior. Better to ignore him, hope he'd get the message, and that eventually, like a child throwing a tantrum, he'd realize what he was doing wasn't working and stop.

And so, despite feeling a wobbly sense of apprehension, I plastered a smile on my face as I rejoined Jake and Charlotte at the side of the pool. "Found it!" I said, with mock cheerfulness, holding up the sunscreen like an Olympic medal. I looked over at Ella and Bentley, who were slathering their young skin with coconut oil, making it glisten in the sun.

"Hand it over, woman," Jake said. He held out his hand, and I dropped the spray can into it, feeling my jaw tremble. He gave me a concerned look. "You okay?"

"Yeah," I said, as brightly as I could. He knew me too well. "A little dehydrated, I think. I should jump in the pool." I paused, wanting to change the subject. "What did you say to Carter?"

"He asked him if he happened to know the age range for statutory rape in Washington!" Charlotte hooted, answering for him.

I laughed. "Oh god, honey. Ella's going to be pissed."

Jake shrugged as he sprayed his long arms with sunscreen. "Just doing my fatherly duty—scaring the crap out of any boy who might date our daughter."

"What's going on with Tiffany?" Charlotte asked. "I saw you guys talking."

"I told her I was happy to listen if she ever needed anyone to talk with about Lizzy or her mom," I said. "I wouldn't wish what she's going through on anyone." I looked over at Tiffany, who was once again lying next to Lizzy. She wasn't the only person putting on a mask, acting like nothing was wrong.

She wasn't the only one afraid that her world might be on the verge of spinning completely out of control.

Twenty
Four

The next few weeks of summer passed quickly, without a word from Andrew. As soon as I put the development that Peter was building on the market, I had offers on over half of the houses, so I was busy meeting with clients and sending paperwork back and forth with other agents, in addition to ferrying Tucker to the job site on some days so he could work for his dad. Every time my phone vibrated, my stomach lurched, afraid that it might be Andrew, but thankfully, he seemed to have gotten whatever it was he had been trying to prove out of his system.

Still, I vigilantly checked the area surrounding our house or my office every time I was outside, looking for any sign of Andrew sitting in his car, waiting to follow me or my family again, but he was nowhere to be found. Gradually, I let myself relax a little, choosing to focus on spending quality time with my husband. With Ella working most nights and Tuck staying with Peter and Kari more often than not, Jake and I went out for dinner a couple of times a week, coming home to a quiet house where we took advantage of the time alone. His new employees were actually able to manage a lot for Jake, now, so he was back to working closer to fifty hours a week instead of the eighty he had been since deciding to expand the company.

"It's kind of weird that we never heard back from Andrew, after that last email," Jake remarked on an early August evening. We were in our bedroom, lying on our backs and holding hands, enjoying that floaty, blissful post-sex space.

Anxiety coursed through me when he mentioned Andrew. "Not really," I said, hoping I sounded convincingly casual. "We told him we were done seeing him, so maybe he felt like there wasn't anything more to say."

"I guess so," Jake said, rolling over onto his side and extracting his hand from mine so he could rest it on my stomach. He tucked his other arm under his pillow and looked at me. "You never told me the details of what it was like to be with him. We had that quickie when you first got home, but that was it."

My insides froze, and I hoped Jake didn't notice how my body suddenly tensed. "Honestly, it wasn't that great," I lied. I turned my head, and his blue eyes bored into mine.

"Even though you stayed with him so long that night?" Jake asked, and I might have been mistaken, but I swear a heard a whisper of suspicion behind his words. That was another thing about lying to someone you loved; you lived on the paranoid edge of fear.

"Yeah," I said, struggling to find a way to explain that particular disparity. "He was sort of a marathon guy, so it took a long time for anything to happen for both of us. It wasn't like he was especially memorable or anything like that." I couldn't say that sex with Andrew was better than sex with my husband, because it wasn't true. However, fucking Andrew *was* different than being with Jake, intoxicating in a way I'd never felt before. That's why it was so dangerous, and why I had to never see Andrew again.

THE next afternoon, I was at the office when I got a call from Diane, the real estate investor for whom I listed all of the houses in the development Peter was in charge of building.

"Hi, Diane," I said, tucking my phone between my ear and shoulder as I sat at my desk with the door closed. I typically worked with it open, but the agent across the hall had a tendency to yell when she was on the phone, making it impossible for me to concentrate. "I was just finishing up another contract for you to sign. Maybe we could meet up later tonight?"

"Are you on the Neighbors app?" she said, ignoring my question. Her tone was sharp, accusatory—it made my stomach twist.

"I am," I said, wondering if someone had posted something derogatory about the development. Peter mentioned that there had been some grumbling from a couple of environmental groups about the project taking down a substantial swath of evergreens, but since Diane had made sure to go through all of the proper permitting and environmental impact processes with the city, there was really nothing anyone could do to stop it from happening.

"I think you'd better look at it," Diane said. "Now."

"Okay," I said, drawing out the word. I grabbed for my wireless mouse and navigated to the Neighbors website on my laptop, which was another way to access everything that was posted on the app.

"I'm calling to let you know that I've decided to go with another agent for the remainder of the houses," Diane said. "I'd appreciate it if you wouldn't fight me on this."

"Wait," I said, a fluttering sense of panic took over my chest. I logged into the Neighbors site, and my eyes instantly went to the post at the top of the list with the heading: JESSICA SNYDER IS A WHORE.

I closed my eyes, hoping they were playing tricks on me. But when I looked again, the bold, black heading was still there. I clicked on the post, feeling like I might vomit. There were several emails—things I'd written on the private, anonymous account I shared with Jake—I had blocked Andrew's email address, but I hadn't gotten around to talking with Jake about deleting the account altogether. The quotes from my emails were filled with graphic descriptions: "I'd love to get you between my legs again" and "I can't wait to feel your cock inside of me." The emails spelled out in detail that I wanted to have sex with men and then tell my husband about it, later. There were pictures of me in the post, too—the discreet versions without a face that we sent to prospective play partners, but for anyone that knew me, it would be easy to recognize my general body shape and curly brown hair. But the most baffling aspect of the post was that it looked like it had been put up *by* me—my moniker on the Neighbors app was simply my name, and there it was, right next to the headline: *Posted by Jessica Snyder.* Someone had clearly hacked into the email Jake and I shared, *and* my Neighbors account.

"Oh my god." My heart thumped an errant rhythm inside my chest as tears pricked my eyes. I almost forgot that Diane was still on the line, and had taken away what would have been a huge chunk of commission from the remaining houses I had to sell in the development. But that was nothing compared to the feverish, desperate terror I felt knowing that this post was being read by the majority of Queen's Ridge residents.

"I hope you think long and hard at what kind of example you're setting for your children," she said. "But at least now I understand why you didn't accept my invitation to visit our church."

"Diane, please," I said. My head was spinning. How many people had already seen the post?

"I've made up my mind," Diane said. She hung up.

I held my phone and stared at the screen, blinking fast, noting that I had received several text messages during my call. I tapped on the one from Charlotte, feeling like I was in a thick fog,

"What the actual fuck?!?" she said. "Have you seen the post on Neighbors? Call me. NOW!!!!"

The tears that had been threatening my eyes began to fall. Everyone was going to know what I'd done. All of my neighbors. My boss. My clients. My friends. How did this *happen*?

Andrew. It had to be him. I didn't know anyone else with a reason to want to hurt me and the technical skills to pull something like this off. But why? Because I rejected him? Would he really be so vindictive?

My phone rang again, and this time, it was Charlotte. I answered, feeling sick, confused, and numb.

"What the fuck is going on?" she said, not bothering to say hello.

"I don't know," I said. My voice cracked. "I didn't post it. Someone hacked into my Neighbors account."

"Then where the hell did the emails come from?"

I was silent, not knowing how to answer.

"Jessica, you have to delete it. Now."

I tried to do just that, but for whatever reason, when I typed in my password that would log me in to the page that usually allowed me to put up new posts or delete old ones, I got an error message. "It's not working," I told Charlotte, in a panic. "It won't accept my password."

"Shit," she said. "Whoever hacked in must have changed it. You should call Tiffany. She's the administrator, right? She should be able to delete your account altogether."

"It's too late," I said. "You know pretty much everyone gets the notifications on their phones when a post goes up. They're all going to think I'm a whore." *Oh god, the kids.* Both Ella and Tucker had the Neighbors app to stay on top of upcoming events for teenagers in the community, as well as for the pure entertainment of reading some of the ridiculous posts. I knew for a fact they both received the notifications in real time, as things went live, because they were usually the ones to tell me what was happening. My *children* were reading these emails. They were seeing the lusty words I'd written to other men; sexy pictures of their mother were plastered across their phone screen. "I have to go," I told Charlotte. Adrenaline charged through my veins, making me feel light-headed. "I have to call the kids and tell them not to look at the post."

"Oh *fuck*," Charlotte said. "I didn't think of that."

"I know. It just hit me." My chin trembled and my stomach roiled.

"Okay," Charlotte said. "Call them. And call Tiffany. Get her to take it down. Or wait. *I'll* call her. I'll tell her you got hacked. She has to know you wouldn't post this kind of bullshit about yourself."

I thanked her, feeling grateful that she hadn't demanded more of an explanation; she simply went into crisis mode, ready to do whatever she could to help. When I hung up, I saw a text from Jake: "What the fuck happened?!?"

"I don't know," I wrote. My entire body shook and my thumbs had a hard time typing out the words on the screen. "But I need to call the kids. I'll call you after." I'd have to tell Jake everything that happened with Andrew. Because how else would I explain this post? I couldn't make up more lies. I needed to tell him the truth.

"Let me call Tuck," he said. "You call Ella. Divide and conquer. Hopefully they haven't seen it yet."

God, please, please, please let them not have seen it. I clicked on the phone icon to call my daughter, and four rings later, she picked up.

"Hi honey," I said as brightly as I could manage, even though tears kept rolling down my hot, flushed cheeks.

"I don't even know what to say to you right now," she said. Her voice was tight.

I felt like I'd been punched. She'd seen it. She knew.

"I didn't post it. Someone hacked into my Neighbors account." My mind flashed to an image of Andrew, and white hot rage began to blur my vision. I was going to *kill* him for doing this. It was one thing to try to make me feel guilty for ending things, but it was a whole different level of fucked-up to break into my private email and then blast my most intimate secrets to my entire community.

"Really, Mom? Because there's another post, now, with screen shots of your texts with some guy named Andrew. Your *name* is on them."

"What?" I exclaimed, and then quickly used my mouse to refresh the Neighbors page. Sure enough, there was another post, directly above the first one, and it included a series of text messages between Andrew and me. Naked pictures of us both. Graphic, sexual descriptions of the things we wanted to do—and had done—to each other.

Oh fuck. Oh fuck oh fuck oh fuck.

"It's so *disgusting*, Mom!" Ella said, and I could hear the tears in her voice, too. "I'm so fucking embarrassed!"

"Oh honey, I'm sorry. I don't know what's happening. I promise I'll figure it out. Charlotte's calling Tiffany right now, asking her to take the posts down."

"It's too late," Ella raged. "Everyone's already seen it. They'll know you cheated on Jake!" Her voice went shrill with those last words, and then she started to sob. "How could you *do* that to him? He's so *good* to you! I thought you guys were so in *love*!"

"We are," I said, desperately wanting to comfort her. How could I have let this happen? Why did I sleep with Andrew? My gut told me not to, and I ignored it. I was a goddamn idiot. "I didn't cheat on Jake. I promise."

"You expect me to believe that?" Ella said. I could feel her fury through the phone. "After seeing all…that *stuff*? Everything you *wrote*? Jesus, Mom!"

"I'm sorry, baby girl," I said. My heart ached inside my chest. "Can we talk about it later, when you get home? I need to make sure that Tiffany is taking care of this." I wanted to find some way to do damage control, at least however much that was possible. Maybe she could prevent Andrew from accessing the Neighbors app? There had to be a way to know who it was that put up the posts, and keep him from doing it.

"I never want to talk about this with you again," Ella said, and then she hung up on me.

I sat at my desk, holding my phone in one hand, in total shock. Then I realized that if Ella had seen the second post, along with everyone else on the app, it was likely that so had Jake. My husband was going to know that I'd been lying to him about Andrew. He would know that I'd been texting this other man—that I'd sent Andrew my dirty thoughts and even dirtier pictures. He would read about how I'd ended up having sex in Andrew's office—*anal* sex—and then kept it a secret from my husband. He would know that I'd lied to him last night, when we'd talked about how being with Andrew hadn't been that great. I felt like a wrecking ball had slammed into my gut.

I closed my eyes and leaned back in my chair, ignoring the impatient buzzing of my phone, knowing that it was likely Charlotte or Jake, calling about the second post. My initial instinct was to run. I wanted to get in my car, drive away, and not look back. How could I face *anyone* after this? How could I walk down the street, go to work, go shopping, and be able to look my neighbors in the eye? I could imagine the juicy, chattering gossip already buzzing throughout Queens Ridge. I was always aware of it, even if I did my best not to participate. I never would have dreamed I'd end up at the center of it all.

But there was no escaping. I would have to talk to Jake. I would have to tell him everything. I'd have to witness the pain and disappointment my dishonesty caused him. I would have to find a way to explain myself, even though no matter how I framed it, there was simply no excuse for what I'd done.

"YOU *knew* him?" Jake said, disbelief widening his blue eyes. We were in our kitchen an hour after we had spoken on the phone when I was still at the office, each of us standing at opposite corners of the granite-topped island, like boxers preparing for a fight. Ella wasn't home, and thankfully, Tucker was still at the job site with his dad.

I'd called and texted Tiffany multiple times, but hadn't received a response. Charlotte called me back and said that she couldn't get through to

Tiffany, either, so I was still in panic mode, trying to figure out how to get the posts removed from the app. I was about to head over to Tiffany's house when Jake had pulled into our driveway, blocking my car in the garage.

"We need to talk," he'd said, with a glowering look. I'd never seen him wear that particular expression before—a nasty concoction of fury and hurt. I'd pressed my lips together and nodded.

"We worked together," I told Jake, now, giving him a look that pled for his understanding. "A long time ago. When I first moved here from Boise. He was the bartender at the restaurant where I waited tables for a few months. I honestly didn't realize it until we met for coffee. It had been almost eighteen years since I'd seen him. He looked like a totally different person."

Jake looked grim. "But you figured it out. And you didn't *tell* me?"

"I didn't think I'd have to, at first," I said, "because I wasn't going to see him again." I paused, feeling the tears begin to cut into my words. My chest felt like it was full of sharp knives. "It's my fault, completely. I should have told you right away. Especially when he called me at the office."

"What?" Jake yelled. "Are you fucking kidding me right now? How did he figure out how to do that? Did you give him our last name?"

"No!" I said, shrinking from his anger. I'd never seen him like this before. I quickly explained how Andrew said he'd found me through a mutual friend on Facebook, but that I later suspected he'd purposely sought me out. "I was a fucking idiot," I said, as an endcap.

"And the texts?" Jake asked. His face was a thundercloud, about to unleash. "The picture of you naked, in front of our bedroom mirror?" I'd been horrified when I saw that picture on the Neighbors app earlier; Andrew had covered my breasts and between my legs with some kind of blurry filter, but my face showed, and it was obvious I wasn't wearing any clothes.

"When you were out to dinner with job candidates at Daniel's Broiler," I said, aching with guilt. "When my mom was still here." I dropped my gaze to the floor. I couldn't look at him anymore. I was too ashamed. "It was wrong, I know. So incredibly wrong. I got sucked in to talking with him. Flirting. He got inside my head. I'm so, so sorry, babe. I fucked up."

"Yeah, you did," he said, angrily. He began to pace back and forth in front of the French doors, and then he stopped short and drove his gaze into me. I could feel it, even though my eyes were still on the floor. "Do you have feelings for him?" His voice shook.

"No," I said, vehemently. "Absolutely not. It was purely physical."

"Then why do this? Why did you *lie*?"

"I don't know. It wasn't like I sat down and rubbed my hands together, concocting ways to get away with it. I made a mistake by not telling you at the beginning. A fucking *huge* one. And then I didn't know how to fix it. I would do anything—*anything*—to take it back."

"You obviously must have felt something if you went to his office and fucked him without telling me about it. You kept that from me." I could taste the bitterness in his voice from across the room.

"I didn't go there for that. I was going to end it. And then it just… happened." I started to cry then, in earnest, putting my face in my hands. "I'm so sorry, baby. I feel like such a piece of shit."

He was silent for a long moment, and then said, quietly, "You're not a piece of shit."

I felt a surge of hope, and looked up at him. His eyes were still on me, and his expression had softened the tiniest bit. Tears streamed down my cheeks as I kept talking. "What I *did* was shit. I really messed up. I made stupid decisions. And I swear to God, I had *zero* romantic feelings toward him. It was physical chemistry. That's it. That was the only thing I felt."

"So the whole you fucking-someone-I-didn't-meet was a bad idea."

I sniffed and wiped my cheeks with the back of my hand. "My not telling you right away that I used to work with him was a bad idea. My agreeing to see him without you meeting him was a bad idea. *None* of this is about you. *I'm* the one who fucked up." I paused. "And now everyone in Queens Ridge thinks I'm a whore." A wave of revulsion washed over me as I thought about the two posts still up on the Neighbors app. My friends and coworkers seeing the words I'd written. The pictures I'd sent. I wrapped my arms tightly across the front of my body. I felt like if I released my grip, I might fall apart. "What did Tuck say?" I asked.

"He didn't answer his phone. I called Peter and made sure that he held on to it for the time being. At least until we can talk with him."

I cringed at the thought of my ex seeing the posts. "Did you tell Peter what's going on?"

"I told him that your Neighbors account had been hacked and someone had posted something offensive that Tuck shouldn't see."

"Okay," I said. But I knew that it was only a matter of time before one of Tuck's friends showed him the pictures and screen shots of the texts between Andrew and me. Now that the posts had been up for a couple of hours, they were part of the internet ether—even if Tiffany took them down and closed my account, someone could have easily taken screen shots of them, or saved the pictures. There was no way to make them disappear altogether. They were out in the world, and linked to my name. The thought made me want to find a hole to crawl into and hide. An ancient shame burned inside my chest. Despite how "strong" I was, I'd still adhered to the generally accepted belief that "nice" girls didn't have voracious sexual appetites. Nice girls didn't fuck men other than their husbands. And now that I had, everyone in my immediate world knew about it. I didn't know how to cope.

"How was Ella?" Jake asked.

"Not good."

"I'm sorry."

"Me, too." I started to cry again, my shoulders shaking, and this time, Jake made his way over to me and took me into his arms. I sobbed into his chest, experiencing a level of remorse and embarrassment I never had before. It felt like I'd been poisoned. "I'm so sorry," I kept saying, my words muffled against my husband's chest. He cupped my head with one hand and rubbed a soothing circle on my back with the other.

"It'll be okay," he said, and I was equally overwhelmed with gratitude for his embrace and disgust at myself, for knowingly putting our marriage in danger.

"You don't hate me?" I asked him, my voice trembling.

"I'm upset," he said, "but I could never hate you. I *do* hate the fucker who put up those posts." He pulled away, his blue eyes flashing with intent. "You know where he lives, right?"

I nodded, feeling a growing sense of trepidation. I didn't like the threatening edge I heard in his voice.

"Take me there," he said.

And even though I didn't want to, even though I was terrified of what would happen when Jake and Andrew came face-to-face, I grabbed my purse and followed my husband, knowing that after everything I'd done, I didn't have the right to tell him no.

Twenty Five

It was rush hour, so it took us almost an hour to get to Andrew's house in Kirkland. While we sat in traffic, I kept trying to get through to Tiffany, but every time I called, it went straight to voicemail and all of my texts to her went unanswered. When we were a few blocks away from Andrew's, a text came in from Nancy, my boss: "I need to see you in my office tomorrow morning. First thing."

"Shit," I muttered, knowing exactly what she was going to want to talk with me about.

"What is it?" Jake asked as he turned the corner onto Andrew's street.

"Nancy wants to talk to me."

"She's on the app?"

"Everyone at the office is." I tried to swallow the sharp knot that had formed in my throat, but to no avail. I wondered if Andrew was even home—it was a little past six-thirty, so I assumed that he would be. I hadn't wanted to text or call to warn him that we were coming. Better to catch him off guard, and hope that we would be able to talk some sense into him and he'd take the posts down.

Jake parked on the street, and then we made our way up the walkway to Andrew's front door. Jake pounded on it. I crossed my arms in front of my chest; my shoulders were hunched forward.

It only took a few seconds for Andrew to open the door, and he had the audacity to look smug when he saw us. He held out his hand. "You must be Jake," he said. "Nice to finally meet you."

Jake batted his hand away. He seemed taller than usual, somehow, more imposing, as though his anger had increased his stature. "You need to take the posts down," he said, through gritted teeth. "Now."

Andrew raised his thick brows. "Posts? What posts?"

My fingers curled into fists at my side. I wanted to hit him. "Don't pretend it wasn't you."

"Wasn't me that…what?" He let his voice trail off, his expression bemused.

Jake took a step toward him and Andrew held up his hands, palms facing us. "Careful, now, Jake. I haven't invited you in. You don't want me to call the police and have you arrested for unlawful entry."

"They're going to have to arrest me for assault if you don't get on your fucking laptop and take down those posts," Jake growled. "I don't know how you did it, but it's illegal. Plan on getting a visit from the police, yourself."

Andrew laughed. "Oh, that's funny. The police don't have time for petty little shit like this."

"So you admit it was you?" I said. Looking at him now, all I felt was disgust. I couldn't believe that I'd let him affect me the way that he did. I couldn't believe I was attracted to him at all.

His dark brown eyes landed on me. "I'm not admitting anything. I'm simply assuming, from what you're saying, that someone posted something about you online that you don't like?" He moved his eyes to Jake. "If that's true, my guess is that whoever did it is technically gifted enough not to leave behind any trace that could lead back to him. Or her." He paused. "Let's just say I've heard of people attaching something called a key-logger to a picture they send someone, like a virus. And that does exactly what it sounds like. It logs every key someone types on their laptop or phone and sends it to the other person's computer. Passwords, even. Once someone has those, everything else is easy. Like *changing* the password so the person whose account it actually is can't log back in."

"You mother *fucker*," Jake said, and it looked like he was about to lunge at Andrew, so I grabbed him by the arm.

"Honey, don't," I pleaded. "He's not worth it."

"That's not what you were thinking when I bent you over my desk and fucked you in the ass," Andrew said.

Jake's fist hit shot out before I could stop it, landing a solid punch. Andrew stumbled backward, his hand clamped over his right cheek.

"God*dammit!*" he yelled, but with a high-pitched edge, as he leaned forward at the waist. I suddenly saw a flash of the geeky bartender I used to know behind his eyes.

"If you ever come near my wife or me again, I'll fucking *kill* you," Jake said. The muscles of his jaw worked under his skin. "Do you understand me?"

Andrew didn't speak, but he nodded, his hand still covering one side of his face. He looked scared, which made me glad.

"Good," Jake continued. "Now, if those posts aren't deleted in the next ten minutes, I'm going to come back here and finish what I started. And if the police show up at my house, talking about charging me with assault, you'll regret it. You'll never see me coming."

I didn't know this side of Jake existed. I hated that my actions had pushed him to this point. But at the same time, it felt like I had never loved him more.

"You're a fucking bastard," I told Andrew, as Jake and I were turning to leave. "And karma is a bitch." I wish I felt as strong as I sounded. "Why did you *do* this?"

"We had something special," he said. "And you threw it away."

"It wasn't special," I snapped. "It was nothing. It was just sex." I looked at Jake—at the violent, dark storm that had taken over his face—and again, I couldn't believe I'd done anything to jeopardize our relationship. The blip of excitement I'd experienced with Andrew was so utterly shallow and meaningless compared to what Jake and I shared. And not only in bed. We shared a *life*, an imperfect, messy, too busy, but amazing life.

Andrew looked as though he might say more, but then glanced at Jake, and thought better of it.

My phone rang as Jake and I had climbed back into his car, and I grabbed it out of my purse. The caller ID showed that it was Tiffany. "I've been trying to reach you for hours," I said, urgently. "I need you to delete my account from Neighbors right away. It's been hacked."

"What?" Tiffany said. Her voice sounded scratchy and muffled, like she'd been crying. "I'm at the hospital with Lizzy."

"Oh my god!" I said. "Is she okay? What happened?"

"She snuck out last night with a college boy who works at the pool. Carter, I think? She drank too much and passed out. A few girls at the party found her in a bedroom and couldn't wake her up, so they got scared and called 911. She has alcohol poisoning. And someone wrote "slut" on her forehead in black ink." Her words stumbled out slowly, awkwardly, as though she couldn't believe what she was saying was true. "Apparently, she had another account on Instagram that Lacy didn't know about. It was worse than the first. I'm reading through her direct messages and the things she talked about *doing* with these boys...what she said she'd let them do to her...." Her voice broke and she trailed off, not finishing her thought.

"Oh god, Tiff, I'm so sorry," I said. Jake touched my arm, questioning. "Is she going to be okay? Was she...?" I trailed off, unable to ask an unfathomable question.

"No," Tiffany said, sniffling. "Thank god. No evidence of that. The doctor said she's going to feel like shit, but she'll be fine. She can go home in the morning."

"I'm so glad. I can't even imagine how scared you must have been. Is Ben with you?"

"He's in Portland, at a car auction, but he's on his way. The boys are with a sitter."

"Do you need anything? I can be there, with you, until Ben shows up." My head was still spinning from everything that had happened over the last few hours, but the thought of Tiffany sitting alone in a hospital waiting room, or next to Lizzy's bed, was heart-breaking.

"No, no, that's okay." Her voice held a forced brightness. "What was that you said about the Neighbors app? I haven't looked at it since this morning."

"I really hate bothering you with this now," I said, "but somebody hacked my account and posted some pretty slanderous stuff. I can't log in.

You're the administrator, so is there any way you could please delete my account altogether?" I didn't want to risk Andrew not taking down the posts. "Only if it's not too much of a hassle. I know you have so much going on…." I flinched, thinking about how she would read the posts first. Even if I asked her not to read them, she would do it anyway. I know I would have, if the tables were turned.

"Okay," Tiffany said. "No problem. I'll do it when we hang up."

"Thank you," I said. Even though the damage had already been done, my body flooded with relief. "I'll check in with you later. And please let me know if I can watch the kids or something, when the sitter has to leave."

"I'm sure Ben will go home after he stops here, but thank you," Tiffany said. "Really. It means a lot." She spoke with sincerity, and I was glad that I had stopped to talk with her at the pool the other day.

"Of course," I said. We hung up, and I saw an all caps text from Charlotte: "WHAT THE FUCK IS GOING ON???"

I quickly tapped out a response: "Too much to text. Tiffany's deleting my account. I'll talk with you later."

"What happened?" Jake asked as he pulled away from the curb. The knuckles on his right hand were already puffy and red; they would likely be bruised by tomorrow morning.

I told him about Lizzy, and that Tiffany was going to delete my account. We drove toward home in total silence after that, a sick feeling still plaguing my stomach. I hoped that our visit to Andrew had convinced him to leave us alone, and that he wouldn't report Jake to the police for assault. I worried that he might use his technical skills to harass us in other, more devious and damaging ways. I worried that the texts and pictures that had been posted would ruin my career. I hadn't even told Jake about losing the last part of the development deal. I wondered how

I was going to explain to my children the complexities of an adult sexual arrangement—that I hadn't been cheating on Jake. In their eyes, I was just a mom, not a woman with desires and needs. I didn't know how to make sense of it for them. Or anyone else, for that matter. The whole of Queens Ridge were, without a doubt, already judging me for what they'd seen about me. They'd judge Jake, too, I was sure, for "letting" his wife fuck other men, but when it comes to sex, no matter how equal the treatment of both men and women is purported to be, I knew that Jake would get off easier than me.

"You okay?" Jake asked as we pulled into our driveway. Ella's car was nowhere to be seen, which concerned me, but then I realized that she was likely at work.

"No," I said. "I'm not." I was exhausted and physically aching, like I'd been flogged. I looked at him, my eyes filling with tears once again. "I fucked everything up. I don't know how to fix it."

He stared ahead for a minute, his arms ramrod straight, hands at ten and two, still gripping the steering wheel. "It's not the end of the world," he finally said.

I nodded, but I couldn't help but feel that he was wrong. That I'd broken something between us past the point of mending, and that our life together might never be the same again.

ELLA didn't come home that night after work. Peter texted me around eleven, saying that she'd come to his house, and wanted to spend the weekend, which was unusual, because she'd already spent the entire week there. Normally, she and Tuck spent the summer weekends with us.

"Did she tell you what happened?" I replied.

"Yeah," he said, with his typical brevity.

"Tuck, too?" I asked, as acid roiled in my stomach. I hadn't eaten anything since lunch; I was too nauseous.

"Yeah. But he didn't see the pictures."

I cringed, knowing that Peter had surely been told what the posts were about, and that Ella had shared the details not only with him, but with her brother.

"It's complicated."

It took a minute for him to respond. "None of my business."

I pressed on. "My account was hacked." But the emails and texts were real; the pictures, too. A fresh wave of embarrassment surged through me.

He didn't reply, and I didn't text anymore him after that.

I looked over at Jake's side of the bed, feeling a sharp pang inside my chest. It was empty, the covers still flat and tucked up under his pillow. Despite the brief comfort he'd given me earlier and confronting Andrew, he had retreated to the guest room for the night.

"I need some space," he said, and I knew it would have been pointless to try to argue. If he had done the same thing to me, I wouldn't have been able to sleep in the same bed with him, either. Maybe not even the same house.

I plugged my phone into the charger on the night stand, turned off the light, and closed my eyes, settling into my pillow. I took deep breaths, trying to relax, but my mind was littered with landmines—every thought I had exploded and sent me right back to the moment when I saw the first post. The horror I'd felt. The pure, unadulterated humiliation. I wondered what was being said about me in other Queens Ridge homes tonight.

I tossed and turned for hours—my body exhausted, my mind wired and alert—until finally, around four in the morning, I decided to get up and attempt to burn off the adrenaline raging through me. I skipped my usual morning coffee—I was jittery enough—and left Jake a note on the counter before heading out the door.

It was barely light. The air was still cool, and in the distance, the sun had peeked up behind the craggy, snow-topped Cascade Mountains, casting a pink and orange haze over the cloudless sky. I pumped my arms as I walked, trying to focus only on my breathing, and the balls of my feet, and then my heels, hitting the pavement. Even as I did, I had to fight off tears. The shame I felt in knowing that my most intimate behavior had been broadcast in such a public matter was astounding. I couldn't believe Andrew had sunk to that level. He had said that the police would never bother to get involved in something as petty as this. But there *had* to be some sort of repercussion, some punishment for what he had done. Wasn't it slanderous? Wasn't it an attack of my character? Wasn't breaking into my email and Neighbors account some kind of cyber-crime? I wondered if I should speak to a lawyer, but then realized if I did, it would only draw more attention to what I had done, and I didn't think I could handle that. Nor would I want to put Jake or the kids through anything more than they were already dealing with.

I wound my way through the neighborhood, until eventually, I found myself only a few blocks away from Charlotte's house. I glanced at my watch, thinking that it was way too early to knock on her front door, but I didn't know where else to go. Home, eventually, and then to the office to meet Nancy as she had requested, but right now, I needed my best friend.

When I knocked on her front door, it took her a few minutes to answer. She was in her pajamas, her hair was a mess, and her eyes were hooded from sleep, but she took one look at my sweaty, beet-red face and reached out her arms. "Oh honey," she said, and pulled me inside, and into a long, hard hug.

I let her hold me, and I began to sob, my tears wetting her shoulder. "Sorry I stink," I said, after the initial wave of sadness had passed. I'd forgotten to swipe on deodorant.

She laughed and released me, then closed the door behind us. "I need coffee," she said. "Come on."

I followed her into the kitchen, where I sat on a barstool and watched as she brewed a big mug from her Keurig machine. "Do you want one?" she asked, and when I said no, she grabbed a bottle of Pellegrino from the fridge and handed it to me before we headed outside to her patio. We sat on the thickly padded, wicker couch, and I took a few huge swallows of water while she drank her first sips of coffee.

"Okay," she said, still holding her mug. "Tell me everything."

And so I did, starting with the night Jake and I met Will at the club. Her eyes widened as she listened to me describe our sexual adventures, the things I had done with Jake, the lovers I'd spent time with on my own. I told her everything that happened with Andrew, how he got inside my head, and how I'd reacted. The things I kept from Jake. How caught up in the thrill of it all I'd been. She nodded when appropriate, but didn't speak until I finished up with what had happened last night, how we'd gone to Andrew's house and Jake had punched him. And that Ella and Tucker were staying with Peter, and Jake had slept in a separate room.

"So you went for a walk," Charlotte said, setting her now-empty mug on the table next to us.

"I had to. I'm fucking exhausted, but I couldn't sleep. I feel like I have ants crawling under my skin. And now I have to go see Nancy and god knows what *she's* going to say. I'm probably going to lose my job."

Charlotte scrunched up her face. "She can't fire you for having a sex life."
She paused. "Which I can't believe you didn't tell me about, by the way."

I frowned. "I know. I'm sorry. I wanted to, so many times, but with
your history with Alex, I was worried what you'd think of me."

She was quiet a moment, picking at the hem of her pajama top.
"That makes sense, I guess. But you weren't technically cheating, right?
Jake was a part of it."

"He was part of *all* of it. Every detail. Up until I started keeping
things from him about Andrew. I kept trying to rationalize that as long
as Jake knew about what was happening in a general way, leaving out a
few things here and there wasn't a big deal. It was stupid. So, so stupid."

"Yeah, well, I get it. I hid my interaction with Bryan from Richard, too."

I searched her face for any hint of judgment. "You don't hate me?"

"No!" Charlotte said, firmly. "Listen. You got fucked over by some
asshole who couldn't take it when you ended things with him. That's it.
You have nothing to be ashamed of. *He* does."

My eyes filled with tears, again. "No one else is going to see it that
way." I worried that Charlotte was she was on my side only because she
loved me. For as long as I'd known her, whenever she talked about Alex's
cheating, she tended to express less fury with him and more toward the
women who slept with her man. The specifics of a sexually charged
situation didn't seem to matter—the blame seemed to fall on the woman
instead of the man.

"So you'll put up an explanation, saying that your account was
hacked."

"But the pictures…the texts…" I cringed and pressed the heels of
my palms against my eyes. "I don't know what to say about them. About
what I did."

"You can say whatever the fuck you want," she insisted. "Your private sex life is nobody's business but yours. What this guy did *violated* you, and you don't owe anyone an explanation for what you choose to do with your body, or in your marriage. You don't have to give everyone a play-by-play of what really happened. All anyone needs to know is that your account was hacked. And then you hold your fucking head up high and let the stupid bitches gossip until they get bored and move on to something else. That's the way it works around here, and you know it."

I nodded and dropped my hands back into my lap, trying to believe that what she had said was true. Maybe I didn't owe most people in Queens Ridge a detailed explanation, but I would need to talk to Peter and the kids. And Nancy, today, to explain how I'd lost the development deal with Diane. I thought about Lizzy, then, too, wondering how she was doing, and promised myself that I would call Tiffany later. I also thought about Jake, sleeping alone in our guestroom, and my chest caved in. What if he wouldn't be able to forgive the fact that I'd lied to him, and more than once? What if he *left* me? I began to cry again, and Charlotte reached out and grabbed my hand.

"Hey," she said, squeezing my fingers. "I know it sucks, but it's going to be okay. I promise. This too shall fucking pass."

We sat together in silence, hand-in-hand, listening to the birds chirping in her backyard, both of us lost in our own thoughts, until I couldn't put it off any longer.

I went home to face the consequences of what I'd done.

Twenty Six

Charlotte drove me to my house because I was too exhausted to walk. "You've got this," she told me right before I climbed out her car. "You're stronger than you know."

I gave her a weak smile. I felt defeated and frail; my muscles ached and my eyes were gritty from lack of sleep. Shame thrummed through me with every breath. "Thanks," I said. "I'll call you later."

She waved at me as she pulled away from the curb, and I trudged inside. The house was quiet as I entered. "Jake?" I called out, my voice echoing in the tall-ceilinged entryway. He didn't answer. I glanced to my right. The door to the guest room was open, and the bed was rumpled, but empty. Panic seized me. Had he packed a bag and left while I was gone? Would I find a note on the counter, saying that he needed some time away?

I walked as fast as I could into the kitchen, but the only note I found on the counter was the one I'd left for him earlier. The air was rich with the scent of recently brewed coffee. And then, I saw him, through the French doors that led to our deck. He sat at the table with one hand on a mug; the steam from the hot liquid rose up in short wisps before they evaporated.

I smoothed my curls—a pointless endeavor after tossing and turning most of the night, followed by my sweaty excursion. "Hi," I said, as I opened the door and stepped outside. His salt-and-pepper hair stuck out all over his head, as though he had tossed and turned, too.

"Hi," he said. His voice was flat. He didn't turn around.

"I went to Charlotte's," I said, staying where I was. Normally, I would come up behind him and throw my arms around his shoulders, kissing the side of his cheek and nuzzling his neck. But I was afraid to touch him—terrified that he'd push me away. "I told her everything."

"Okay." He lifted his mug, took a sip, and then carefully set it back onto the table.

I crossed my arms over my chest, trying to ignore the rattling sensation in my chest. I loved him so much. I was desperate for him to say that he forgave me, but it was too soon. I couldn't push him. "I didn't sleep."

"Me neither," he said. "I heard you leave."

I felt another stitch of panic, worried that he had thought I might have gone to see Andrew again. If he had been the one to lie to me, that would have been the first place my mind would go. "You saw my note, right?"

"Yes."

"I'm so sorry, babe." My voice cracked, and once again, tears stung my eyes. "I know it's not enough and it doesn't fix anything, but you have to know that I never meant to hurt you."

"Right. You just figured I'd never know what you did."

I opened my mouth to protest, but then didn't speak a word, because that was exactly what I'd figured. I wanted to hide the mistake I'd made, the sins of omission I'd committed. I wanted to bury them, down deep, hoping they would never see the light of day. I hadn't counted on light's natural tendency to seek darkness out. The sun rises, slowly erasing the night, and eventually, so does the truth, illuminating a lie.

"I was wrong," I finally said. "In every sense of the word." He didn't respond, so I continued. "How's your hand?"

He held it up and I gasped at the dark purple and red, exaggerated swell of his knuckles. I'd never witnessed anyone punch someone else, let alone the aftermath of the act. I wondered what Andrew's face looked like this morning; my guess was that it wasn't good. "Let me get you some ice."

"It's fine."

"You might have broken something," I pressed. "You should probably get it checked."

"It's *fine!*" he said. His voice was like thunder.

"Sorry," I said, meekly. The tension between us was unbearable. In the years we'd been together, he'd never spoken to me in that tone or slept anywhere but next to me, unless he had to travel for work. He'd never had any reason to. I'd put everything we had together at risk, and for what? The temporary thrill of a few empty compliments from, and stolen moments with an attractive, charismatic man? What an idiot I had been. A tear rolled down my cheek and I quickly wiped it away.

"I put up a post on Neighbors," Jake said, ignoring my apology. "I said your account was hacked. I asked people to please respect our family's privacy."

"Oh, thank you." I exhaled a breath I hadn't realized I'd been holding. "I need to know something. Do you feel like I cheated on you?" It felt strange, having this serious conversation with the back of his head, but I didn't want to risk going over to him and having him stop talking to me altogether.

He sighed. "It's a weird line, Jess. On one hand, I knew you were fucking him, but I didn't know that you used to know him or that you were texting each other like that. Was that cheating, technically? Probably not. But you did break my trust by not telling me everything that was going on, so, I don't know what to think or feel right now. I'm processing."

I nodded, remembering a conversation we'd had early on in our relationship about the difference between what men and women typically need when they're in conflict.

"Men are basically primal," he told me. "We need to go into our cave and have time to work out whatever we're thinking and feeling before we can talk about it."

"And women process what we're thinking and feeling *by* talking it out," I said. "So how do we make that work? I'll go nuts if we're fighting and you shut down and refuse to talk."

He had smiled. "Just give me a little time to work it out inside my own head, first. Because the *worst* thing you can do is come marching into my 'cave,' demanding a conversation. I'll come out when I'm good and ready, and not before then."

"Okay, Fred Flintstone," I'd said, teasingly, and I remembered how hard he had laughed.

During the rare, serious arguments we'd had since then, I learned that if I respected his need for time in his "cave," if I backed off and let him come to me when he'd had a chance to calm down, we came to a quicker, less stressful resolution. But if I pushed him to talk, he only pulled away more, became angrier, and it took longer for us to sort things out.

"I'm meeting with Nancy in a bit," I told him. "And then I need to talk with the kids."

"What are you going to say?"

"I don't know. The truth, I guess. Or at least an abbreviated version of it." I paused. "Do you want to be there?" I held my breath again, hoping that he would say yes, that it was still important to him that we remain a united front, at least when it came to Ella and Tuck.

He finally turned around, then, and gave me a grim look. There were dark circles under his blue eyes and his complexion was sallow, as though he were ill. "No," he said. "But I will be."

My bottom lip trembled. "Thank you." I wanted to rush toward him, to throw myself into his arms. But his face was a closed door. "I'm going to get dressed," I told him, but he didn't answer. He had already turned away from me again, staring out into the gradually brightening sky.

An hour later, I'd had two cups of coffee and was in my car, on my way to the office. It was still early for a Saturday, only eight o'clock, so I hoped that there wouldn't be any other people at their desks. I checked my phone after I pulled into the parking lot, but there were no new texts or calls, nothing from my clients or any of my friends. Typically, my phone would light up on the weekend, clients asking me questions and friends reaching out to see if Jake and I had any plans. I flinched knowing that this lack of communication was likely due to every single one of them having seen the posts Andrew put up. The headline—JESSICA SYNDER IS A WHORE—blinked like a bright red neon sign inside my head.

The last thing I felt like doing was talking to Nancy, but I forced myself to go inside and straight to her office, where I found her already sitting on the couch across from her desk. She rose when I entered, and I took in what I knew she considered a casual Saturday outfit: slim-fitting, black linen pants, a loose white tunic, and strappy black sandals. Her brown bob was perfectly coiffed, as usual, one side tucked behind her ear, and she wore her signature red lipstick with no other makeup.

"Good morning," she said. "Thanks for coming in."

"Of course," I said, having a hard time meeting her intense, knowing gaze. We both sat down, she on the couch, and me in a chair across from her. I held my hands together in my lap and straightened my spine, trying to appear more confident than I felt.

"Diane called me last night," she said, pointedly. "After her conversation with you."

"I'm so sorry—" I started to say, but she cut me off.

"Please, let me finish," she said, and I nodded. She leaned forward before going on, resting her elbows on her knees. "You know I've always been fond of you. More fond than I usually am of my agents. I've watched you blossom from a young and inexperienced single mother to a strong and extremely capable businesswoman. Your sales record can't be beat. And while you work under the name of Kendall Properties, you're actually an independent contractor, and I can't control what you do with your business. Or your personal life."

I swallowed hard. It took everything in me not to let my eyes drop to the ground, bracing myself for what she was going to say to me next. She'd seen the posts, and was going to ask me to leave the company. I was going to lose my job.

"I'm sorry for what happened to you on Neighbors," she said. Her gray eyes were suddenly full of compassion, and I relaxed, the tiniest bit. "I can't imagine what you must be feeling right now. It's horrible, that kind of violation of your privacy. But I want you to know that it doesn't matter to me. Diane made a stink, demanding that I let you go, and I basically told her to stick it where the sun doesn't shine."

Relief rushed through me and I had to fight off the tears of gratitude that rose in my eyes. "Oh god, Nancy," I said. "Thank you. I thought you were going to fire me."

"I wouldn't do that," she said.

"This whole thing was something Jake and I explored together," I said, anxious to defend myself. But she held up her hand.

"It's none of my business, and I'm in no place to judge. I'm just happy I did all my stupid shit before the dawn of social media. Let me tell you, if some of the things I did during my first divorce had been posted online, it wouldn't have been pretty. I probably would have lost my business."

I nodded, intensely curious to know what she was referring to, but it wasn't the time to ask. I was grateful that she wasn't going to ask me to sever my connection to Kendall Properties.

"I asked to see you in person because I really want to be sure you're prepared to deal with office gossip," she said. "Because you know it will happen. They might not say anything to your face, but there will no doubt be some tension and behind-your-back chatter going on. It might make it difficult to come to work for a while."

I nodded, and fell back against my chair, wishing I could take time off, but being self-employed, I couldn't afford to. I had upwards of seven deals in process, with well over six-figures due to come in. I couldn't sacrifice that, especially with the loss of the rest of the houses Peter was building for Diane.

"I'll manage," I said. "I can work from home a bit more, if I have to. Until this all blows over." As an agent, I didn't actually need to be in the office except for when I had floor hours, but having a place other than home helped me keep at least the illusion of separation between my work and personal life, so I typically made an appearance at Kendall Properties at least for a few hours every day. I enjoyed talking with other agents, answering questions for the newer ones, and taking up Nancy on any bits of money-making wisdom she had to offer. I imagined that now, with my personal life made so public, chatting with my coworkers wouldn't be nearly as enjoyable.

"That sounds good," Nancy said. "Let me know if you need anything."

"Thank you." I stood up, then, and so did she. We didn't have a hugging kind of relationship, so I held out my hand, and she shook it.

"You'll get through this," she said, encouragingly, as I made my way to her door.

"Thank you," I said, again, and then I went back out to my car. I knew that Peter was an early riser, even on the weekend, so before I drove to his house, I called him. "Are the kids up, yet?" I asked, when he answered the phone. I heard the TV on in the background, then a screeching Ruby, and Kari's sharp, but muffled response.

"Yeah, but barely," Peter said, gruffly.

"Is it okay for me and Jake to come over? I need to talk to them."

"Yeah," Peter said, and I thanked him. I texted Jake, letting him know that I was headed over to Peter's house, and he answered right away, saying that he'd meet me there. I was already drained from the tumult of the last sixteen hours or so, more tired than I think I'd ever been. But I didn't have a choice. I had to talk with the kids.

It only took me fifteen minutes to get to Peter's house from the office. I parked on the street, and waited for Jake, wanting us to go inside together. While I was sitting there, I got a text from Ella.

"I don't feel like talking," it said.

I took a deep breath before responding. "I don't either, but we need to. It won't take long. I'm waiting for Jake."

"I don't want to talk with him, either!" she said, and before I could reply, Jake's SUV rounded the corner. He parked on the opposite side of the street from me, and I got out and shut my car door as he approached.

"Thanks for coming," I said, trying to read his face for what he might be feeling. His lips were drawn in a hard, straight line. He had showered and changed into a pair of tan cargo shorts and a white T-shirt. He looked as tired as I felt.

"What did Nancy say?" he asked as we walked toward Peter and Kari's front door. I told him, quickly, and he nodded in acknowledgment, but didn't say anything more.

I rapped on the door, lightly, and heard Ruby yelling, unintelligibly. There was a loud, but inaudible response, and a moment later, Peter welcomed us inside. He had built this house for him and Kari, back before Ruby was born. It had an enormous entryway that led directly into an open-spaced kitchen/family room, where Ella and Tuck sat on a large sectional couch, their eyes glued to the huge flat screen that was hung over the fireplace, where cartoons were playing. Ruby was at the square dining room table, which was in between the kitchen and couch. She was on a chair with a small bowl in front of her, wearing an Elsa-from-Frozen light blue nightie. Her brown, angel-puff of hair made it clear she had only recently gotten out of bed. At six years old, she was petite, like her mother, and according to Ella and Tucker, stubborn like her dad.

"Hi, you two," Kari said from her spot in front of the kitchen sink. She looked tired, too, that almost indescribable bone-tiredness I remembered so well from both of the first trimesters of my pregnancies.

Her blond hair was in a messy bun and she wore a red and baggy Wright Contractors T-shirt.

Both Jake and I said good morning at the same time, trying to ignore the thick tension in the room. Neither of the kids greeted us.

"Thanks for letting us come over so early," I said, looking at both Peter and Kari.

"I have *yogurt!*" Ruby announced, and accidentally knocked her bowl to the floor, splattering her breakfast everywhere.

Kari sighed. "Let me clean her up and we'll get out of your way," she said. "Can you help me, honey?" She looked at Peter, but he shook his head.

"I've got a meeting at the job site at nine-thirty," he said. He grabbed his keys from the counter, and I felt a pinch of empathetic anger on Kari's account, remembering how he so often used to leave me to take care of the kids on my own when we were married, too.

"Can I talk to you for a sec?" I asked Peter, and Jake gave me a quick, concerned look. "It's fine," I told my husband, and then I followed my ex outside, to his truck, which was parked in the driveway.

"So, I know this is all really crazy," I began, and as I had with Nancy, I tried to appear more confident than I felt.

Peter adjusted his baseball cap and looked away from me. "Like I said, none of my business."

"Well, it is, kind of," I countered, not letting him escape the conversation just yet. "Because of the kids. If they talk with you about it, I hope you'll reiterate that what was posted should have stayed private, but my email and my Neighbors account were hacked. Maybe use it as a way to talk to them about being careful what they put online. And if you can, try not to bad-mouth me."

"You think I would?" Peter said, slightly raising his black brows. His voice was rough.

I took in a deep breath and then released it. "No. Sorry. This is all really hard." My chest felt hollow, and tears stung my eyes.

"You okay?"

"Not really."

"You will be." He met my gaze and I felt a flicker of comfort—as though we were friends, or at least, as ex-spouses who shared a past and had brought two beautiful children into the world together, something akin to it.

"Thank you," I whispered.

He bobbed his head, his lips pressed together before he spoke. "So Jake hit the guy?"

"How did you know?" I asked, taken aback.

Peter made a fist.

"Oh, right," I said. I'd never thought of him as especially observant, but it wasn't the first time he had surprised me. "Anyway, I'm going to talk with them, and hope they come home with me, so we can work out how to handle all of this. I'm worried what their friends are going to say."

"They can stay, if they want," Peter said. "And good luck. Ella is pissed."

I cringed. "I know. What about Tuck?"

Peter shrugged. "He's embarrassed. He doesn't want to talk about it." He gave me a long look. "I don't blame him."

I sighed. "Yeah, well, that makes two of us."

He left, and I reentered the house to find the TV off and Jake sitting on the couch with Ella and Tuck. Kari and Ruby had disappeared, upstairs, presumably, for a bath, because I could hear water running and the pitter-patter of her bare feet as she ran up and down above us.

"Hey guys," I said, going to join my family. I sat down on the far corner of the sectional, a cushion away from Jake. The kids sat opposite of us, and both had their arms crossed over their chests, refusing to look at me. "Look, I know this sucks. And I'm so sorry it happened. I can't tell you how sorry I am. But we need to talk about it, at least a little, so I can help you figure out how to handle it."

"Your mom's right," Jake said, and I felt grateful for his support, considering what I'd put him through. I took it as a small sign that he had the capacity to forgive me; that we were still a team.

"What'd you do to your hand?" Tuck asked him. He still wouldn't look at me.

"That doesn't matter," Jake said.

"What matters is that mom had sex with other guys," Ella said. "Someone named *Andrew*." She spit out his name like it was poison.

"So you hit him?" Tuck asked Jake. He sounded impressed.

"I did," Jake admitted. "I shouldn't have, but my anger got the better of me."

"He stood up for me," I said.

Ella narrowed her eyes as she finally gazed in my direction. "I don't know why he would," she said. "You sent him disgusting text messages and naked pictures. It's so fucking embarrassing, I can't *stand* it!" Her face turned red, and tears shone in her eyes.

"Oh honey," I said, fighting back my own tears. "I'm sorry. But you have to know that it wasn't an affair. It's more complicated than that. Your step-dad…" I trailed off, unsure of how much I should tell them. They were teenagers, and for the most part, open with me about sex, as long as I kept it general and educational. I knew this conversation was as excruciating for them as it was for me. Maybe more so.

"I knew what your mom was doing," Jake said, saving me. "It was something we decided to do, together. But it was never meant for anyone else to know about. This man got angry, and hacked into your mom's email and Neighbors account."

Ella and Tuck were silent.

"So that's all you need to say, if anyone brings it up," I said. "That my accounts were hacked, and everything that happened was private and should have stayed that way."

"And that you should be careful what you do online," Tuck piped up. He looked at me with his light green eyes and frowned. "You weren't very smart, Mom."

I gave him a closed lipped smile. "You're right. I wasn't. I made a huge mistake and I'm sorrier for it than I can say. I'm sorry you guys have to deal with any of this. You shouldn't have to. I wish I could make it all go away." I looked at my daughter. "Are you guys ready to come home?" All I could think about was turning off my phone and curling up on the couch with my kids and husband. We could watch movies all day, then order pizza for dinner and finish off the ice cream I'd bought for us the other day. We could cocoon in the house and pretend, at least for the weekend, that none of this had happened. Even if things weren't perfect between me and Jake, I wanted to be near him.

"I'm staying here," Ella said. She lifted her chin almost imperceptibly, defiantly the same way she had when she was Ruby's age, and refusing to put on her shoes or make her bed. "I'll stop by later and get more clothes before work tonight."

"That's fine," Jake said, and I shot him a sidelong glance. We hadn't talked about whether the kids would come home with us, but since they'd already spent the majority of the week with Peter and Kari, I'd assumed that they would come home for the weekend.

"Yeah, I'm supposed to help Dad with yardwork, later," Tuck said.

"And Kari needs help with Ruby," Ella said. "I promised her I'd take her to the park."

"Oh," I said, trying not to let my disappointment show. "Okay. So I'll see you later, at the house? When you pick up some more clothes?"

"Probably," Ella said, nonchalantly. "I won't be there very long."

Jake stood up and looked at the kids. "You can text or call us if you need to," he said. "If you want to talk about this more."

"I won't," Ella said. "I don't ever want to talk about it again."

I winced, internally, at the anger behind her words, but knew that like Jake, I would need to give her time to work through her feelings over what had happened. Maybe it was better that Jake and I had time alone this weekend, anyway. We could talk when we needed to, or just be in the house together. I could bake something, and make us an extra fancy meal. I'd break out the expensive bottle of Merlot my parents had given us for an anniversary gift and we'd get a little drunk, which was usually when we had some of our best talks. The booze lowered both of our defenses and our true feelings came spilling out.

"Okay," I said again, as I stood up, too. "Let me know if you need anything. I love you both so much. And I really am sorry."

"Love you, too," Tuck said, but Ella remained silent. She grabbed the remote and turned the TV back on. I wanted to hug them both, but figured that I shouldn't push it.

"Tell Kari thanks again for letting us come over," I said, and Jake and I left the house. "Well, that sucked," I said to him as we made our way to our cars.

"Yeah, it wasn't great." He jangled his keys in his hand. "I think I'm going to hang out with Kevin for a few hours. Go play some basketball and get some lunch." Kevin was a friend of Jake's from the days he used to work for Microsoft, right after he moved to Seattle. They didn't get together often, but I knew Jake felt comfortable talking with him, though I hated knowing what they would likely discuss, today.

"Oh," I said. This time, I couldn't hide my disappointment. "Aren't you exhausted?"

He shrugged. "I'll live."

"Are you really, really sure you don't hate me?" I asked, and tears once again sprung to my eyes.

"Jess...," he said, drawing out my name. "Please. You know that I don't. I'm just upset. You broke the most important rule—telling me everything. And look what happened."

"I know." My bottom lip trembled, and I wiped away a tear that rolled down my cheek. "You're the most important thing in my life, baby—outside of the kids—and I hate *so* much that I hurt you. I wish we had never done *any* of this."

He regarded me for a moment before speaking. "I don't wish that. But I do wish you'd come home from coffee with him and told me a funny story about how this guy ended up being someone you used to work with. We could have laughed about it, and that would have been that."

I nodded, keeping my mouth closed, trying not to break down in front of my ex-husband's house. "I wish that, too," I finally said, looking at him with teary eyes.

"I know," Jake said, softly, and then he sighed. "I'm going to go."

"Okay," I said, and then I watched him cross the street and get into his car, wondering how long he'd be gone. Hoping that he wouldn't decide to stay away for good.

Twenty
Seven

I stopped by the grocery store on the way home, planning to make Jake his favorite dinner in the hopes that he wouldn't end up staying at Kevin's house overnight. He never had before, but we were in an unprecedented situation. I didn't know what to expect.

It was only a little past ten when I pulled into the Whole Foods parking lot, and I quickly headed inside, hoping I wouldn't run into anyone I knew. I kept my head down as I grabbed a cart and pushed it toward the back of the store to the seafood counter, where I would pick up a couple of pounds of fresh crab to make the crab cakes Jake loved, along with a creamy, Thai sweet chili sauce. I rounded the corner from the frozen food section when I felt someone staring at me. I looked up, and it was more than someone—it was two mothers of girls on Ella's dance team, women I knew only well enough to smile and say hello. They stood about ten feet away from me with their heads leaned in, close together. One of them said something under her breath, and the other laughed, covering her mouth with one hand. Their eyes never left me.

"Hi, Jessica," the one who had spoken said, with a quick wave. "I'm surprised to see you out and about today."

My face was on fire, and I gripped the handle of the shopping cart tightly enough that it hurt my fingers. They knew. Of course they knew. They were looking at me and thinking about the pictures of my naked body and the intimate words I'd written. They were judging me. They thought I was a whore.

I kept walking, trying to ignore the feeling of their eyes still on me as I ordered the crab, and then rushed around the store, throwing the ingredients I would need into my cart. I didn't make eye contact with anyone, even the cashier as I stood at the register, waiting for my groceries to be rung up.

"Any plans this beautiful Saturday?" the cashier asked.

I finally looked up. She was a younger woman, maybe in her early twenties, with short, spiky black hair, pale skin, and a nose ring. "Nothing much," I said, shakily, searching her face for any evidence that she knew who I was. "Just making some crab cakes, and baking a lemon tart." The dessert was Jake's favorite, and I usually only made it for his birthday, because he ended up wanting to eat the entire thing in one sitting, but I hoped coming home to find it on the counter later might soften his anger toward me. That might have been taking the notion that the way to a man's heart is through his stomach a bit too far, but I felt desperate enough to give it a chance.

"Yum," the cashier said with a smile. "What time should I be over?"

I laughed, feeling my body relax. Maybe *everyone* in Queens Ridge wasn't on the Neighbors app. Maybe some people in the community would still be kind to me.

I wished her a nice day, and on my way out of the store, I saw Ben, Tiffany's husband, in the parking lot, climbing out of his enormous, double cabbed, bright red truck with the "Mitchell Motors" logo painted in white and silver on the side. I immediately thought about Lizzy, wondering how she was doing, and if she had been released from the hospital. I also wondered if Ben had seen the posts about me, but I forced myself to ignore the trepidation I felt and walked toward him.

"Hey, Ben," I said, as I approached his truck. He had just shoved his cell phone into his front pocket.

He looked at me with hooded gray eyes. He looked like he hadn't slept, either. "Jessica. Hi." He paused. "What are you doing here?"

I smiled, and held up my shopping bags.

He laughed, but it was a forced thing. "Oh, right, right. Sorry. I'm a little out of it this morning."

"I can imagine," I said, feeling the weight of my own fatigue like wet sand packed beneath my skin. He wasn't acting like he had seen the posts, but he could simply be too distracted by his daughter's stint in the ER to show it. "I talked with Tiffany last night. She told me about Lizzy. How is she?"

"She's home," Ben said. "Just barely. Tiff sent me to pick up a few things, but I forgot the list." He looked lost, and patted his back pockets, as though he might find the misplaced scrap of paper there.

"You can shoot her a text," I said, gently. "She can remind you what to get."

"Good idea," he said, giving me a grateful smile. "Thanks. I don't know where my head is. The kids kept me up most the night."

"The little buggers can do that," I said, imagining that this might be the first time Ben had been solely responsible for taking care of his twins, who were still in elementary school. "I'm happy to help any way that I can. I can watch the kids if you guys need to talk with Lizzy alone. Or if you need a break."

"That's really nice of you," Ben said. "I appreciate it." He lifted a hand as a farewell, and then headed toward the entrance of the store.

I made my way to my own car, and then home. Part of me hoped that Jake's car would be in the driveway—that he'd changed his mind about going to Kevin's house and decided to come home to me. But the driveway was empty, and so I parked inside the garage—there was only enough space for one of our cars in it, and Jake had always insisted that I use it so I would never have to run from my car to the house with the rain that fell in Seattle almost six months a year. He was the best man I'd ever known; how could I have done anything to possibly lose him?

I was still exhausted as I unpacked my groceries, blinking heavily as I made sure the crab was well-picked over before I began forming it into small, cylindrical cakes that I would later coat in egg and panko breadcrumbs. I never used any filler in this particular dish, like most restaurants did. The sweetness of the seafood was accented by the creamy, tangy spiciness of the Thai chili sauce I served alongside it, and I usually made a crunchy Romaine salad tossed with apple cider vinaigrette to complete the meal.

After I whipped up the sauce, I made the tart, discovering that I accidentally had doubled the recipe for the lemon filling. I quickly made another batch of tart dough, while the first one baked. Within an hour, I had crab cakes prepped in the fridge, ready to fry later, when Jake came home, and two lemon tarts cooling on the counter. I then threw together a pasta dish with some meatball marinara I already had in the freezer, and enough salad to go along with it. Without pausing to think much about what I was doing, I grabbed my phone and called Tiffany. I was certain I was going to voicemail, but at the last second, she picked up.

"Hi," I said, after she greeted me. "I'm sorry to bother you again, but I wanted to see if it would be okay for me to bring over some dinner for you guys. I saw Ben at the store, but I can't imagine either of you are going to feel up to cooking today." I held my breath, waiting for her to tell me no, to launch into a diatribe about the posts Andrew had put up about me, chastising me for setting such a horrible example for the girls in Queens Ridge, including Lizzy.

But instead, I heard her breathe a sigh of relief. "Really?" she asked, tremulously. "I fed the boys cereal for lunch, but Ben came home and asked what I was going to make for dinner and I didn't know what to tell him." Her voice broke. "I keep trying to talk with Lizzy, but she won't unlock her bedroom door. I'm just sitting outside, waiting."

"I'll be there in a few minutes," I said. Distraction was what I needed; the last place I wanted to be was alone, inside my own head.

I packed up the pasta and the salad in big Tupperware containers, and then carried them, along with the second lemon tart, out to my car. I left Jake another note, so he would know where I'd gone in case he decided to come home, and ten minutes later, I stood in front of Ben and Tiffany's elaborate, double front doors. My hands were full, so I used my elbow to ring the bell, and a moment later, Ben welcomed me inside.

"You didn't have to do this," he said, taking the containers from me. I'd balanced the tart on top, and once we were in the kitchen, he set the entire stack carefully onto the counter. I looked out the window to the backyard and saw the twins standing on the grass in their swim trunks, spraying each other with Super-Soakers. Their blond heads were darkened and damp, and their tan skin glistened in the mid afternoon sun. When the water from the bright plastic guns hit them, they shrieked and laughed.

"I know," I told Ben. "But I wanted to. You guys have had a rough night."

He paused and gave me a meaningful look. "So have you."

I blushed, furiously, and dropped my eyes to the ground. *Shit.* I had hoped he hadn't seen the posts.

"Sorry," he said. "I figured I should address the elephant in the room." He chuckled, awkwardly, and reached down, below the pudge of his beer belly, to heft up his shorts. Change jingled in his pockets. "I say let your freak flag fly. Screw what anybody else thinks."

"I appreciate that," I said. Despite the awkward delivery, the latter part of what he'd said was good advice, though I wasn't sure I'd be able to take it. "Where's Tiff?"

"Upstairs, outside of Lizzy's room. She hasn't left there since I got back from the store." He waved, and headed outside to join his boys.

I quickly put the dinner I'd brought into their fridge—Ben had left the food out on the counter—and then made my way back into the living room and up the stairs.

"Tiffany?" I said as I rounded a corner, and then I saw her, sitting on the floor with her knees drawn up to her chest. I almost didn't recognize her. She was pale and her face was bare.

"Hi," she said, rising to greet me. She wore black leggings and baggy T-shirt; her blond hair hung in straggled pieces around her narrow face.

I hugged her, thinking it would feel awkward since we'd never done it before, but instead, she leaned in, her skinny fingers clutching my back, and held onto me for a long moment.

"Thanks for coming," she said, when we parted.

"Who's that?" Lizzy called out from behind her closed bedroom door.

"It's Jessica, Ella's mom," Tiff replied. "She was nice enough to bring over dinner. Come out and say hi." She kept her eyes on the door as she spoke, her expression equally pained and hopeful.

Lizzy didn't respond.

"Hi, Lizzy," I said, in the same slightly-louder-than-normal voice that Tiffany had used. "I'm sorry you're not feeling well." She wasn't sick, exactly, but I couldn't imagine that the after-effects of alcohol poisoning were all that pleasant.

"I'm sorry you fucked a bunch of strangers!" Lizzy replied, sarcastically.

"Elizabeth Mitchell!" Tiffany said in a sharp tone.

I put a hand on Tiffany's arm. "That's okay," I said. "She's upset."

"No, it's not," Tiffany insisted. She took a step closer to the door and set her forehead upon it. "You apologize to Jessica, right *now*."

A moment later, there was a clicking sound, the door unlocking, and it flew open, causing Tiffany to stumble forward. Her arms flew out, catching herself on the door jamb right before crashing into her daughter.

Lizzy stood in front of us then, one hand still on the door knob, looking as though she actually *was* sick. Her skin held a ghostly pallor, and her blond hair was matted all around her head. The thin skin under her blue eyes was stained purple, which only highlighted the word SLUT that was written on her forehead in jagged black lettering. I could tell that someone—probably a nurse at the hospital—had attempted to scrub it away, but it was still legible. Seeing it made my heart ache.

"I saw what you wrote," Lizzy said, in a defiant tone. "And the pictures."

"That's none of our business," Tiffany said, but then I interrupted her.

"Yeah, it's pretty horrible, having everyone see all of that. Someone hacked my account because they were angry at me. I'm pretty humiliated right now." I kept my gaze on Lizzy, trusting my instincts to be honest with her, as I had been with my own kids. If I'd learned anything from parenting Ella, it was that teenage girls could smell bullshit a mile away.

Lizzy searched my face, an appraising look in her eyes, and then, seemingly satisfied with what she saw, she stepped back and opened the door, wide. "*She* can come in," she said. She squinted at Tiffany. "Not *you*."

Tiffany looked hurt, but then quickly rearranged her face into a more passive expression. "Fine," she said. "I'll be in the family room." She glanced at me, and pointed past the stairs. "Down the hall, and to the left." Their home was similar to, though much larger than, ours, with two family rooms—one right off the kitchen, and another upstairs.

I entered Lizzy's room, and she closed the door behind me. I looked around the space that was almost as big as the master I shared with Jake, taking in the pale turquoise paint and white accents. She had a queen-size canopy bed, which I didn't even know they made, and a wall that was made up entirely of shelves, filled with what had to be several hundred books.

"You like to read?" I asked, turning to look at her. She had dropped onto her bed, leaning on the stack of fluffy pillows that were set against the headboard, her legs outstretched.

"Yeah," she said. She grabbed another pillow and hugged it tightly to her chest.

"What's your favorite book?" I reached for the chair that was tucked under a white desk and then sat down about five feet away from the bed.

She shrugged. "I don't really have one."

I waited, unsure why, exactly, she wanted me there. My eyes were still heavy, and my body cried out for my own bed, but the events of the last twenty-four hours had led me to this point, and I felt like I needed to see it through. Anything was better than sitting alone in my empty house, without Jake or the kids, wondering if my husband was going to come home.

"I like to read because I can pretend I'm the characters instead of me," she said, quietly. Her gaze landed on her bookshelves, and then me, expectant.

"I get that," I said, because it was true. "I'd sure like to be someone else right now."

"Why did you write those things to other guys?" she asked. "You're married."

I sighed, and crossed my legs, setting my hands loosely in my lap. "It's complicated, but Jake and I have a more…adventurous sex life than most people. What I wrote was extremely private, and not meant for anyone else to see." I thought about how I hadn't meant for Jake to see the texts or pictures I'd sent Andrew, either, and a twitch began to pulse under my right eye. What if he really didn't come home tonight? What would I do? The muscles of my throat thickened, and I swallowed hard to keep from crying in front of Lizzy.

"See, *you* get it," Lizzy said. "I like sex, too, but everyone else just thinks I'm a slut." Her blue eyes glossed with tears, and she wiped at them, angrily, and then rubbed the palm of her right hand vigorously back and forth over her forehead, as though trying to erase the word that someone had written.

"It's okay to like sex," I said, measuring my words carefully. I didn't want her to feel like I was judging her, too. "I really liked it when I was your age, too." I told her about Ryan, and how my parents had walked in on us. "I didn't really even like *him* all that much. I just wanted to do things with him so I would know what it was like."

"I've already had sex," Lizzy said, carefully, scanning my face for any hint of condemnation. "Like, a lot."

I nodded, but didn't comment; again, not wanting her to feel judged. "I lost my virginity when I was a junior." I told her. "It wasn't the greatest experience. He was my boyfriend, but I felt like he didn't really care if I enjoyed it. It almost was like I wasn't even there." I thought back to that night at my boyfriend's house. We were alone for a few hours—I'd lied to my parents about studying at the library with friends—and when we were making out, I told him I wanted to have sex. A few minutes later, the condom was on and he was inside me. About ten seconds after that, it was over, and I was pretty overwhelmed with disappointment."

"That's how I felt," Lizzy said, and tears shone in her blue eyes. "So I was like, what's the big deal?"

"Oh honey," I said. "You should know that it's totally different when you're in a committed, adult relationship like the one I have with Jake. The sex we have is reciprocal. We give to each other and share how good it feels. There's an emotional connection and so much trust." *Trust that I'd broken*, I thought. Lizzy's eyes were fixed on mine, listening. "At your age, boys, especially, are only looking for physical relief for themselves. They don't necessarily have the ability to form the kind of respectful, loving relationship that makes sex so good between two people. A lot of the time, girls want that connection and then end up feeling used when a boy just wants sex." I paused, and gave her a compassionate look. "Have you ever felt that way? Like a boy has used you?"

She stared at me in silence for a moment, and then nodded as she frowned. "But it also feels good," she said. "Sometimes I like it."

"Of course you do," I said. "Sex is supposed to feel good. But it feels even better when you share it with someone who really cares about you, and who wants it to be a great experience for you, too—not just for them." I got up, then, and went to sit next to her, on the edge of her bed. "You deserve to have someone care about you like that, Lizzy. I know it can feel really special when a boy you don't know very well flirts with you and kisses you and wants to have sex with you. I know that feeling. I promise you that I do." My mind flashed to Andrew's face—the way he'd looked at me and I felt like I'd been drugged. How easily I'd allowed that feeling to override my common sense.

"Then why did you write those emails and those texts to that Andrew guy?" Lizzy asked, as though she had sensed me thinking about him. "If you and Jake are so happy and sex is better with someone who loves you, why were you sexting with someone else?"

"Because Jake and I made a choice," I said. "And exploring that kind of thing was something we had agreed to do together, as a couple." I decided it was too much to try and explain the intricate details—the fundamental rule of our arrangement that I'd broken. Lizzy didn't need to know all of that.

"Like a threesome?" Lizzy asked, tilting her blond head.

"Yeah," I said. I knew from my conversations with Ella and Tuck that teenagers these days were far savvier and informed when it came to sex than I had ever been. "But I never would have been able to handle something like that when I was your age. I was too insecure, and didn't really know myself well enough, yet. What we did isn't wrong, but it's probably not something a teenager should do."

"Carter was so *nice* to me," Lizzy said, dropping her eyes to her lap. She picked at one corner of the pillow she still hugged to her chest. "He followed my account on Instagram and was always commenting on how hot I was, how pretty he thought my eyes were. Then he saw me at the pool the other day and sent me a direct message saying that couldn't stop thinking about me. We talked about all the sex stuff we could do together and he made me feel so good about myself, especially when he asked to come to the party. But when we got there, he was too busy flirting with other, older girls to even *talk* to me. So I started flirting with his friends, and some other guys I knew from my school, taking shots and pounding beers." She shuddered, as though her body was reacting to the memory of that unnatural influx of alcohol. "That's all I remember. I woke up in the hospital feeling shittier than I ever had before, with my mom sitting next to me, crying."

"That must have been so awful for you," I said.

"It still *is*!" she said. She pressed the heels of her palms into her eyes, as though trying to push back tears. "They put this fucking word on my forehead and took pictures! They sent it to *everyone*! I've been getting texts about it all *morning*!" She began to sob.

This was news to me; neither Tiffany nor Ben had mentioned the photos. "Oh, honey," I said, reaching out to rub her leg. "I'm so sorry. I know *exactly* how you feel."

She sniffled and looked up at me. "I know you do. That's why I wanted to talk to you. My mom doesn't understand."

"I think she might, if you gave her a chance," I said. "She loves you. She might not always know how to show it, but I promise you, I'm a mom, too, and there's nothing in the world more important to me than making sure my kids are okay."

Lizzy pondered this, and then spoke. "Would you talk to her first?"

"If you think it would help, of course." I suddenly wished that there was someone I could ask to talk with Jake that might help him forgive me. Maybe we'd need to go to counseling, like Charlotte and Richard.

"I want you to think about something, though," I said to Lizzy. "I know what happened to you last night feels like the absolute worst thing in the world. I know you're embarrassed and humiliated, because that's how I feel about what happened to me, too." I paused, took her hand in mine, and squeezed. "But it really could have been so much worse. Those boys could have hurt you. They could have done things to you while you were passed out. What they did do was *terrible*—unforgivable, really—but when it overwhelms you, when you feel like you can't handle how bad it feels, try to keep it in perspective. Screw the people who talk behind your back. They don't know you, or understand who you really are. And remember that you're not alone. It will eventually blow over, and I'm here for you, until then, whenever you might need me. Okay? Your mom is, too."

As she nodded, and I realized I needed to take a bit of my own advice, too. What Andrew had done to me was horrifying, but like Jake had said last night, it wasn't the end of the world. My kids were physically fine; I had my job and my best friend; nobody in my family was suffering from a life-threatening illness. What other people thought of my less than traditional sex life didn't matter. What mattered was my marriage, and that my children were okay. Yes, it might take time for the kids to forgive me and for Jake to get over how I'd hurt him, but I had to believe that our relationship was strong enough to weather this particular storm. I couldn't let myself believe anything else.

"You look like you could use a shower," I said, rising from Lizzy's bed. "Why don't you clean up, and I'll go talk with your mom?"

"Can I get your phone number, first?" she asked, reaching for her cell, which was on her nightstand. "So we can text?"

"Sure," I said. She swiped the screen a few times, and then handed her phone to me. I quickly tapped in my number as a new contact, and then gave it back to her. "Reach out anytime, day or night. I'll answer as soon as I can."

I gave Lizzy a quick hug, and then left her room, shutting the door behind me. Fatigue threatened to take me down—I felt dizzied by it, and everything inside me screamed that I should go home and sleep. But first, I needed to know why Tiffany, a woman I wasn't especially close with—a woman whom I'd judged way too many times—had chosen to be on my side.

Twenty
Eight

The Mitchells' upstairs family room was enormous—a rectangular space on the second floor that spanned the entire length of the front of their house. I found Tiffany curled up in the corner of a large, overstuffed couch, her head resting on a thick pillow and a blanket drawn up around her shoulders. At first, I thought she might be asleep, but she popped upright when I entered the room.

"How is she?" she asked, concern etched across her face.

"Upset," I said. "Embarrassed and confused." I made my way over to her and sat down a few cushions away. Ben's loud voice rose up from the backyard, muffled, along with the screeching laughter of his sons as the three of them played. Sun streamed in through the windows, creating dancing rainbows on the plush, cream-colored carpet. The brightness of the day seemed at odds with my darker mood. "They sound like they're having fun out there." I nodded toward the wall facing the backyard.

"Yeah," Tiffany said with a wan smile. "He can be a really good dad, when he wants to. But I had to seriously beg for him not to go into the dealership on a Saturday." She frowned, then, and shook her head. "I can't believe this is happening. Do you think she's going to be okay?"

"I do," I said. "She's afraid that you won't understand how she's feeling, but I told her that you love her more than anything, and would do anything to help her get through this." It felt a little strange, having a conversation this intimate with her, but I could relate to this version of Tiffany.

I quickly explained that the boys at the party had taken photos and texted them to others, and Tiffany's hand momentarily flew to her mouth. "That's why she wanted to talk with you," she said. "Because of the posts."

"Right." My cheeks flushed. I couldn't believe that this time yesterday, I was sitting in my office, working. It felt like I'd aged a hundred years since then. "I talked with her about how embarrassed I am right now, but that I'm going to do my best not to care what other people say behind my back, and that she shouldn't, either."

"People are assholes," Tiffany said, darkly.

"Yeah, they are."

"What can I do to help her?" Tiffany asked. "What would help *you* right now?"

"Can you build a time machine?" I said, only partially joking. I wanted to go back and change my decision to keep things about Andrew from Jake. If I had, none of this would be happening.

"But really," Tiffany pressed. "What do I do?"

"I think you're doing it," I said. "You're showing her you're not going to let her go through this alone or that you're going to ignore what happened. She may fight it and tell you to go away, but by staying close to her anyway, you're giving her exactly what she needs. She'll open up eventually. I think the key is to not tell her what she *should* be doing or feeling. Just listen. Tell her what happened sucks, but that she's strong enough to get through it. That you'll love her no matter what."

Tiffany nodded, crossing her thin arms over her chest and rubbed the outside of her biceps. "Should I take her to counseling?"

"Maybe. But let her make her own decision about it. She's feeling powerless, and needs to regain some sense of control." I felt that way, too.

"Thank you so much," Tiffany said. Her pale blue eyes were full of gratitude. "I can't believe you're here when you're dealing with your own...issues. It means a lot."

I gave her a half-hearted smile, because that was all I had energy to do. "It's been good for me to get out of my head."

"Are you doing okay?" Tiffany asked. "How's Jake?"

I shook my head and dropped my gaze to the carpet, trying to fight off the scratchy ache of impending tears in my throat.

"Oh, no," she said. "I'm so sorry. You guys are such a great couple."

"Thank you," I said. "It's all so complicated."

"I'm sure you'll work it out," Tiffany said, sounding way more convinced than I felt. "Whoever hacked into your accounts was obviously trying to hurt you. I hope karma bites them in the ass."

"Jake punched him," I said, venturing that I could trust her with this piece of information.

Her eyes widened. "Really? That's kind of awesome, in a horrible, you're in a fucked up situation kind of way."

I chuckled. The cuss word sounded strange coming out of Tiffany's mouth, but I liked it. I felt a sliver of relief.

"You were kind to me, the other day at the pool," Tiffany said. "I don't have a lot of friends." She laughed, but it came out harshly. "I try—I really do. I plan events and put up posts about the neighborhood and talk with other people all the time, but I never seem to make real connections."

This was a side of Tiffany I'd never seen before. Her defenses were down; she wasn't trying to hide a thing. I decided to tell her the truth. "I guess I've had a hard time connecting with you, sometimes, but it's only because your life always seems so picture-perfect. When I saw you at the pool, struggling with Lizzy, I felt for you. I *related* to you." I paused. "I do, now, too. What happened to Lizzy at the party was a traumatic thing. I can only imagine how scared you were when the hospital called."

"I was terrified," she said. "When I logged into Neighbors to delete your account and saw what had been posted, I realized that you were in the middle of your own total nightmare, yet you still took the time to talk with me and even offered to take care of the kids." She teared up. "I can't tell you what that meant to me. And then you call again, today, and show up with dinner and you talk with Lizzy…" Her voice cracked and she shook her head. "Sorry."

"That's okay," I said. "I've been crying off and on for the last twenty-four hours. I haven't slept."

She laughed, even as a tear rolled down her cheek. "You must be exhausted."

"I am." Simply saying the words seemed to intensify the heaviness in my eyelids and limbs. "I should probably go home and try to get some sleep." But then something else hit me. "How's your mom doing? Charlotte mentioned you had to find a home for her."

Tiffany bobbed her head. "She's okay. Slowly getting adjusted. The facility has a wonderful staff, who are really good about keeping her to a routine, which seems to help her be less confused and agitated." She waved her hand in the air, toward the window. "That was pretty much impossible around here, with the kids and all their craziness."

"I think it's amazing you took care of her as long as you did," I said. "Truly. You're a good daughter. And mom."

"Thank you," she said, softly, and we both stood up. "Let me walk you out."

I let her lead the way to the front door, and outside to her porch. As I said goodbye and walked to my car, I thought about how I didn't know what would be waiting for me when I got home, but at that point, I was too exhausted to care. Sleep was what I needed. What might happen after that, there was no way to know.

I held my breath as I rounded the corner of our street, fully expecting to find the driveway empty. It was almost four o'clock, and I hadn't heard from Jake since that morning, when we stood in front of Peter and Kari's house. Normally, he'd only hang out with Kevin for a few hours, but what if he went into his "cave" and decided to never come out?

But his black SUV was there, glinting in the late afternoon sun. A flood of relief washed over me, immediately followed by a pulsing anxiety. He was home, but what did that mean? Was he packing a bag? Was he simply going to leave again?

I pulled into the garage and rushed inside. Throwing my gaze around the kitchen, I saw him lying on the couch in the family room, on his side, asleep. His breathing was regular and deep, and I thought better of waking him up. I needed to rest, too. At least he wasn't in a hurry to leave again. At least he'd come home.

I stared at him a moment, taking all of him in, feeling as though my heart might burst. I loved the slightly crooked bent of his nose; the length of his dark lashes and the now-more-salt-than-pepper of his hair. I loved the way his upper lip was slightly thinner than the bottom one, and the fan of lines at the corners of his eyes, etched there by so many years of smiling. His chest rose and fell as he slept, and I longed to put my head upon it, to feel the steady and reassuring beat of his heart—the comforting lullaby that so often soothed me to sleep.

Instead, I left him to sleep in peace, and I tiptoed upstairs to our bedroom, where with a few stumbling movements, I tore off my clothes and climbed beneath the covers. The shades were still drawn from the night before, so the room was dark, save for the straight, sharp slashes of light peeking around the window frames. But it likely wouldn't have mattered if the sun had been shining directly into my face—at that point, nothing would have kept me awake. My head hit the pillow and the next thing I knew, I woke to find Jake sitting on the bed next to me, watching me.

"Hey," I said, groggily. I rubbed my eyes, which were still heavy with sleep. "What time is it?"

"Almost midnight," he said. "When did you get back?"

"Around four, I think." I sat up and leaned against the backboard. The room was dark, but I could still make out my husband's face. "You were passed out on the couch. I didn't want to wake you."

"Thanks for leaving a note," he said. "How's Lizzy?"

"She had a rough night," I said, quickly explaining the details I'd learned once I got there, about the pictures the boys took being sent out to all of their friends.

"It was good that she had you to talk to, then," Jake said. "And nice of you to take them dinner."

"It was good to keep busy," I said. "I needed a distraction." I paused.

"I prepped crab cakes, too."

"I saw." He stared at me, searching my face.

"How's Kevin?" I asked. Making small talk seemed silly, considering the weight of what we'd been through since yesterday, but I didn't want to push him to talk about what had happened. Or maybe I was simply too afraid what he might say if I did.

"A little obnoxious, actually. He really didn't understand how I could be into what we did. I couldn't take it for very long, so I went for a drive, instead."

It was unsettling, thinking about my husband's friend passing judgment on our sex life, but not as troubling as the knowledge that I'd betrayed Jake's trust. "Where'd you go?"

"Franklin Falls."

My eyes flooded with tears. Franklin Falls was where he'd asked me to marry him—a beautiful gem of a hidden spot off of I-90, about a mile hike in from the main road. He'd taken me there early on a Sunday morning almost twelve years ago, and I'd grumbled on the way there, calling him a bastard for making me get out of bed before nine on a weekend when the kids were with their dad. But then, when we got to the waterfall, which was hidden amongst towering gatherings of evergreens and giant, verdant ferns, he got down on one knee and held up the ring he'd picked out—a simple, round stone in a silver band. "I can't imagine my life without you," he said, "or the kids. Please, marry me, Jessica. There's no one else for me in the world."

Remembering that moment made the tears slip down my cheek. "That was an amazing day."

"Yeah," he said. "I needed to remember how I felt."

I looked at him, my stomach churning. "And how was that?"

He held my gaze, looking as serious as I could ever remember him being. "More in love with you and happier than any man had a right to be."

My bottom lips trembled, then, and more tears fell.

"The way I grew up," Jake said, "with my mom and her flavor-of-the-week boyfriends, I never really understood what it was to love someone. I thought I'd been in love a few times before we met, but then you came along and it was so different. Everything with us just *clicked*. We finished each other's sentences, remember? We laughed at all the same things. We saw the world the same way. I looked into your gorgeous eyes and I felt like I had finally found a *home*."

"Oh, baby," I said, through my tears, hoping that he wasn't saying all of this as a preamble to saying that I'd broken something between us that was beyond repair. "I felt the same way. I still do."

"I'm mad that you didn't tell me the truth about Andrew from the start," he said, ignoring me. "I'm hurt and don't really understand why you did it. It's not like you, at *all*."

"I made a mistake," I whispered. "A terrible, fucked-up mistake. I wish I could take it back."

"I believe you," he said. "I'm still upset, but I think you got caught up in something and you made some stupid decisions. But it's going to take me some time to get over it."

"I know." I wanted so much to reach over and take his hand, but I was too afraid he'd pull away. "I'm willing to do anything to fix this. We can go to counseling, if you want. Or I'll go alone. Whatever it takes, however long it takes. I can't lose you."

He was quiet, and I held my breath, everything hinging on what he came out of his mouth, next.

"I can't lose you, either," he finally said, and then he reached over, lacing his fingers through mine.

In that moment, as we sat together in the dark, connecting in the smallest of ways, I knew, despite the damage I'd done, that Jake and I were going to get past this. We had been lucky for a long time to not have any major conflicts in our marriage, but because of that—because we had spent almost twelve good years together building a strong foundation of love and trust and consistency—this one issue, however terrible it might be, was not enough to crash us to the ground. We had been shaken, and I would need to get to the root of why I made the choices I did, but in the end, I would survive it, with the man I had chosen, above all others, by my side.

Epilogue

The last thing you need to know about me is that I love my husband.

When I look at him, now, what I feel is deeper and more meaningful than anything I can put into words. And it did take time, as we both knew it would, for me to earn back his trust.

We didn't sleep in the same room for more than three months. He needed the space, and I needed to give it to him. It was heart-wrenching, every single time, saying goodnight to him at the bottom of the stairs.

"Let me take the guestroom," I told him, more than once. "You take our bed." It seemed a pittance of an offering, but I was willing to do anything, make any sacrifice, no matter how small, if it meant that things would begin to improve between us.

But he insisted on remaining downstairs, some mornings leaving for the office before I woke up. Most days, we didn't talk until we both got home for work, save for the occasional logistical text about what was going on with the kids or who was going to pick up groceries. I cried most evenings, in what felt like the solitary confinement of our room, my chest aching with remorse, with fear that Jake might change his mind and decide that he couldn't forgive me, after all.

We didn't kiss, let alone have sex, until an evening in early October, a little over two months after Andrew posted on Neighbors. I'd just climbed in bed, and saw Jake's shadow appear in the doorway, backlit from the hallway overhead light.

"Are you okay?" I ventured, sitting up and snapping on the bedside lamp. My heartbeat thudded like a steel drum.

But instead of answering, Jake strode toward me and reached for the base of the lamp, turning the room dark again. He put his hands on both sides of my head, clutching it in his grip, and then leaned down to kiss me, fervently.

"Jake," I said against his lips, but he responded only by deepening his kiss, and then lay on top of me. I could feel him on my thigh, so I spread my legs, instantly ready for him. The weight of him, the scent of his skin was so familiar and comforting, I almost began to cry. He yanked down the thin shorts I wore, as I jerked his pants down, too. He grabbed my wrists and pinned them on either side of my head, and then without warning, without the normal outpouring of foreplay we'd always preferred, he shoved inside me. I gasped from the pleasure of it, and the memories of every moment our bodies had shared together came flooding back.

He bit the spot where my neck met my shoulder, almost hard enough to hurt, and then shifted his body so his chest was lifted off mine, staring me directly in the eye. His hands remained tightly squeezing my wrists; I couldn't move my arms, and I didn't want to.

"You're mine," he said, as he thrusted with more intent than I could ever remember before. It felt like he was on a mission, and taking my body back was his goal.

"Yours," I said, lifting my hips to meet him, feeling my orgasm build from a place deep inside me that only Jake had ever been able to reach—the place from where my love for him had blossomed and grown into something bigger than me, bigger than the both of us. I gave myself over to him; I let him take control. I liked that it didn't feel as though I had a choice.

We continued to move, not saying another word, our gazes riveted together. I tensed, and began to go over the edge just moments before Jake shuddered and moaned, pounding himself inside of me as though he were trying to leave a brand.

He rolled off of me almost immediately, releasing my wrists, and onto his back. Not an inch of his skin touched mine. I was reminded of how I'd done the same with the other men I'd been with; my intimacy with them ceased the moment the two of us had come, and I would walk out the door not long after that. Except with Andrew, of course; one of the many mistakes I made with him. But in that moment, in bed with my husband, I yearned for nothing more than to curl up against his side—to bask in his body's warmth and the security of his arm encircling me and his protective hand resting on the small of my back. I wanted that, but I was too afraid if I reached for him, he might push me away.

"I love you," I said, instead, with as much feeling as I could muster. I couldn't deny the pleasure I'd felt with the way he'd taken me, but I didn't know what it meant. I didn't know what had led him to come to me that particular night, and I was too terrified to ask. All I knew was that I didn't want him to leave.

"We need to find a counselor," he said, in a flat voice. "I don't think we can work through this on our own."

"Yes," I said, feeling heartened; a little hopeful. "Okay. Let's do it." Though I'd suggested the same thing the day after the whole nightmare with Andrew came to a head, we had yet to act on finding someone, choosing instead to see if time and a little distance from each other could heal our wounds. But time alone is not a cure-all, so Charlotte and Richard's therapist gave us a referral, and two days later, we went to our first appointment. A month after that, Jake returned to our bed.

In the end, we were in therapy once a week for three months, during which time I understood again and again that it wasn't the sex I'd had with Andrew that had hurt my husband: it was the fact that I'd hidden things from him—that I'd concealed the nature of the connection I felt with someone else. And so, in repentance, I gave Jake access to every part of me, whenever he wanted it. He had the password on my emails and phone, and could check them as often as he liked, though he seldom did. We agreed to take a long break from any sexual encounters outside of our marriage, and focused instead solely on each other. We spent time with the kids, even though for the first several months, both Ella and Tucker wanted to stay at Peter and Kari's more often than with us, something that was painful for me, but I needed—and our counselor advised—to allow them the space to do. Tucker came around more quickly than Ella, who took almost six months before she would hug me, again. When she finally did, it led to tears and some very meaningful conversations about slut-shaming and a grown woman's right to have sex with whomever she wanted, however she chose.

As it t turned out, my sex life wasn't a topic of interest in Queens Ridge for as long as I feared it might be. There was chatter, of course.

For months after Andrew hacked my accounts, my coworkers would often stop talking when I entered a room, and Charlotte had shut down more than one gossipy conversation about me at the various functions she planned. But there were no overt, terrible consequences—none of my clients fired me, other than Diane. Thankfully, we never heard from Andrew, again.

Tiffany became one of my staunchest allies, telling everyone what a help I'd been to both her and her daughter, reaffirming, if anyone brought the subject up, that the hack of my accounts had been a malicious, vengeful act, and what I did behind closed doors with my husband was our business, and ours alone. Gradually, she started spending more time with Charlotte and me, dropping the occasional F-bomb and drinking martinis with us at the Tipsy Sailor on Friday nights. She even cut down on her Neighbors' postings realizing more and more how it made her come across. After a fairly rough few months dealing with the fall-out of what had happened to her at the party, Lizzy was doing better, too, trying to develop friendships with other girls her age instead of searching for affirmation from boys. Even though she was now off at the University of Washington, she and I still texted on occasion, and in giving her advice on how to let go of any shame or embarrassment the incident had caused her, I learned to give that same generosity to myself.

In addition to our couple's therapy session, I began to see a separate counselor on my own, where I talked about some of my own issues, especially around my sexuality. I told her about my early, overwhelming desires and feelings of shame that seemed to come right along with them—how my mother's words, "you don't want to be *that* kind of girl," had become etched into my psyche, so even after all the openness Jake and I experienced together—the sexual adventures we had—when Andrew outed me, I was taken right back to that moment with my parents when they walked in on me with Ryan's tongue in my mouth and my hand on his dick. The moment I decided that my enormous curiosity about, and appetite for, sexual exploration was wrong.

"Am I normal?" I asked my therapist, Diane, during that same session. She was a lovely woman in her early fifties, with short black hair and flawless skin. She possessed a level of calmness I found comforting, but also, a no-nonsense, tell-it-like-it-is demeanor, so I never worried that she was coddling me. She helped me examine the mistakes I'd made with Andrew, but never crucified me for them. She was all about taking action to improve myself, instead of allowing me to wallow around in self-pity. She was exactly what I needed.

"That's the wrong question," she said, as she crossed her slender legs, carefully balancing the yellow legal pad she held in her lap. "The right question is, are you normal for *you*—your particular set of life circumstances, how you were raised, and how, when you found your brother's magazines, you were exposed to not-so-Puritanical ideas of sex. How you internalized that, and your parents' focus on practicality and logic instead of emotion."

"Do you think that's why I was capable of having sex with men without needing to feel something for them, first?" I asked, pondering what she'd just said. "The way my parents were with each other?"

She shrugged. "Maybe. Or maybe you just really like sex, and like you told me, the only way you were able to explore this kind of dynamic with Jake was because he already filled your emotional needs. I've said it once, and I'll say it again. What you did with your husband wasn't wrong. What *was* wrong was not being totally open with him about every single detail when you met Andrew, as you agreed you would be. And once you hid that first detail, it became easier to hide the next. That's how we all justify the things we shouldn't do. We rationalize. We make excuses for our bad behavior, and then one bad choice leads to another. It's not hard to do." She gave me a big smile. "The *good* news is that you realized pretty quickly that you couldn't, and shouldn't, go on seeing him. You didn't let it get to a place where you actually did develop feelings for him. What you had with Andrew was mental and physical stimulation. You didn't love him. Right?"

"Right." Jake and I had discussed this point with our mutual therapist more than once. I think knowing that—understanding that very clear delineation, in addition to having me reiterate it over and over again that my heart was, and had always remained his—was what made it possible for Jake to forgive me. To believe that however difficult this entire episode in our life had been, we would only grow stronger for it.

It also forced me to confess something I had resisted articulating for too long: I needed him to take control more often in the bedroom, even when I tried to fight to take it back.

"I know one of the things you love about me is how strong I am," I told him. "But always having to be the strong one gets to be tiring. Once in a while, I need you to take the reins, even if you have to yank them out of my hands."

"I can do that," Jake said. Later that night, he proved it, and not long after that, we decided that we felt connected enough as a couple again that we could stop going to therapy. Our work wasn't over, but we were finally on solid ground again. And so today, almost two years after the private details of our sex life was outed to all of Queens Ridge, he and I stood in the bathroom room, getting ready to go meet someone new.

"Are you sure you're good with this?" I asked him for what had to be the hundredth time in the last couple of weeks.

He looked at me in the mirror and smiled. "I'm sure. You don't have to keep asking."

"Sorry," I said. It was difficult, sometimes, to let go of how much I'd hurt him.

He came over to stand behind me, then, and put his hands on my hips. "Stop apologizing," he whispered, his blue eyes still on mine in the mirror. "I forgave you a long time ago."

We'd decided that we would dip our toe back in slowly, with the understanding that I would not be having sex with anyone without Jake there, too. We hadn't ruled it out as a possibility, later, but for now, this was what Jake was comfortable with—it was what we had talked about for the last few months, our naked bodies pressed together at night, working each other up into a heated, passion-filled frenzy,.

We knew this way of life wasn't for everyone. After everything that happened, we more than understood the risks. But we knew each other so much better now—and I, for one, certainly better understood myself.

"We're not perfect," Jake said about our marriage, not long after we entered counseling, "but we are perfect for each other."

I couldn't agree with him more.

THE END

Acknowledgments

In the era of #Metoo and Time's Up, we are finally having more honest conversations than ever about how women experience negative sexual encounters. As essential as these discussions are, it is equally essential that we talk about women having good sex. We need positive portrayals of women who take ownership over their sexuality, who embrace it as a very real and necessary part of their identity, and of partnerships in which female pleasure is valued as highly as male gratification. Without that, how can we ever hope to get to the root of such complex issues as toxic masculinity, sexual harassment, and rape culture?

It was with this goal in mind that I began writing Tell Me Everything. At first, I was unsure how to explore this subject in depth, so I must first thank Sarah Cantin. She insisted that what I was writing was vital and important and worthwhile. Thanks also to Haley Weaver for her positivity, responsiveness, and support.

As always, I must thank my agency team for always having my best interests in mind, including Victoria Sanders, (queen-bee, agent-extraordinaire herself), Bernadette Baker-Baughman, Diane Dickensheid, Jessica Spivey, and Allison Leshowitz. Twenty years and still going strong with Victoria, I can honestly say she has been my rock, as well as my lovely, funny, intensely brilliant friend and trusted publishing-world guru. The Pool-boy, Street Urchins, and I wouldn't know what to do without you.

Thanks to my early readers, who provided me with amazing insight and emotional encouragement: Tina Skilton, Liz Fenton, Lisa Steinke, Taylor Jenkins Reid, Andrea Dunlop, Caroline Kepnes, Jen Lancaster, Tammy Greenwood, Carol Mason, and Sarah Strohmeyer. To every other writer in my tribe, thank you. I'm honored to know you all.

Being a writer is a somewhat isolating job, so I am incredibly grateful to my social media family, especially those who make it a point to reach out to me and let me know how my writing has affected them. Thank you for opening up and trusting your worlds and feelings with me. I promise to keep them safe.

Thanks also to my other friends and family, the ones who witness the day-to-day struggle of me attempting to birth a book. Thanks especially to my husband, Stephan, who smiles and orders take-out when I'm so deep in the weeds of a story that he comes home to no dinner and a wife with questionable hygiene.

And finally, my gratitude must reach across the Universe into the great beyond. This book would have never come to be without the constant loving support of one of my dearest, closest friends, Kristie Miller, who passed away in September 2017 after a life-long struggle with Cystic Fibrosis, despite a double-lung transplant meant to save her. In our Odd Couple friendship, Kristie was the Felix to my Oscar—a sweet, kind Christian woman to my (big-hearted) cussing heathen. She was also one of my first readers for Tell Me Everything, and after getting through three chapters of the rough draft, she called me, laughing. "Oh, boy," she said. "This one's a doozy." She paused then, before adding, "Get back to work. I need to read more."

Unfortunately, Kristie's health kept her from having that chance, and her death struck unexpectedly in the middle of working on this book. My soul ached so deeply, I wasn't sure I could finish. But then her voice entered my head each morning, as I sat down in front of my computer: "Get back to work." Never one to deny her, I lit a candle and did as she said. I miss her every minute, but I know that she is always with me, cheering me on, telling me to simply take the next indicated step—write the next indicated word.

I love you, Kristie. This one was for you.